PARADISE FOUND . . .
THEN LOST

Weak almost to fainting, Carol Page wiped her breath from the viewport to peer out. It was confusing—a world like a color-negative, all light coming from below, with strange-hued shadows above. So beautiful. Only trees and shrubs were around her—a wilderness of trees. And they stretched on and on, she knew, to the horizon. She could just see the lighted sparkle of running river water, *free water*.

A paradise—save only for the lethal radio-activity, which had her scanning dial stuck against its high edge. A paradise—but not for her.

Out of the Everywhere

AND OTHER EXTRAORDINARY VISIONS

JAMES TIPTREE, JR.

A Del Rey Book

BALLANTINE BOOKS • NEW YORK

A Del Rey Book
Published by Ballantine Books

Library of Congress Catalog Card Number: 81-67774

ISBN 0-345-28485-2

Manufactured in the United States of America

First Edition: December 1981

Cover art by Rick Sternbach

Acknowledgments

"Angel Fix" copyright © 1974 by Alice B. Sheldon (first published in *Worlds of If*, July–August, 1974).

"Beaver Tears" copyright © 1976 by Alice B. Sheldon (first published in *Galaxy*, May 1976).

"Your Faces, O My Sisters! Your Faces, Filled of Light!" copyright © 1976 by Alice B. Sheldon (first published in *Aurora: Beyond Equality*, Vonda McIntyre and Susan Anderson, eds., Fawcett, 1976).

"The Screwfly Solution" copyright © 1977 by Alice B. Sheldon (first published in *Analog Science Fiction/Science Fact*, June 1977).

"Time-Sharing Angel" copyright © 1977 by James Tiptree, Jr. (first published in *The Magazine of Fantasy and Science Fiction*, October 1977).

"We Who Stole the *Dream*" copyright © 1978 by James Tiptree, Jr. (first published in *Stellar #4 Science Fiction Stories*, Judy-Lynn del Rey, ed., Del Rey Books, 1978).

"Slow Music" copyright © 1980 by James Tiptree, Jr. (first published in *Interfaces*, Ursula LeGuin and Virginia Kidd, eds., Ace, 1980).

"A Source of Innocent Merriment" copyright © 1980 by James Tiptree, Jr. (first published in *Universe 10*, Terry Carr, ed., Doubleday, 1980).

To Robert A. Harper, prince of men and healers, without whose gift for patiently transforming tragedy to farce, these pages would conclude with an obituary; and to his wife Mimi for ESP kindness and help.

Contents

* These four stories were originally published under the pseudonym Raccoona Sheldon.
** First publication.

Angel Fix

By not much of a coincidence, when an alien finally landed on Earth he fell into the hands of a good guy.

In fact he was just folding up his parabort heatsheet in Martin Brumbacher, Sr.'s back forty when young Marty came around the alder clump and saw him.

"Hi," said Marty uncertainly, looking at the alien's yellow helmet and the khaki drawers on his skinny little legs, and the mess of gloop on the ground. "Are you, uh, with the survey?"

"*Como 'sta Usted?*" said the alien. "*Ich bin ein Berliner. Mukka hai!*" He slapped his helmet. "Ah! Hi there. Well, yes, you might say so. Mind holding this end?"

He passed one corner of the heatsheet to Marty and backed off to stretch it, gripping the edge in his humanoid teeth and kicking the middle to make it fold. He wasn't much taller than Marty.

"You sure have some junk," said Marty, holding his end. "That looks like a flying saucer."

" 'On't 'ake 'em 'ike they used to." The alien took the edge out of his mouth and folded some more, shaking his head. "No quality control." He held out his hand for Marty's end.

"Our milker jams all the time," Marty said sympathetically. He looked closely at the alien's hand and his eyes popped.

The alien wrestled the heatsheet into a lump that suddenly became a toroid, jammed in a few more items, and sat down on it, panting and gazing at Marty with large brown eyes above his droopy mustache. The toroid sizzled faintly. Marty stared back.

"Nice place you have here," the alien inhaled appreci-

1

atively. "Lots of *fremth*. You call those cows, right? I thought they were extinct."

"No, they're Ayeshires." Marty swallowed a couple of times. "Uh. Welcome to Earth. I guess."

"Hey, thanks!" The alien grinned and offered the hand. He had a pretty good grin. Marty shook; it felt okay, but hot.

"I suppose you want to see the President or somebody."

"Oh good heavens, no, just a personal pleasure trip. No formalities, please." The alien was still watching Marty carefully. Then he smiled in a relieved way. "I see you're one of the good guys."

"What do you mean?"

"Just checked you out on my Ethical Vibesponder." He pointed to a winky place on his hat. "You test out real high. Honest, brave, truthful, kind, the whole profile. Lucky for me. I mean, a lot of people are hostile to strangers." He shrugged apologetically. "I don't have any secret zap rays or anything."

Marty could believe that, loooking at him. "Yeah. It wouldn't be so good if you landed by Matt's tavern. Or the sheriff."

The alien nodded sadly. Then he brightened. "We have a saying. Every good guy knows at least one other good guy. I mean, I really would like to interact a little while I'm here, if you know somebody else who might accept me."

Marty thought. "Well, I guess Whelan would accept you. I saw his car by the creek. But he isn't anybody important, he's only the warden."

The alien winked. "It is also written, good guys don't win the *phooplesnatch*. Take me to your friend."

So Marty led the alien down to the creek, at the same time asking him a million questions about where was he from and so on which the alien answered as well as he could, astronomy not being Marty's strong subject.

Beside the pasture gate stood a muddy old station wagon. A muddy durable-looking man was coming up from the creek carrying something. The alien stopped.

"Whelan! Hey, Whelan!" Marty scrambled down, talking.

Whelan just kept on walking. When he reached the car

he opened the back and threw in a No. 2 trap on a chain. Then he reached back inside and took out a piece of paw and threw it in the bushes. "Bastards," he said. "Going to kill every goddam thing." He wiped his hands on his pants and turned to the alien.

"What can I do for you, sir? Whelan's the name."

"How do you do, Sir Whelan?" The alien smiled tentatively. "My name is, ah, Joe. Joe Smith. I'm from quite a ways away. I was hoping I could meet a few of you people and, well, talk." He slapped the side of his helmet, frowning.

"Yeah?"

"Really quite a long way." The alien slapped his hat again, harder. A wisp of vapor arose from the winky place. *"Damn,"* he said.

"He is an *extra*terrestrial!" said Marty. "I told you."

"Yeah?" Whelan grinned and pushed his bush hat down over his nose.

"I really am." The alien gazed up at what he could see of Whelan's eyes under the hat. "I see you understand bodily structure, Sir Whelan. Perhaps if I show you—"

He held up his hands, unfolding the extra parts. Whelan stopped grinning. "There is more," the alien said shyly, starting to unzipper. He looked at Marty. "Perhaps if we just stepped to the other side of the car?"

"Hey," said Marty indignantly. But they stepped around to where he couldn't see anything but the alien's back.

When they returned Whelan's hat was on the back of his neck and he was rubbing his head.

"Listen, this is too much for me. You have to see the President or somebody. I better take you to the courthouse."

"Oh, please, no." The alien clasped his hands. "May we not just converse, personally?"

"I told him about the sheriff," Marty said.

Whelan nodded, not taking his eyes off the little alien. "What did you want to talk about?"

The alien's mustache trembled. "It's all very informal, Sir Whelan. A mere whim. We happened to notice the way things were going here—I mean, you seemed to be having a few difficulties. Not your fault, indeed not!" He smiled hopefully. "So I thought I'd drop by and offer a small measure of help, person-to-person as it were. That is, if you want it, of course."

"Who's we?" Whelan demanded.

"Oh, merely myself and two very close friends. We happened to be out this way on a pleasure jaunt. Absolutely nothing official in *any* way, I assure you."

"What kind of help? Hold it, Marty."

The alien made an embarrassed gesture. "It's only a tiny thing. You might not want it at all."

"Try me."

"Gladly. But—" The alien peered hard at Whelan. "I see you do realize how dangerous it can be to inject something totally foreign into an environment? The possible consequences?"

Whelan nodded.

"If I could assemble a few, well, understanding people. As I said to Marty, good guys. And present it to you as a group? You could talk it over and decide if it seemed desirable."

"I guess that makes sense," said Whelan slowly.

"He says every good guy knows another good guy," Marty put in.

The alien nodded eagerly. "Sir Whelan, could you possibly spare the time to lead us to another trustworthy person? You see I can only stay a few hours; our vehicle is only a pleasure-scooter. Perhaps you know someone who is familiar with a wide range of people?"

"Just plain Whelan's okay," Whelan was starting a different sort of grin. "Sure, why not." He rubbed his head. "Someone I trust who knows a lot of people? Well, there's my wife, but she's at the high school. Doc Murrey? He talks too much. Wait. How about Marion Legersky over at the clinic? She knows a million people and she doesn't talk."

"She's always talking," objected Marty.

"Yeah, but she doesn't say anything. She's okay."

"Oh, thank you!" said the alien. "Do we travel in this?"

They made room among the minnow traps, shovels, wire cutters, flashlights, blankets, chains, and other stuff in the wagon. "Hold on, Marty," said Whelan. "Your pa know where you are?"

"I'll yell as we go by."

"Do that." Whelan revved up the wagon. When they passed the Brumbacher gate at the top of the hill Marty stuck his head out and yelled. Nobody yelled back.

"Lovely place you have here," the alien sighed. "Terrific *fremth*. Dreadful to think you might ruin it."

Whelan grunted. "What is *fremth?*"

"Oh, it's a condition you get from the general electromagnetic configuration. Van Allen something? I never could understand the explanation. Some planets have it, some don't. I personally love it."

He wiggled his thin shoulders. Whelan made a racing corner and zoomed onto the blacktop. The alien clutched at the door. "Do you always proceed so, ah, speedily?"

"Sometimes he goes a lot speedilier, don't you, Whelan? Whelan has to catch poachers," Marty told the alien. "Did you catch that real bad one yet, Whelan?"

"Don't talk about it," said Whelan. "Listen, can't you give me a hint about this help you're offering us?"

The alien twinkled shyly, like wait-for-Christmas. Marty could see he wasn't frightened any more. "What would you like?"

"Oh, Christ. Don't quote me, Marty. Well, for starters —go back a couple of centuries and put a flaming sign in the sky saying anybody who dumps anything anywhere has to eat it. And anybody begetting more than two kids should castrate himself. And petroleum can only be extracted in the dark of the moon by left-handed virgins— that kind of thing."

"And Germany shouldn't lose the war," put in Marty. "Hey, Joe, can you? Can you?"

The alien's big brown eyes looked sad and his mustache drooped. "Oh, my dear friends, I hope I have not aroused false hopes. I can't assist you on that sort of scale. I wish I could. Time travel . . ."

"All I want is to save the planet before it's too late," Whelan muttered. "Any woman wearing natural fur should have her nose cut off."

"Goodness." The alien swallowed nervously. "Yes, I do sympathize. I fear that what I have to offer will seem very insignificant."

They swerved around the freezer-plant and rolled up Maple Street.

"Here we are."

The clinic was a one-story brick box in some grass. As they got out the front door opened and a coat came flying out with a girl halfway into it.

"Marion! Hey—Miss Legersky!"

"Whelan!" The girl whirled around. "Hi, Marty! Listen, excuse me, I have a *date.* Paul called me to go to the game in Green Bay! There's the bus, I'm gone!"

She got her other arm in the coat, dropped her pocketbook, and scooped it up running. The Greyhound was down the block in front of Matt's Tavern, chuffing out stink.

Inside the clinic the phone started to ring.

Miss Legersky stopped as if an arrow had hit her and spun around.

"Brenda? Where *are* you? She's late—" She went charging back into the clinic. When they followed her in she was saying, "Yes, Mrs. Floyd . . . No, Mrs. Floyd . . . I'll tell the doctor just as *soon* as he comes in, Mrs. Floyd, good-bye now—what? Oh, yes, Mrs. Floyd, I truly will—"

Outside, the bus was making noises.

"Right. *Yes,* Mrs. Floyd! Good-bye!" She ran back to the door. They all watched the bus pull out.

Miss Legersky slowly took off her coat. "It could have been an emergency." She sighed and looked around at them, her jaw out. She had beautiful skin. "What's with you all?"

There was a short silence and then everybody started telling her at once.

"What? What?" She looked back and forth and focused on the alien. *"What?"*

"Show her," Marty yelled, pulling at him.

"I think you better take a look, Marion," Whelan said. "Being a nurse and all. The teeth," he told the alien.

The alien opened his mouth. His head was a little below hers. Marty went around behind and looked. In back of the alien's front teeth were green and black zigzags.

"Do you mind if I touch that?" Miss Legersky said faintly. "I'll wash my hands."

"The frontals are artificial," said the alien.

When she put her finger in she pulled it right out.

"Your temperature!" she cried. "You're burning up!"

"Quite normal." The alien seemed a little embarrassed. Whelan started telling her about the other things. When the alien unfolded his fingers, Miss Legersky began grinning in a wild sort of way like a dog laughing.

"I have a third, ah, eye, too." The alien tapped his forehead. "Would it be all right to save that for later? It hurts to pull the cover off."

"I saw him *land!*" Marty declared. "Well, practically. He has a flying saucer, it's by our gravel pit. Only he made it shrink."

Miss Legersky was grinning even more wildly. "You, you—you're from outer space! You really are? *Where?*"

"Well, it's over by the Hillihilevio Complex. I don't know what you call it. That way," he pointed, grinning too. Everybody was grinning.

"Why? Why'd you come? Do you know about us? Hey, don't you have to see the President or the UN or something?"

"Oh, no, please!" They all explained at once.

"You want to meet my good guy?" She messed her hair around. "Well, you made a start. Who, who? Oh, wow, my old boss in O.E.D. would be perfect, but he's in Detroit. *Who?*"

"Perhaps there is someone you take counsel with about your problems?" the alien suggested.

"My problems? Wow. Well, there's three families didn't get milk since January, Mrs. Riccardi gave me some milk powder. But she's kind of erratic. Problems . . . Whelan, did you hear the sheriff is throwing Mrs. Kovacs off her farm, she's eighty-one and blind? Wait! Cleever. Cleever!" She seized the phone.

"If only he's there, if he hasn't quit or something. He's the new P.D.," she told them. "Courthouse? Mary? Is Cleever there? Look, tell him to wait, please, it's urgent! I'm coming over right away, okay, Mary?" She hung up. "Oh my God—Brenda! Where is she?"

"Hey," said a voice in the doorway, "I'm sorry I'm late, my polish wouldn't dry. What's doing? I mean, goodbye," Brenda added as they all rushed out past her and piled into Whelan's car.

Whelan took off backward so as not to pass the tavern

and swooshed around Ray's junkyard onto county road C, with Marion chattering, "Oh, wow, is this real? Can you help us? Can you really, really?"

"It's just a tiny thing," the alien said humbly. "It may not be anything you want at all."

"What *I* want? Oh, hey, I can't—Whelan, is this *real?*"

"Could be," Whelan said cautiously. "Courthouse, right?"

"My goodness, the *fremth*," the alien sighed. "You just can't imagine. Glorious."

"*Fremth* is Van Allen belts," Marty explained. "He digs it. Hey, Joe, what's your planet like? Is it all right if I call you Joe? Are you from the Galactic Federation?"

"What's that?" the alien asked. "Oh, yes, please, Joe."

"Hello, Joe, I'm Marion. Look, Whelan, there's the Moellers, they lost their food stamps. Next time you confiscate some meat could you—"

"They have too goddam many kids," Whelan said. "Besides, it's illegal. Okay."

The wagon shot over the old bridge and past the Hecker-Giodano pulp works and around the Foxy Cabins and the Frigo cheese factory into the back end of town. The courthouse had a pizza-colored tower. Whelan turned into some service ruts and parked behind a couple of rusty school buses.

"Close as we go." They all climbed out and hurried around the buses and across the parking lot to the courthouse's back porch. Inside next to the garbage cans was a door saying EDGAR CLEEVER, JR. PUBLIC DEFENDER.

"Cleever!" Marion rushed them all in and started introducing. Cleever was a long tea-colored young man with a mean expression. He said "How do" all around, sneering impartially.

"Oh, Cleever, you won't believe this, but Joe's from outer space. I mean, he isn't from Earth. He came to *help* us, isn't that tremendous?"

Cleever's squint stopped on the alien.

"I saw him land," said Marty.

"He *showed* us, Cleever. I mean, I believe it. I really do!"

Cleever squinted at Whelan. Whelan cleared his throat. "Looks like," he said.

Cleever's eyes narrowed to two black pinholes focused on the alien. "Doesn't he talk? Where's his interstellar translator?"

"Actually I don't have one," the alien spoke up timidly. "It isn't really necessary."

"Ah, the faint British accent," said Cleever. "What'd you say his name was?"

"Joe Smith," Whelan told him uncomfortably.

"Well, it's really more like *Sorajosojojorghthu*," the alien interjected. "Joe seemed easier. I just made up the Smith part."

"So what are you selling? This isn't my day for jollity." Cleever picked up some papers but one ear stayed trained on the alien.

"Oh dear," the alien swallowed. "Obviously I must first satisfy you that I really am from off-planet."

"Good thinking."

"Well, of course, minor physical aspects—" The alien held out his hands and wiggled everything. "But I see that isn't really convincing."

"No," said Cleever shortly.

"I feared not." The alien started tugging at his zippers. Marty just got a glimpse of black, wet-looking things before Whelan hauled him away. Marion took two steps back, her eyes bugging out.

Cleever just looked in silence. His mouth drew down at the ends into two angry cuts. He blinked twice and slowly shook his head.

"Sorry. I really am sorry. But no."

The alien sighed, zipping up. He started to pick at his forehead, wincing a little. A big piece of skin peeled away. Above his nose was a jelly place.

"That's not an eye," said Marty indignantly.

The alien was holding a plastic cup to his forehead. He leaned his head down and bounced a couple of times. When he straightened up everybody could see.

"Oooh," breathed Marion.

It wasn't like his other eyes but more like a soft, shiny little animal looking out, straight at Cleever. His other eyes looked at Cleever, too.

Cleever stared back with terrible ferocity. His fingers hit three drumtaps on the desk. Presently the third eye left Cleever and swiveled around to look at them all. It winked.

Cleever cleared his throat, once, twice. He stretched a hand out toward the alien. The alien nodded and leaned across the desk. Very carefully, Cleever touched the eye. It sort of ducked. Cleever pulled back and exhaled, scowling viciously.

"Okay." He shook himself. "Okay. Provisionally. Now what? What's the scenario? Not the ultimatum, by any chance?"

"Oh, mercy no," said the alien. "Oh, no! Purely a friendly call. Look, would it be all right if I put this back? It's a bit . . ."

"Go ahead. What's your friendly calling on behalf of? The last friendly aliens we had here didn't turn out so good."

"He says he wants to give us something," said Whelan.

"Aha," Cleever snorted.

The alien had his head back, putting the jelly in.

"We," he said muffledly. "I mean, my two companions and I happened to pass nearby and we couldn't help noticing that things weren't too happy with you. Quite distressing, in fact. Perilous." He smooshed the skin back. "Does this look all right? We've had our calamities too, alas. So I recalled something—a very small item, you understand—that might be helpful and I thought I'd drop by to see if you cared to try it."

"How much?" Cleever demanded.

"Oh Cleever," Marion protested. "He's not selling anything—he wants to help."

"That's right," the alien told him eagerly. "We have a saying, The good guys have to link together."

"Good guys. What's that supposed to mean? I don't dig the black-hat-white-hat line myself."

"Yes, forgive me. A slang expression. How to put it?" The alien chewed on his big mustache. "Well, in situations like yours one does find persons—so few, alas—who are trying to help rather than seeking status or power or material—"

"You keep saying help. What do you mean? Everybody thinks he's helping. General Custer was helping."

"Of course." The alien peered at him anxiously.

"Would it help—excuse me—could I say, people to whom the pain felt by others is real? All the pain, the waste. Empathetic, is that it? So real that they try to, well, stop it?"

"That's beautiful," said Marion.

"Okay, okay," Cleever grunted. "So what do you want?"

"To make my modest offer of assistance."

"Make it."

The alien looked around, counting. "I had hoped for at least one more . . . for diversity. . . ." His voice trailed off timidly.

"He wants like a panel," Whelan explained. "To decide if it would mess things up."

"Who do you want? Ralph Nader? The Sierra Club? Billy Graham? Bella Abzug?"

"He wants your good guy!" said Marty.

The alien nodded. "If you could possibly lead us to someone, well, experienced in the larger ethical implications? Not an official, please. Someone you would trust with a secret of great power."

"Oh, wow!" said Marion.

"Larger ethical implications." Cleever shook his head slowly, staring hard at the alien. "Well, maybe. Provided any of this is real, which I doubt. Let me think. Judge Ball was on my orals, he knows every implication there is. I guess I trust the old bastard. I'd love to see his face—" Cleever was slashing around in his desk. Suddenly he stopped. "Listen, if this turns out funny I'm going to rip you apart. You know that?"

The alien quailed. "Oh, I *assure* you . . ."

"Be warned." Cleever picked up the phone. "Oh hell, no way. He's in Denver. Next week?"

"Oh dear, it does have to be sooner. Today, actually. My friends were very emphatic."

"I should have my brain serviced," Cleever sneered at the alien. "Look, why don't you go save the world someplace else?"

"Hey!" said Marion. "Dr. Lukas. How about him? I was in his seminar, I trust him. He resigned from N.I.H. because of, you know, Cleever. I told you."

"Lukas? Isn't he in some kind of scientific advisory crap now?"

"He's down at State annex. Pike River, it's only forty miles."

"Call him."

"Oh God, I couldn't," she wailed. But when Cleever got through to Lukas's secretary Marion made quite a good speech about how she was an ex-student and something of tremendous scientific significance had come up and could they please have ten minutes of his time? When the secretary gave in and said yes, Cleever hung his Gone Hunting sign on the door and they all tore out and jumped into Whelan's wagon with the minnow bait and stuff.

"What makes you trust Lukas, Marion?" Cleever asked as the party hurtled down Interstate 101. It was a gorgeous Northlands day. The alien was fluttering his hand out the window and asking Marty the names of things.

"Oh, I don't know," Marion laughed. "The flinch, I guess."

"What flinch?"

"You know. Like all the stuff in the news and after a while you can't react anymore, it's all so horrible, but you go on flinching. Like, twenty million babies starving to death someplace, flinch. Old people abused in stinking nursing homes, flinch, flinch. Eighty billion for new super-bombs, flinch-flinch-flinch. You flinch, Cleever. I see you."

"Chippewas don't flinch," Cleever snapped. Then he said, "Oh, shit."

A siren bansheed up deafeningly behind them.

"It's him. Oh, *no*."

They rolled onto the verge and waited. Boots clumped. Then Whelan's window was filled with a khaki-colored bag of rocks. It had badges and belts on it.

"Hello, folks."

"Hello, Sheriff," Whelan said tonelessly.

"I got to talk to you, boy. What kind of shit you trying to pull with Charlie Orr? 'Scuse me, miss." The sheriff's large face came down to see who belonged to the legs. When he saw he stopped smiling, which was on the whole an improvement.

"Orr had eight deer carcasses or parts thereof in his panel," Whelan told him.

"He says you tried to drive him off the road at over one hundred miles per hour."

"Well, he didn't want to stop. I had my flasher going. I just eased up behind and nudged him a little."

"Goddam dangerous driving. That car of yours could kill somebody." The sheriff was still bent down, taking them all in with his round blue eyes. "You got stuff on this car that's illegal, Whelan. You setting up to be a law-enforcement officer? I got to write you up, boy."

Whelan said nothing.

"Quite a party, I see. Say, you're Brumbacher's boy. Your pa know you're going around with these people?"

"We told him," said Marty.

"Yeah? I think I'll tell him, too. You—" He jerked his chin at the alien. "You new in town?"

"Oh yes sir! I truly am!" They could feel the alien quivering. "Merely passing through, really!"

"Keep it that way. He your lawyer?"

"Oh dear me, no indeed! I—" Cleever nudged him and he shut up.

"Birds of a feather," grunted the sheriff. He pulled his head back out. "I want you in my office first thing tomorrow, Whelan. Hear? And bring this unsafe vehicle with you."

"The charge stands against Orr," Whelan said.

"Sure, sure." The sheriff chuckled and slapped the car roof. At that instant the alien sneezed, or something. A big ring of lavender light whipped through the wagon and out the window.

The sheriff's face zoomed down at them.

"You got fireworks in this car!"

"Oh, no! No!" cried everybody but Cleever.

The sheriff slapped the roof again, hard. "All right, everybody out." He jerked the door open by Marion.

"Warrant?" said Cleever.

The sheriff rolled his lips and spit out some gum.

"On my authority as sheriff of this county I'm ordering you to assist an officer of the law in performance of his duties. Namely, checking possession of illegal fireworks. Out." He grabbed Marion's arm.

Cleever started unfolding himself. "Let go of her, Claude."

"Look!" cried the alien, pointing ahead.

A car was roaring at them fast, some kind of soap-dish body on big fat tires. Hairy heads were blowing out of the top.

"Haughgh!" said the sheriff, letting go of Marion.

The strange car was almost on top of them. It fishtailed onto the gravel, showering stones, and screeched back into the road by the sheriff's cruiser. *Ping-g-g!*

The sheriff bellowed and took off for his car. The kids got straightened out and clouted down the road. There were big letters painted on the back. The cruiser tore into a U-turn and took after them, throwing gravel all over.

Whelan started up and whooshed them out of there.

"Never saw them before," he said. "What was that, a built-up VW?"

"It said 'Love.'" Marion giggled. "In purple. Oh, wow, was he mad. I hope he doesn't catch them."

"It did not," Marty told her. "It said Claude Eats Dandruff."

"I saw it. Love."

"Actually, it said White Man Drop Dead," said Cleever. "And it was a green '67 Pontiac."

"I'm sorry," said the alien. "It's hard with so many people. I blur."

"Huh?"

"You mean *you* did that?" Cleever said.

The alien smiled modestly. "Well, I thought—I *hope* it was all right?"

"Oh, it was perfect! Oh, wow! Ho ho ho!" cried Marion.

"You mean they weren't, they— Hey!" Marty bounced around to face the alien. "Do some more! Do some monsters!"

"Oh, I'm not very good at it. It has to be in one's head. That is, the person's head, I mean." He tugged his mustache again. "Ah, Miss Legersky—"

"Marion."

"Marion . . . I must apologize. That phone call. Mrs., ah, Floyd. That was me."

"What do you mean? I *heard* her."

"No, really. Nobody called. I did it from your head. I'm so sorry."

"You mean Mrs. Floyd never called? But—but, *why?*"

"I had to be sure about you," the alien said pleadingly. "My—my device seems to have quit working."

"His ethical vibrator," Marty explained. "It's in his hat. I saw smoke, Joe."

"Yes. Absolute junk. So I thought, make a test. The worst thing a person is worried about. I'm terribly sorry."

"You mean, to see if I'd answer." She rumpled her hair, staring blankly at the scenery, which was rushing by behind some Wonder Bread ads. "Cleever, just when I was leaving, I mean, *Paul* asked me—I guess he did," she looked around. The alien nodded. "Anyway, Brenda was late and Mrs. Floyd called—only it wasn't Mrs. Floyd. But the voice and all—"

"I *am* so sorry." The alien's big brown eyes glistened. "Your mating ritual . . ." he said miserably.

"Oh, Joe, it doesn't matter." She patted his hand. "I wouldn't have missed this for anything. And you're trying to help us."

"I *do* hope you won't be disappointed." He clasped her hand. "It's such a tiny thing."

"You have beautiful eyes, Joe." She hugged his shoulders. He beamed.

"Testing," Cleever said. "I don't recall you trying anything on me. Why not? Professional courtesy?"

"Oh, I *looked* at you," the alien told him shyly.

"It occurs to me," Cleever was squinting again. "Maybe we should have some kind of test. Just for openers, does everybody see this guy the way I do? Whelan, mind telling us what Joe here looks like?"

They all started describing the alien and checking and arguing, while they flew past the oil-loading rack and across the Soo tracks and around Earl's Trailer Court and over the bridge into Pine River.

"Oh, Cleever, what does it *matter* about his earlobes," Marion said. "We all see him. Slow down, Whelan, there's the campus."

"I don't know," Cleever said darkly as they rolled into the parking area under a lot of maples. "I wish my grandpa was here with his Windigo trap." The alien shuddered.

"Life Sciences, she said." Marion pointed. "That motel-looking one."

They scrambled out from among the axes and jerry cans and trooped into the Life Sciences motel and found T. H. LUKAS, PH.D., M.D. on a door. Inside was a small office about ten degrees below zero.

"The air conditioner," his secretary sneezed. "Go right on in."

"Oh, it's fine," the alien assured her. "Really brings out the *fremth.*" He followed them into Lukas' cubbyhole, shivering pleasurably.

Lukas turned out to be a sturdy little man with a white pompadour, like a serious show pony.

"Take over, Marion," Cleever said.

"Oh, wow," said Marion and plunged at it. Just as she was saying "outer space" the door opened and the secretary walked in carrying a yellow paper.

"Excuse me."

Lukas opened it and started reading. As he read he slowly backed himself up until he hit the wall. The paper shook a little and his face paled.

Marty suddenly made a loud inhale and Whelan clamped him from behind.

"Shall I send an answer?" The secretary didn't look well, either.

"No . . . Oh, yes, of course, Miss Timmons. Ah. Dear Harry. Sincere—no, many congratulations on your appointment. You have all my support. Signed Theo."

"Doctor Lukas, I—I'm so sorry."

He made a vague gesture. "Thank you, Miss Timmons. These things . . . One must hope, the realization of power sometimes ameliorates. . . ."

"I know what the realization of power will do for *him.*" Miss Timmons marched out.

Lukas smiled a little effortfully and pulled himself back to his desk. "Do forgive me—Miss Legersky, isn't it? Please continue."

She'd just started to talk when the alien murmured something and quickly sidled out the door. "Oops," said Cleever, and whipped out after him. Marion went on talking.

When they came back in Lukas was standing up.

"You . . .?" He peered at the alien, shaking his white head and smiling tiredly.

"The eye," said Cleever. "Show him."

"It isn't really necessary now." The alien's mustache seemed to have perked up.

"I know. You better tell him that, too. She'll send that wire."

"Oh, no," the alien shook his head, smoothing his mustache. "I have an electronic sweet tooth," he confided. Then he sobered. "Doctor Lukas, I must apologize for your distress. That telegram does not exist."

"What?"

"Oh, *Joe!*" cried Marion.

"Really. Look on your desk, where you put it. Nothing there."

There wasn't. Lukas ran around looking, with his eyebrows going higher and higher.

"That's his thing," Cleever explained. "Testing. He says he uses the worst thing you can think of."

"Only in emergencies," said the alien. "It's very draining. Please forgive me."

"Amazing!" Lukas blinked and began to smile. "Well! Yes, my goodness! That certainly is a feat, Mr. Joe, is it? But, regretfully, I cannot accept it as, ah . . ."

"Of course," the alien agreed.

So they showed him everything, with Lukas getting more and more excited. By the time they were doing the eye his eyebrows were up by his pompadour and he was peering at the alien with a pocket lens.

"A pineal analog? Impossible, see the ancillary structures . . . Why, that isn't hair, either—" The eye swiveled, apparently enjoying itself.

"We should get to the business," Whelan interrupted. "I'd like to see this gismo he has."

"Button up, Joe. Somebody might come in."

"Well, well, well!" Lukas repeated while the alien put himself together. "Well! Now. Whom to call first?"

"No, no! No!" They told him. The alien began to explain about how this was a private thing he wanted to offer to a small group. He was choosing his words with great care, glancing nervously at Cleever.

"—persons of, how shall I express it? Of altruistic temperament, of low dominance-submission orientation? Unexploitative?"

Lukas looked puzzled.

"I see in your mind the terms 'nonagonistic behavior.' Pronounced et-epimeletic tendencies?"

"Ah," Lukas replied. "You mean the good guys!"

Marion giggled.

"But how marvelous! You offer to help us? You really mean this?"

"In a small way." The alien started feeling around in his clothing. "A very small way. That is if you . . ." He frowned, tried another place.

Lukas was gazing over their heads. "An inhibition, perhaps, against destroying each other? Such as Lorenz—so poetically if quite unfoundedly—believes is to be seen among wolves? We do seem to need it more than wolves." Absently he rubbed a tattooed place on his arm. "Is such a thing possible?" He demanded urgently, "Can you stop man destroying man?"

"There goes the planet," said Whelan.

The alien's face was sorrowful. "Doctor Lukas, I regret. What you suggest *is* possible, in a way. But it would require—oh, to begin with, an official project, a huge organization, funding, authorizations, coordinations, impact studies. . . . I see you understand."

Cleever snorted.

"Yes." Lukas breathed out slowly. "I understand."

"I'm so sorry about your family," the alien said softly.

Lukas started. "You really do read minds?"

"When the thought is so prominent."

"And you can't bring back the dead either, I'm sure. Or—could—" Lukas's face changed. "Oh, no. Forgive me. But now, let us see! What do you bring?"

The alien pulled out a small crumpled packet which promptly swelled up into a lobed pouch.

"It's quite safe," the alien said. "Now, the point is—"

There was a very fast knock on the door as Miss Timmons came in.

"Doctor Lukas, may I use your phone? My line is dead."

"Oh," said the alien. "Ah, Doctor Lukas."

"So that's what you were doing," Cleever said. "Sir, maybe you should mention about the telegram."

"Of course. Miss Timmons, it won't be necessary to send

that wire. I have determined that the message was an, ah, error."

"A joke," Cleever added grimly.

"What a perverted, horrible—"

"Yes, yes, it's quite all right." Lukas smiled at her. She glared at each of them in turn and strode out.

"I should repair it," the alien said anxiously.

"Later, we don't want any calls."

"True. Well, as I was saying, the point is fatigue."

"Fatigue?" they echoed blankly.

"Yes, on the part of the good guys. We have a saying, the good guys get all the unclean matter."

"I follow you," said Whelan.

"And we say also, good guys are stupid enough to care. So they keep trying. But there are so few of them and they are always suffering hurts and defeats and unclean matter. A terrible strain. They become tired."

He looked around. Nobody nodded; nobody had to.

"And so they wear out, they weaken. Unable to go on. Perhaps dead. The society suffers, error and evil triumph. So I thought to bring you refreshment, for the good guys."

"Drugs," grunted Cleever. *"Shit."*

"Oh, no!" The alien looked shocked. "Tell me—have none of you experienced a desire to go *away* for a time? To have a secret beautiful place free from evil and greed, without—is 'hassles' the word? Wait—" He looked at Marion. "Where there is only sympathy and understanding and the deer and the antelope play?"

"Ohhh," breathed Marion. "You mean like vacations?" Then her smile faded. "I went to Yellowstone. It's wall-to-wall crud."

"A travel agent." Cleever's teeth showed.

"Oh, please, this is a gift! A very modest gift, I'm afraid. But you see," the alien said earnestly, "we have *experienced* these problems. Really. We learned that if one can relieve the stress for a time one returns refreshed. Renewed! Able to carry on, to accomplish more. To flourish like the green tree."

"Hey Joe, where is it?" Marty asked. "How do we go?"

"Observe, please." The alien opened a lobe of the bundle. An object fell out. "No, wait; wrong culture." He pushed it back and tried another.

"That looked like an Afro comb," Marion said. Everybody was peering madly.

"I do *hope* you like it." The alien pulled out a shiny little thing.

"Car keys?"

"For camouflage. Unremarkable and owned by everyone, is it not? Now, if you will move back from the center of the room—good, good. See. I hold the key up, so, and tap upon it. Twelve times."

His finger made twelve even taps.

"Ooohh! Ahhh!"

In the middle of the room stood a faint, shimmery bubble about the size of a big refrigerator.

"That is the gate. Now, to enter—"

"Wait a minute," said Whelan. "What's in there?"

"Oh, nothing at the moment. See—it's quite empty." The alien walked into the bubble and out again, waving his arms. "It synchronizes two points. You go in here and come out there. I forget the technical name, time-independent-null-dimensional-something. Our transportation industry makes it."

"Does it work?" asked Marty.

"Oh yes. They haven't recalled one for ages."

"I thought you came here in a flying saucer," Cleever said.

"Oh, naturally. I didn't need a *permanent* hookup, you wouldn't build a highway just for one—"

"Okay."

"Where does it go? I want to try it," Marty and Marion said together.

"No," Cleever and Whelan spoke as one.

Lukas advanced on the bubble and thrust his hand in. "I am the oldest; I am expendable. I shall test it."

"Oh, no, Doctor Lukas—"

But the alien was already showing him. "When you are inside, tap the key again like this." He tapped three slow, three fast, three slow. "Your emergency signal, I believe? To come back, just re-enter and repeat the taps." He handed Lukas the key. "Please come right back, won't you? Your friends are bound to worry. Oh, I do hope he likes it," the alien added as Lukas advanced into the bubble.

They saw his pompadour lift slightly, like a brush charge. He held up the key and tapped it. Nothing happened.

The alien put his head in and said something. Cleever snickered.

"It has to be quite forceful," the alien said apologetically when his head came out. "This is a used model. But very reliable, I assure you."

"Sure, sure," said Cleever. They could see Lukas tapping hard.

All of a sudden he and the bubble weren't there anymore.

"Holy mother of us all," whispered Whelan.

"Is he all right?" asked Marion breathlessly just as the door opened and Miss Timmons' head came in.

"Is everything all right, Professor? Doctor Lukas! Where is he?"

"He stepped out for a minute," Marty said loudly. "Hah hah hah!" Whelan grabbed him.

"D-didn't you see him go by?" said Marion. "He said he'd be right back."

The phone in the outer office rang. Miss Timmons looked to and fro wildly and finally backed out. Cleever went over and leaned on the door.

"All right, you. *Get him back*," Cleever snarled.

"Oh, I *can't*—" The alien took one look and scooted behind Marion. "Please, do not—"

The bubble and Lukas suddenly popped back in the middle of the room. Lukas stepped out slowly, a strange expression on his face.

"Virgin . . ." he said to the alien. "It's virgin, isn't it? The air—" He sniffed. "I hadn't realized it was so foul here. But so lonely . . ." He turned to the others. "Yes. You find yourself in a large, a very large pavilion. Looking out upon a virgin world. All quite empty."

"The reception area. We put it up," the alien said. "Did you like it?"

"Let me, let us," the others clamored.

"Of course!" The alien handed keys around. "May I

suggest you go in pairs? The bubbles must be in different spots, you see. Perhaps if we push this desk?"

As they pushed Miss Timmons began to pound on the door. Lukas stuck his head out. "Elvira, do not be alarmed. Everything is quite all right. We're working on something."

He turned back just in time to see Marion and Cleever go bubble-pop. The next minute Whelan and Marty were gone, too.

Lukas leaned on the desk, puffing a bit. "Do you think," he asked the alien, "Elvira—Miss Timmons has been with me for years. Might it be possible—?"

"Oh, I *want* you to bring friends!" the alien beamed. "And your friends shall bring friends, as many as possible shall have refreshment! But—Doctor Lukas, this is very serious; you must impress it on them after I have gone: *The gate is for good guys only.* You see, there is a scanning device, I have no idea how it works. It's sensitive to, well, emotions. If a person who emanates hate or cruelty or greed tries to use it, it goes null. Ffft!" He gestured. "Key, person, all gone. So you see why I was so careful in testing you."

"The needle's eye," Lukas marveled. "God in Heaven, it's the needle's eye." He looked sharply at the alien.

"Oh, no, no!" said the alien, backing up a little. "An ordinary being, I assure you. A mere technological convenience."

"I see . . ." Lukas rubbed his arm absently. "Well, surely if I passed Elvira need not fear." He frowned. "But how is it you have such a planet empty? It seemed a paradise."

"No *fremth*," the alien told him. "So many are like that, your place here is quite an exception. The magnetic field forms," he explained, as Marion and Cleever popped back into the room.

They came out both talking at once.

"Did you like it?" the alien asked eagerly.

Marion just kept on saying, "Oh, oh, oh." Cleever took a deep breath.

"Yeah. When do the developers arrive?"

"It appears they don't!" Lukas was telling them what

the alien had said when Marty and Whelan popped out in the corner.

"Man," said Whelan. "Did you see those mountains? Sure hated to come back."

"And the big lake," shouted Marty. "Is that the *ocean*? Hey, Cleever, I bet there's *buffalo* there!"

"Chippewas don't dig buffalo," Cleever told him. He seemed unusually springy on his feet.

"And the flowers, the sun," Marion sighed. "I bet you could grow stuff in that meadow by just throwing down seeds."

"Wait," Whelan said. "How do we know the soil isn't poisonous to us? Or the water, how about that?"

"Completely compatible," the alien assured them. "Of course we only sampled here and there, but you and I are much alike. Very common. Be cautious. I did eat quite a few fruits. Delicious!"

"You were there?"

"When we made the pavilions. Now please—*did* you like it? Will it provide refreshment? Do you think it will help?"

"Oh, yes! Yes! Yes!" They were all grinning, even Cleever. Marion hugged the little alien. "You've made such a beautiful thing for us, how can we ever thank you?"

The alien glowed, beamed, tugged his mustache. "Oh, it was nothing. Foam, mostly. You may have to fix the roof. Oh dear," he looked at Whelan. "The time! Could you take me back to my ship?"

"This I *must* see." Doctor Lukas raised his voice surprisingly. "Miss Timmons! Elvira! Cancel everything for today—and wait!"

They all swarmed out clasping their keys and climbed in among Whelan's water samples and bumper jacks. When they were bowling back up 101 the alien said, "Now I mustn't forget anything." And he went over what he'd told Lukas about bringing their friends but being careful about it.

"Imagine!" said Marion. "A whole planet full of only good guys!"

"Not too damn full," said Whelan.

"Can I bring my raccoon?" Marty asked.

"There goes the ecological balance," Whelan groaned. But he kept on grinning.

"Raccoons are good guys!"

"Before we get into an ethical evaluation of raccoons let's see if there's anything more he should tell us," said Cleever.

"I nearly forgot," the alien said, "There's a key dispenser by the washrooms. I think you should always carry two, don't you? In case you lose one."

"What happens if the wrong guy finds a key?"

"Oh, it's most unlikely anyone would perform the code by chance. But if he did, well, that would be the end of that, I'm afraid."

"Hey," Marion said, "let's give the sheriff one!"

The alien looked at her. She caught his eye and her head began to go back and forth, no. "It was just a thought."

"Watch those thoughts," said Cleever.

"I wouldn't *contaminate* it!" she said indignantly. "Oh, I can't wait. I'm going to find some of that fruit for Mrs. Kovacs."

The alien sighed happily. "I'm *so* gratified. If only my next stop goes as well."

"Where? Who?" they asked.

"We thought, a nucleus in each large land mass, you know. Just time. I go down that way—Brazil, is it? And one more place. I have it coded."

"That explains the Afro combs," Cleever muttered. "You won't be too lonesome, Doctor."

"But *good* guys," Marion reminded him.

"I thought I saw something move just as we were leaving," Whelan said. "Over on the far side."

"Really! Oh, how marvelous, that means one of my friends has found a suitable group. What good news. We worried about that." He smiled bravely. "We're quite vulnerable. You *are* somewhat intimidating, you know."

Marion hugged him some more and they alternately chattered in bursts, then fell silent in excited thoughts while Whelan zoomed them back up the highway and bounced into the shortcut to Marty's father's farm.

"We're going to kick ourselves for not asking you a

couple of million things," Cleever said as they rushed over the last hill. "Oh Jesus. In the yard."

They peered out as the Brumbacher farm went by.

The sheriff's cruiser was standing by the pigsty.

"Keep on going!" Marty yelled. "The creek's out of sight."

"He's going to bust out after us in two shakes." Whelan kept going, watching the mirror. "There! He's running out of the barn."

"Quickly," the alien was wriggling around, pulling tubes out of his suit. "If you will just drop me where we came out. I can use my invisibility inducer." He pulled out some grids. "I hope."

"Can't you make a monster?" Marty asked as they shot down the hill.

The alien connected things frantically. "I'm so tired. This is much easier—if it works."

Behind them they heard the sheriff's car, *Vrrooomm.*

"We shan't see your vehicle," said Lukas disappointedly.

"We won't see *you* again," Marion cried. "Oh, Joe dear! Please come back!"

The alien was pushing part of his apparatus into his mouth. His eyes rolled appealingly and he tried to nod. Whelan stood on the brakes. They were by the creek gate.

The *vrroomm* got louder.

"Here he comes. Hurry, Joe!"

The alien scrambled out. His invisibility thing uncurled down around his shoulders like an over-wrought tuba. He straightened up and started working various buttons. Nothing happened.

"Hurry, Joe! *Hurry!*"

The alien's eyes popped, he fiddled and punched feverishly, backing into the gate to push it ajar. A siren blared to life at the top of the hill.

"Look, he's shimmering! He's thinning out!"

"Oh, good-bye, good-bye! Dear Joe, thank you!"

The sheriff's car was scorching down the hill, warble horn going.

"Good luck, Joe! Oh, thank you!"

"Hey—his *foot!*"

The alien had melted into a heat-wavy place in the air except for one solid foot. It ended in a pinkish blur. The foot stamped a couple of times and they heard a faint voice, apparently swearing.

Just as the cruiser growled up beside them the foot turned and started hopping through the gate.

"Marty, you better get out," said Whelan through his teeth. "Just bringing him home," he shouted at the sheriff.

Everybody was trying not to look at the solitary foot leaping down the pasture path. "See you later," they said to Marty as he climbed out and headed back up the road to his house.

The sheriff's face came down to the window.

"You—the guy with the fireworks. Okay, out."

"I am Professor Theodore Lukas of the state university department of Life Sciences," said Lukas stiffly. "Mr. Whelan is assisting me in a scientific investigation."

"Professor, huh?" The sheriff's blue stare jabbed around. Then, surprisingly, he straightened up and slapped the roof.

"All right, move on. Move on, you're blocking the road."

"He's overdue at Matt's about now," Whelan explained as they moved briskly on. "Oh, man. Know what I'm going to do? Soon as we get the professor home I'm going to pick up some groceries and take Helen back on the old logging road. Nobody'll find the car. We're going to have ourselves a weekend in Heaven!"

"You won't be alone," they laughed.

"I hope to Christ these keys work better than his invisibility whoosis," said Cleever.

"We'll have to watch out for Marty." Marion was sniffling a little. "Oh, I wonder, will he ever come back? He was such a *sweet* person."

"It just occurred to me," Cleever remarked reflectively. "He never did use that thing himself."

"Oh, *Cleever!*"

Back in the pasture the alien was humming happily as he expanded the modules of his little ship. He was thinking about coming back. Every so often he stood up and shivered, letting the *fremth* do its stuff.

When he had everything assembled he opened his communicator circuits, keeping one eye on an Ayrshire heifer who was becoming curious. An excited voice answered him.

"You can't guess what I ran into," the voice chattered in his own language. "A whole town full of heavy *disarmament* types! From all over. Place called Geneva. One of them's already planning to move his family out. How'd you do? Hey, is the *fremth* this good where you are?"

"Fantastic," said the alien known as Joe. "My group went beautifully, such nice people. I feel sure that they and their friends will decide to leave this planet permanently after a very few visits."

"Mine, too," the voice chuckled. "And as we always say, when all the good guys go, good-bye planet. How's Shushli doing? If he's having the same luck we'll have this place ready to go in no time."

"Shushli here," said a new voice. "I'm doing great, in fact I'm running out of keys. City called Gorski. Pathetic, isn't it? Absolutely ripe. I tell you, there won't be a sane mind left on this planet in a couple of their ridiculously short generations."

"Yeah," said Joe happily. "I just hope the sickies don't mess the place too badly before they wipe themselves out. Well, I must move along. Shoo!—not you, a cow. An animal." Joe stood up and took one last shiver. "Listen, guys, we better start thinking about our sales brochures. And be sure to stick an official seal on your recorders, will you? You know—folks will never believe the *fremth*."

Beaver Tears

HOME LATE, HOT and tired. Tonight he treats himself to Chivas Regal and the last of the excellent roast beef Jenny had left him in the icebox. A garlic pickle, black bread to go with it. Cheese, sage cheddar; not quite as good as the ads, but okay.

He flops tiredly by the TV, twirls the dials. Too late, good night for NBC. Fade to some *National Geographic* thing. Chewing, he watches the character explaining how to tranquilize beavers. The beavers look toothy, inscrutable. Marlboro music. Men are putting the beavers in bags, the bags in baskets on a packhorse. Beavers are ecological. He gathers they are being taken up a strip-mined mountain to be released. There they will start right in doing their beaver thing, making dams, catching silt, rebuilding the forests. Very neat; miracles of nature.

He has another Chivas Regal, wondering if the beavers in the bags like each other. When the man turns them loose they hump off wildly in different directions. A couple act damaged but the camera pans quickly to an okay beaver disappearing up a dry gulch, synchronized with Disney music. Next week, Spearing the Giant Manta.

He kills the commercial and wanders out onto the dark patio. Still hot. Lights all around now. This was all woodland when he and Jenny came out five years ago. Supposed to be five-acre zoning, but the commission ran in a sewer line and changed that.

He studies what can be seen of the sky above the lights. Summer storm building up over Bald Peak, west of town. Big sheet flash. A loud blare of amped-up C&W is coming from the Bannermans' patio, another of their interminable parties. "Bashes," Joan Bannerman calls them, grinning with postmenopausal gaiety. The Bannermans have two oafish teenaged sons. Joan dresses like their sister. Prides herself on her figure. Riding behind them on their Harley-Davidsons to the post office, for God's sake. Wagon wheels and cow skulls around their big swimming pool.

He sighs, appreciating Jenny, even appreciating the baby at this distance. No, that isn't fair, he's a good little guy. In two more days she'll be back, Jenny and Jimmy. . . . He grunts uxoriously, scratching his arse on the redwood table. Two more nights. To Grandmother's house we go. Only why the hell does Grandmother live in Santa Barbara? Good thing overall, though. Feeling mellow now he whistles softly at an awakened mockingbird that is answering the Bannerman stampede.

There's one dark patch of woods left, around the Jacksons' house. Last black family left out here. Ex-farmland. They own their land. Probably sell out soon. Nice neighbors; six kids, no noise at all. Doubtless being kept awake by middle-class honky uproar.

A massive flickering over Bald Peak now, quite a display. Jenny says there's no such thing as "summer" lightning, merely a storm somewhere else. If so it's a good one, maybe it'll bring rain. We need it; water table is way down, wells going dry since they've paved half the county. Should get the weather forecast, he thinks, and on impulse goes back in and flips on the radio weather station. On the fritz again, nothing but squeals. Without Jenny everything goes to hell fast.

He spins to a news channel, gets some kind of science-fiction late show, more static. Jenny will fix it. Two more nights. Should he finish up the whiskey?

He decides against it; heavy day tomorrow. Thursday always the worst of the week, never ask anybody for anything on Thursdays. The Bannerman bedlam seems to be increasing. Shrieks and loud male bellowing through the PA. Goddam it, outdoor PA systems are illegal now, one good thing. Should he go over there and remonstrate? No, wait for Jenny, she does that kind of thing better. Especially if it wakes up the baby.

He grins lonesomely, closing windows on the Bannerman side. Thank God it's cooling off, but the air really stinks. Gassy. Imagine smog out here, he thinks disgustedly, sliding shut the patio doors. The last thing he remembers is a sudden stillness from the Bannerman patio. . . .

. . . A mean slick hardness under his cheek. He rejects it, wills it to become smooth bedsheets. Too hard—a floor, say the patio tiles. Please God, let it be tiles, let it be a coronary even. I hurt. It's a minor coronary, that's all.

But the pain isn't in his chest, it's in his leg. His arm, too. And oh yes, the jaw, which he has tried imperceptibly to move. Very bad; he decides against trying to move anything else, lies with his eyes shut. *I did fight—*

He abolishes thought, tries to wrap unconsciousness around him. But the drug, gas, whatever, is wearing thin. The horrible slick floor under his face has begun to hum, buzzes through his bones like an angry insect. *I did fight—*

And at that moment he sees it all again, the awful view from the conveyor or whatever it was, when he had waked to find himself sprawled on metal mesh which was carrying him higher and higher above the early dawn countryside. High-pitched whine of machinery . . . He remembers blurrily raising his head, seeing the dim lumps of other bodies ascending behind him. And then as the thing stopped two or three hundred feet up in nowhere, he had turned and seen the cliff of metal alongside. The dark cliff, the darker gaping port, and THEM. Coming for him, reaching with *things—*

In that instant he realized with total lucidity that he was here while Jenny and his child were in California two thousand miles away; he will never conceivably see either of them again if he does not act. He leaps, throws himself hurtfully across alien machinery, trying to scramble away, slide down—if necessary fall down—anything not to be taken by THEM, into THAT—but it's too late, things have seized and coiled around him as he struggles. He flails, kicks, and bites metal until the nauseating fog blotted his world.

Yes, I fought, he forms now with his lips on hardness, refusing to open his eyes, to admit any of this. But he cannot shut out the humming, and above it the susurrus of other breathing around him. Something or somebody is making a high thin rasping sound, *Ekkk-hnhnhn, Ek-kkk-hhhn,* like a delirious chicken.

The drumming under his head is louder, is making his jaw hurt intolerably. Teeth are broken from grinding on metal or moving metallic flesh. He has a searing memory of sentient coils against his body and vomit suddenly shoots up his throat, literally jumps against his teeth. Projectile vomiting, he remembers this is called. Without moving he lets it trickle out, retasting decomposed whiskey.

Against his will, vision has penetrated between the lashes of his good eye. A dim gray light, which seems to be coming from the slickness of the floor. In his line of sight is a bare tanned ankle. Involuntarily he follows the young line of the leg in faded jeans. Beyond the jeans is a mauve t-shirt, a heavy mane of reddish-gold hair. It is not Jenny. The girl is lying face down, breathing okay. The rasping whine is coming from beyond her.

Very slowly he lets his eyes open. He can see a corner of the cell or compartment. The wall is shiny like the floor. A cargo space. The ship probably is full of them.

Crouched against the wall in a curious squatting posture is a woman. In the dim underlighting her face looks like a frog. Then he recognizes her: Joan Bannerman. She is making the gasping.

After a moment he realizes that there is another figure in the far corner of his field of vision. By squinting over his shoulder, not moving his head, he can see a face down by the floor. It is looking at Joan Bannerman, a round brown face, screwed into a toothy rigid mask. A memory from another world flicks him; the beavers on TV. But this is not a beaver, it is a human child. Finally he remembers. She is Evelyn, or Jacqueline, one of the Jacksons' kids. About eight. She is clutching her arm, which seems to have bled heavily. He will have to face reality now, he knows; he must move, get up, help the child.

But as he thinks this, a huge clanging rush of sound rocks the chamber, almost tears him loose from consciousness. Pain rips through him, while in the deeps of his heart a shutter closes forever on a world of green and sunlight. The ship is taking off. *Jenny, Jimmy.* Gone, lock it away. Bite down.

Dizzy, trying not to vomit again, he thinks, we did it. Whatever it was, we did our human thing. We fixed it the way they liked. Concrete, carbon monoxide, the sea full of plastic and oil, who knows. What we do. It's fixed up for them. So now they're moving some of us along to start fixing up another. Hundreds, maybe thousands of us. Beavers. A batch per so many zillion square miles, per planet even, who knows?

With that the drug or anesthetic wears completely away and the pain from his thigh and his broken face becomes unbearable. His leg must be splintered, really he needs medical care. A groan escapes him. He tries to turn sidewise, wondering if Joan Bannerman can help him, or maybe the strange girl on the floor.

Joan Bannerman is staring blindly, muttering "Harry, Harry," with her fingers in her mouth. No help there. The girl?

The girl is moving now, he sees, waking up. Apparently not hurt. She rolls over with luxurious sleepy ease and farts loudly.

"Mom?"

Oh God, it is not a girl at all. It is Oscar Bannerman.

"Mom!" Oscar repeats querulously. His mother does not react. Suddenly a hand comes from nowhere and slaps her on the face. Jesus—there's another youth here, squatting by the wall beyond Joan. It's not her other son, it's that friend of theirs who shot the cat. Billy Dee something.

Joan Bannerman comes jerkily to life and starts patting her youngest, still crooning "Harry . . ."

"Okay, Mom." Oscar shrugs off her hand. He and Billy Dee get groggily up on their feet, staring around. Their eyes are not empathic.

Beneath the pain a deathly hysteria is rising in him. The aliens, he thinks, do not seem to know much about human biology. Or they don't care. Maybe they use some easy mark like hair, maybe they thought Oscar was a female. . . . One prepubescent and one wombless female, to colonize what? Their ecological operations must be on such a large scale that little slipups like this don't matter. We dump millions of trout from planes, some of them live.

"You okay, Ossie?" Billy Dee inquires.

Oscar farts again, giggles. Billy Dee nods in approval, his small, slightly crossed eyes roving between the black child and the wounded man on the floor, himself.

No one says anything. In the silence rise faint clangors of alien might. The little Jackson girl has her flat terrified stare fixed on Billy Dee. And now another, final presence is perceptible behind her in the dim cell.

Please God, he thinks, let it be someone okay. Painfully he twists his head to see.

It is her thirteen-year-old brother Payton, a lithe black youth crouched death-still with a glinting object in one hand.

No. Letting himself sink down through pain's claws, he decides this is not going to be one of the successful ones.

Your Faces, O My Sisters!
Your Faces Filled of Light!

HOT SUMMER NIGHT, big raindrops falling faster now as she swings along the concrete expressway, high over the old dead city. Lightning is sizzling and cracking over the lake behind her. Beautiful! The flashes jump the roofs of the city to life below her, miles of cube buildings gray and sharp-edged in the glare. People lived here once, all the way to the horizons. Smiling, she thinks of all those walls and windows full of people, living in turbulence and terror. Incredible.

She's passing a great billboard-thing dangling and banging in the wind. Part of a big grinning face: O-N-D-E-R-B-R-E-A, whatever that was, bright as day. She strides along enjoying the cool rain on her bare head. No need to pull up her parka for a few minutes yet, the freshness is so great. All headaches completely gone. The sisters were wrong, she's perfectly fine. There was no reason to wait any longer, with the messages in her pack and Des Moines out there ahead. They didn't realize how walking rests you.

Sandals just getting wet, she notes. It feels good, but she mustn't let them get wet through, they'll chafe and start a blister. Couriers have to think of things like that. In a few minutes she'll climb down one of the ramps and take shelter.

There's ramps along here every half-mile or so, over the old city. Chi-cago or She-cago, which was it. She should find out, she's been this way several times now. Courier to the West. The lake behind her is Michigam, Michi-gami, the shining Big Sea Water. Satisfied, she figures she has come nearly seventy miles already since she left the hostel yesterday, and only one hitch. I'm not even tired. That beautiful old sister, she thinks. I'd have liked to talk with her more. Like the wise old Nokomis. That's the trouble, I always want to stop and explore the beautiful places and people, and I always want to get on too, get to the next. Couriers see so much. Someday she'll come back here and have a good swim in the lake, loaf and ramble around the old city. So much to see, no danger except from falling walls, she's expert at watching that. Some sisters say there are dog packs here, she doesn't believe it. And even if there are, they wouldn't be dangerous. Animals aren't dangerous if you know what to do. No dangers left at all, in the whole free wide world!

She shakes the rain out of her face, smiling up at the blowing night. To be a courier, what a great life! Rambling woman, on the road. Heyo, sister! Any mail, any messages for Des Moines and points west? Travel, travel on. But she is traveling in really heavy downpour now, she sees. She squeezes past a heap of old wrecked "cars" and splash! one foot goes in ankle-deep. The rain is drumming little fountains all over the old roadway. Time to get under; she reaches back and pulls the parka hood up from under her pack, thinking how alive the highway looks in the flashing lightning and rain. This road must have been full of the "cars" once, all of them shiny new, roaring along probably quite close together, belching gases, shining their lights, using all this space. She can almost hear them, poor crazy creatures. *Rrrr-oom!* A blazing bolt slaps down quite near her, strobes on and off. Whew! That was close. She chuckles, feeling briefly dizzy in the ozone. Ah, here's a ramp right by her, it looks okay.

Followed by a strange whirling light shaft, some trick of the storm, she ducks aside and runs lightly down from the Stevenson Expressway into the Thirty-fifth Street underpass.

"Gone." Patrolman Lugioni cuts the flasher, lets the siren growl diminuendo. The cruiser accelerates in the curb lane, broadcasting its need of a ring job. "Shitass kids out hitching on a night like this." He shakes his head.

Al, the driver, feels under his leg for the pack of smokes. "I thought it was a girl."

"Who can tell," Lugioni grunts. Lightning is cracking

everywhere, it's a cloudburst. All around them the Saturday night madhouse tears on, every car towing a big bustle of dirty water in the lights of the car behind.

—Dry under the overpass, but it's really dark in here between the lightning flashes. She pushes back her parka, walks on carefully avoiding wrecks and debris. With all that flashing, her night vision won't develop. Too bad, she has keen night vision. Takes forty-five minutes to come up fully, she knows a lot of stuff like that.

She's under a long elevated roadway down the center of an old street, it seems to go on for miles straight ahead. Almost straight west, good. Outside on both sides the open street is jumping with rain, splashing up white like plaster grass as the lightning cracks. *Boom! Barooomm-m-m!* The Midwest has great storms. She loves the wild uproar, she loves footing through a storm. All for her! How she'd like to strip and run out into it. Get a good bath, clean off all the dust and sweat. Her stuff would keep dry in here. Hey, shall I? . . . Almost she does, but she isn't really that dirty yet and she should get on, she lost so much time at that hostel. Couriers have to act responsible. She makes herself pad soberly along dodging junk in the dark, thinking, now here's the kind of place a horse would be no good.

She has always this perennial debate with herself about getting a horse. Some of the couriers like to ride. It probably *is* faster, she thinks. But not much, not much. Most people have no idea how fast walking goes, I'm up and moving while they're still fussing with the horse. And so much trouble, feeding them, worrying about their feet. You can carry more, of course. But the real point is how isolated it makes you. No more hitching, no more fun of getting to know all kinds of sisters. Like that wise motherly sister back there who picked her up coming into the city. Sort of a strange dialect, but I could understand her and the love showed through. A mother . . . Maybe I'll be a mother someday, she thinks. But not yet. Or I'll be the good old Nokomis. *The wrinkled old Nokomis, many things Nokomis taught her.* . . . And those horses she had, I never saw horses go like that. Must be some tremendous farms around here. Tomorrow when she's out of the city she'll get up on a high place where she can really look over the country. If I see a good horsefarm I'll remember. A horse would be useful if I take the next route, the route going all the way west, across the Rockies. But Des Moines is far enough now. Des Moines is just right, on my own good legs.

"She was one of *them*, one of those bra-burners," Mrs. Olmsted says pursily, sliding gingerly out of her plastic raincoat. She undoes her plastic Rainflower bonnet. "Oh God, my set."

"You don't usually pick up hitchers, Mom." Bee is sitting in the dinette, doing her nails with Plum Love.

"It was starting to storm," the mother says defensively, hustling into the genuine Birdseye kitchen area. "She had a big knapsack on her back. Oh, to tell you the truth, I thought it was a Boy Scout. That's why I stopped."

"Ha ha ha."

"I dropped her right at Stony Island. That's as far as we go, I said. She kept talking crazy about my face."

"Probably stoned. She'll get murdered out there."

"Bee, I told you, I wish you wouldn't use that word. I don't want to know about it, I have no sympathy at all. She's made her bed, I say. Now, where's the Fricolator lid?"

"In the bathroom. What about your face?"

"What's it doing in the bathroom?"

"I used it to soak my fluffbrush, it's the only thing the right shape. What'd she say about your face?"

"Oh, Bee, your father would murder you. That's no way to do, we eat out of that." Her voice fades and rises, still protesting, as she comes back with the lid.

"My hair isn't poison, Mom. Besides, the heat will fix it. You know my hair is pure hell when it rains, I have to look good at the office."

"I wish you wouldn't swear, either."

"What did she say about your face, Mom?"

"Oh, my face. Well! 'Your face has wisdom,' she says in this crazy way. 'Mother-lines full of wisdom and light.' *Lines*. Talk about rude! She called me the wrinkled old somebody. I told her what I thought about girls hitchhiking, believe me I told her. Here, help me clear this off, your father will be home any minute. You know what she said?"

"What did she say? Here, hand me that."

"She asked, did I mean dogs? *Dogs!* 'There is no fear,' she says, 'there is no fear on the whole wide earth.' And she kept asking me where did I get the horses. I guess that's some word they have, she meant the Buick."

"Stoned, I told you. Poor kid."

"Bee, *please*. What I say is, a girl like that is asking for it. Just asking for whatever she gets. I don't care what you say, there are certain rules. I have no sympathy, no sympathy at all."

"You can say that again."

—Her sandals are damp but okay. Good leather, she sewed and oiled them herself. When she's real old she'll have a little cabin by the road somewhere, make sandals and stuff for the sisters going by. How would I get the leather, she thinks. She could probably deal with one of the peddler sisters. Or can she tan it herself? It isn't so hard. Have to look that up some time.

The rain is still coming down hard, it's nice and cool now. She notices she has been scuffling through drifts of old paper, making it sail away into the gusty wind. All kinds of trash, here and everywhere. How they must have lived. The flashing outside is lighting up a solid wall of ruined buildings. Big black empty windows, some kind of factory. A piece of paper blows up and sticks on her neck. She peels it off, looks at it as she walks. In the lightning she can see it's a picture. Two sisters hugging. Neat. They're dressed in funny old clothes. And the small sister has such a weird look, all painted up and strange. Like she was pretending to smile. A picture from the troubles, obviously.

As she tucks it in her pocket she sees there's a light, right ahead between the pillars of the overpass. A hand-lantern, it moves. Somebody in here too, taking shelter. How great! Maybe they even live here, will have tales to tell! She hastens toward the light, calling the courier's cry:

"Heyo, sister! Any mail, any messages? Des Moines and going west!"

Yes—she sees there are two of them, wrapped up in

rain gear, leaning on one of the old "cars." Probably travelers too. She calls again.

"Hello?" One of them replies hesitantly. They must be worried by the storm, some sisters are. She'll reassure them, nothing to be afraid of, nothing at all. How she loves to meet new sisters, that's the beautiest part of a courier's life. Eagerly she strides through papers and puddles and comes into the circle of their light.

"But who can we report it *to*, Don? You aren't even known here, city police wouldn't pay any attention."

He shrugs regretfully, knowing his wife is right.

"One more unfortunate, weary of breath, rashly importunate, gone to her death."

"What's that from?"

"Oh, Hood. Thomas Hood. When the Thames used to be full of ruined women."

"Wandering around in this district at night, it's suicide. We're not so safe here ourselves, you know. Do you think that AAA tow truck will really come?"

"They said they would. They have quite a few calls ahead of us. Nobody's moving out there, she'll probably be safe as long as this downpour lasts, anyway. We'll get inside when it eases up."

"Yes . . . I wish we could have done something, Don. She seemed so, I don't know, not just a tramp."

"We couldn't very well hit her over the head and take her in, you know. Besides, she was a fairly strong-looking little piece, if you noticed."

"Yes . . . Don, she *was* crazy, wasn't she? She didn't hear one thing you said. Calling you Sister. And that ad she showed us, she said it was two women. That's sick, isn't it—I mean, seriously disturbed? Not just drugs?"

He laughs ruefully. "Questions I'd love to be able to answer. These things interact, it's tough to unscramble. But yes, for what it's worth, my intuition says it was functional. Of course my intuition got some help, you heard her say she'd been in a hospital or hostel somewhere. . . . If I had to bet, Pam, I'd say post-ECS. That placid waxy cast to the face. Capillary patches. A lot of rapid eye movement. Typical."

"You mean, she's had electric shock."

"My guess."

"And we just let her walk away. . . . You know, I don't think that truck is coming at all. I think they just say yes and forget it. I've heard the triple-A is a terrible fraud."

"Got to give them time on a night like this."

"Ummm . . . I wonder where she is now."

"Hey, look, the rain's letting up. We better hop inside and lock the doors."

"Right, sister."

"Don't you start that, I warn you. Lock that back window, too."

"Don . . ."

"Yeah, what?"

"Don, she seemed so, I don't know. Happy and free. She—she was *fun*."

"That's the sick part, honey."

—The rain is letting up now, she sees. How convenient, because the sheltering ramp is now veering away to the north. She follows the median strip of the old avenue out into the open, not bothering to put the parka up. It's a wrecked part of the city, everything knocked down flat for a few blocks, but the street is okay. In the new quiet she can hear the lake waves smacking the shore, miles behind. Really have to stop and camp here a while some trip, she thinks, skirting a wreck or two on the center strip. By the Shining Big Sea Waters.

Was it Michi-Gami or Gitche-Gumee? No matter; she loves the whole idea of Hiawatha. In fact she always felt she *was* the sister Hiawatha somehow; it's one of the few pieces from the old days that makes any sense to her. Growing up learning all the ways of the beautiful things, the names of the wild creatures, learning lovingly all the richness, learning how. There are words for it, some of the sisters talk so beautifully. But that's not her way, words; she just knows what's the way that feels right. The good way, and herself rambling through the wonderful world. Maybe she's a little superficial, but it takes all kinds. I'm the *working* kind, she thinks proudly. Responsible, too, a courier. Speaking of which, she's at a Y; better make sure she's still headed west, these old streets can twist you.

She stops and opens her belt compass, watches the dim green needle steady. There! Right that way. And what luck, in the last flickers of lightning she can see trees a couple of blocks ahead. Maybe a park!

How fast these storms go; she dodges across a wreck-filled intersection, and starts trotting for the sheer joy of strength and health down the open median toward the park. Yes, it looks like a long strip of greenery, heading due west for quite a ways. She'll have nice walking. Somewhere ahead she'll hit another of the old freeways, the Kennedy or the Dan Ryan, that'll take her out of the city. Bound to be traffic on them too, in the morning. She'll get a hitch from a grain cart maybe, or maybe a peddler. Or maybe something she's never seen before, one more of the surprises of the happy world.

Jogging, feeling her feet fall fast and free, she thinks with respect of the two sisters she met back there under the ramp. The big one was some kind of healer, from down South. So loving together, making jokes. But I'm not going to get sick anymore, I'm really well. Proud of the vitality in her, she strides swiftly across the last intersection and spots a path meandering into the overgrown strip of park. Maybe I can go barefoot in there, no glass, she thinks. The last lightning flash helps her as she heads in under the dripping trees.

The biker cuts off his spotlight fast, accelerates past the park entrance. She looked okay, little and running. Scared. But something about her bothers him. Not quite right. Maybe she's meeting somebody in there?

He's running alone tonight, the rain freaked them all out. Alone isn't so good. But maybe she's alone, too? Small and alone . . .

Gunning up Archer Avenue, he decides to cut back once through the park crossover, check it out. The main thing is not to get the bike scratched up.

—Beautiful cool clean breeze on her face, and clouds are breaking up. Old moon is trying to shine out! The path is deep in leaves here, okay to get the sandals off and dry them awhile.

She balances one-legged, unbuckling. The left one is

soaked, all right. She hangs them over her pack and steps out barefoot. Great.

Out beyond the trees the buildings are reared up high on both sides now, old cubes and towers sticking up at the racing clouds, glints of moonlight where the glass windows are still in. Fantastic. She casts a loving thought back toward the long-dead ones who had built all this. The Men, the city-builders. So complex and weird, so different from the good natural way. Too bad they never lived to know the beautiful peaceful free world. But they wouldn't have liked it, probably. They were sick, poor things. But maybe they could have been different; they were people too, she muses.

Suddenly she is startled by the passage of something crashing across the path ahead, and without thinking springs nimbly into a big bush. Lightning, growling noises —in a minute it fades away. A deer, maybe, she wonders, rubbing her head. But what was the noise? One of those dogs, maybe? Could it be a dog pack?

Hmmm. She rubs harder, frowning because the headache seems to have come back. Like a knife blade in her temple. Ouch! It's really bad again, it's making her dizzy. She blinks, sees the buildings beyond the park blaze up brightly—squares of yellow light everywhere like a million windows. Oh no, not the bad hallucinations again. No, she's well now!

But yes, it is—and great lights seem to be suddenly everywhere, a roar of noise breaks out all around her in the dead streets, things are rushing and clanging. Maybe she isn't quite as well as she thought.

Grunting softly with pain, she strips a bunch of cool wet leaves, presses it against her forehead, the veins in her neck. Pressure. That's what it is, the air pressure must have changed fast in the storm. She'll be all right in a few minutes. . . . Even the memory of the deer seems strange, as if she'd glimpsed some kind of crazy machine with a sister riding on it. Crazy! The uproar around her has voices in it, too, a ghostly whistle blows. . . . Go away, dreams. . . .

She stands quietly, pressing the coolness to her temples, willing the noisy hallucination to leave. Slowly it does; subsides, fades, vanishes. Leaving her in peace back in the normal, happy world. She's okay, that was nothing at all!

She tosses the leaves down and strikes out on the path, remembering—whew!—how bad it had been when she was back there at the hostel. All because of that funny flu or whatever that made her gut swell up so. Bad dreams all the time, real horrible hallucinations. Admit it; couriers do catch things. But it's worth it.

The sisters had been so scared. How they kept questioning her. Are you dreaming now? Do you see it now, dear? Making her describe it, like she was a historical play. They must read too much history, she thinks, splashing through a puddle, scaring up some little night-thing. A frog, probably, out in the rain like me. And all that talk about babies. Babies . . . Well, a baby might be nice, someday. Not till after a lot more trips, though. Right now she's a walking sister, traveling on, heading for Des Moines and points west!

Left-right, left-right, her slim strong legs carry her Indian style, every bit of her feeling good now in the rain-fresh night. Not a scrap weary; she loves her tough enduring wiry body. To be a courier, surely that's the best life of all. To be young and night-walking in the great free moonlit world. Heyo, sisters! She grins to herself, padding light-foot. Any messages, any mail?

"Of course she's not dangerous, Officer," the doctor says authoritatively. The doctor is a heavy, jolly-looking woman with a big Vuitton carryall parked on the desk. The haggard young man slumped in a lounger over at the side stares tiredly, says nothing.

"Jeans, green parka, knapsack, sandals. May have credit cards," the detective repeats, writing in his notebook. "Hair?"

"Short. Just growing out, in fact; it was shaved during treatment. I realize that isn't much to go on."

The policeman juts his lip out noncommittally, writing. Why can't they keep track of their patients, a big place like this? One medium-height, medium-looking girl in jeans and a parka . . .

"You see, she is quite, quite helpless," the heavy woman

says seriously, fingering her desk calendar. "The delusional system has expanded."

"You were supposed to break that up," the young man says suddenly, not looking up. "My wife was, I mean, when I brought her here . . ."

His voice is stale with exhausted anger, this has all been said before. The psychiatrist sighs briefly, says nothing.

"The delusion, is it dangerous? Is she hostile?" the detective asks hopefully.

"No. I told you. It takes the form of a belief that she's living in another world where everybody is her friend. She's completely trusting, you'll have no difficulty."

"Oh." He puts the notebook away with finality, getting up. The psychiatrist goes with him to the door. Out of earshot of the husband she says quietly, "I'll be at my office number when you've checked the morgue."

"Yeah."

He leaves, and she walks back to the desk, where the young man is now staring unseeingly at a drift of Polaroid snaps. The one on top shows a young brown-haired woman in a yellow dress in a garden somewhere.

—Moon riding high now in the summer night, cutting through a race of little silver clouds, making shafts of light wheel over the still city. She can see where the park is ending up ahead, there's a wreck-strewn traffic circle. She swings along strongly, feeling now just the first satisfying edge of tiredness, just enough to make her enjoy her own nimble endurance. Right-and-a-left-and-a-right-and-a-left, toes-in Indian style, that trains the tendons. She can go on forever.

Now here's the traffic circle, better watch out for metal and glass underfoot. She waits for a bright patch of moonlight and trots across to the center, hearing one faint hallucinatory screech or roar somewhere. No, no more of *that*. She grins at herself firmly, making her way around the pieces of an old statue toppled here. *That is but the owl and owlet, talking in their native language,* something *Hiawatha's Sisters*. I'd like to talk with them in their native language, she thinks—and speaking of which, she sees to her delight there's a human figure on the far side of the circle. What, another sister out nightwalking too!

"Heyo, sister!"

"Hi," the other replies. It's a Midwest person, she can tell. She must live here, can tell about the old city!

Eagerly she darts between the heaps in the roadway, joyfully comes to the beautiful sister, her face so filled in light.

"Where heading? Out to ramble? I'm a courier," she explains, taking the sister's arm. So much joy, a world of friends. "Any messages, any mail?" she laughs.

And they stride on together, free-swinging down the median strip of the old avenue to keep away from falling stuff in the peaceful old ruins. Over to one side is a bent sign saying TO DAN RYAN EXPRESSWAY, O'HARE AIRPORT. On the heading for Des Moines and points west!

"I don't remember," the girl, or woman, repeats hoarsely, frowning. "I really don't remember, it was all strange. My head was really fucked up, I mean, all I wanted was to get back and sack out, the last john was a bummer. I mean, I didn't know the area. You know? I asked her could she give me some change."

"What did she say? Did she have money with her?" the older man asks with deadly patience. His wife is sitting on the leather sofa, her mouth trembling a little.

"I don't remember, really. I mean, she was talking but she wasn't listening, I could see she was behind the heavy stuff. She offered me some chocolate. Oh shit, she was gone. Excuse me. She was really gone. I thought she was —well, she kept saying, y'know. Then she gave me all her cards."

The man looks down at them silently, lying on the coffee table. His daughter's married name embossed on the brown Saks plastic.

"So when I saw the paper I thought I should, well, you know." She gets up, smoothing her white Levi's. "It wasn't just the reward. She . . . Thanks anyway."

"Yes," he says automatically. "We do thank you, Miss Jackson, was it."

"Yes," his wife echoes shakily.

Miss Jackson, or whatever, looks around at the woman, the man, the elegantly lived-in library; hitches her white shoulder bag.

"I tried to tell her," she says vaguely. "She said, about going west. She wouldn't . . . I'm sorry."

"Yes, thank you." He's ushering her to the door. "I'm afraid there wasn't anything anyone could do."

"She wasn't in this world."

"No."

When the door closes behind her the older woman makes an uncertain noise and then says heavily, "Why?"

Her husband shakes his head, performs a non-act of straightening the credit cards, putting them on another table.

"We'll have to call Henry, when he gets back from—"

"*Why?*" the wife repeats as if angry. "*Why* did she? What did she want? Always running away. Freedom. Doesn't she know you can't have freedom? Why isn't this world good enough for her? She had everything. If I can take it why can't she?"

He has nothing to say, only moves near her and briefly touches her shoulder.

"Why didn't Doctor Albers *do* something? All those drugs, those shocks, it just made her worse. Henry never should have taken her there, it's all his fault—"

"I guess Henry was desperate," her husband says in a gray tone.

"She was all right when she was with us."

"Maria. Maria, please. She was out of her head. He had to do something. She wouldn't even recognize her own baby."

His wife nods, trembling harder. "My little girl, my little girl . . ."

—Glorious how bright it is now, she pads along still barefoot on the concrete median, tipping her head back to watch the moon racing above the flying clouds, imparting life and motion to the silent street, almost as if it was alive again. Now watch it, she cautions herself cheerfully —and watch the footing too, no telling what kind of sharp stuff is lying out here. No more dreaming about the old days, that was what gave her the fever-nightmares. Dreaming she was stuck back in history like a caged-up animal. An "affluent young suburban matron," whatever that was. All those weird people, telling her. Don't go outside, don't do this, don't do that, don't open the door, don't breathe. Danger everywhere.

How did they *live,* she wonders, seeing the concrete good and clean underfoot. Those poor old sisters, never being free, never even being able to go walking! Well, those dreams really made history live and breathe for her, that was sure. So vivid—whew! Maybe some poor old sister's soul has touched hers, maybe something mystical like that. She frowns faintly, feeling a stab of pressure in her forehead.

Now really, watch it! She scolds herself, hoisting up the pack straps, flapping the drying parka. All secure. She breaks into a slow, light-footed jog, just because she feels so good. Cities are so full of history. Time to forget all that, just appreciate being alive. Hello, moon! Hello, sky! She trots on carefully, tickled by it all, seeing a moon's-eye view of herself: one small purposeful dot resolutely moving west. Courier to Des Moines. All alone in the big friendly night world, greeting the occasional night-bird sisters. One traveling woman, going on through.

She notes a bad scatter of debris ahead and slows to pick her way with care through the "cars," not wanting to put her sandals back on yet. It's so bright—and hello! The sky really is brightening in the East behind her. Sunrise in another hour or so.

She's been on the road about twenty hours but she isn't really weary at all, she could go on all day if it didn't get so hot. She peers ahead, looking for signs of the Ryan Freeway that'll carry her west. What she'll do is stop and have a snack in the sunrise, maybe boil up some tea. And then go on awhile until it heats up, time to find a nice cool ruin and hole up for the day. Hey, maybe she can make O'Hare! She stayed there once before, it's neat.

She has enough rations in her pack to go at least two days easy, she figures. But she's short on chocolate now; have to get some at the next settlement if they have it. Sweet stuff is good for calories when you're exercising. She pads on, musing about the sister she shared her chocolate with while they walked together after the park. Such a free sweet face, all the sisters are so great but this one was especially interesting, living here studying the old days. She knew so much, all those stories, whew! Imagine when people had to sell their sex organs to the Men just to eat!

It's too much for her, she thinks, grinning. Leave that to the students. I'm an action person, yes. A courier, a traveler, moving along looking at it all, the wonder-filled world. Sampling, enjoying, footing it over the miles. Right-and-a-left-and-a-right-and-a-left on the old road-ways. A courier's feet are tough and brown as oak. *Of all beasts she learned the language, learned their names and all their secrets. Talked with them whene'er she met them*—a great rhythm for hiking, with a fresh breeze behind her and the moon setting ahead!

The breeze is making the old buildings on both sides creak and clank too, she notices. Better stay out here in the middle, even if it's getting narrow. The houses are really crowded in along here, all sagging and trashy. "Slums," probably. Where the crazy people lived on top of each other. What a mess it must have been; interesting to her but rotten for them. Well, they're gone now, she thinks, dodging around a heap of broken junk in the in-tersection, starting down the center strip of the next long block.

But something isn't gone, she notices; footsteps that have been pad-padding along after her for a while are still there. An animal, one of the poor dogs, she thinks. Fol-lowing her. Oh well, they must do all right in here, with rats and such.

She whirls around a couple of times, but sees nothing. It must be scared. What's its native language, she won-ders, and forgets about it as she sees ahead, unmistak-able, the misty silhouette of a freeway overpass. Hey, is that the Ryan already?

She casts a glance up at the floating-down moon, sees the sky is paling fast. And the left side of the street is passing an empty cleared place, the going looks all right there. She decides to cross over.

Yes, it's good walking, and she settles into her easy barefoot swing, letting one last loving thought go back to the poor maddened people who once strove here, who somehow out of their anguish managed to send their genes down to her, to give her happy life: courier going west! With the dawn wind in her hair and the sun coming up to light the whole free world!

"A routine surveillance assignment," the young police-woman, Floyd, says carefully.

"A stakeout." The bald reporter nods.

"Well, yes. We were assigned to surveil the subject building entrance. Officer Alioto and myself were seated in the parked car."

"So you saw the assault."

"No," she says stiffly. "We did not observe anything unusual. Naturally we observed the pedestrians, I mean the female subject and the alleged—alleged assailants, they were moving west at the time."

"You saw four punks following her."

"Well, it could look that way."

"You saw them going after her and you just sat there."

"We carried out our *orders*," she tells him. "We were assigned to surveil the building. We did not observe any alleged attack, nobody was running."

"You see the four of them jump this girl and you don't call that an attack?"

"We did not observe it. We were two blocks away."

"You could have seen if you wanted to," he says tiredly. "You could have cruised one block, you could have tapped the horn."

"I told you we were on a covert detail. You can't expect an officer to destroy his cover every time some little tramp runs down the street."

"You're a woman," he says wonderingly. "You'd sit there and let a girl get it."

"I'm not a nursemaid," she protests angrily. "I don't care if she was crazy. A spoiled brat if you ask me, all those women's lib freaks. I work. Who does she think she is, running on the street at night? She thinks the police have nothing more important to do than that?"

—Sunrise coming on sure enough though it's still dark down here. The magic hour. And that stupid dog or dogs are still coming on too, she notes. Pad-pad-pad, they've crossed over to the sidewalk behind her. Well, dogs don't attack people, it's just like those false wolf scares. *Learn of every beast its nature, learn their names and all their secrets*. They're just lonesome and curious, it's their nature to follow people. Tag along and veer off if I say boo.

She strides along, debating whether she should put her wet sandals on or whether it's going to stay this clean. If so she can make it barefoot up to the expressway ramp— and it *is* the Ryan, she can see the big sign now. Great, that'll be the perfect place to make her breakfast, just about sunrise. Better remember to pick up a couple of dry sticks and some paper under the ramp, not much to burn on those skyways.

Ignoring the footfalls pattering behind, she lets her mind go back pleasurably to the great breakfasts she's had. All the sunrise views, how she loves that. Like the morning on the old Ohio Turnpike, when all the owls hooted at once, and the mists turned pink and rose up and there was the shining river all spread out below her. Beautiful. Even with the mosquitoes. If you're going to appreciate life you can't let little things like mosquitoes bother you. . . . That was before her peculiar sickness, when she was at the hostel. So many good hostels she's stopped at, all the interesting different settlements and farms, all the great sister-people. Someday she'll do the whole west route, know people everywhere. . . . Pad-pad-pad, she hears them again momentarily, rubs away a tiny ache in her temple. *Boo,* she chuckles to herself, feeling her bare feet falling sturdy and swift, left-and-a-right-and-a-left, carrying her over the miles, across the free beautiful friendly Earth. O my sisters, living in light!

Pictures flit through her head, all the places she wants to visit. The Western mountains, the real big ones. And the great real Sea. Maybe she'll visit the grave of the Last Man when she's out there, too. That would be interesting. See the park where he lived, hear the tapes of his voice and all. Of course he probably wasn't the actually last Man, just the one they knew about. It would be really something to hear such a different person's voice.

Pad-pad-pad—louder, closer than before. They're going to be a nuisance if they follow her up the ramp and hang around her breakfast.

"Boo!" she shouts, laughing, swinging around at them. They scatter so fast she can barely glimpse dark shapes vanishing into the old walls. Good. "Boo!" she shouts again, sorry to have to drive them away, and swings back on course, satisfied.

The buildings are beside her now, but they're pretty intact, no glass she can see underfoot. In fact, the glass is still in the old store windows here. She glances in curiously as she passes, heaps of moldy stuff and faded pictures and printing. "Ads." Lots of sisters' faces, all looking so weird and fake-grinning. One window has nothing but dummy heads in it, all with strange-looking imitation hair or something on them. Fantastic.

—But here they come again behind her, pad-pad-pad, and she really ought to discourage them before they decide to stick with her up the freeway.

"Boo, boo! No—" Just as she's turning on them something fast and dark springs and strikes or snaps at her arm! And before she can react she sees they are suddenly all around her, ahead of her—rearing up weirdly, just like people!

"Get *out!*" she shouts, feeling a rush of something unknown—anger?—sending heat through her, this is almost like one of the dreams! But hardness strikes her neck, staggers her, with roaring in her ears.

She hits out awkwardly, feels herself slammed down on concrete—pain—her head is hurt. And she is striking, trying to fend them off, realizing unbelieving that the brutes are tugging at her, terribly strong, pulling her legs and arms apart, spread-eagling her.

"Sisters!" she shouts, really being hurt now, struggling strongly. "*Sisters!* Help!" But something gags her so that she can only choke, while she feels them tearing at her clothes, her belly. *No, no*—she understands with horror that they really are going to bite her, to eat her flesh, and remembers from somewhere that wild dogs tear out the victim's guts first.

A great wave of anger convulses her against their fangs, she knows this is a stupid accident, a mistake—but her blood is fountaining everywhere, and the pain, the *pain!* All in a moment she is being killed, she knows now she is going to die here.

—But as a truly terrible agony cuts into her crotch and entrails, she sees or thinks she sees—yes!—in the light, in

the patches of sky between the terrible bodies of her at-
tackers, she can see them coming—see far off but clear
the beautiful faces of her sisters speeding to save her, to
avenge her! O my sisters, yes—it will be all right now,
she knows, choking in her blood. They will finish these
animals. And my knapsack, my messages—somewhere
inside the pain and the dying she knows it is all right, it
will be all fixed when they get here; the beloved sisters
will save her, this is just an accident—and soon she, or
someone like her, will be going on again, will be footing
over the wide free Earth, courier to Des Moines and
points west—

The Screwfly Solution

THE YOUNG MAN sitting at 2° N, 75° W sent a casually venomous glance up at the nonfunctional shoofly *ventilador* and went on reading his letter. He was sweating heavily, stripped to his shorts in the hotbox of what passed for a hotel room in Cuyapán.

How do other wives *do* it? I stay busy-busy with the Ann Arbor grant review programs and the seminar, saying brightly 'Oh yes, Alan is in Colombia setting up a biological pest-control program, isn't it wonderful?' But inside I imagine you surrounded by nineteen-year-old raven-haired cooing beauties, every one panting with social dedication and filthy rich. And forty inches of bosom busting out of her delicate lingerie. I even figured it in centimeters, that's 101.6 centimeters of busting. Oh, darling, darling, do what you want only *come home safe*.

Alan grinned fondly, briefly imagining the only body he longed for. His girl, his magic Anne. Then he got up to open the window another cautious notch. A long pale mournful face looked in—a goat. The room opened on the goatpen, the stench was vile. Air, anyway. He picked up the letter.

Everything is just about as you left it, except that the Peedsville horror seems to be getting worse. They're calling it the Sons of Adam cult now. Why can't they *do* something, even if it is a religion? The Red Cross has set up a refugee camp in Ashton, Georgia. Imagine, refugees in the U.S.A. I heard two little girls were carried out all slashed up. Oh, Alan.

Which reminds me, Barney came over with a wad of clippings he wants me to send you. I'm putting them in a separate envelope; I know what happens to very fat letters in foreign POs. He says, in case you don't get them, what do the following have in common? Peedsville, Sao Paulo, Phoenix, San Diego, Shanghai, New Delhi, Tripoli, Brisbane, Johannesburg and Lubbock, Texas. He says the hint is, remember where the Intertropical Convergence Zone is now. That makes no sense to me, maybe it will to your superior ecological brain. All I could see about the clippings was that they were fairly horrible accounts of murders or massacres of women. The worst was the New Delhi one, about "rafts of female corpses" in the river. The funniest (!) was the Texas Army officer who shot his wife, three daughters and his aunt, because God told him to clean the place up.

Barney's such an old dear, he's coming over Sunday to help me take off the downspout and see what's blocking it. He's dancing on air right now; since you left, his spruce budworm-moth antipheromone program finally paid off. You know he tested over 2,000 compounds? Well, it seems that good old 2,097 *really* works. When I asked him what it does he just giggles, you know how shy he is with women. Anyway, it seems that a one-shot spray program will save the forests, without harming a single other thing. Birds and people can eat it all day, he says.

Well, sweetheart, that's all the news except Amy goes back to Chicago to school Sunday. The place will be a tomb, I'll miss her frightfully in spite of her being at the stage where I'm her worst enemy. The sullen sexy subteens, Angie says. Amy sends love to her daddy. I send you my whole heart, all that words can't say.

Your Anne

Alan put the letter safely in his note file and glanced over the rest of the thin packet of mail, refusing to let himself dream of home and Anne. Barney's "fat envelope" wasn't there. He threw himself on the rumpled bed, yanking off the light cord a minute before the town generator went off for the night. In the darkness the list of places Barney had mentioned spread themselves around a misty globe that turned, troublingly, in his mind. Something . . .

But then the memory of the hideously parasitized children he had worked with at the clinic that day took possession of his thoughts. He set himself to considering the data he must collect. *Look for the vulnerable link in the behavioral chain*—how often Barney—Dr. Barnhard Braithwaite—had pounded it into his skull. Where was it, where? In the morning he would start work on bigger canefly cages. . . .

At that moment, five thousand miles north, Anne was writing:

Oh, darling, darling, your first three letters are here, they all came together. I *knew* you were writing. Forget what I said about swarthy heiresses, that was all a joke. My darling I know, I know . . . us. Those dreadful canefly larvae, those poor little kids. If you weren't my husband I'd think you were a saint or something. (I do anyway.)

I have your letters pinned up all over the house, makes it a lot less lonely. No real news here except things feel kind of quiet and spooky. Barney and I got the downspout out, it was full of a big rotted hoard of squirrel nuts. They must have been dropping them down the top, I'll put a wire over it. (Don't worry, I'll use a ladder this time.)

Barney's in an odd, grim mood. He's taking this Sons of Adam thing very seriously, it seems he's going to be on the investigation committee if that ever gets off the ground. The weird part is that nobody seems to be doing anything, as if it's just too big. Selina Peters has been printing some acid comments, like: When one man kills his wife you call it murder, but when enough do it we call it a life-style. I think it's spreading, but nobody knows because the media have been asked to downplay it. Barney says it's being viewed as a form of contagious hysteria. He insisted I send you this ghastly interview, printed on thin paper. It's *not* going to be published, of course. The quietness is worse, though, it's like something terrible was going on just out of sight. After reading Barney's thing I called up Pauline in San Diego to make sure she was all right. She sounded funny, as if she wasn't saying everything . . . my own sister. Just after she said things were great she suddenly asked if she could come and stay here awhile next month. I said come right away, but she wants to sell her house first. I wish she'd hurry.

The diesel car is okay now, it just needed its filter changed. I had to go out to Springfield to get one but Eddie installed it for only $2.50. He's going to bankrupt his garage.

In case you didn't guess, those places of Barney's are all about latitude 30° N or S—the horse latitudes. When I said not exactly, he said remember the Equatorial Convergence Zone shifts in winter, and to add in Libya, Osaka, and a place I forget—wait, Alice Springs, Australia. What has this to do with anything, I asked. He said, "Nothing—I hope." I leave it to you, great brains like Barney can be weird.

Oh my dearest, here's all of me to all of you. Your letters make life possible. But don't feel you *have* to, I can tell how tired you must be. Just know we're together, always everywhere.

Your Anne

Oh PS I had to open this to put Barney's thing in, it wasn't the secret police. Here it is. All love again. A.

In the goat-infested room where Alan read this, rain was drumming on the roof. He put the letter to his nose to catch the faint perfume once more, and folded it away. Then he pulled out the yellow flimsy Barney had sent and began to read, frowning.

PEEDSVILLE CULT/SONS OF ADAM SPECIAL. Statement by driver Sgt. Willard Mews, Globe Fork, Ark. We hit the roadblock about 80 miles west of Jacksonville. Major John Heinz of Ashton was expecting us, he gave us an escort of two riot vehicles headed by Capt. T. Parr. Major Heinz appeared shocked to see that the N.I.H. medical team included two women doctors. He warned us in the strongest terms of the danger. So Dr. Patsy

Putnam (Urbana, Ill.), the psychologist, decided to
stay behind at the Army cordon. But Dr. Elaine Fay
(Clinton, N.J.) insisted on going with us, saying she
was the epi-something (epidemiologist).

We drove behind one of the riot cars at 30 m.p.h. for
about an hour without seeing anything unusual. There
were two big signs saying SONS OF ADAM—LIBERATED
ZONE. We passed some small pecan-packing plants and
a citrus-processing plant. The men there looked at us
but did not do anything unusual. I didn't see any children or women of course. Just outside Peedsville we
stopped at a big barrier made of oil drums in front of a
large citrus warehouse. This area is old, sort of a
shantytown and trailer park. The new part of town with
the shopping center and developments is about a mile
farther on. A warehouse worker with a shotgun came
out and told us to wait for the mayor. I don't think he
saw Dr. Elaine Fay then, she was sitting sort of bent
down in back.

Mayor Blount drove up in a police cruiser and our
chief, Dr. Premack, explained our mission from the
Surgeon General. Dr. Premack was very careful not to
make any remarks insulting to the mayor's religion.
Mayor Blount agreed to let the party go on into Peedsville to take samples of the soil and water and so on
and talk to the doctor who lives there. The mayor was
about 6′ 2″, weight maybe 230 or 240, tanned, with
grayish hair. He was smiling and chuckling in a
friendly manner.

Then he looked inside the car and saw Dr. Elaine
Fay and he blew up. He started yelling we had to all
get the hell back. But Dr. Premack talked to him and
cooled him down and finally the mayor said Dr. Fay
should go into the warehouse office and stay there with
the door closed. I had to stay there too and see she
didn't come out, and one of the mayor's men would
drive the party.

So the medical people and the mayor and one of the
riot vehicles went on into Peedsville and I took Dr. Fay
back into the warehouse office and sat down. It was
real hot and stuffy. Dr. Fay opened a window, but
when I heard her trying to talk to an old man outside I

told her she couldn't do that and closed the window. The old man went away. Then she wanted to talk to me but I told her I did not feel like conversing. I felt it was real wrong, her being there.

So then she started looking through the office files and reading papers there. I told her that was a bad idea, she shouldn't do that. She said the government expected her to investigate. She showed me a booklet or magazine they had there, it was called *Man Listens to God* by Reverend McIllhenny. They had a carton full in the office. I started reading it and Dr. Fay said she wanted to wash her hands. So I took her back along a kind of enclosed hallway beside the conveyor to where the toilet was. There were no doors or windows so I went back. After a while she called out that there was a cot back there, she was going to lie down. I figured that was all right because of the no windows; also, I was glad to be rid of her company.

When I got to reading the book it was very intriguing. It was very deep thinking about how man is now on trial with God and if we fulfill our duty God will bless us with a real new life on Earth. The signs and portents show it. It wasn't like, you know, Sunday-school stuff. It was deep.

After a while I heard some music and saw the soldiers from the other riot car were across the street by the gas tanks, sitting in the shade of some trees and kidding with the workers from the plant. One of them was playing a guitar, not electric, just plain. It looked so peaceful.

Then Mayor Blount drove up alone in the cruiser and came in. When he saw I was reading the book he smiled at me sort of fatherly, but he looked tense. He asked me where Dr. Fay was and I told him she was lying down in back. He said that was okay. Then he kind of sighed and went back down the hall, closing the door behind him. I sat and listened to the guitar man, trying to hear what he was singing. I felt really hungry, my lunch was in Dr. Premack's car.

After a while the door opened and Mayor Blount came back in. He looked terrible, his clothes were messed up and he had bloody scrape marks on his face.

He didn't say anything, he just looked at me hard and fierce, like he might have been disoriented. I saw his zipper was open and there was blood on his clothing and also on his (private parts).

I didn't feel frightened, I felt something important had happened. I tried to get him to sit down. But he motioned me to follow him back down the hall, to where Dr. Fay was. "You must see," he said. He went into the toilet and I went into a kind of little room there, where the cot was. The light was fairly good, reflected off the tin roof from where the walls stopped. I saw Dr. Fay lying on the cot in a peaceful appearance. She was lying straight, her clothing was to some extent different but her legs were together. I was glad to see that. Her blouse was pulled up and I saw there was a cut or incision on her abdomen. The blood was coming out there, or it had been coming out there, like a mouth. It wasn't moving at this time. Also her throat was cut open.

I returned to the office. Mayor Blount was sitting down, looking very tired. He had cleaned himself off. He said, "I did it for you. Do you understand?"

He seemed like my father. I can't say it better than that. I realized he was under a terrible strain, he had taken a lot on himself for me. He went on to explain how Dr. Fay was very dangerous, she was what they call a cripto-female (crypto?), the most dangerous kind. He had exposed her and purified the situation. He was very straightforward, I didn't feel confused at all, I knew he had done what was right.

We discussed the book, how man must purify himself and show God a clean world. He said some people raise the question of how can man reproduce without women but such people miss the point. The point is that as long as man depends on the old filthy animal way God won't help him. When man gets rid of his animal part which is woman, this is the signal God is awaiting. Then God will reveal the new true clean way, maybe angels will come bringing new souls, or maybe we will live forever, but it is not our place to speculate, only to obey. He said some men here had seen an Angel of the Lord. This was very deep, it seemed like it echoed inside me, I felt it was an inspiration.

Then the medical party drove up and I told Dr. Premack that Dr. Fay had been taken care of and sent away, and I got in the car to drive them out of the Liberated Zone. However four of the six soldiers from the roadblock refused to leave. Capt. Parr tried to argue them out of it but finally agreed they could stay to guard the oil-drum barrier.

I would have liked to stay too, the place was so peaceful, but they needed me to drive the car. If I had known there would be all this hassle I never would have done them the favor. I am not crazy and I have not done anything wrong and my lawyer will get me out. That is all I have to say.

In Cuyapán the hot afternoon rain had temporarily ceased. As Alan's fingers let go of Sgt. Willard Mews's wretched document he caught sight of pencil-scrawled words in the margin. Barney's spider hand. He squinted.

"Man's religion and metaphysics are the voices of his glands. Schönweiser, 1878."

Who the devil Schönweiser was Alan didn't know, but he knew what Barney was conveying. This murderous crackpot religion of McWhosis was a symptom, not a cause. Barney believed something was physically affecting the Peedsville men, generating psychosis, and a local religious demagogue had sprung up to "explain" it.

Well, maybe. But cause or effect, Alan thought only of one thing: eight hundred miles from Peedsville to Ann Arbor. Anne should be safe. She *had* to be.

He threw himself on the lumpy cot, his mind going back exultantly to his work. At the cost of a million bites and cane cuts he was pretty sure he'd found the weak link in the canefly cycle. The male mass-mating behavior, the comparative scarcity of ovulant females. It would be the screwfly solution all over again with the sexes reversed. Concentrate the pheromone, release sterilized females. Luckily the breeding populations were comparatively isolated. In a couple of seasons they ought to have it. Have to let them go on spraying poison meanwhile, of course; damn pity, it was slaughtering everything and getting in the water, and the caneflies had evolved to immunity anyway. But in a couple of seasons, maybe three, they could drop the canefly populations below reproductive viability. No more tormented human bodies with those stinking larvae in the nasal passages and brain. . . . He drifted off for a nap, grinning.

Up north, Anne was biting her lip in shame and pain.

Sweetheart, I shouldn't admit it but your wife is s̶c̶a̶r̶e̶d̶ a bit jittery. Just female nerves or something, nothing to worry about. Everything is normal up here. It's so eerily normal, nothing in the papers, nothing anywhere except what I hear through Barney and Lillian. But Pauline's phone won't answer out in San Diego; the fifth day some strange man yelled at me and banged the phone down. Maybe she's sold her house—but why wouldn't she call?

Lillian's on some kind of Save-the-Women committee, like we were an endangered species, ha-ha—you know Lillian. It seems the Red Cross has started setting up camps. But she says, after the first rush, only a trickle are coming out of what they call "the affected areas." Not many children, either, even little boys. And they have some air photos around Lubbock showing what look like mass graves. Oh, Alan . . . so far it seems to be mostly spreading west, but something's happening in St. Louis, they're cut off. So many places seem to have just vanished from the news, I had a nightmare that there isn't a woman left alive down there. And nobody's *doing* anything. They talked about spraying with tranquilizers for a while and then that died out. What could it do? Somebody at the UN has proposed a convention on—you won't believe this—*femicide*. It sounds like a deodorant spray.

Excuse me, honey, I seem to be a little hysterical. George Searles came back from Georgia talking about God's Will—Searles the lifelong atheist. Alan, something crazy is happening.

But there aren't any facts. Nothing. The Surgeon General issued a report on the bodies of the Rahway Rip-Breast Team—I guess I didn't tell you about that. Anyway, they could find no pathology. Milton Baines wrote a letter saying in the present state of the art we can't distinguish the brain of a saint from a psychopathic killer, so how could they expect to find what they don't know how to look for?

Well, enough of these jitters. It'll be all over by the time you get back, just history. Everything's fine here, I fixed the car's muffler again. And Amy's coming home for the vacations, *that'll* get my mind off faraway problems.

Oh, something amusing to end with—Angie told me what Barney's enzyme does to the spruce budworm. It seems it blocks the male from turning around after he connects with the female, so he mates with her *head* instead. Like clockwork with a cog missing. There're going to be some pretty puzzled female spruceworms. Now why couldn't Barney tell me that? He really is such a sweet shy old dear. He's given me some stuff to put in, as usual. I didn't read it.

Now don't worry, my darling, everything's fine.

I love you, I love you so.

Always, all ways your Anne

Two weeks later in Cuyapán when Barney's enclosures slid out of the envelope, Alan didn't read them, either. He stuffed them into the pocket of his bush jacket with a shaking hand and started bundling his notes together on the rickety table, with a scrawled note to Sister Dominique on top. The hell with the canefly, the hell with everything except that tremor in his fearless Anne's firm handwriting. The hell with being five thousand miles away from his woman, his child, while some deadly madness raged. He crammed his meager belongings into his duffel. If he hurried he could catch the bus through to Bogotá and maybe make the Miami flight.

He made it to Miami but the planes north were jammed. He failed a quick standby; six hours to wait. Time to call Anne. When the call got through some difficulty he was unprepared for the rush of joy and relief that burst along the wires.

"Thank God—I can't believe it—oh, Alan, my darling, are you really—I can't believe—"

He found he was repeating too, and all mixed up with

the canefly data. They were both laughing hysterically when he finally hung up.

Six hours. He settled in a frayed plastic chair opposite *Aerolineas Argentinas,* his mind half back at the clinic, half on the throngs moving by him. Something was oddly different here, he perceived presently. Where was the decorative fauna he usually enjoyed in Miami, the parade of young girls in crotch-tight pastel jeans? The flounces, boots, wild hats and hairdos, and startling expanses of newly tanned skin, the brilliant fabrics barely confining the bob of breasts and buttocks? Not here—but wait; looking closely, he glimpsed two young faces hidden under unbecoming parkas, their bodies draped in bulky nondescript skirts. In fact, all down the long vista he could see the same thing: hooded ponchos, heaped-on clothes and baggy pants, dull colors. A new style? No, he thought not. It seemed to him their movements suggested furtiveness, timidity. And they moved in groups. He watched a lone girl struggle to catch up with others ahead of her, apparently strangers. They accepted her wordlessly.

They're frightened, he thought. Afraid of attracting notice. Even that gray-haired matron in a pantsuit resolutely leading a flock of kids was glancing around nervously.

And at the Argentine desk opposite he saw another odd thing; two lines had a big sign over them: MUJERES. Women. They were crowded with the shapeless forms and very quiet.

The men seemed to be behaving normally; hurrying, lounging, griping, and joking in the lines as they kicked their luggage along. But Alan felt an undercurrent of tension, like an irritant in the air. Outside the line of storefronts behind him a few isolated men seemed to be handing out tracts. An airport attendant spoke to the nearest man; he merely shrugged and moved a few doors down.

To distract himself Alan picked up a *Miami Herald* from the next seat. It was surprisingly thin. The international news occupied him for a while; he had seen none for weeks. It too had a strange empty quality, even the bad news seemed to have dried up. The African war which had been going on seemed to be over, or went unreported. A trade summit meeting was haggling over grain and steel prices. He found himself at the obituary pages, columns of close-set type dominated by the photo of an unknown defunct ex-senator. Then his eye fell on two announcements at the bottom of the page. One was too flowery for quick comprehension, but the other stated in bold plain type:

THE FORSETTE FUNERAL HOME REGRETFULLY ANNOUNCES
IT WILL NO LONGER ACCEPT FEMALE CADAVERS

Slowly he folded the paper, staring at it numbly. On the back was an item headed *Navigational Hazard Warning,* in the shipping news. Without really taking it in, he read:

AP/Nassau: The excursion liner *Carib Swallow* reached port under tow today after striking an obstruction in the Gulf Stream off Cape Hatteras. The obstruction was identified as part of a commercial trawler's seine floated by female corpses. This confirms reports from Florida and the Gulf of the use of such seines, some of them over a mile in length. Similar reports coming from the Pacific coast and as far away as Japan indicate a growing hazard to coastwise shipping.

Alan flung the thing into the trash receptacle and sat rubbing his forehead and eyes. Thank God he had followed his impulse to come home. He felt totally disoriented, as though he had landed by error on another planet. Four and a half hours more to wait. . . . At length he recalled the stuff from Barney he had thrust in his pocket, and pulled it out and smoothed it.

The top item seemed to be from the *Ann Arbor News.* Dr. Lillian Dash, together with several hundred other members of her organization, had been arrested for demonstrating without a permit in front of the White House. They had started a fire in a garbage can, which was considered particularly heinous. A number of women's groups had participated; the total struck Alan as more like thousands than hundreds. Extraordinary security precautions were being taken, despite the fact that the President was out of town at the time.

The next item had to be Barney's acerbic humor.

UP/Vatican City 19 June. Pope John IV today intimated that he does not plan to comment officially on the so-called Pauline Purification cults advocating the elimination of women as a means of justifying man to God. A spokesman emphasized that the Church takes no position on these cults but repudiates any doctrine involving a "challenge" to or from God to reveal His further plans for man.

Cardinal Fazzoli, spokesman for the European Pauline movement, reaffirmed his view that the Scriptures define woman as merely a temporary companion and instrument of man. Women, he states, are nowhere defined as human, but merely as a transitional expedient or state. "The time of transition to full humanity is at hand," he concluded.

The next item appeared to be a thin-paper Xerox from a recent issue of *Science:*

SUMMARY REPORT OF THE AD HOC
EMERGENCY COMMITTEE ON FEMICIDE

The recent worldwide though localized outbreaks of femicide appear to represent a recurrence of similar outbreaks by groups or sects which are not uncommon in world history in times of psychic stress. In this case the root cause is undoubtedly the speed of social and technological change, augmented by population pressure, and the spread and scope are aggravated by instantaneous world communications, thus exposing more susceptible persons. It is not viewed as a medical or epidemiological problem; no physical pathology has been found. Rather it is more akin to the various manias which swept Europe in the seventeenth century, e.g., the Dancing Manias, and like them, should run its course and disappear. The chiliastic cults which have sprung up around the affected areas appear to be unrelated, having in common only the idea that a new means of human reproduction will be revealed as a result of the "purifying" elimination of women.

We recommend that (1) inflammatory and sensational reporting be suspended; (2) refugee centers be set up and maintained for women escapees from the focal areas; (3) containment of affected areas by military cordon be continued and enforced; and (4) after a cooling-down period and the subsidence of the mania, qualified mental-health teams and appropriate professional personnel go in to undertake rehabilitation.

SUMMARY OF THE MINORITY
REPORT OF THE AD HOC COMMITTEE

The nine members signing this report agree that there is no evidence for epidemiological contagion of femicide in the strict sense. *However,* the geographical relation of the focal areas of outbreak strongly suggest that they cannot be dismissed as purely psychosocial phenomena. The initial outbreaks have occurred around the globe near the 30th parallel, the area of principal atmospheric downflow of upper winds coming from the Intertropical Convergence Zone. An agent or condition in the upper equatorial atmosphere would thus be expected to reach ground level along the 30th parallel, with certain seasonal variations. One principal variation is that the downflow moves north over the East Asian continent during the late winter months, and those areas south of it (Arabia, Western India, parts of North Africa) have in fact been free of outbreaks until recently, when the downflow zone moved south. A similar downflow occurs in the Southern Hemisphere, and outbreaks have been reported along the 30th parallel running through Pretoria and Alice Springs, Australia. (Information from Argentina is currently unavailable.)

This geographical correlation cannot be dismissed, and it is therefore urged that an intensified search for a physical cause be instituted. It is also urgently recommended that the rate of spread from known focal points be correlated with wind conditions. A watch for similar outbreaks along the secondary down-welling zones at 60° north and south should be kept.

(signed for the minority)
Barnhard Braithwaite

Alan grinned reminiscently at his old friend's name, which seemed to restore normalcy and stability to the world. It looked as if Barney was on to something, too, despite the prevalence of horses' asses. He frowned, puzzling it out.

Then his face slowly changed as he thought how it would be, going home to Anne. In a few short hours his arms would be around her, the tall, secretly beautiful body that had come to obsess him. Theirs had been a late-blooming love. They'd married, he supposed now, out of friendship, even out of friends' pressure. Everyone said they were made for each other, he big and chunky and blond, she willowy brunette; both shy, highly controlled, cerebral types. For the first few years the friendship had held, but sex hadn't been all that much. Conventional necessity. Politely reassuring each other, privately—he could say it now—disappointing.

But then, when Amy was a toddler, something had happened. A miraculous inner portal of sensuality had slowly opened to them, a liberation into their own secret unsuspected heaven of fully physical bliss. . . . Jesus, but it had been a wrench when the Colombia thing had come up. Only their absolute sureness of each other had made him take it. And now, to be about to have her again, trebly desirable from the spice of separation—feeling-seeing-hearing-smelling-grasping. He shifted in his seat to conceal his body's excitement, half mesmerized by fantasy.

And Amy would be there, too; he grinned at the memory of that prepubescent little body plastered against him. She was going to be a handful, all right. His manhood understood Amy a lot better than her mother did; no cerebral phase for Amy . . . But Anne, his exquisite shy one, with whom he'd found the way into the almost unendurable transports of the flesh . . . First the conventional greeting, he thought; the news, the unspoken, savored, mounting excitement behind their eyes; the light touches; then the seeking of their own room, the falling clothes, the caresses, gentle at first—the flesh, the *nakedness*—the delicate teasing, the grasp, the first thrust—

A terrible alarm bell went off in his head. Exploded from his dream, he stared around, then finally down at his hands. *What was he doing with his open clasp knife in his fist?*

Stunned, he felt for the last shreds of his fantasy, and realized that the tactile images had not been of caresses, but of a frail neck strangling in his fist, the thrust had been the plunge of a blade seeking vitals. In his arms, legs, phantasms of striking and trampling bones cracking. And Amy—

Oh God, Oh God—

Not sex, blood lust.

That was what he had been dreaming. The sex was there, but it was driving some engine of death.

Numbly he put the knife away, thinking only over and over, it's got me. It's got me. Whatever it is, it's got me. *I can't go home.*

After an unknown time he got up and made his way to the United counter to turn in his ticket. The line was long. As he waited, his mind cleared a little. What could he do, here in Miami? Wouldn't it be better to get back to Ann Arbor and turn himself in to Barney? Barney could help him, if anyone could. Yes, that was best. But first he had to warn Anne.

The connection took even longer this time. When Anne finally answered he found himself blurting unintelligibly, it took awhile to make her understand he wasn't talking about a plane delay.

"I tell you, I've caught it. Listen, Anne, for God's sake. If I should come to the house don't let me come near you. I mean it. I mean it. I'm going to the lab, but I might lose control and try to get to you. Is Barney there?"

"Yes, but darling—"

"Listen. Maybe he can fix me, maybe this'll wear off. But I'm not safe. Anne, Anne, I'd kill you, can you understand? Get a—get a weapon. I'll try not to come to the house. But if I do, don't let me get near you. Or Amy. It's a sickness, it's real. Treat me—treat me like a fucking wild animal. Anne, say you understand, say you'll do it."

They were both crying when he hung up.

He went shaking back to sit and wait. After a time his head seemed to clear a little more. *Doctor, try to think.* The first thing he thought of was to take the loathsome knife and throw it down a trash slot. As he did so he realized there was one more piece of Barney's material in his pocket. He uncrumpled it; it seemed to be a clipping from *Nature*.

At the top was Barney's scrawl: "Only guy making sense. U.K. infected now, Oslo, Copenhagen out of communication. Damfools still won't listen. Stay put."

Communication from Professor Ian MacIntyre, Glasgow Univ.

A potential difficulty for our species has always been implicit in the close linkage between the behavioral expression of aggression/predation and sexual reproduction in the male. This close linkage involves (a) many of the same neuromuscular pathways which are utilized both in predatory and sexual pursuit, grasping, mounting, etc., and (b) similar states of adrenergic arousal which are activated in both. The same linkage is seen in the males of many other species; in some, the expression of aggression and copulation alternate or even coexist, an all-too-familiar example being the common house cat. Males of many species bite, claw, bruise, tread, or otherwise assault receptive females during the act of intercourse; indeed, in some species the male attack is necessary for female ovulation to occur.

In many if not all species it is the aggressive behavior which appears first, and then changes to copulatory behavior when the appropriate signal is presented (*e.g.,* the three-tined stickleback and the European robin). Lacking the inhibiting signal, the male's fighting response continues and the female is attacked or driven off.

It seems therefore appropriate to speculate that the present crisis might be caused by some substance, perhaps at the viral or enzymatic level, which effects a failure of the switching or triggering function in the higher primates. (Note: Zoo gorillas and chimpanzees have recently been observed to attack or destroy their mates; rhesus not.) Such a dysfunction could be expressed by the failure of mating behavior to modify or supervene over the aggressive/predatory response; *i.e.,* sexual stimulation would produce attack only, the stimulation discharging itself through the destruction of the stimulating object.

In this connection it might be noted that exactly this condition is a commonplace of male functional pathology, in those cases where murder occurs as a response to and apparent completion of, sexual desire.

It should be emphasized that the aggression/copulation linkage discussed here is specific to the male; the female response (*e.g.*, lordotic reflex) being of a different nature.

Alan sat holding the crumpled sheet a long time; the dry, stilted Scottish phrases seemed to help clear his head, despite the sense of brooding tension all around him. Well, if pollution or whatever had produced some substance, it could presumably be countered, filtered, neutralized. Very very carefully, he let himself consider his life with Anne, his sexuality. Yes; much of their loveplay could be viewed as genitalized, sexually gentled savagery. Play-predation . . . He turned his mind quickly away. Some writer's phrase occurred to him: "The panic element in all sex." Who? Fritz Leiber? The violation of social distance, maybe; another threatening element. Whatever, it's our weak link, he thought. Our vulnerability . . . The dreadful feeling of *rightness* he had experienced when he found himself knife in hand, fantasizing violence, came back to him. As though it was the right, the only way. Was that what Barney's budworms felt when they mated with their females wrong-end-to?

At long length, he became aware of body need and sought a toilet. The place was empty, except for what he took to be a heap of clothes blocking the door of the far stall. Then he saw the red-brown pool in which it lay, and the bluish mounds of bare, thin buttocks. He backed out, not breathing, and fled into the nearest crowd, knowing he was not the first to have done so.

Of course. Any sexual drive. Boys, men, too.

At the next washroom he watched to see men enter and leave normally before he ventured in.

Afterward he returned to sit, waiting, repeating over and over to himself: *Go to the lab. Don't go home. Go straight to the lab.* Three more hours; he sat numbly at 26° N, 81° W, breathing, breathing. . . .

Dear diary. Big scene tonite, Daddy came home!!! Only he acted so funny, he had the taxi wait and just held onto the doorway, he wouldn't touch me or let us come near him. (I mean funny weird, not funny ha-ha.) He said, I have something to tell you, this is getting worse not better. I'm going to sleep in the lab but I want you to get out, Anne, Anne, I can't trust myself anymore. First thing in the morning you both get on the plane for Martha's and stay there. So I thought he had to be joking, I mean with the dance next week and Aunt Martha lives in Whitehorse where there's nothing nothing nothing. So I was yelling and Mother was yelling and Daddy was groaning, Go now! And then he started crying. Crying!!! So I realized, wow, this is serious, and I started to go over to him but Mother yanked me back and then I saw she had this big *knife!!!* And she shoved me in back of her and started crying too: Oh Alan, Oh Alan, like she was insane. So I said, Daddy, I'll never leave you, it felt like the perfect thing to say. And it was thrilling, he looked at me real sad and deep like I was a grown-up while Mother was treating me like I was a mere infant as usual. But Mother ruined it raving, Alan the child is mad, darling go. So he ran out of the door yelling, Be gone, Take the car, Get out before I come back.

Oh I forgot to say I was wearing what but my gooby green with my curltites still on, wouldn't you know of all the shitty luck, how could I have known such a beautiful scene was ahead we never know life's cruel whimsy. And Mother is dragging out suitcases yelling, Pack your things hurry! So she's going I guess but I am not repeat not going to spend the fall sitting in Aunt Martha's grain silo and lose the dance and all my summer credits. And Daddy was trying to *communicate* with us, right? I think their relationship is obsolete. So when she goes upstairs I am splitting. I am going to go over to the lab and see Daddy.

Oh PS Diane tore my yellow jeans she promised me I could use her pink ones ha-ha that'll be the day.

* * *

I ripped that page out of Amy's diary when I heard the squad car coming. I never opened her diary before but when I found she'd gone I looked. . . . Oh, my darling little girl. She went to him, my little girl, my poor little fool child. Maybe if I'd taken time to explain, maybe—

Excuse me, Barney. The stuff is wearing off, the shots they gave me. I didn't feel anything. I mean, I knew somebody's daughter went to see her father and he killed her. And cut his throat. But it didn't mean anything.

Alan's note, they gave me that but then they took it away. Why did they have to do that? His last handwriting, the last words he wrote before his hand picked up the, before he—

I remember it. *"Sudden and light as that, the bonds gave. And we learned of finalities besides the grave. The bonds of our humanity have broken, we are finished. I love—"*

I'm all right, Barney, really. Who wrote that, Robert Frost? *The bonds gave.* . . . Oh, he said, tell Barney: *The terrible rightness.* What does that mean?

You can't answer that, Barney dear. I'm just writing this to stay sane, I'll put it in your hidey-hole. Thank you, thank you, Barney dear. Even as blurry as I was, I knew it was you. All the time you were cutting off my hair and rubbing dirt on my face, I knew it was right because it was you. Barney, I never thought of you as those horrible words you said. You were always Dear Barney.

By the time the stuff wore off I had done everything you said, the gas, the groceries. Now I'm here in your cabin. With those clothes you made me put on—I guess I do look like a boy, the gas man called me "Mister."

I still can't really realize, I have to stop myself from rushing back. But you saved my life, I know that. The first trip in I got a paper, I saw where they bombed the Apostle Islands refuge. And it had about those three women stealing the Air Force plane and bombing Dallas, too. Of course they shot them down, over the Gulf. Isn't it strange how we do nothing? Just get killed by ones and twos. Or more, now they've started on the refuges. . . . Like hypnotized rabbits. We're a toothless race.

Do you know I never said "we" meaning women before? "We" was always me and Alan, and Amy of course. Being killed selectively encourages group identification. . . . You see how sane-headed I am.

But I still can't really realize.

My first trip in was for salt and kerosene. I went to that little Red Deer store and got my stuff from the old man in the back, as you told me—you see, I remembered! He called me "Boy" but I think maybe he suspects. He knows I'm staying at your cabin.

Anyway, some men and boys came in the front. They were all so *normal*, laughing and kidding. I just couldn't believe, Barney. In fact I started to go out past them when I heard one of them say, "Heinz saw an angel." An *angel*. So I stopped and listened. They said it was big and sparkly. Coming to see if man is carrying out God's will, one of them said. And he said, Moosenee is now a liberated zone, and all up by Hudson Bay. I turned and got out the back, fast. The old man had heard them, too. He said to me quietly, I'll miss the kids.

Hudson Bay, Barney, that means it's coming from the north too, doesn't it? That must be about 60°.

But I have to go back once again, to get some fish hooks. I can't live on bread. Last week I found a deer some poacher had killed, just the head and legs. I made a stew. It was a doe. Her eyes; I wonder if mine look like that now.

I went to get the fishhooks today. It was bad, I can't ever go back. There were some men in front again, but they were different. Mean and tense. No boys. And there was a new sign out in front, I couldn't see it; maybe it says Liberated Zone, too.

The old man gave me the hooks quick and whispered to me, "Boy, them woods'll be full of hunters next week." I almost ran out.

About a mile down the road a blue pickup started to chase me. I guess he wasn't from around there, I ran the VW into a logging draw and he roared on by. After a long while I drove out and came on back, but I left the car about a mile from here and hiked in. It's surprising how hard it is to pile enough brush to hide a yellow VW.

Barney, I can't stay here. I'm eating perch raw so nobody will see my smoke, but those hunters will be coming through. I'm going to move my sleeping bag out to the swamp by that big rock, I don't think many people go there.

Since the last lines I moved out. It feels safer. Oh, Barney, how did this *happen*?

Fast, that's how. Six months ago I was Dr. Anne Alstein. Now I'm a widow and bereaved mother, dirty and hungry, squatting in a swamp in mortal fear. Funny if I'm the last woman left alive on Earth. I guess the last one around here, anyway. Maybe some are holed up in the Himalayas, or sneaking through the wreck of New York City. How can we last?

We can't.

And I can't survive the winter here, Barney. It gets to 40° below. I'd have to have a fire, they'd see the smoke. Even if I worked my way south, the woods end in a couple hundred miles. I'd be potted like a duck. No. No use. Maybe somebody is trying something somewhere, but it won't reach here in time . . . and what do I have to live for?

No. I'll just make a good end, say up on that rock where I can see the stars. After I go back and leave this for you. I'll wait to see the beautiful color in the trees one last time.

Good-bye, dearest dearest Barney.

I know what I'll scratch for an epitaph.

HERE LIES THE SECOND MEANEST
PRIMATE ON EARTH

I guess nobody will ever read this, unless I get the nerve and energy to take it back to Barney's. Probably I won't. Leave it in a Baggie, I have one here; maybe Barney will come and look. I'm up on the big rock now. The moon is going to rise soon, I'll do it then. Mosquitoes, be patient. You'll have all you want.

The thing I have to write down is that I saw an angel, too. This morning. It was big and sparkly, like the man said; like a Christmas tree without the tree. But I knew it was real because the frogs stopped croaking and two blue jays gave alarm calls. That's important; it was *really there*.

I watched it, sitting under my rock. It didn't move much. It sort of bent over and picked up something, leaves or twigs, I couldn't see. Then it did something with them around its middle, like putting them into an invisible sample pocket.

Let me repeat—it was *there*. Barney, if you're reading this, *there are things here*. And I think they've done whatever it is to us. Made us kill ourselves off.

Why? Well, it's a nice place, if it wasn't for people. How do you get rid of people? Bombs, death rays—all very primitive. Leave a big mess. Destroy everything, craters, radioactivity, ruin the place.

This way there's no muss, no fuss. Just like what we did to the screwfly. Pinpoint the weak link, wait a bit while we do it for them. Only a few bones around; make good fertilizer.

Barney dear, good-bye. I saw it. It was there.

But it wasn't an angel.

I think I saw a real estate agent.

Time-Sharing Angel

IT'S NOT TRUE there are no angels; the young woman named Jolyone Schram spoke to one, with results that have astounded us all.

Whether what Jolyone talked to was actually an angel in the classic sense, we'll never know, of course; unless it returns, which seems unlikely. Certainly it was a space-borne Something of great power, a principle of the outer void, perhaps, a wandering sentience—possibly even, as some might claim, an interstellar commuter out of his usual way. Whatever it may have been, it heard Jolyone, and this is the manner of that event.

On the night it happened Jolyone was trying not to cry, while her teeth played music.

She was at her nightly job of news clipper and general gofer on the fifth floor of WPNQ's new building. Far up above her head towered WPNQ's new transmitter, which had just been erected on what had been the last wooded ridge behind L.A. The new transmitter was powered up to cut through everything near it on the L.A. bands. It was so strong that while Jolyone stapled Telex flimsies, the big filling in her right molar clearly brought in Stevie Smith.

"I was much farther out than you thought, and not waving but drowning," sang her tooth. Jolyone's eyes blinked tears and her chin trembled, but it wasn't the song doing it.

The fact is that right there in Hal Hodge's office Jolyone was passionately mourning the death of Earth, which she had just foreseen.

She was nineteen years old.

The day before she had taken off to drive up the coast and over to the piney-woods valley where she'd spent a lot of happy time as a kid. Her semiroommate had just split, semiamiably, and she needed some peace. She felt she'd been away from earth and woods too long.

It was dark before she got close, but she couldn't help noticing that there seemed to be a lot more houses than on her last trip. Finally the misty trees closed around her headlights, and the road was its bad old self. By midnight she drove over the ridge and pulled onto the verge. The mist was so thick she decided to nap till dawn and see the sunrise. All around was the peaceful smell of woods. A hoot owl called and was answered. As Jolyone drifted off to sleep, she could just hear the little brook purling through a cave she used to hide out in when she was little. She smiled, remembering.

Jolyone never saw the sun rise there.

In the first pale light she was jolted awake by the starting roar of a big diesel not a hundred yards away. It was joined by another, and another, and another—and before she was sure she wasn't in a nightmare, from the other side the high wicked yowl of chain saws burst out.

Hands on her ears, Jolyone peered out at the thinning mist. Treetops were waving and crashing. She saw a line of giant earth movers advancing past her straight across the valley. A horrifying great misty mountain of trees, rocks, earth, everything was spewing out of the monsters' blades. Behind them stretched raw gravel.

Aghast, Jolyone whirled in her seat, trying to disbelieve the devastation. From nowhere a back-hoe bucket rose up beside her, so close that she could see a small dusty body still struggling in the rocks. A kit fox, her eyes noted numbly.

With a wordless moan she threw the VW in gear and shot back over the ridge. As she went she saw she had spent the night under a huge signboard painted with a man's grinning face: A THOUSAND MORE HAPPY HOMES BY HAPPY HARRY JOEL.

"Oh no, *oh no*," Jolyone wept to herself as she drove shakenly down toward the coast. The darkness had fooled her coming in, she saw. There weren't just a few more houses among the trees. From horizon to horizon the foothills were covered by houses, houses, houses everywhere, with only a thin line of dried trees by the old road. Her valley had been the last patch of woods left.

"How could they, it was so, so—" she whispered incoherently, trying to find a word for all lost defenseless beauty, for all that she had loved deeply without really knowing it, and believed would always endure.

When she finally got onto the freeway approaches, the hurt was calmer. It was a fine sunny day. As she sailed up the ramp into the southbound lanes, she noticed something else she had missed the night before. The sea up north had a funny black-looking scum edge on it. An oil slick?

"It's the biggest one yet," the girl at the Burgerchef rest stop told her, nodding proprietarily. "They say it killed all those seal otters or whatever—hey, don't you want your Supercheese?"

Jolyone drove on back to her job, trying to lose herself in the long thrumming hypnosis of the freeway traffic. The sun shone whitely on her from the thickening veils of the sky; trucks, cars, vans roared beside her, ahead, behind. The grief that had shaken her calmed to the rhythm of driving on and on. But, somewhere underneath, her mind kept chewing on it.

A thousand new homes, on top of all those other thousands . . . Jolyone had once heard her generation described as "the baby boom's baby boom." She'd always intended, in a vague way, to have kids. But now all the bits and pieces of her standard education began to add up. The "ecology"—it wasn't something distant, somewhere else with strip mines. It was the awful devastation of her lovely valley, the broken little body in the backhoe bucket. And that oil slick . . she herself was driving a car right now. Probably she would have used some of the oil that spilled. It was being brought for people like her. For thousands, millions of people just like her.

To get away from the idea she tuned the radio to catch the end of Hal Hodge's newsbreak. Nothing but a filler about some mountains in Nepal that had slid down because the people had used up all the trees for firewood. Then she switched to WPNQ's Pop Hour, and she thankfully let thought go with the dreamy beat. *Twenty-nine colors of blue . . .*

The miles passed.

Finally she was turning into the station parking lot. Mimi Lavery was subbing for Hal on the evening news; Jolyone listened critically, hoping Mimi would pitch her voice low. Mimi ended with another filler, something about how the population was going up again and was expected to double in thirty years, and cut to a taped ad for condominiums in the Rockies.

And right then, all in the second between parking the Volks and pulling out her car keys, it happened.

Jolyone Schram *knew*.

It came to her as a vision of a billion-headed monstrous wave, a huge spreading flood of multiplying people, people unending, forming in their billions a great devouring mindless incubus that spread around the green ball of Earth—blotting out everything, eating everything, using everything, expanding and destroying without limit on a finite surface. Hordes of individually innocent people made frightful by their numbers bulged out into and under the oceans, tunneled underground, flowed over the mountains, surging and covering everything everywhere. Billions of heads gaped, grinned at her, billions of hands reached and grasped blindly as the torrent of bodies flooded over the world.

That was what was happening, slower or faster, all around her. And it would continue, faster and faster, to the oncoming end.

Jolyone gasped, falling back into the car seat. She was a gentle girl, unsuited to apocalyptic visions. But she had also an innocent fact-mindedness; she actually believed in numbers. All in that terrible instant she saw what the numbers meant. *Doubling in thirty years*—and then doubling again and again, quicker each time. It was happening. Not somewhere else in some remote lifetime, but right here and now. She was seeing it begin. With all the singleness of her nineteen-year-old mind she suddenly, totally believed.

And all in that same second it came to her how much she would suffer and how helpless she was. How could she live in that tumult of people, without room or peace, with no refuge to escape to? But she couldn't stop it, no one could—she saw that, too. People just wouldn't stop having kids, she knew that in her blood. Pointing a gun at a President wouldn't save the redwoods; all those organizations to save a river or a mountain wouldn't delay matters much. Because nothing could stop those *numbers*. In the cold time-light of her vision she saw the flurries of protest, speeches, little movements, hopes and local successes and good intentions—all swept away by the relentless multitudes, like the line of buckling trees she had seen go down in the valley. Numbers talk. Nothing can stop it, really, she thought. Everything I love will go.

She sat trembling, too shaken to cry. After a while things eased a little. Since there seemed to be nothing else to do, she picked up the fallen car keys and went on in to her job.

In the studio no one noticed her. It was an off night. A couple of engineers were still trying to fix that oscillation in the booster circuits; they had a panel torn down.

Jolyone went leadenly about her work, sorting the Telex pile, putting back the used tapes, answering phones in the empty offices, doing zombielike whatever she was asked. Her teeth whispered the late sports roundup. The vision that had hit her didn't go away. It surrounded her head like a ghostly projection, making the real world outside as thin as a momentary dream. Every now and then her eyes leaked uncontrollably when she thought of something dear to her that wouldn't be around much longer. High-rise developers were already buying up the scraggly old garden block she and her friends lived in. That was just one first soft nudging edge of the terrible future she had foreseen. With all the clarity of her nineteen years Jolyone was saying good-bye to something deep and vital, to hope itself maybe.

At 10:30 Hal Hodge's usual batch of almost-celebrities came in for Tonight Talk. One of them was a science-fiction writer, a short, jumpy older man, neurotically worried that his car would be towed away. Jolyone got him some Kleenex for his cold, gave them all coffee, and put them into Hal's hands during the station break.

As she shut the door, one of the equipment men called her over to the torn-out board.

"Hold this a sec." He handed her a big complicated

jack trailing cables. "Don't let it touch anything, that's right. Look, when I say 'break,' you push that circuit breaker up here with your other hand. Got it?"

Jolyone nodded; she was having trouble with her eyes again.

The engineer dived down and wriggled in under the panel. Jolyone stood holding the thing. Her teeth were even louder here; she heard Hal Hodge's sincerely interested voice. "What are people like us going to be doing a hundred years from now, Bill?"

"Standing on each other's throats," the science-fiction writer said in her tooth, and sneezed.

The whole horrible vision came back onto Jolyone, and with it something worse she hadn't seen before. "Oh, no, no, no," she whispered, feeling a big tear start down her cheek. She couldn't wipe it.

What she had seen were the expressions on that oncoming mountain of people. Their faces snarled, mouths gnashing in hatred, leering in triumph, wailing in desperate loss; eyes narrowed in cold calculation; hands clutched knives or guns and fought as the tide rolled over them. Here a few combined for a moment in furious victory, only to go under as new faces overrode them. From under every foot rose the weak cries of the trampled and dying. Nowhere in all that panorama of strife was kindness, nowhere was anything she thought of as human— only the war of all against all raging on the despoiled earth.

When we've destroyed everything we'll be animals, she thought. A great sob rose in her throat compounded of doomed beauty and the hideous revelation that what she had taken for the reality of people was a fragile dream about to perish. *"No,"* she choked.

"Hit it!" barked the engineer from under the board.

Blind and shaking, Jolyone reached across the open board. Tears ran unheeded down her jaw and splashed complex electrolytes where no such things should be. In anguish, Jolyone whispered a prayer to the empty air. "Make it stop, *please.*"

There was a sudden total silence that crackled.

"Piontwxq?" said her filling sharply in the stillness. *"Eh! Stop what?"*

"Make us stop," Jolyone repeated crazily, unaware that her cry was howling out on unknown frequencies, unaware of anything except her pain. "Make us stop making more people before we kill everything! Oh, *please* don't let it happen, don't let all the beautiful world be killed!"

"*Wait,*" said the tiny voice in her jawbone. Jolyone's eyes suddenly got as big as Hal Hodge's mouth. "*Oh, very well,*" the voice went on. "*You can stop crying now.*"

It sounded far away and preoccupied, and it wasn't speaking English, although Jolyone never knew that.

"Oh!" she gasped. "Who—wha—?"

"Holy crap!" The engineer exploded out from under the panel and started grabbing things. Hal Hodge shot from the booth and collided with the sound man, both of them yelling. In the uproar Jolyone saw the science-fiction writer scuttle out clutching his car keys and shaking his head.

Then she was being chewed out for letting the hyper-mixed touch the goobilizer, and it was all entirely too much.

Meanwhile, twenty-two thousand miles out in space, the Something—being, djinn, essence, or what have you —completed a tiny swift adjustment to the last of our synchronized satellites. Then he or she or it zipped into a parabolic pass down through earth's atmosphere. As it hurtled down, it opened something that wasn't a brief-case. The orbit noded over the Andes and something very small dropped into a crevasse.

Next instant, our visitor was out again and receding into the depths of space with the thing that wasn't a brief-case tucked under its—well, whatever it was under. Could you have translated the expression on what might have been its face, you would have been reminded of the look worn by a passing grown-up who has stopped to re-trieve a kid's lost ball.

And that's the last we've known of it to this day.

But as the next morning's light spread round the world, we all know what was revealed.

In every home, every apartment or igloo or cave or grass hut from Fiji to New York to Archangel, the scene was the same. One baby and only one awoke—the youngest. All the other children lay unstirring; on mats, in beds or hammocks or cribs or fur piles, all but the youngest lay apparently asleep.

A moment later started the billion-throated scream that followed the sunrise round the world. Mothers discovered the sleeping children's flesh was cool, their chests were silent. No breath moved their lips. Girls and boys from two to twenty, all siblings of whatever age, lay moveless and cold. Even the grown ones not at home were found lying lifeless.

Death, it seemed, had reaped the earth of all but the last-borns.

But among the frantic parents were a few persistent ones who held mirrors to the still lips and listened longer at the cooling breasts. And finally it was known: the children were not dead. Slower than glaciers, breath moved in them. Slower than the ooze of rock, their blood flowed still and the infinitely languorous hearts squeezed and relaxed. They were not dead but sleeping—or rather, as their temperatures fell and fell, it was understood that this was a sleep like hibernation, but deeper than any ever known.

And they could not be waked or revived. Doctors, shamans, mothers en masse attacked the sleepers with heat or cold or shock, with any or every stimulus that could possibly or impossibly break the spell. Nothing worked. Days passed, but not a heartbeat quickened, no breath came a millisecond faster.

All over the world, fathers gazed upon the rows of their comatose offspring and went looking for drink. Distracted mothers alternated between caring for their waking youngest and futilely trying to awaken the rest.

Only those homes with a single child were unaffected. But in many such, another child was on the way. And it was soon found that whenever the mother gave birth, as the newborn cry squalled out, the eyelids of the older baby fell upon its cheeks. By the time the new baby had started to nurse, the former only child was cooling into hibernation. It seemed that in every home only one child, the youngest, could wake to cry and feed and play in normalcy. All around it, in every hut, hospital, sampan or split-level, the older siblings lay in cold trance.

Desperation mounted with the days; all other issues faded to insignificance. Were the Earth and the hearts of its people to be filled with the living dead?

And then the first sleeper woke.

It was, at any rate, the first one known, and it happened on Day Fourteen in the well-filled trailer of the McEvoys in Pawnet, West Virginia. As the sun rose, a young voice that had been silent for a fortnight spoke.

"Maw! Maw, I'm hongry."

Mrs. McEvoy rushed into the front room where her sleeping brood was laid out on every surface. Denny, her next-to-youngest, was starting to scream in fright because he had touched his cold brother Earl. She clutched him and felt of him while he wriggled; he seemed perfectly all right.

"Earlene!" called her sister. "I can't wake the baby. I think she's coolin' off."

And sure enough, little Debbie McEvoy was sliding into the chill of hibernation and could not be roused.

The waking of a child was world news; the media led a mass descent upon little Dennis. It was soon established that he was his normal self with no memory of his missing fortnight.

Among the crowd was a lanky, quizzical man named Springer. Like Jolyone, he believed in numbers. He ascertained that there were eighteen living McEvoy children, and his face became more puzzled than ever.

"You, ah, don't happen to have any more children, do you, Mrs. McEvoy?"

Earlene McEvoy's face clamped shut.

But her neighbors were not so reticent, and Springer soon discovered that there had been a period, or periods, of extra-McEvoy activity in Earlene's life. The results thereof were now living, or rather, sleeping, with various distant relatives. He was also impressed by the robust health Mrs. McEvoy had imparted to all her young.

"Twenty-six," he mused. "Twenty-six alive from one mother. Remarkable. And there's twenty-six fortnights in a year, give or take a few hours."

To Mrs. McEvoy he said only, "I'd keep my eye on Dennis about a week from Saturday."

"Why?"

"It's only a hunch, Mrs. McEvoy. He just might go back to sleep then."

"Don't talk like that, mister."

But, sure enough, on Saturday week young Dennis was cooling back to hibernation while his next-oldest sister woke up.

By then it wasn't a surprise, because living families of less than twenty-six are common and enough other children were waking up to make the arithmetic plain. Saturday week was Day Twenty-eight; on that morning, the next-youngest child of every family of thirteen was waking up while the youngest slid into stasis.

It was clear what had happened, at least in its first incredible outlines.

No one had been killed.

No one had been hurt, except by overzealous efforts to wake them.

No one had been prevented from having as many children as her heart, mores, ignorance, or vulnerability dictated. (It was noted with varying emotions that the Affliction seemed to count only mothers as parents.)

What had happened was time-sharing.

Every child, it appeared, would have its turn at being awake, and this was shortly found to be true. The problem was that the length of time it stayed awake depended on how many siblings it had. All the children of each mother shared out the year, each getting more or less depending on their number; the twenty-six offspring of Earlene got only a fortnight apiece while each child of a pair waked for six months. Only children were unaffected. Thus each mother had always one waking child—and one only.

But were the children of large families to be robbed of most of their lives? Was even the child of a two-child family to lose half its life asleep?

The answer slowly came back: No.

It required time to be sure, of course. But right from the start people had their suspicions, because even the smallest hibernating infants did not seem to grow. Hair and nails did not lengthen, even small cuts did not heal. Older children awoke with their last meals undigested and their last waking preoccupations on their lips. In sleeping women, pregnancies did not advance. Scientists watched, measured, argued, and finally the startling fact was understood: those who hibernated did not perceptibly age. Only waking hours counted as life.

This meant—this meant—with a worldwide gasp it was realized that the sleepers' lives would be long. Even the children of a pair would take twice as long as normal to grow up and then, presumably, would go on to live twice the usual span. And as for those from larger families—

For two days the McEvoys were in the news again when it was realized that Earlene's brood might live, if all survived, for fifteen hundred years—each doing so two weeks at a time. Then a woman in Afghanistan was delivered of her thirtieth living child. People drew in their breaths, contemplating a baby who could live, in twelve-day installments, for three thousand years.

The world was upside down.

It's hard to remember how it went, the chaos in all our heads as the tired old problems were overwhelmed by new ones. Different problems everywhere, of course. In the hungry nations millions of young mouths closed peacefully, while a million tasks went undone because the child workers were sleeping. A dozen nasty little wars subsided across their hibernating armies. In the industrialized world the loss of millions of young consumers ushered in the great Sleepers' Depression that's with us still. The reality of zero pop growth came crunching down on us all.

And beyond the economic immediacies rose the great human questions. Who will care for the sleeping multitudes when their parents age and die? How do you educate kids in monthly or six-monthly increments? What will we do with teenagers who are going to be teenagers for centuries ahead? Sibling rivalry has taken on new and fearful dimensions as children realize that they sleep because their brothers and sisters wake; mercifully many can understand that their hibernation also means long life. Everything has subtly changed in myriad ways. Even fiction and soap operas have taken on a whole new content: can a girl who wakes only in summer find happiness with a boy who wakes through summers and autumns, too?

All over the world, groups of the young people who waken at the same time are forming, to be replaced when the next group wakes. Perhaps alternative cultures will develop on the same terrain. Or perhaps the visible futility of having additional children will do what no other arguments could. The number of people who believe that this is temporary gets less every year. It seems the "angel" has wrought well, having the superior technology you'd expect of angels.

Meanwhile a strange sense of quiet pervades our life. The decibels seem to have fallen and the grass could be coming back. In every family, only one child at a time coos or squalls or begs for the car keys or mugs old ladies or competes for jobs or medical school. Only one young body in each home consumes food or firewood or gasoline or orthodontistry or plastic toys. And each child as it wakes gets the full attention of its adults.

A peaceful trip, while it lasts. Happy Harry Joel's thousand new homes went into receivership half-built, though of course nothing could be done about the kit foxes.

As for Jolyone Schram, who had started it all, she has had several good job offers, being an awake-all-the-time only child. She spends a lot of time just breathing and listening to the growing green. The terrible vision faded away. But she never told anybody what happened. Except one night in Point Lobos Park; when she saw I was harmless, she told me.

We were sitting by a dusty eucalyptus clump, looking out to where the rocks drown in the shimmering moonlit Pacific.

"The thing is," she said, frowning, "I was thinking. Take sixteen people, say. That's eight couples."

I saw she still believed in numbers.

"So they have children. But only one apiece is awake at a time. So that's like it's really just one child. And then say the eight children marry, that's four couples. And they have one waking child each, that's four. And they grow up and marry, that's two couples. So it comes down to really two children. I mean, it's half each time . . . of course that takes a long time."

"A long time," I agreed.

"But when the two children grow up and marry, they have one child. I mean, it *counts* as one child. And that's all."

"Looks that way."

She pushed back her hair, frowning harder in the moonlight. "Of course there's billions of people, not just sixteen, so it's a *really* long way off. And maybe something's wrong with my idea, I mean, they'll all wake up eventually. But . . . I wonder if the—the person I spoke to, I wonder if they thought of that?"

"No telling, is there?"

The sea sighed and glittered peacefully, making long shining curves around the rocks. There was no sign of any oil. There wasn't much litter on the grass, and the highway behind us was unusually empty.

Jolyone sat staring out with her chin on her knees. "Maybe whoever it was will come back and change things in time. Or maybe I should tell people and try to call it somehow."

"Would you know how?"

"No."

"There's a lot of time for somebody else to worry about all that," I offered.

We sat in silence for a while. Then she sighed and stretched out on the grass; a strange, private, gentle girl.

"Funny . . . I feel like I'd almost got run over. It feels good to—to *be*. Maybe the thing is, I should just go on and enjoy it."

"Why not?"

And that's exactly what she went on and did.

We Who Stole the *Dream*

*The children could survive only twelve minims in the
sealed containers.*

JILSHAT PUSHED THE heavy cargo loader as fast as she
dared through the darkness, praying that she would not
attract the attention of the Terran guard under the flood-
lights ahead. The last time she passed he had roused and
looked at her with his frightening pale alien eyes. Then,
her truck had carried only fermenting containers full of
amlat fruit.

Now, curled in one of the containers, lay hidden her
only-born, her son Jemnal. Four minims at least had already been used up in the loading and weighing sheds.
It would take four more, maybe five, to push the load out
to the ship, where her people would send it up on the
cargo conveyor. And more time yet for her people in the
ship to find Jemnal and rescue him. Jilshat pushed
faster, her weak gray humanoid legs trembling.

As she came into the lighted gate the Terran turned
his head and saw her.

Jilshat cringed away, trying to make herself even
smaller, trying not to run. Oh, why had she not taken
Jemnal out in an earlier load? The other mothers had
taken theirs. But she had been afraid. At the last minute
her faith had failed. It had not seemed possible that what
had been planned so long and prepared for so painfully
could actually be coming true, that her people, her poor
feeble, dwarf Joilani, could really overpower and subdue
the mighty Terrans in that cargo ship. Yet there the big
ship stood in its cone of lights, all apparently quiet. The
impossible must have been done, or there would have
been disturbance. The other young must be safe. Yes—

now she could make out empty cargo trucks hidden in the shadows; their pushers must have already mounted into the ship. It was really and truly happening, their great escape to freedom—or to death . . . And now she was almost past the guard, almost safe.

"Oy!"

She tried not to hear the harsh Terran bark, hurried faster. But in three giant strides he loomed up before her, so that she had to halt.

"You deaf?" he asked in the Terran of his time and place. Jilshat could barely understand; she had been a worker in the far *amlat* fields. All she could think of was the time draining inexorably away, while he tapped the containers with the butt of his weapon, never taking his eyes off her. Her huge dark-lashed Joilani gaze implored him mutely; in her terror, she forgot the warnings, and her small dove-gray face contorted in that rictus of anguish the Terrans called a "smile." Weirdly, he smiled back, as if in pain, too.

"I wo'king, seh," she managed to bring out. A minim gone now, almost two. If he did not let her go at once her child was surely doomed. Almost she could hear a faint mew, as if the drugged baby was already struggling for breath.

"I go, seh! Men in ship ang'ee!" Her smile broadened, dimpled in agony to what she could not know was a mask of allure.

"Let 'em wait. You know, you're not bad-looking for a Juloo *moolie?*" He made a strange *hahnha* sound in his throat. "It's my duty to check the natives for arms. Take that off." He poked up her dingy *jelmah* with the snout of his weapon.

Three minims. She tore the *jelmah* off, exposing her wide-hipped, short-legged little gray form, with its double dugs and bulging pouch. A few heartbeats more and it would be too late, Jemnal would die. She could still save him—she could force the clamps and rip that smothering lid away. Her baby was still alive in there. But if she did so all would be discovered; she would betray them all. *Jailasanatha*, she prayed. Let me have love's courage. O my Joilani, give me strength to let him die. I pay for my unbelief.

"Turn around."

Grinning in grief and horror, she obeyed.

"That's better, you look almost human. Ah, Lord, I've been out too long. C'mere." She felt his hand on her buttocks. "You think that's fun, hey? What's your name, *moolie?*"

The last possible minim had run out. Numb with despair, Jilshat murmured a phrase that meant *Mother of the Dead.*

"Joobly-woobly—" His voice changed. "Well, well! And where did *you* come from?"

Too late, too late: Lal, the damaged female, minced swiftly to them. Her face was shaved and painted pink and red; she swirled open a bright *jelmah* to reveal a body grotesquely tinted and bound to imitate the pictures the Terrans worshiped. Her face was wreathed in a studied smile.

"Me Lal." She flirted her fingers to release the flower essence the Terrans seemed to love. "You want I make fik-fik foh you?"

The instant Jilshat felt the guard's attention leave her, she flung her whole strength against the heavy truck and rushed naked with it out across the endless field, staggering beyond the limit of breath and heart, knowing it was too late, unable not to hope. Around her in the shadows the last burdened Joilani filtered toward the ship. Behind them the guard was being drawn by Lal into the shelter of the gatehouse.

At the last moment he glanced back and scowled.

"Hey, those Juloos shouldn't be going into the ship that way."

"Men say come. Say move cans." Lal reached up and caressed his throat, slid skillful Joilani fingers into his turgid alien crotch. "Fik-fik," she crooned, smiling irresistibly. The guard shrugged, and turned back to her with a chuckle.

The ship stood unwatched. It was an aging *amlat* freighter, a flying factory, carefully chosen because its huge cargo hold was heated and pressurized to make the fruit ferment en route, so that some enzyme the Terrans valued would be ready when it made port. That hold could be lived in, and the *amlat* fruit would multiply a thousandfold in the food-converter cycle. Also, the ship was the commonest type to visit here; over the decades the Joilani ship cleaners had been able to piece together, detail by painful detail, an almost complete image of the operating controls.

This one was old and shabby. Its Terran Star of Empire and identifying symbols were badly in need of paint. Of its name the first word had been eroded away, leaving only the alien letters, . . . N'S DREAM. Some Terran's dream once; it was now the Joilani's.

But it was not Lal's Dream. Ahead of Lal lay only pain and death. She was useless as a breeder; her short twin birth channels had been ruptured by huge hard Terran members, and the delicate spongy tissue that was the Joilani womb had been damaged beyond recovery. So Lal had chosen the greater love, to serve her people with one last torment. In her hair flower was the poison that would let her die when the *Dream* was safely away.

It was not safe yet. Over the guard's great bulk upon her Lal could glimpse the lights of the other ship on the field, the station's patrol cruiser. By the worst of luck, it was just readying for its periodic off-planet reconnaissance.

To our misfortune, when the Dream *was loaded, the Terran warship stood ready to lift off, so that it could intercept us before we could escape by entering what the Terrans called tau-space. Here we failed.*

Old Jalun hobbled as smartly as he could out across the Patrol's section of the spaceport, to the cruiser. He was wearing the white jacket and female *jelmah* in which the Terrans dressed their mess servants, and he carried a small, napkin-wrapped object. Overhead three fast-moving moonlets were converging, sending triple shadows around his frail form. They faded as he came into the lights of the cruiser's lock.

A big Terran was doing something to the cruiser's lock tumblers. As Jalun struggled up the giant steps, he saw that the spacer wore a sidearm. Good. Then he recognized the spacer, and an un-Joilani flood of hatred made his twin hearts pound. This was the Terran who had raped Jalun's granddaughter, and broken her brother's spine with a kick when the boy came to her rescue. Jalun fought down his feelings, grimacing in pain. *Jailasanatha; let me not offend Oneness.*

"Where you think you're going, Smiley? What you got there?"

He did not recognize Jalun; to Terrans all Joilani looked alike.

"Commandeh say foh you, seh. Say, celeb'ation. Say take to offiseh fi'st."

"Let's see."

Trembling with the effort to control himself, smiling painfully from ear to ear, Jalun unfolded a corner of the cloth.

The spacer peered, whistled. "If that's what I think it is, sweet stars of home. Lieutenant!" he shouted, hustling Jalun up and into the ship. "Look what the boss sent us!"

In the wardroom the lieutenant and another spacer were checking over the micro-source charts. The lieutenant also was wearing a weapons belt—good again. Listening carefully, Jalun's keen Joilani hearing could detect no other Terrans on the ship. He bowed deeply, still smiling his hate, and unwrapped his packet before the lieutenant.

Nestled in snowy linen lay a small tear-shaped amethyst flask.

"Commandeh say, foh you. Say must d'ink now, is open."

The lieutenant whistled in his turn, and picked the flask up reverently.

"Do you know what this is, old Smiley?"

"No, seh," Jalun lied.

"What is it, sir?" the third spacer asked. Jalun could see that he was very young.

"This, sonny, is the most unbelievable, most precious, most delectable drink that will ever pass your dewy gullet. Haven't you ever heard of Stars Tears?"

The youngster stared at the flask, his face clouding.

"And Smiley's right," the lieutenant went on. "Once it's open, you have to drink it right away. Well, I guess we've done all we need to tonight. I must say, the old man left us a generous go. Why did he say he sent this, Juloo boy?"

"Celeb'ation, seh. Say his celeb'ation, his day."

"Some celebration. Well, let us not quibble over miracles. Jon, produce three liquor cups. *Clean* ones."

"Yes*sir!*" The big spacer rummaged in the lockers overhead.

Standing child-size among these huge Terrans, Jalun was overcome again by the contrast between their size and strength and perfection and his own weak-limbed, frail, slope-shouldered little form. Among his people he had been accounted a strong youth; even now he was among the ablest. But to these mighty Terrans, Joilani strength was a joke. Perhaps they were right; perhaps he was of an inferior race, fit only to be slaves. . . . But then Jalun remembered what he knew, and straightened his short spine. The younger spacer was saying something.

"Lieutenant, sir, if that's really Stars Tears I can't drink it."

"You can't *drink* it? Why not?"

"I promised. I, uh, swore."

"You'd promise such an insane thing?"

"My—my mother," the youngster said miserably.

The two others shouted with laughter.

"You're a long way from home now, son," the lieutenant said kindly. "What am I saying, Jon? We'd be delighted to take yours. But I just can't bear to see a man pass up the most beautiful thing in life, and I mean bar none. Forget Mommy and prepare your soul for bliss. That's an order. . . . All right, Smiley boy, equal shares. And if you spill one drop I'll *dicty* both your little *pnonks,* hear?"

"Yes seh." Carefully Jalun poured the loathsome liquor into the small cups.

"You ever tasted this, Juloo?"

"No seh."

"And never will. All right, now scat. Ah-h-h . . . Well, here's to our next station, may it have real live poogy on it."

Jalun went silently back down into the shadows of the gangway, paused where he could just see the spacers lift their cups and drink. Hate and disgust choked him, though he had seen it often: Terrans eagerly drinking Stars Tears. It was the very symbol of their oblivious cruelty, their fall from *Jailasanatha*. They could not be excused for ignorance; too many of them had told Jalun how Stars Tears was made. It was not tears precisely, but the body secretions of a race of beautiful, frail winged creatures on a very distant world. Under physical or mental pain their glands exuded this liquid which the Terrans found so deliciously intoxicating. To obtain it, a mated pair were captured and slowly tortured to death in each other's sight. Jalun had been told atrocious details which he could not bear to recall.

Now he watched, marveling that the hate burning in his eyes did not alert the Terrans. He was quite certain that the drug was tasteless and did no harm; careful trials over the long years had proved that. The problem was that it took from two to five minims to work. The last-affected Terran might have time to raise an alarm. Jalun would die to prevent that—if he could.

The three spacers' faces had changed; their eyes shone.

"You see, son?" the lieutenant asked huskily.

The boy nodded, his rapt gaze on nowhere.

Suddenly the big spacer Jon lunged up and said thickly, "What—?" Then he slumped down with his head on one outstretched arm.

"Hey! Hey, Jon!" The lieutenant rose, reaching toward him. But then he too was falling heavily across the ward-room table. That left only the staring boy.

Would he act, would he seize the caller? Jalun gathered himself to spring, knowing he could do little but die in those strong hands.

But the boy only repeated, "What? . . . What?" Lost in a private dream, he leaned back, slid downward, and began to snore.

Jalun darted up to them and snatched the weapons from the two huge lax bodies. Then he scrambled up to the cruiser's control room, summoning all the memorized knowledge that had been gained over the slow years. Yes—that was the transmitter. He wrestled its hood off and began firing into its works. The blast of the weapon frightened him, but he kept on till all was charred and melted.

The flight computer next. Here he had trouble burning in, but soon achieved what seemed to be sufficient damage. A nearby metal case fastened to what was now the ceiling bothered him. It had not been included in his instructions—because the Joilani had not learned of the cruiser's new backup capability. Jalun gave it only a perfunctory blast, and turned to the weapons console.

Emotions he had never felt before were exploding in him, obscuring sight and reason. He fired at wild random across the board, concentrating on whatever would explode or melt, not realizing that he had left the heavy-weapons wiring essentially undamaged. Pinned-up pictures of the grotesque Terran females, which had done his people so much harm, he flamed to ashes.

Then he did the most foolish thing.

Instead of hurrying straight back down through the wardroom, he paused to stare at the slack face of the spacer who had savaged his young. His weapon was hot in his hand. Madness took Jalun: he burned through face and skull. The release of a lifetime's helpless hatred seemed to drive him on wings of flame. Beyond all reality, he killed the other two Terrans without pausing and hurried on down.

He was quite insane with rage and self-loathing when he reached the reactor chambers. Forgetting the hours of painful memorization of the use of the waldo arms, he went straight in through the shielding port to the pile itself. Here he began to tug with his bare hands at the damping rods, as if he were a suited Terran. But his Joilani strength was far too weak, and he could barely move them. He raged, fired at the pile, tugged again, his body bare to the full fury of radiation.

When presently the rest of the Terran crew poured into the ship they found a living corpse clawing madly at the pile. He had removed only four rods; instead of a meltdown he had achieved nothing at all.

The engineer took one look at Jalun through the vitrex and swung the heavy waldo arm over to smash him into the wall. Then he replaced the rods, checked his readouts, and signaled: Ready to lift.

* * *

*There was also great danger that the Terrans would
signal to one of their mighty warships, which alone can
send a missile seeking through tau-space. An act of infamy
was faced.*

The Elder Jayakal entered the communications chamber just as the Terran operator completed his regular
transmission for the period. That had been carefully
planned. First, it would insure the longest possible interval before other stations became alarmed. Equally important, the Joilani had been unable to discover a way of
entry to the chamber when the operator was not there.

"Hey, Pops, what do you think you're doing? You
know you're not supposed to be in here. Scoot!"

Jayakal smiled broadly in the pain of his heart. This
Terran She'gan had been kind to the Joilani in his rough
way. Kind and respectful. He knew them by their proper
names; he had never abused their females; he fed
cleanly, and did not drink abomination. He had even
inquired, with decorum, into the sacred concepts:
Jailasanatha, the Living-with-in-honor, the Oneness-of-
love. Old Jayakal's flexible cheekbones drew upward in
a beaming rictus of shame.

"O gentle friend, I come to share with you," he said
ritually.

"You know I don't really divvy your speech. Now you
have to get out."

Jayakal knew no Terran word for *sharing;* perhaps
there was none.

"F'iend, I b'ing you thing."

"Yeah, well bring it me *outside*." Seeing that the old
Jolani did not move, the operator rose to usher him out.
But memory stirred; his understanding of the true meaning of that smile penetrated. "What is it, Jayakal? What
you got there?"

Jayakal brought the heavy load in his hands forward.
"Death."

"What—where did you get that? Oh, holy mother, get
away from me! That thing is armed! *The pin is out*—"

The laboriously pilfered and hoarded excavating plastic had been well and truly assembled; the igniter had

been properly attached. In the ensuing explosion fragments of the whole transmitter complex, mingled with those of Jayakal and his Terran friend, rained down across the Terran compound and out among the *amlat* fields.

Spacers and station personnel erupted out of the post bars, at first uncertain in the darkness what to do. Then they saw torches flaring and bobbing around the transformer sheds. Small gray figures were running, leaping, howling, throwing missiles that flamed.

"The crotting Juloos are after the power plant! Come on!"

Other diversions were planned. The names of the Old Ones and damaged females who died thus for us are inscribed on the sacred rolls. We can only pray that they found quick and merciful deaths.

The station commander's weapons belt hung over the chair by his bed. All through the acts of shame and pain Sosalal had been watching it, waiting for her chance. If only Bislat, the commander's "boy," could come in to help her! But he could not—he was needed at the ship.

The commander's lust was still unsated. He gulped a drink from the vile little purple flask, and squinted his small Terran eyes meaningfully at her. Sosalal smiled, and offered her trembling, grotesquely disfigured body once more. But no: he wanted her to stimulate him. She set her empathic Joilani fingers, her shuddering mouth, to do their work, hoping that the promised sound would come soon, praying that the commander's communicator would not buzz with news of the attempt failed. Why oh why was it taking so long? She wished she could have one last sight of the Terran's great magical star projection, which showed at one far side those blessed, incredible symbols of her people. Somewhere out there, so very far away, was Joilani home space—maybe even, she thought wildly, while her body labored at its hurtful task, maybe a Joilani empire!

Now he wished to enter her. She was almost inured to the pain; her damaged body had healed in a form pleasing to this Terran. She was only the commander's fourth "girl." There had been other commanders, some better, some worse, and "girls" beyond counting, as far back as the Joilani records ran. It had been "girls" like herself and "boys" like Bislat who had first seen the great three-dimensional luminous star swarms in the commander's private room—and brought back to their people the unbelievable news: somewhere, a Joilani homeland still lived!

Greatly daring, a "girl" had once asked about those Joilani symbols. Her commander had shrugged. "That stuff! It's the hell and gone the other side of the system, take half your life to get there. I don't know a thing about 'em. Probably somebody just stuck 'em in. They aren't Juloos, that's for sure."

Yet there the symbols blazed, tiny replicas of the ancient Joilani Sun-in-splendor. It could mean only one thing, that the old myth was true: that they were not natives to this world, but descendants of a colony left by Joilani who traveled space as the Terrans did. And that those great Joilani yet lived!

If only they could reach them. But how, how?

Could they somehow send a message? All but impossible. And even if they did, how could their kind rescue them from the midst of Terran might?

No. Hopeless as it seemed, they must get themselves out and reach Joilani space by their own efforts.

And so the great plan had been born and grown, over years, over lifetimes. Painfully, furtively, bit by bit, Joilani servants and bar attendants and ship cleaners and *amlat* loaders had discovered and brought back the magic numbers, and their meaning: the tau-space coordinates that would take them to those stars. From discarded manuals, from spacers' talk, they had pieced together the fantastic concept of tau-space itself. Sometimes an almighty Terran would find a naive Joilani question amusing enough to answer. Those allowed inside the ships brought back tiny fragments of the workings of the Terran magic. Joilani who were humble "boys" by day and "girls" by night, became clandestine students and teachers, fitting together the mysteries of their overlords, reducing them from magic to comprehension. Preparing, planning in minutest detail, sustained only by substance-less hope, they readied for their epic, incredible flight.

And now the lived-for moment had come.

Or had it? Why was it taking so long? Suffering as she had so often smilingly suffered before, Sosalal despaired. Surely nothing would, nothing could change. It was all a dream; all would go on as it always had, the degradation and the pain. . . . The commander indicated new desires; careless with grief, Sosalal complied.

"Watch it!" He slapped her head so that her vision spun.

"Excuse, seh."

"You're getting a bit long in the tooth, Sosi." He meant that literally: mature Joilani teeth were large. "You better start training a younger *moolie*. Or have 'em pulled."

"Yes seh."

"You scratch me again and I'll pull 'em myself— Holy Jebulibar, what's that?"

A flash from the window lit the room, followed by a rumbling that rattled the walls. The commander tossed her aside and ran to look out.

It had come! It was really true! *Hurry*. She scrambled to the chair.

"Good God Almighty, it looks like the transmitter blew. Wha—"

He had whirled toward his communicator, his clothes, and found himself facing the mouth of his own weapon held in Sosalal's trembling hands. He was too astounded to react. When she pressed the firing stud he dropped with his chest blown open, the blank frown still on his face.

Sosalal too was astounded, moving in a dream. She had killed. Really killed a Terran. A living being. "I come to share," she whispered ritually. Gazing at the fiery light in the window, she turned the weapon to her own head and pressed the firing stud.

Nothing happened.

What could be wrong? The dream broke, leaving her in dreadful reality. Frantically she poked and probed at the strange object. Was there some mechanism needed to reset it? She was unaware of the meaning of the red charge dot—the commander had grown too careless to recharge his weapon after his last game hunt. Now it was empty.

Sosalal was still struggling with the thing when the door burst open and she felt herself seized and struck all but senseless. Amid the boots and the shouting, her wrist glands leaked scarlet Joilani tears as she foresaw the slow and merciless death that would now be hers.

They had just started to question her when she heard it: the deep rolling rumble of a ship lifting off. The *Dream* was away—her people had done it, they were saved! Through her pain she heard a Terran voice say, "Juloo-town is empty! All the young ones are on that ship." Under the blows of her tormentors her twin hearts leaped with joy.

But a moment later all exultation died; she heard the louder fires of the Terran cruiser bursting into the sky. The *Dream* had failed, then: they would be pursued and killed. Desolate, she willed herself to die in the Terrans' hands. But her life resisted, and her broken body lived long enough to sense the thunderous concussion from the sky that must be the destruction of her race. She died believing all hope was dead. Still, she had told her questioners nothing.

Great dangers came to those who essayed to lift the Dream.

"If you monkeys are seriously planning to try to fly this ship you better set that trim lever first or we'll all be killed."

It was the Terran pilot speaking—the third to be captured, so they had not needed to stop his mouth.

"Go on, push it! It's in landing attitude now, that red one. I don't want to be smashed up."

Young Jivadh, dwarfed in the huge pilot's chair, desperately reviewed his laboriously built-up memory engram of this ship's controls. Red lever, red lever . . . He was not quite sure. He twisted around to look at their captives. Incredible to see the three great bodies lying bound and helpless against the wall, which should soon become the floor. From the seat beside him Bislat held his weapon trained on them. It was one of the two stolen Terran weapons which they had long hoarded for this, their greatest task: the capture of the Terrans on the *Dream*. The first spacer had not believed they were serious until Jivadh had burned through his boots.

Now he lay groaning intermittently, muffled by the gag. When he caught Jivadh's gaze he nodded vehemently in confirmation of the pilot's warning.

"I left it in landing attitude," the pilot repeated. "If you try to lift that way we'll all die!" The third captive nodded, too.

Jivadh's mind raced over and over the remembered pattern. The *Dream* was an old, unstandardized ship. Jivadh continued with the ignition procedure, not touching the red lever.

"Push it, you fool!" the pilot shouted. "Holy mother, do you want to die?"

Bislat was looking nervously from Jivadh to the Terrans. He too had learned the patterns of the *amlat* freighters, but not as well.

"Jivadh, are you *sure?*"

"I cannot be certain. I think on the old ships that is an emergency device which will change or empty the fuels so that they cannot fire. What they call *abort*. See the Terran symbol *a*."

The pilot had caught the words.

"It's not abort, it's attitude! *A* for attitude, *attitude*, you monkey. Push it over or we'll crash!"

The other two nodded urgently.

Jivadh's whole body was flushed blue and trembling with tension. His memories seemed to recede, blur, spin. Never before had a Joilani disbelieved, disobeyed a Terran order. Desperate, he clung to one fading fragment of a yellowed chart in his mind.

"I think not," he said slowly.

Taking his people's whole life in his delicate fingers, he punched the ignition-and-lift sequence into real time.

Clickings—a clank of metal below—a growling hiss that grew swiftly to an intolerable roar beneath them. The old freighter creaked, strained, gave a sickening lurch. Were they about to crash? Jivadh's soul died a thousand deaths.

But the horizon around them stayed level. The *Dream* was shuddering upward, straight up, moving faster and faster as she staggered and leaped toward space. All landmarks fell away—they were in flight! Jivadh, crushed against his supports, exulted. They had not crashed! He had been right: the Terran had been lying.

All outer sound fell away. The *Dream* had cleared atmosphere, and was driving for the stars!

But not alone.

Just as the pressure was easing, just as joy was echoing through the ship and the first of his comrades were struggling up to tell him all was well below, just as a Healer was moving to aid the Terran's burned foot—a loud Terran voice roared through the cabin.

"Halt, you in the *Dream!* Retrofire. Go into orbit for boarding or we'll shoot you down."

The Joilani shrank back. Jivadh saw that the voice was coming from the transceiver, which he had turned on as part of the liftoff procedures.

"That's the patrol," the Terran pilot told him. "They're coming up behind us. You have to quit now, monkey boy. They really will blow us out of space."

A sharp clucking started in an instrument to Jivadh's right. MASS PROXIMITY INDICATOR, he read. Involuntarily he turned to the Terran pilot.

"That's nothing, just one of those damn moons. Listen, you *have* to backfire. I'm not fooling this time. I'll tell you what to do."

"Go into orbit for boarding!" the great voice boomed.

But Jivadh had turned away, was busy doing something else. It was not right. Undoubtedly he would kill them all—but he knew what his people would wish.

"Last warning. We will now fire," the cruiser's voice said coldly.

"They mean it!" the Terran pilot screamed. "For God's sake let me talk to them, let me acknowledge!" The other Terrans were glaring, thrashing in their bonds. This fear was genuine, Jivadh saw, quite different from the lies before. What he had to do was not difficult, but it would take time. He fumbled the transceiver switch open and spoke into it, ignoring Bislat's horrified eyes.

"We will stop. Please wait. It is difficult."

"That's the boy!" The pilot was panting with relief. "All right now. See that delta-V estimator, under the thrust dial? Oh, it's too feking complicated. Let me at it, you might as well."

Jivadh ignored him, continuing with his doomed task. Reverently he fed in the coordinates, the sacred coordinates etched in his mind since childhood, the numbers that might possibly, if they could have done it right, have brought them out of tau-space among Joilani stars.

"We will give you three minims to comply," the voice said.

"Listen, they *mean* it!" the pilot cried. "What are you doing? Let me up!"

Jivadh went on. The mass-proximity gauge clucked louder; he ignored that, too. When he turned to the small tau-console the pilot suddenly understood.

"No! Oh, *no!*" he screamed. "Oh, for God's sake don't do that! You crotting idiot, if you go tau this close to the planet we'll be squashed right into its mass!" His voice had risen to a shriek; the other two were uttering wordless roars and writhing.

They were undoubtedly right, Jivadh thought bleakly. One moment's glory—and now the end.

"We fire in one more minim," came the cruiser's toneless roar.

"Stop! Don't! No!" the pilot yelled.

Jivadh looked at Bislat. The other had realized what he was doing; now he gave the true Joilani smile of pursed lips and made the ritual sign of Acceptance-of-ending. The Joilani in the passage understood that; a sighing silence rustled back through the ship.

"Fire one," the cruiser voice said briskly.

Jivadh slammed the tau-tumbler home.

An alarm shrieked and cut off, all colors vanished, the very structure of space throbbed wildly—as, by a million-to-one chance, the three most massive nearby moons occulted one another in line with the tiny extra energies of the cruiser and its detonating missile, in such a way that for one micromicrominim the *Dream* stood at a seminull point with the planetary mass. In that fleeting instant she flung out her tau-field, folded the normal dimensions around her, and shot like a squeezed pip into the discontinuity of being which was tau.

Nearby space-time was rocked by the explosion; concussion swept the moons and across the planet beneath. So narrow was the *Dream*'s moment of safe passage that a fin of bright metal from the cruiser and a rock with earth and herbs on it were later found intricately meshed into the substance of her stern cargo hold, to the great wonder of the Joilani.

Meanwhile the rejoicing was so great that it could be expressed in only one way: all over the ship, the Joilani lifted their voices in the sacred song.

They were free! The *Dream* had made it into tau-space, where no enemy could find them! They were safely on their way.

Safely on their way—to an unknown destination, over an unknown time, with pitifully limited supplies of water, food, and air.

Here begins the log of the passage of the Dream *through tau-space, which, although timeless, required finite time.* . . .

Jatkan let the precious old scroll roll up and laid it carefully aside, to touch the hand of a co-mate. He had been one of the babies in the *amlat* containers; sometimes he thought he remembered the great night of their escape. Certainly he remembered a sense of rejoicing, a feeling of dread nightmare blown away.

"The waiting is long," said his youngest co-mate, who was little more than a child. "Tell us again about the Terran monsters."

"They weren't monsters, only very alien," he corrected the child gently. His eyes met those of Salasvati, who was entertaining her young co-mates at the porthole of the tiny records chamber. It came to Jatkan that when he and Salas were old, they might be the last Joilani who had ever really seen a Terran. Certainly the last to have any sense of their terror and might, and the degradations of slavery burned into their parents' souls. Surely this is good, he thought, but is it not also a loss, in some strange way?

"—reddish, or sometimes yellow or brownish, almost

hairless, with small bright eyes," he was telling the child. "And big, about the distance to that porthole there. And one day, when the three who were on the *Dream* were allowed out to exercise, they rushed into the control room and changed the—the *gyroscope* setting, so that the ship began to spin around faster and faster, and everybody fell down and was pressed flat into the walls. They were counting on their greater strength, you see."

"So that they could seize the *Dream* and break out of tau-space into Terran stars!" His two female co-mates recited in unison: "But old Jivadh saved us."

"Yes. But he was young Jivadh then. By great good luck he was at the central column, right where the old weapons were kept, that no one had touched for hundreds of days."

A co-mate smiled. "The luck of the Joilani."

"No," Jatkan told her. "We must not grow superstitious. It was simple chance."

"And he *killed them all!*" the child burst out excitedly. A hush fell.

"Never use that word so lightly," Jatkan said sternly. "Think what you are meaning, little one. *Jailasanatha—*"

As he admonished the child, his mind noted again the incongruity of his words: the "little one" was already as large as he, as he in turn was larger and stronger than his parents. This could only be due to the children's eating the Terran-mixed food from the ship's recycler, however scanty. When the older ones saw how the young grew, it confirmed another old myth: that their ancestors had once been giants, who had diminished through some lack in the planet's soil. Was every old myth-legend coming true at once?

Meanwhile he was trying once more to explain to the child, and to the others, the true horror of the decision Jivadh had faced, and Jivadh's frenzy of anguish when he was prevented from killing himself in atonement. Jatkan's memory was scarred by that day. First the smash against the walls, the confusion—the explosions—their release; and then the endless hours of ritual argument, persuading Jivadh that his knowledge of the ship was too precious to lose. The pain in Jivadh's voice as he confessed: "I thought also in selfishness, that we would have their water, their food, their air."

"That is why he doesn't take his fair share of food, and sleeps on the bare steel."

"And why he's always so sad," the child said, frowning with the effort to truly understand.

"Yes." But Jatkan knew that he could never really understand; nobody could who had not seen the horror of violently dead flesh that once was living, even though alien and hostile. The three corpses had been consigned with due ritual to the recycling bins, as they did with their own. By now all the Joilani must bear some particles in their flesh that once were Terran. Ironic.

A shadow passed his mind. A few days ago he had been certain that these young ones, and their children's children, would never need know what it was to kill. Now he was not quite so certain. . . . He brushed the thought away.

"Has the log been kept right up to now?" asked Salasvati from the port. Like Jatkan, she was having difficulty keeping her young co-mates quiet during this solemn wait.

"Oh yes."

Jatkan's fingers delicately riffled through the motley pages of the current logbook on the stand. It had been sewn together from whatever last scraps and charts they could find. The clear Joilani script flashed out at him on page after page: "Hunger . . . rations cut . . . broken, water low . . . repairs . . . adult rations cut again . . . oxygen low . . . the children . . . water reduced . . . the children need . . . how much more can we . . . end soon; not enough . . . when . . ."

Yes, that had been his whole life, all their lives: dwindling life sustenance in the great rotating cylinder that was their world. The unrelenting uncertainty: would they ever break out? And if so, where? Or would it go on till they all died here in the timeless, lightless void?

And the rare weird events, things almost seen, like the strange light ghost ship that had suddenly bloomed beside them with ungraspably alien creatures peering from its parts—and as suddenly vanished again.

Somewhere in the *Dream*'s magical computers circuits

were clicking toward the predestined coordinates, but no one knew how to check on the program's progress, or even whether it still functioned. The merciless stress of waiting told upon them all in different ways, as the hundred-day cycles passed into thousands. Some grew totally silent; some whispered endless ritual; some busied themselves with the most minute tasks. Old Bislat had been their leader here; his courage and cheer were indomitable. But it was Jivadh, despite his dreadful deed, despite his self-imposed silence and reclusion, who was somehow still the symbol of their faith. It was not that he had lifted the *Dream*, had saved them not once but twice; it was the sensed trueness of his heart . . . Jatkan, turning the old pages, reflected that perhaps it had all been easiest for the children, who had known no other life but only waiting for the Day.

And then—the changed writing on the last page spoke for itself—there had come the miracle, the first of the Days. All unexpectedly, as they were preparing for the three-thousandth-and-something sleep period, the ship had shuddered, and unfamiliar meshing sounds had rumbled around them. They had all sprung up wildly, reeling in disorientation. Great strainings of metal, frightening clanks—and the old ship disengaged her tau-field, to unfold her volume into normal space.

But what space! Stars—the suns of legend—blazed in every porthole, some against deep blackness, some shrouded in glorious clouds of light! Children and adults alike raced from port to port, crying out in wonder and delight.

It was only slowly that realization came: they were still alone in limitless, empty, unknown space, among unknown beings and forces, still perishingly short of all that was needful to life.

The long-planned actions were taken. The transmitter was set to send out the Joilani distress call, at what old Jivadh believed was maximum reach. A brave party went outside, onto the hull, in crazily modified Terran spacesuits. They painted over the ugly Terran star, changing it to a huge Sun-in-splendor. Over the Terran words they wrote the Joilani word for *Dream*. If they were still in the Terran Empire, all was now doubly lost.

"My mother went outside," said Jatkan's oldest co-mate proudly. "It was dangerous and daring and very hard work."

"Yes." Jatkan touched her lovingly.

"I wish I could go outside now," said the youngest.

"You will. Wait."

"It's *always* 'wait.' We're waiting now."

"Yes."

Waiting—oh yes, they had waited, with conditions growing ever worse and hope more faint. Knowing no other course, they set out at crawling pace for the nearest bright star. Few believed they were waiting for anything more than death.

Until that day—the greatest of Days—when a strange spark burst suddenly into being ahead, and grew into a great ship bearing down upon them.

And they had seen the Sun-in-splendor on her bow.

Even the youngest child would remember that forever.

How the stranger had almost magically closed and grappled them, and forced the long-corroded main lock. And they of the *Dream* had seen all dreams come true, as in a rush of sweet air the strange Joilani—the true, real Joilani—had come aboard. Joilani—but giants, as big as Terrans, strong and upright, glowing with health, their hands upraised in the ancient greeting. How they had narrowed their nostrils at the *Dream's* foul air! How they had blinked in wonderment as the song of thanksgiving rose around them!

Through it all, their leader had patiently repeated in strange but understandable accents, "I am *Khanrid* Jemnal Vizadh. Who *are* you people?" And when a tiny old Joilani female had rushed to him with leaves torn from the hydroponics bed and tried to wreathe him, crying, "Jemnal! Jemnal my lost son! Oh, my son, my son!" he had smiled embarrassedly, and stooped to embrace her, calling her "Mother," before he put her gently aside.

And then the explanations, the incredulity, as the great Joilani had spread out to examine the *Dream*, each with his train of awestruck admirers. They had scanned the old charts, and opened and traced the tau-program with casual skill. They too seemed excited; the *Dream*, it seemed, had performed an unparalleled deed. One of the giants had begun questioning them: arcane, incomprehensible questions as to types of Terran ships they had seen, the colors and insignia numbers on the Terrans' clothes. "Later, later," *Khanrid* Jemnal had said. And then had begun the practical measures of bringing in food and water, and recharging the air supply.

"We will plot your course to the sector base," he told them. "Three of our people will go with you when you are ready."

In all the excitement Jatkan found it hard to recall exactly when he had noticed that their Joilani saviors all were armed.

"They are patrol spacers," old Bislat said wonderingly. "*Khanrid* is a military title. That ship is a warship, a protector of the Joilani Federation of Worlds."

He had to explain to the young ones what that meant.

"It means we are no longer helpless!" His old eyes glowed. "It means that our faith, our Gentleness-in-honor, our *Jailasanatha* way, can never again be trodden to the dirt by brute might!"

Jatkan, whose feet could not remember treading dirt, yet understood. A marveling exultation grew in them all. Even old Jivadh's face softened briefly from its customary grim composure.

Female Joilani came aboard—new marvels. Beautiful giantesses, who did strange and sometimes uncomfortable things to them all. Jatkan learned new words: *inoculation, infestation, antisepsis.* His clothes and the others' were briefly taken away, and returned looking and smelling quite different. He overheard *Khanrid* Jemnal speaking to one of the goddesses.

"I know, *Khanlal.* You'd like to strip out this hull and blow everything but their bare bodies out to space. But you must understand that we are touching history here. These rags, this whole pathetic warren, is hot, living history. Evidence, too, if you like. No. Clean them up, depingee them, inoculate and dust and spray all you want. But leave it looking just the way it is."

"But, *Khanrid*—"

"That's it."

Jatkan had not long to puzzle over that; it was the day of their great visit to the wonderful warship. There they saw and touched marvels, all giant-size. And then were fed a splendid meal, and afterward all joined in singing, and they learned new words for some of the old Joilani songs. When they finally returned, the *Dream* seemed to be permeated with a most peculiar odor which made them all sneeze for days. Soon afterward they noticed that they were doing a lot less scratching; the fritlings that had been a part of their lives seemed to be gone.

"They sent them away," Jatkan's mother explained. "It seems they are not good on ships."

"They were killed," old Jivadh broke his silence to remark tonelessly.

The three great Joilani spacers who were to get them safely to the sector base came aboard then. *Khanrid* Jemnal introduced them. "And now I must say good-bye. You will receive a warm welcome."

When they sang him and the others farewell it was almost as emotional as on the first day.

Their three guardians had been busy at mysterious tasks in the *Dream*'s workings. Old Bislat and some of the other males watched them keenly, trying to understand, but Jivadh seemed no longer to care. Soon they were plunged back into tau-space, but how different this time, with ample air and water and food for all! In only ten sleep periods the now-familiar shudder ran through the *Dream* again, and they broke out into daylight with a blue sun blinding in the ports.

A planet loomed up beside them. The Joilani pilot took them down into the shadow-darkened limb, sinking toward a gigantic spaceport. Ships beyond count stood there, ablaze with lights, and beyond the field itself stretched a vast jeweled webwork, like myriad earthly stars.

Jatkan learned a new word: *city*. He could hardly wait to see it in the day.

Almost at once the *Dream*'s five Elders had been ceremoniously escorted out, to visit the High Elders of this wondrous place. They went in a strange kind of landship. Looking after them, the *Dream*'s people could see that a lighted barrier of some sort had been installed around the ship. Now they were awaiting their return.

"They're taking so long," Jatkan's youngest co-mate complained. He was getting drowsy.

"Let us look out again," Jatkan proposed. "May we exchange places, Salasvati?"

"With pleasure."

Jatkan led his little family to the port as Salasvati's moved back, awkward in the unfamiliar sternward weight.

"Look, out beyond—there are people!"

It was true. Jatkan saw what seemed to be an endless multitude of Joilani in the night, hundreds upon hundreds upon hundreds of pale gray faces beyond the barrier, all turned toward the *Dream*.

"We are history," he quoted *Khanrid* Jemnal.

"What's that?"

"An important event, I think. See—here come our Elders now!"

There was a commotion, a parting in the throng, and the landship which had taken the Elders away came slowly out into the free space around the *Dream*.

"Come look, Salasvati!"

Craning and crowding, they could just make out their Elders and their giant escorts emerging from the landship, and taking warm ritual leaving of each other.

"Hurry, they'll tell us all about it in the Center!"

It was difficult, with the ship in this new position and everything hanging wrong. Their parents were already sitting sideways in the doors of the center shaft. The youngsters scrambled to whatever perches or laps they could find. The party of Elders could be heard making their slow way up from below, climbing the long-unused central ladders to where they could speak to all.

As they came into view Jatkan could see how weary they were, and how their dark eyes radiated excitement, exultation. Yet with a queer tautness or tension stretching their cheekbones, too, he thought.

"We were indeed warmly received," old Bislat said when all had reached the central space. "We saw wonders it will take days to describe. All of you will see them too, in due time. We were taken to meet the High Elders here, and ate the evening meal with them." He paused briefly. "We were also questioned, by one particular Elder, about the Terrans we have known. It seems that our knowledge is important, old as it is. All of you who remember our previous life must set yourselves to recalling every sort of small detail. The colors of their spacers' clothing, their ornaments of rank, the names and appearance of their ships that came and went." He smiled wonderingly. "It was . . . strange . . . to hear Terrans spoken of so lightly, even scornfully. We think now that their great Empire is not so mighty as we believed. Pehaps it has grown too old, or too big. Our people"—he spoke with his hands clasped in thanksgiving—"our people do not fear them."

A wordless, incredulous gasp of joy rose from the listeners around the shaft.

"Yes." Bislat stilled them. "Now, as to what is ahead for us. We are, you must understand, a great wonder to them. It seems our flight here from so far away was extraordinary, and has moved them very much. But we are also, well, so very different—like people from another age. It is not only our size. Their very children know more than we do of practical daily things. We could not quietly go out and dwell among the people of this city or the lands around it, even though they are our own Joilani, of the faith. We Elders have seen enough to understand that, and you will, too. Some of you may already have thought on this, have you not?"

A thoughtful murmur of assent echoed his words from door after door. Even Jatkan realized that he had been wondering about this, somewhere under his conscious mind.

"In time, of course, it will be different. Our young, or their young, will be as they are, and we all can learn."

He smiled deeply. But Jatkan found his gaze caught by old Jivadh's face. Jivadh was not smiling; his gaze was cast down, and his expression was tense and sad. Indeed, something of the same strain seemed to lie upon them all, even Bislat. What could be wrong?

Bislat was continuing, his voice strong and cheerful. "So they have found for us a fertile land, an empty land on a beautiful world. The *Dream* will stay here, as a permanent memorial of our great flight. They will take us there in another ship, with all that we need, and with people who will stay to help and teach us." His hands met again in thanksgiving; his voice rang out reverently. "So begins our new life of freedom, safe among Joilani stars, among our people of the faith."

Just as his listeners began quietly to hum the sacred song, old Jivadh raised his head.

"Of the faith, Bislat?" he asked harshly.

The singers hushed in puzzlement.

"You saw the Gardens of the Way." Bislat's tone was strangely brusque. "You saw the sacred texts emblazoned, you saw the Meditators—"

"I saw many splendid places," Jivadh cut him off. "With idle attendants richly gowned."

"It is nowhere written that the Way must be shabbily served," Bislat protested. "The richness is a proof of its honor here."

"And before one of those sacred places of devotion," Jivadh went on implacably, "I saw Joilani as old as I, in rags almost as poor as mine, toiling with heavy burdens. You did not mention that, Bislat. For that matter, you did not mention how strangely young these High Elders of our people here are. Think on it. It can only mean that the old wisdom is not enough, that new enterprises not of the Way are in movement here."

"But, Jivadh," another Elder put in, "there is so much here that we are not yet able to understand. Surely, when we know more—"

"There is much that Bislat refuses to understand," Jivadh said curtly. "He also has omitted to say what we were offered."

"No, Jivadh! Do not, we implore you." Bislat's voice trembled. "We agreed, for the good of all—"

"*I* did not agree." Jivadh turned to the tiers of listeners. His haggard gaze swept past them, seeming to look far beyond.

"O my people," he said somberly, "the *Dream* has not come home. It may be that it has no home. What we have come to is the Joilani Federation of Worlds, a mighty, growing power among the stars. We are safe here, yes. But Federation, Empire, perhaps it is all the same in the end. Bislat has told you that these so-called Elders kindly gave us to eat. But he has not told you what the High Elder offered us to drink."

"They said it was confiscated!" Bislat cried.

"Does that matter? Our high Joilani, our people of the faith—" Jivadh's eyelids closed in sadness; his voice broke to a hoarse rasp. *"Our Joilani . . .* were drinking Stars Tears."

Slow Music

Caoilte tossing his burning hair
and Niamh calling "Away, come away;
Empty your heart of its mortal dream. . . .
We come between man and the deed of his hand,
We come between him and the hope of his heart."
—W.B. Yeats

LIGHTS CAME ON as Jakko walked down the lawn past the house; elegantly concealed spots and floods which made the night into a great intimate room. Overhead the big conifers formed a furry nave drooping toward the black lake below the bluff ahead. This had been a beloved home, he saw; every luxurious device was subdued to preserve the beauty of the forested shore. He walked on a carpet of violets and mosses, in his hand the map that had guided him here from the city.

It was the stillness before dawn. A long-winged night bird swirled in to catch a last moth in the dome of light. Before him shone a bright spear point. Jakko saw it was the phosphorescent tip of a mast against the stars. He went down velvety steps to find a small sailboat floating at the dock like a silver leaf reflected on a dark mirror.

In silence he stepped on board, touched the mast.

A gossamer sail spread its fan, the mooring parted soundlessly. The dawn breeze barely filled the sail, but the craft moved smoothly out, leaving a glassy line of wake. Jakko half-poised to jump. He knew nothing of such playtoys, he should go back and find another boat. As he did so, the shore lights went out, leaving him in darkness. He turned and saw Regulus rising ahead where the channel must be. Still, this was not the craft for him. He tugged at the tiller and sail, meaning to turn it back.

116

But the little boat ran smoothly on, and then he noticed the lights of a small computer glowing by the mast. He relaxed; this was no toy, the boat was fully programmed and he could guess what the course must be. He stood examining the sky, a statue-man gliding across reflected night.

The eastern horizon changed, veiled its stars as he neared it. He could see the channel now, a silvery cut straight ahead between dark banks. The boat ran over glittering shallows where something splashed hugely, and headed into the shining lane. As it did so, all silver changed to lead and the stars were gone. Day was coming. A great pearl-colored blush spread upward before him, developed bands of lavender and rays of coral-gold fire melting to green iridescence overhead. The boat was now gliding on a ribbon of fiery light between black-silhouetted banks. Jakko looked back and saw dazzling cloud-cities heaped behind him in the west. The vast imminence of sunrise. He sighed aloud.

He understood that all this demonstration of glory was nothing but the effects of dust and vapor in the thin skin of air around a small planet, whereon he crawled wingless. No vastness brooded; the planet was merely turning with him into the rays of its mediocre primary. His family, everyone, knew that on the River he would encounter the Galaxy itself in glory. Suns beyond count, magnificence to which this was nothing. And yet—and yet to him this was not nothing. It was intimately his, man-sized. He made an ambiguous sound in his throat. He resented the trivialization of this beauty, and he resented being moved by it. So he passed along, idly holding the sail rope like a man leashing the living wind, his face troubled and very young.

The little craft ran on unerringly, threading the winding sheen of the canal. As the sun rose, Jakko began to hear a faint drone ahead. The sea surf. He thought of the persons who must have made this voyage before him: the ship's family, savoring their final days of mortality. A happy voyage, a picnic. The thought reminded him that he was hungry; the last groundcar's synthesizer had been faulty.

He tied the rope and searched. The boat had replenished its water, but there was only one food bar. Jakko lay down in the cushioned well and ate and drank comfortably, while the sky turned turquoise and then cobalt. Presently they emerged into an enormous lagoon and began to run south between low islands. Jakko trailed his hand and tasted brackish salt. When the boat turned east again and made for a seaward opening, he became doubly certain. The craft was programmed for the River, like almost everything else on the world he knew.

Sure enough, the tiny bark ran through an inlet and straight out into the chop beyond a long beach, extruded outriggers, and passed like a cork over the reef foam onto the deep green swells beyond. Here it pitched once and steadied; Jakko guessed it had thrust down a keel. Then it turned south and began to run along outside the reef, steady as a knife cut with the wind on its quarter. Going Riverward for sure. The nearest River-place was here called Vidalita or Beata, or sometimes Falaz, meaning "illusion." It was far south and inland. Jakko guessed they were making for a landing where a moveway met the sea. He had still time to think, to struggle with the trouble under his mind.

But as the sun turned the boat into a trim white-gold bird flying over green transparency, Jakko's eyes closed and he slept, protected by invisible deflectors from the bow-spray. Once he opened his eyes and saw a painted fish tearing along magically in the standing wave below his head. He smiled and slept again, dreaming of a great wave dying, a wave that was a many-headed beast. His face became sad and his lips moved soundlessly, as if repeating. "No . . . no . . ."

When he woke they were sailing quite close by a long bluff on his right. In the cliff ahead was a big white building or tower, only a little ruined. Suddenly he caught sight of a figure moving on the beach before it. A living human? He jumped up to look. He had not seen a strange human person in many years.

Yes—it was a live person, strangely colored gold and black. He waved wildly.

The person on the beach slowly raised an arm.

Alight with excitement, Jakko switched off the computer and grabbed the rudder and sail. The line of reef surf seemed open here. He turned the boat shoreward, riding on a big swell. But the wave left him. He veered erratically, and the surf behind broached into the boat, overturning it and throwing him out. He knew how to swim; he surfaced and struck out strongly for the shore, spluttering brine. Presently he was wading out onto the white beach, a short, strongly built, reddened young male person with pale hair and water-blue eyes.

The stranger was walking hesitantly toward him. Jakko saw it was a thin, dark-skinned girl wearing a curious netted hat. Her body was wrapped in orange silk and she carried heavy gloves in one hand. Three nervous moondogs followed her. He began turning water out of his shorts pockets as she came up.

"Your . . . boat," she said in the language of that time. Her voice was low and uncertain.

They both turned to look at the confused place by the reef where the sailboat floated half-submerged.

"I turned it off. The computer." His words came jerkily too, they were both unused to speech.

"It will come ashore down there." She pointed, still studying him in a wary, preoccupied way. She was much smaller than he. "Why did you turn? Aren't you going to the River?"

"No." He coughed. "Well, yes, in a way. My father wants me to say good-bye. They left while I was traveling."

"You're not . . . ready?"

"No. I don't—" He broke off. "Are you staying alone here?"

"Yes. I'm not going, either."

They stood awkwardly in the sea wind. Jakko noticed that the three moondogs were lined up single file, tiptoeing upwind toward him with their eyes closed, sniffing. They were not, of course, from the moon, but they looked it, being white and oddly shaped.

"It's a treat for them," the girl said. "Something different." Her voice was stronger now. After a pause she added, "You can stay here for a while if you want. I'll show you but I have to finish my work first."

"Thank you," he remembered to say.

As they climbed steps cut in the bluff Jakko asked, "What are you working at?"

"Oh, everything. Right now it's bees."

"Bees!" he marveled. "They made what—honey? I thought they were all gone."

"I have a lot of old things." She kept glancing at him intently as they climbed. "Are you quite healthy?"

"Oh yes. Why not? I'm all alpha so far as I know. Everybody is."

"Was," she corrected. "Here are my bee skeps."

They came around a low wall and stopped by five small wicker huts. A buzzing insect whizzed by Jakko's face, coming from some feathery shrubs. He saw that the bloom-tipped foliage was alive with the golden humming things. Recalling that they could sting, he stepped back.

"You better go around the other way." She pointed. "They might hurt a stranger." She pulled her veil down, hiding her face. Just as he turned away, she added, "I thought you might impregnate me."

He wheeled back, not really able to react because of the distracting bees. "But isn't that terribly complicated?"

"I don't think so. I have the pills." She pulled on her gloves.

"Yes, the pills. I know." He frowned. "But you'd have to stay, I mean one just can't—"

"I know that. I have to do my bees now. We can talk later."

"Of course." He started away and suddenly turned back.

"Look!" He didn't know her name. "You, look!"

"What?" She was a strange little figure, black and orange with huge hands and a big veil-muffled head. "What?"

"I felt it. Just then, desire. Can't you see?"

They both gazed at his wet shorts.

"I guess not," he said finally. "But I felt it, I swear. Sexual desire."

She pushed back her veil, frowning. "It will stay, won't it? Or come back? This isn't a very good place. I mean, the bees. And it's no use without the pills."

"That's so."

He went away then, walking carefully because of the

tension around his pubic bone. Like a keel, snug and tight. His whole body felt reorganized. It had been years since he'd felt flashes like that, not since he was fifteen at least. Most people never did. That was variously thought to be because of the River, or from their parents' surviving the Poison Centuries, or because the general alpha strain was so forebrain-dominant. It gave him an archaic, secret pride. Maybe he was a throwback.

He passed under cool archways, and found himself in a green, protected place behind the seaward wall. A garden, he saw, looking round surprised at clumps of large tied-up fruiting plants, peculiar trees with green balls at their tops, disorderly rows of rather unaesthetic greenery. Tentatively he identified tomatoes, peppers, a feathery leaf which he thought had an edible root. A utilitarian planting. His uncle had once amused the family by doing something of the sort, but not on this scale. Jakko shook his head.

In the center of the garden stood a round stone coping with a primitive apparatus on top. He walked over and looked down. Water, a bucket on a rope. Then he saw that there was also an ordinary tap. He opened it and drank, looking at the odd implements leaning on the coping. Earth tools. He did not really want to think about what the strange woman had said.

A shadow moved by his foot. The largest moondog had come quite close, inhaling dreamily. "Hello," he said to it. Some of these dogs could talk a little. This one opened its eyes wide but said nothing.

He stared about, wiping his mouth, feeling his clothes almost dry now in the hot sun. On three sides the garden was surrounded by arcades; above him on the ruined side was a square cracked masonry tower with no roof. A large place, whatever it was. He walked into the shade of the nearest arcade, which turned out to be littered with myriad disassembled or partly assembled objects: tools, containers, who knew what. Her "work"? The place felt strange, vibrant and busy. He realized he had entered only empty houses on his year-long journey. This one was alive, lived-in. Messy. It hummed like the bee skeps. He turned down a cool corridor, looking into rooms piled with more stuff. In one, three white animals he couldn't identify were asleep in a heap of cloth on a bed. They moved their ears at him like big pale shells but did not awaken.

He heard staccato noises and came out into another courtyard where plump white birds walked with jerking heads. "Chickens!" he decided, delighted by the irrational variety of this place. He went from there into a large room with windows on the sea, and heard a door close.

It was the woman, or girl, coming to him, holding her hat and gloves. Her hair was a dark curly cap, her head elegantly small; an effect he had always admired. He remembered something to say.

"I'm called Jakko. What's your name?"

"Jakko." She tasted the sound. "Hello, Jakko. I'm Peachthief." She smiled very briefly, entirely changing her face.

"Peachthief." On impulse he moved toward her, holding out his hands. She tucked her bundle under her arm and took both of his. They stood like that a moment, not quite looking at each other. Jakko felt excited. Not sexually, but more as if the air was electrically charged.

"Well." She took her hands away and began unwrapping a leafy wad. "I brought a honeycomb even if it isn't quite ready." She showed him a sticky-looking frame with two dead bees on it. "Come on."

She walked rapidly out into another corridor and entered a shiny room he thought might be a laboratory.

"My food room," she told him. Again Jakko was amazed. There stood a synthesizer, to be sure, but beside it were shelves full of pots and bags and jars and containers of all descriptions. Unknown implements lay about and there was a fireplace which had been partly sealed up. Bunches of plant parts hung from racks overhead. He identified some brownish ovoids in a bowl as eggs. From the chickens?

Peachthief was cleaning the honeycomb with a manually operated knife. "I use the wax for my loom, and for candles. Light."

"What's wrong with the lights?"

"Nothing." She turned around, gesturing emphatically with the knife. "Don't you understand? All these machines, they'll go. They won't run forever. They'll break or wear out or run down. There won't *be* any, anymore. Then we'll have to use natural things."

"But that won't be for centuries!" he protested. "Decades, anyhow. They're all still going, they'll last for us."

"For you," she said scornfully. "Not for me. I intend to stay. With my children." She turned her back on him and added in a friendlier voice, "Besides, the old things are aesthetic. I'll show you, when it gets dark."

"But you haven't any children! Have you?" He was purely astonished.

"Not yet." Her back was still turned.

"I'm hungry," he said, and went to work the synthesizer. He made it give him a bar with a hard filler; for some reason he wanted to crunch it in his teeth.

She finished with the honey and turned around. "Have you ever had a natural meal?"

"Oh yes," he said, chewing. "One of my uncles tried that. It was very nice," he added politely.

She looked at him sharply and smiled again, on—off. They went out of the food room. The afternoon was fading into great gold and orange streamers above the courtyard, colored like Peachthief's garment.

"You can sleep here." She opened a slatted door. The room was small and bare, with a window on the sea.

"There isn't any bed," he objected.

She opened a chest and took out a big wad of string. "Hang this end on that hook over there."

When she hung up the other end he saw it was a large mesh hammock.

"That's what I sleep in. They're comfortable. Try it."

He climbed in awkwardly. The thing came up around him like a bag. She gave a short sweet laugh as brief as her smile.

"No, you lie on the diagonal. Like this." She tugged his legs, sending a peculiar shudder through him. "That straightens it, see?"

It would probably be all right, he decided, struggling out. Peachthief was pointing to a covered pail.

"That's for your wastes. It goes on the garden, in the end."

He was appalled, but said nothing, letting her lead him out through a room with glass tanks in the walls to a big screened-in porch fronting the ocean. It was badly in need of cleaners. The sky was glorious with opalescent domes and spires, reflections of the sunset behind them, painting amazing colors on the sea.

"This is where I eat."

"What is this place?"

"It was a sea station last, I think. Station Juliet. They monitored the fish and the ocean traffic, and rescued people and so on."

He was distracted by noticing long convergent doveblue rays like mysterious paths into the horizon; cloud shadows cast across the world. Beauty of the dust. Why must it move him so?

"—even a medical section," she was saying. "I really could have babies, I mean in case of trouble."

"You don't mean it." He felt only irritation now. "I don't feel any more desire," he told her.

She shrugged. "I don't either. We'll talk about it later on."

"Have you always lived here?"

"Oh, no." She began taking pots and dishes out of an insulated case. The three moondogs had joined them silently; she set bowls before them. They lapped, stealing glances at Jakko. They were, he knew, very strong despite their sticklike appearance.

"Let's sit here." She plumped down on one end of the lounge and began biting forcefully into a crusty thing like a slab of drybar. He noticed she had magnificent teeth. Her dark skin set them off beautifully, as it enhanced her eyes. He had never met anyone so different in every way from himself and his family. He vacillated between interest and a vague alarm.

"Try some of the honey." She handed him a container and spoon. It looked quite clean. He tasted it eagerly; honey was much spoken of in antique writings. At first he sensed nothing but a waxy sliding, but then an overpowering sweetness enveloped his tongue, quite unlike the sweets he was used to. It did not die away but seemed to run up his nose and almost into his ears, in a peculiar physical way. An *animal* food. He took some more, gingerly.

"I didn't offer you my bread. It needs some chemical, I don't know what. To make it lighter."

"Don't you have an access terminal?"

"Something's wrong with part of it," she said with her mouth full. "Maybe I don't work it right. We never had a big one like this, my tribe were travelers. They believed in sensory experiences." She nodded, licking her fingers. "They went to the River when I was fourteen."

"That's very young to be alone. My people waited till this year, my eighteenth birthday."

"I wasn't alone. I had two older cousins. But they wanted to take an aircar up north, to the part of the River called Rideout. I stayed here. I mean, we never stopped traveling, we never *lived* anywhere. I wanted to do like the plants, make roots."

"I could look at your program," he offered. "I've seen a lot of different models, I spent nearly a year in cities."

"What I need is a cow. Or a goat."

"Why?"

"For the milk. I need a pair, I guess."

Another animal thing; he winced a little. But it was pleasant, sitting here in the deep blue light beside her, hearing the surf plash quietly below.

"I saw quite a number of horses," he told her. "Don't they use milk?"

"I don't think horses are much good for milk." She sighed in an alert, busy way. He had the impression that her head was tremendously energic, humming with plans and intentions. Suddenly she looked up and began making a high squeaky noise between her front teeth, "Sssswwt! Sssswwwt!"

Startled, he saw a white flying thing swooping above them, and then two more. They whirled so wildly he ducked.

"That's right," she said to them. "Get busy."

"What are they?"

"My bats. They eat mosquitoes and insects." She squeaked again and the biggest bat was suddenly clinging to her hand, licking honey. It had a small, fiercely complicated face.

Jakko relaxed again. This place and its strange inhabitant were giving him remarkable memories for the

River, anyway. He noticed a faint glow moving where the dark sky joined the darker sea.

"What's that?"

"Oh, the seatrain. It goes to the River landing."

"Are there people on it?"

"Not anymore. Look, I'll show you." She jumped up and was opening a console in the corner, when a sweet computer voice spoke into the air.

"Seatrain Foxtrot Niner calling Station Juliet! Come in, Station Juliet!"

"It hasn't done that for years," Peachthief said. She tripped tumblers. "Seatrain, this is Station Juliet, I hear you. Do you have a problem?"

"Affirmative. Passenger is engaging in nonstandard activities. He-slash-she does not conform to parameters. Request instructions."

Peachthief thought a minute. Then she grinned. "Is your passenger moving on four legs?"

"Affirmative! Affirmative!" Seatrain Foxtrot sounded relieved.

"Supply it with bowls of meat food and water on the floor and do not interfere with it. Juliet out."

She clicked off, and they watched the far web of lights go by on the horizon, carrying an animal.

"Probably a dog following the smell of people," Peachthief said. "I hope it gets off all right. . . . We're quite a wide genetic spread," she went on in a different voice. "I mean, you're so light, and body type and all."

"I noticed that."

"It would give good heterosis. Vigor."

She was talking about being impregnated, about the fantasy child. He felt angry.

"Look, you don't know what you're saying. Don't you realize you'd have to stay and raise it for years? You'd be ethically and morally bound. And the River places are shrinking fast, you must know that. Maybe you'd be too late."

"Yes," she said somberly. "Now it's sucked everybody out it's going. But I still mean to stay."

"But you'd hate it, even if there's still time. My mother hated it, toward the end. She felt she had begun to deteri-

orate energically, that her life would be lessened. And me
—what about me? I mean, I should stay, too."

"You'd only have to stay a month. For my ovulation.
The male parent isn't ethically bound."

"Yes, but I think that's wrong. My father stayed. He
never said he minded it, but he must have."

"You only have to do a month," she said sullenly. "I
thought you weren't going on the River right now."

"I'm not. I just don't want to feel bound, I want to
travel. To see more of the world, first. After I say good-
bye."

She made an angry sound. "You have no insight.
You're going, all right. You just don't want to admit it.
You're going just like Mungo and Ferrocil."

"Who are they?"

"People who came by. Males, like you. Mungo was last
year, I guess. He had an aircar. He said he was going to
stay, he talked and talked. But two days later he went
right on again. To the River. Ferrocil was earlier, he was
walking through. Until he stole my bicycle."

A sudden note of fury in her voice startled him; she
seemed to have some peculiar primitive relation to her
bicycle, to her *things*.

"Did you want them to impregnate you, too?" Jakko
noticed an odd intensity in his own voice as well.

"Oh, I was thinking about it, with Mungo." Suddenly
she turned on him, her eyes wide open in the dimness like
white-ringed jewels. "Look! Once and for all, I'm not going! I'm alive, I'm a human woman. I am going to stay
on this earth and do human things. I'm going to make
young ones to carry on the race, even if I have to die
here. You can go on out, you—you pitiful shadows!"

Her voice rang in the dark room, jarring him down to
his sleeping marrow. He sat silent as though some deep
buried bell had tolled.

She was breathing hard. Then she moved, and to his
surprise a small live flame sprang up between her cupped
hands, making the room a cave.

"That's a candle. That's me. Now go ahead, make fun
like Mungo did."

"I'm not making fun," he said, shocked. "It's just that
I don't know what to think. Maybe you're right. I really

. . . I really don't want to go, in one way," he said haltingly. "I love this earth, too. But it's all so fast. Let me . . ."

His voice trailed off.

"Tell me about your family," she said, quietly now.

"Oh, they studied. They tried every access you can imagine. Ancient languages, history, lore. My aunt made poems in English. . . . The layers of the earth, the names of body cells and tissues, jewels, everything. Especially stars. They made us memorize star maps. So we'll know where we are, you know, for a while. At least the earth-names. My father kept saying, when you go on the River you can't come back and look anything up. All you have is what you remember. Of course you could ask others, but there'll be so much more, so much new. . . ."

He fell silent, wondering for the millionth time: is it possible that I shall go out forever between the stars, in the great streaming company of strange sentiences?

"How many children were in your tribe?" Peachthief was asking.

"Six. I was the youngest."

"The others all went on the River?"

"I don't know. When I came back from the cities the whole family had gone on, but maybe they'll wait a while, too. My father left a letter asking me to come and say good-bye, and to bring him anything new I learned. They say you go slowly, you know. If I hurry there'll still be enough of his mind left there to tell him what I saw."

"What did you see? We were at a city once," Peachthief said dreamily. "But I was too young, I don't remember anything but people."

"The people are all gone now. Empty, every one. But everything works, the lights change, the moveways run. I didn't believe everybody was gone until I checked the central control offices. Oh, there were so many wonderful devices." He sighed. "The beauty, the complexity. Fantastic what people made." He sighed again, thinking of the wonderful technology, the creations abandoned, running down. "One strange thing. In the biggest city I saw, old Chio, almost every entertainment screen had the same tape running."

"What was it?"

"A girl, a young girl with long hair. Almost to her feet, I've never seen such hair. She was laying it out on a sort of table, with her head down. But no sound, I think the audio was broken. Then she poured a liquid all over very slowly. And then she lit it, she set fire to herself. It flamed and exploded and burned her all up. I think it was real." He shuddered. "I could see inside her mouth, her tongue going all black and twisted. It was horrible. Running over and over, everywhere. Stuck."

She made a revolted sound. "So you want to tell that to your father, to his ghost or whatever?"

"Yes. It's all new data, it could be important."

"Oh yes," she said scornfully. Then she grinned at him. "What about me? Am I new data, too? A woman who isn't going to the River? A woman who is going to stay here and make babies? Maybe I'm the last."

"That's very important," he said slowly, feeling a deep confusion in his gut. "But I can't believe, I mean, you—"

"*I mean it.*" She spoke with infinite conviction. "I'm going to live here and have babies by you or some other man if you won't stay, and teach them to live on the earth naturally."

Suddenly he believed her. A totally new emotion was rising up in him, carrying with it sunrises and nameless bonds with earth that hurt in a painless way; as though a rusted door was opening within him. Maybe this was what he had been groping for.

"I think—I think maybe I'll help you. Maybe I'll stay with you, for a while at least. Our—our children."

"You'll stay a month?" she asked wonderingly. "Really?"

"No, I mean I could stay longer. To make more and see them and help raise them, like Father did. After I come back from saying good-bye I'll really stay."

Her face changed. She bent to him and took his face between her slim dark hands.

"Jakko, listen. If you go to the River you'll never come back. No one ever does. I'll never see you again. We have to do it now, before you go."

"But a month is too long!" he protested. "My father's mind won't be there, I'm already terribly late."

She glared into his eyes a minute and then released

him, stepping back with her brief sweet laugh. "Yes, and it's already late for bed. Come on."

She led him back to the room, carrying the candles, and he marveled anew at the clutter of strange activities she had assembled. "What's that?"

"My weaving room." Yawning, she reached in and held up a small, rough-looking cloth. "I made this."

It was ugly, he thought; ugly and pathetic. Why make such useless things? But he was too tired to argue.

She left him to cleanse himself perfunctorily by the well in the moonlit courtyard, after showing him another waste-place right in the garden. Other peoples' wastes smelled bad, he noticed sleepily. Maybe that was the cause of all the ancient wars.

In his room he tumbled into his hammock and fell asleep instantly. His dreams that night were chaotic; crowds, storms, jostling, and echoing through strange dimensions. His last image was of a great whirlwind that bore in its forehead a jewel that was a sleeping woman, curled like an embryo.

He waked in the pink light of dawn to find her brown face bending over him, smiling impishly. He had the impression she had been watching him, and jumped quickly out of the hammock.

"Lazy," she said. "I've found the sailboat. Hurry up and eat."

She handed him a wooden plate of bright natural fruits and led him out into the sunrise garden.

When they got down to the beach she led him south, and there was the little craft sliding to and fro, overturned in the shallows amid its tangle of sail. The keel was still protruding. They furled the sail in clumsily, and towed it out to deeper water to right it.

"I want this for the children," Peachthief kept repeating excitedly. "They can get fish, too. Oh how they'll love it!"

"Stand your weight on the keel and grab the side-rail," Jakko told her, doing the same. He noticed that her silks had come loose from her breasts, which were high and wide-pointed, quite unlike those of his tribe. The sight distracted him, his thighs felt unwieldy, and he missed his handhold as the craft righted itself and ducked

him. When he came up he saw Peachthief scrambling
aboard like a cat, clinging tight to the mast.

"The sail! Pull the sail up," he shouted, and got another faceful of water. But she had heard him, the sail
was trembling open like a great wing, silhouetting her
shining dark body. For the first time Jakko noticed the
boat's name, on the stern: *Gojack*. He smiled. An omen.

Gojack was starting to move smoothly away, toward
the reef.

"The rudder!" he bellowed. "Turn the rudder and come
back."

Peachthief moved to the tiller and pulled at it; he could
see her strain. But *Gojack* continued to move away from
him into the wind, faster and faster toward the surf. He
remembered she had been handling the mast where the
computer was.

"Stop the computer! Turn it off, turn it off!"

She couldn't possibly hear him. Jakko saw her in frantic activity, wrenching at the tiller, grabbing ropes, trying
physically to push down the sail. Then she seemed to notice the computer, but evidently could not decipher it.
Meanwhile *Gojack* fled steadily on and out, resuming its
interrupted journey to the River. Jakko realized with horror that she would soon be in dangerous water; the surf
was thundering on coral heads.

"Jump! Come back, jump off!" He was swimming after
them as fast as he could, his progress agonizingly slow. He
glimpsed her still wrestling with the boat, screaming something he couldn't hear.

"JUMP!"

And finally she did, but only to try jerking *Gojack*
around by its mooring lines. The boat faltered and jibbed,
but then went strongly on, towing the threshing girl.

"Let go! Let go!" A wave broke over his head.

When he could see again he found she had at last let
go and was swimming aimlessly, watching *Gojack* crest
the surf and wing away. At last she turned back toward
shore, and Jakko swam to intercept her. He was gripped
by an unknown emotion so strong it discoordinated him.
As his feet touched bottom he realized it was rage.

She waded to him, her face contorted by weeping. "The
children's boat," she wailed. "I lost the children's boat—"

"You're crazy," he shouted. "There aren't any children."

"I lost it—" She flung herself on his chest, crying. He thumped her back, her sides, repeating furiously, "Crazy! You're insane!"

She wailed louder, squirming against him, small and naked and frail. Suddenly he found himself flinging her down onto the wet sand, falling on top of her with his swollen sex crushed between their bellies. For a moment all was confusion, and then the shock of it sobered him. He raised to look under himself and Peachthief stared too, round-eyed.

"Do you w-want to, now?"

In that instant he wanted nothing more than to thrust himself into her, but a sandy wavelet splashed over them and he was suddenly aware of chafing wet cloth and Peachthief gagging brine. The magic waned. He got awkwardly to his knees.

"I thought you were going to be drowned," he told her, angry again.

"I wanted it so, for—for them. . . ." She was still crying softly, looking up desolately at him. He understood she wasn't really meaning just the sailboat. A feeling of inexorable involvement spread through him. This mad little being had created some kind of energy vortex around her, into which he was being sucked along with animals, vegetables, chickens, crowds of unknown things; only *Gojack* had escaped her.

"I'll find it," she was muttering, wringing out her silks, staring beyond the reef at the tiny dwindling gleam. He looked down at her, so fanatic and so vulnerable, and his inner landscape tilted frighteningly, revealing some ancient-new dimension.

"I'll stay with you," he said hoarsely. He cleared his throat, hearing his voice shake. "I mean I'll really stay, I won't go to the River at all. We'll make them, our babies now."

She stared up at him openmouthed. "But your father! You promised!"

"My father stayed," he said painfully. "It's—it's right, I think."

She came close and grabbed his arms in her small hands.

"Oh, Jakko! But no, listen—*I'll go with you*. We can start a baby as we go, I'm sure of that. Then you can talk to your father and keep your promise and I'll be there to make sure you come back!"

"But you'd be—you'd be pregnant!" he cried in alarm. "You'd be in danger of taking an embryo on the River!"

She laughed proudly. "Can't you get it through your head that I will *not* go on the River? I'll just watch you and pull you out. I'll see you get back here. For a while, anyway," she added soberly. Then she brightened. "Hey, we'll see all kinds of things. Maybe I can find a cow or some goats on the way! Yes, yes! It's a perfect idea."

She faced him, glowing. Tentatively she brought her lips up to his, and they kissed inexpertly, tasting salt. He felt no desire, but only some deep resonance, like a confirmation in the earth. The three moondogs were watching mournfully.

"Now let's eat!" She began towing him toward the cliff steps. "We can start the pills right now. Oh, I have so much to do! But I'll fix everything, we'll leave tomorrow."

She was like a whirlwind. In the food room she pounced on a small gold-colored pillbox and opened it to show a mound of glowing green and red capsules.

"The red ones with the male symbol are for you."

She took a green one, and they swallowed solemnly, sharing a water mug. He noticed that the seal on the box had been broken, and thought of that stranger, Mungo, she had mentioned. How far had her plans gone with him? An unpleasant emotion he had never felt before rose in Jakko's stomach. He sensed that he was heading into more dubious realms of experience than he had quite contemplated, and took his foodbar and walked away through the arcades to cool down.

When he came upon her again she seemed to be incredibly busy, folding and filling and wrapping things, closing windows and tying doors open. Her intense relations with things again . . . He felt obscurely irritated and was pleased to have had a superior idea.

"We need a map," he told her. "Mine was in the boat."

"Oh, great idea. Look in the old control room, it's down

those stairs. It's kind of scary." She began putting oil on her loom.

He went down a white ramp that became a tunnel stairway, and came finally through a heavily armored portal to a circular room deep inside the rock, dimly illumined by portholes sunk in long shafts. From here he could hear the hum of the station energy source. As his eyes adjusted he made out a bank of sensor screens and one big console standing alone. It seemed to have been smashed open; some kind of sealant had been poured over the works.

He had seen a place like this before; he understood at once that from here had been controlled terrible ancient weapons that flew. Probably they still stood waiting in their hidden holes behind the station. But the master control was long dead. As he approached the console he saw that someone had scratched in the cooling sealant. He could make out only the words:—WAR NO MORE. Undoubtedly this was a shrine of the very old days.

He found a light switch that filled the place with cool glare, and began exploring side alleys. Antique gear, suits, cupboards full of masks and crumbling packets he couldn't identify. Among them was something useful—two cloth containers to carry stuff on one's back, only a little mildewed. But where were the maps?

Finally he found one on the control-room wall, right where he had come in. Someone had updated it with scrawled notations. With a tremor he realized how very old this must be; it dated from before the Rivers had touched earth. He could hardly grasp it.

Studying it, he saw that there was indeed a big landing dock not far south, and from there a moveway ran inland about a hundred kilometers to an airpark. If Peachthief could walk twenty-five kilometers they could make the landing by evening, and if the cars were still running the rest would be quick. All the moveways he'd seen had live cars on them. From the airpark a dotted line ran southwest across mountains to a big red circle with a cross in it, marked VIDA! That would be the River. They would just have to hope something on the airpark would fly, otherwise it would be a long climb.

His compass was still on his belt. He memorized the

directions and went back upstairs. The courtyard was already saffron under great sunset flags.

Peachthief was squatting by the well, apparently having a conference with her animals. Jakko noticed some more white creatures he hadn't seen before, who seemed to live in an open hutch. They had long pinkish ears and mobile noses. Rabbits, or hares perhaps?

Two of the strange white animals he had seen sleeping were now under a bench, chirruping irritably at Peachthief.

"My raccoons," she told Jakko. "They're mad because I woke them up too soon." She said something in a high voice Jakko couldn't understand, and the biggest raccoon shook his head up and down in a supercilious way.

"The chickens will be all right," Peachthief said. "Lotor knows how to feed them, to get the eggs. And they can all work the water lever." The other raccoon nodded crossly, too.

"The rabbits are a terrible problem." Peachthief frowned. "You just haven't much sense, Eusebia," she said fondly, stroking the doe. "I'll have to fix something."

The big raccoon was warbling at her; Jakko thought he caught the word "dog-g-g."

"He wants to know who will settle their disputes with the dogs," Peachthief reported. At this, one of the moon-dogs came forward and said thickly, "We go-o." It was the first word Jakko had heard him speak.

"Oh, good!" Peachthief cried. "Well, that's that!" She bounced up and began pouring something from a bucket on a line of plants. The white raccoons ran off silently with a humping gait.

"I'm so glad you're coming, Tycho," she told the dog. "Especially if I have to come back alone with a baby inside. But they say you're very vigorous—at first, anyway."

"You aren't coming back alone," Jakko told her. She smiled a brilliant, noncommittal flash. He noticed she was dressed differently; her body didn't show so much, and she kept her gaze away from him in an almost timid way. But she became very excited when he showed her the backpacks.

"Oh, good. Now we won't have to roll the blankets around our waists. It gets cool at night, you know."

"Does it ever rain?"

"Not this time of year. What we mainly need is lighters and food and water. And a good knife each. Did you find the map?"

He showed it. "Can you walk, I mean really hike if we have to? Do you have shoes?"

"Oh yes. I walk a lot. Especially since Ferrocil stole my bike."

The venom in her tone amused him. The ferocity with which she provisioned her small habitat!

"Men build monuments, women build nests," he quoted from somewhere.

"I don't know what kind of monument Ferrocil built with my bicycle," she said tartly.

"You're a savage," he said, feeling a peculiar ache that came out as a chuckle.

"The race can use some savages. We better eat now and go to sleep so we can start early."

At supper in the sunset-filled porch they scarcely talked. Dreamily Jakko watched the white bats embroidering flight on the air. When he looked down at Peachthief he caught her gazing at him before she quickly lowered her eyes. It came to him that they might eat hundreds, thousands of meals here; maybe all his life. And there could be a child—children—running about. He had never seen small humans younger than himself. It was all too much to take in, unreal. He went back to watching the bats.

That night she accompanied him to his hammock and stood by, shy but stubborn, while he got settled. Then he suddenly felt her hands sliding on his body, toward his groin. At first he thought it was something clinical, but then he realized she meant sex. His blood began to pound.

"May I come in beside you? The hammock is quite strong."

"Yes," he said thickly, reaching for her arm.

But as her weight came in by him she said in a practical voice, "I have to start knotting a small hammock, first thing. Child-size."

It broke his mood.

"Look. I'm sorry, but I've changed my mind. You go on back to yours, we should get sleep now."

"All right." The weight lifted away.

With a peculiar mix of sadness and satisfaction he heard her light footsteps leaving him alone. That night he dreamed strange sensory crescendos, a tumescent earth and air; a woman who lay with her smiling lips in pale-green water, awaiting him, while thin black birds of sunrise stalked to the edge of the sea.

Next morning they ate by candles, and set out as the eastern sky was just turning rose-gray. The ancient white coral roadway was good walking. Peachthief swung right along beside him, her backpack riding smooth. The moon-dogs pattered soberly behind.

Jakko found himself absorbed in gazing at the brightening landscape. Jungle-covered hills rose away on their right, the sea lay below on their left, sheened and glittering with the coming sunrise. When a diamond chip of sun broke out of the horizon he almost shouted aloud for the brilliance of it; the palm trees beyond the road lit up like golden torches, the edges of every frond and stone were startlingly clear and jewel-like. For a moment he wondered if he could have taken some hallucinogen.

They paced on steadily in a dream of growing light and heat. The day wind came up, and torn white clouds began to blow over them, bringing momentary coolnesses. Their walking fell into the rhythm Jakko loved, broken only occasionally by crumbled places in the road. At such spots they would often be surprised to find the moondogs sitting waiting for them, having quietly left the road and circled ahead through the scrub on business of their own. Peachthief kept up sturdily, only once stopping to look back at the far white spark of Station Juliet, almost melted in the shimmering horizon.

"This is as far as I've gone south," she told him.

He drank some water and made her drink too, and they went on. The road began to wind, rising and falling gently. When he next glanced back the station was gone. The extraordinary luminous clarity of the world was still delighting him.

When noon came he judged they were well over halfway to the landing. They sat down on some rubble under the palms to eat and drink, and Peachthief fed the moondogs. Then she took out the fertility-pill box. They each took theirs in silence, oddly solemn. Then she grinned.

"I'll give you something for dessert."

She unhitched a crooked knife from her belt and went searching around in the rocks, to come back with a big yellow-brown palm nut. Jakko watched her attack it with rather alarming vigor; she husked it and then used a rock to drive the point home.

"Here." She handed it to him. "Drink out of that hole." He felt a sloshing inside; when he lifted it and drank it tasted hairy and gritty and nothing in particular. But sharp too, like the day. Peachthief was methodically striking the thing around and around its middle. Suddenly it fell apart, revealing vividly white meat. She pried out a piece.

"Eat this. It's full of protein."

The nutmeat was sweet and sharply organic.

"This is a coconut!" he suddenly remembered.

"Yes. I won't starve, coming back."

He refused to argue, but only got up to go on. Peachthief holstered her knife and followed, munching on a coconut piece. They went on so in silence a long time, letting the rhythm carry them. Once when a lizard waddled across the road Peachthief said to the moondog at her heels, "Tycho, you'll have to learn to catch and eat those one day soon." The moondogs all looked dubiously at the lizard but said nothing. Jakko felt shocked and pushed the thought away.

They were now walking with the sun westering slowly to their right. A flight of big orange birds with blue beaks flapped squawking out of a roadside tree, where they were apparently building some structure. Cloud shadows fled across the world, making blue and bronze reflections in the sea. Jakko still felt his sensory impressions almost painfully keen; a sunray made the surf line into a chain of diamonds, and the translucent green of the near shallows below them seemed to enchant his eyes. Every vista ached with light, as if to utter some silent meaning.

He was walking in a trance, only aware that the road had been sound and level for some time, when Peachthief uttered a sharp cry.

"My bicycle! There's my bicycle!" She began to run; Jakko saw shiny metal sticking out of a narrow gulch in the roadway. When he came up to her she was pulling a machine out from beside the roadwall.

"The front wheel— Oh, he bent it! He must have been going too fast and wrecked it here. That Ferrocil! But I'll fix it, I'm sure I can fix it at the station. I'll push it back with me on the way home."

While she was mourning her machine Jakko looked around and over the low coping of the roadwall. Sheer cliff down there, with the sun just touching a rocky beach below. Something was stuck among the rocks—a tangle of whitish sticks, cloth, a round thing. Feeling his stomach knot, Jakko stared down at it, unwillingly discovering that the round thing had eyeholes, a U-shaped open mouth, blowing strands of hair. He had never seen a dead body before (nobody had), but he had seen pictures of human bones. Shakenly he realized what this had to be: Ferrocil. He must have been thrown over the coping when he hit that crack. Now he was dead, long dead. He would never go on the River. All that had been in that head was perished, gone forever.

Scarcely knowing what he was doing, Jakko grabbed Peachthief by the shoulders, saying roughly, "Come on! Come on!" When she resisted confusedly, he took her by the arm and began forcibly pulling her away from where she might look down. Her flesh felt burning hot and vibrant, the whole world was blasting colors and sounds and smells at him. Images of dead Ferrocil mingled with the piercing scent of some flowers on the roadway. Suddenly an idea struck him; he stopped.

"Listen. Are you sure those pills aren't hallucinaids? I've only had two and everything feels crazy."

"Three," Peachthief said abstractedly. She took his hand and pressed it on her back. "Do that again, run your hand down my back."

Bewildered, he obeyed. As his hand passed her silk shirt onto her thin shorts he felt her body move under it in a way that made him jerk away.

"Feel? Did you feel it? The lordotic reflex," she said proudly. "Female sexuality. It's starting."

"What do you mean, three?"

"You had three pills. I gave you one that first night, in the honey."

"What? But—but—" He struggled to voice the enormity of her violation, pure fury welling up in him. Chok-

ing, he lifted his hand and struck her buttocks the hardest blow he could, sending her staggering. It was the first time he had ever struck a person. A moondog growled, but he didn't care.

"Don't you ever—never—play a trick like—" He yanked at her shoulders, meaning to slap her face. His hand clutched a breast instead; he saw her hair blowing like dead Ferrocil's. A frightening sense of mortality combined with pride surged through him, lighting a fire in his loins. The deadness of Ferrocil suddenly seemed violently exciting. He, Jakko, was alive! Ignoring all sanity he flung himself on Peachthief, bearing her down on the road among the flowers. As he struggled to tear open their shorts he was dimly aware that she was helping him. His engorged penis was all reality; he fought past obstructions and then was suddenly, crookedly *in* her, fierce pleasure building. It exploded through him and then had burst out into his vitals, leaving him spent.

Blinking, fighting for clarity, he raised himself up and off her body. She lay wide-legged and disheveled, sobbing or gasping in a strange way, but smiling, too. Revulsion sent a sick taste in his throat.

"There's your baby," he said roughly. He found his canteen and drank. The three moondogs had retreated and were sitting in a row, staring solemnly.

"May I have some, please?" Her voice was very low; she sat up, began fixing her clothes. He passed her the water and they got up.

"It's sundown," she said. "Should we camp here?"

"No!" Savagely he started on, not caring that she had to run to catch up. Was this the way the ancients lived? Whirled by violent passions, indecent, uncaring? His doing sex so close to the poor dead person seemed unbelievable. And the world was still assaulting all his senses; when she stumbled against him he could feel again the thrilling pull of her flesh, and shuddered. They walked in silence awhile; he sensed that she was more tired than he, but he wanted only to get as far away as possible.

"I'm not taking any more of those pills," he broke silence at last.

"But you have to! It takes a month to be sure."

"I don't care."

"But, ohhh—"

He said nothing more. They were walking across a twilit headland now. Suddenly the road turned, and they came out above a great bay.

The waters below were crowded with boats of all kinds, bobbing emptily where they had been abandoned. Some still had lights that made faint jewels in the opalescent air. Somewhere among them must be *Gojack*. The last light from the west gleamed on the rails of a moveway running down to the landing.

"Look, there's the seatrain." Peachthief pointed. "I hope the dog or whatever got ashore. . . . I can find a sailboat down there, there's lots."

Jakko shrugged. Then he noticed movement among the shadows of the landing station and forgot his anger long enough to say, "See there! Is that a live man?"

They peered hard. Presently the figure crossed a light place, and they could see it was a person going slowly among the stalled waycars. He would stop with one awhile and then waver on.

"There's something wrong with him," Peachthief said.

Presently the stranger's shadow merged with a car, and they saw it begin to move. It went slowly at first, and then accelerated out to the center lanes, slid up the gleaming rails and passed beyond them to disappear into the western hills.

"The way's working!" Jakko exclaimed. "We'll camp up here and go over to the way station in the morning, it's closer."

He was feeling so pleased with the moveway that he talked easily with Peachthief over their foodbar dinner, telling her about the cities and asking her what places her tribe had seen. But when she wanted to put their blankets down together he said no, and took his away to a ledge farther up. The three moondogs lay down by her with their noses on their paws, facing him.

His mood turned to self-disgust again; remorse mingled with queasy surges of half-enjoyable animality. He put his arm over his head to shut out the brilliant moonlight and longed to forget everything, wishing the sky held only cold quiet stars. When he finally slept he didn't dream at all, but woke with ominous tollings in his inner ear. *The Horse is hungry,* deep voices chanted. *The Woman is bad!*

He roused Peachthief before sunrise. They ate and set off overland to the hill station; it was rough going until they stumbled onto an old limerock path. The moondogs ranged wide around them, appearing pleased. When they came out at the station shunt they found it crowded with cars.

The power pack of the first one was dead. So was the next, and the next. Jakko understood what the stranger at the landing had been doing; looking for a live car. The dead cars here stretched away out of sight up the siding; a miserable sight.

"We should go back to the landing," Peachthief said. "He found a good one there."

Jakko privately agreed, but irrationality smoldered in him. He squinted into the hazy distance.

"I'm going up to the switch end."

"But it's so far, we'll have to come all the way back—"

He only strode off; she followed. It was a long way, round a curve and over a rise, dead cars beside them all the way. They were almost at the main tracks when Jakko saw what he had been hoping for: a slight jolting motion in the line. New cars were still coming in ahead, butting the dead ones.

"Oh, fine!"

They went on down to the newest-arrived car and all climbed in, the moondogs taking up position on the opposite seat. When Jakko began to work the controls that would take them out to the main line, the car bleated an automatic alarm. A voder voice threatened to report him to Central. Despite its protests, Jakko swerved the car across the switches, where it fell silent and began to accelerate smoothly onto the outbound express lane.

"You really do know how to work these things," Peachthief said admiringly.

"You should learn."

"Why? They'll all be dead soon. I know how to bicycle."

He clamped his lips, thinking of Ferrocil's white bones. They fled on silently into the hills, passing a few more station jams. Jakko's perceptions still seemed too sharp, the sensory world too meaning-filled.

Presently they felt hungry, and found that the car's automatics were all working well. They had a protein drink and a pleasantly fruity bar, and Peachthief found bars for the dogs. The track was rising into mountains now; the car whirled smoothly through tunnels and came out in passes, offering wonderful views. Now and then they had glimpses of a great plain far ahead. The familiar knot of sadness gathered inside Jakko, stronger than usual. To think that all this wonderful system would run down and die in a jumble of rust . . . He had a fantasy of himself somehow maintaining it, but the memory of Peachthief's pathetic woven cloth mocked at him. Everything was a mistake, a terrible mistake. He wanted only to leave, to escape to rationality and peace. If she had drugged him he wasn't responsible for what he'd promised. He wasn't bound. Yet the sadness redoubled, wouldn't let him go.

When she got out the pillbox and offered it he shook his head violently. "No!"

"But you *promised*—"

"No. I hate what it does."

She stared at him in silence, swallowing hers defiantly. "Maybe there'll be some other men by the River," she said after a while. "We saw one."

He shrugged and pretended to fall asleep.

Just as he was really drowsing the car's warning alarm trilled and they braked smoothly to a halt.

"Oh, look ahead—the way's gone! What is it?"

"A rockslide. An avalanche from the mountains, I think."

They got out among other empty cars that were waiting their prescribed pause before returning. Beyond the last one the way ended in an endless tumble of rocks and shale. Jakko made out a faint footpath leading on.

"Well, we walk. Let's get the packs, and some food and water."

While they were back in the car working the synthesizer, Peachthief looked out the window and frowned. After Jakko finished she punched a different code and some brownish lumps rolled into her hand.

"What's that?"

"You'll see." She winked at him.

As they started on the trail a small herd of horses appeared, coming toward them. The two humans politely scrambled up out of their way. The lead horse was a large yellow male. When he came to Peachthief he stopped and thrust his big head up at her.

"Zhu-gar, zhu-gar," he said sloppily. At this all the other horses crowded up and began saying "zhu-ga, zu-cah," in varying degrees of clarity.

"This *I* know," said Peachthief to Jakko. She turned to the yellow stallion. "Take us on your backs around these rocks. Then we'll give you sugar."

"Zhu-gar," insisted the horse, looking mean.

"Yes, sugar. *After* you take us around the rocks to the rails."

The horse rolled his eyes unpleasantly, but he turned back down. There was some commotion, and two mares were pushed forward.

"Riding horseback is done by means of a saddle and bridle," protested Jakko.

"Also this way. Come on." Peachthief vaulted nimbly onto the back of the smaller mare.

Jakko reluctantly struggled onto the fat round back of the other mare. To his horror, as he got himself astride she put up her head and screamed shrilly.

"You'll get sugar, too," Peachthief told her. The animal subsided, and they started off along the rocky trail, single file. Jakko had to admit it was much faster than afoot, but he kept sliding backward.

"Hang onto her mane, that hairy place there," Peachthief called back to him, laughing. "I know how to run a few things too, see?"

When the path widened the yellow stallion trotted up alongside Peachthief.

"I thinking," he said importantly.

"Yes, what?"

"I push you down and eat zhugar now."

"All horses think that," Peachthief told him. "No good. It doesn't work."

The yellow horse dropped back, and Jakko heard him making horse-talk with an old gray-roan animal at the rear. Then he shouldered by to Peachthief again and said, "Why no good I push you down?"

"Two reasons," said Peachthief. "First, if you knock me down you'll never get any more sugar. All the humans will know you're bad and they won't ride on you anymore. So no more sugar, never again."

"No more hoomans," the big yellow horse said scornfully. "Hoomans finish."

"You're wrong there, too. There'll be a lot more humans. I am making them, see?" She patted her stomach.

The trail narrowed again and the yellow horse dropped back. When he could come alongside he sidled by Jakko's mare.

"I think I push you down now."

Peachthief turned around.

"You didn't hear my other reason," she called to him.

The horse grunted evilly.

"The other reason is that my three friends there will bite your stomach open if you try." She pointed up to where the three moondogs had appeared on a rock as if by magic, grinning toothily.

Jakko's mare screamed again even louder, and the gray roan in back made a haw-haw sound. The yellow horse lifted his tail and trotted forward to the head of the line, extruding manure as he passed Peachthief.

They went on around the great rockslide without further talk. Jakko was becoming increasingly uncomfortable; he would gladly have got off and gone slower on his own two legs. Now and then they broke into a jog-trot, which was so painful he longed to yell to Peachthief to make them stop. But he kept silent. As they rounded some huge boulders he was rewarded by a distant view of the unmistakable towers of an airpark, to their left on the plain below.

At long last the rockslide ended, quite near a station. They stopped among a line of stalled cars. Jakko slid off gratefully, remembering to say "Thank you" to the mare. Walking proved to be uncomfortable, too.

"See if there's a good car before I get off!" Peachthief yelled.

The second one he came to was live. He shouted at her.

Next moment he saw trouble among the horses. The big yellow beast charged in, neighing and kicking. Peachthief came darting out of the melée with the moondogs, and fell into the car beside him, laughing.

"I gave our mares all the sugar," she chuckled. Then she sobered. "I think mares *are* good for milk. I told them to come to the station with me when I come back. If that big bully will let them."

"How will they get in a car?" he asked stupidly.

"Why, I'll be walking, I can't run these things."

"But I'll be with you." He didn't feel convinced.

"What for, if you don't want to make babies? You won't be here."

"Well then, why are you coming with me?"

"I'm looking for a cow," she said scornfully. "Or a goat. Or a man."

They said no more until the car turned into the airpark station. Jakko counted over twenty apparently live ships floating at their towers. Many more hung sagging, and some towers had toppled. The field moveways were obviously dead.

"I think we have to find hats," he told Peachthief.

"Why?"

"So the service alarms won't go off when we walk around. Most places are like that."

"Oh."

In the office by the gates they found a pile of crew hats laid out, a thoughtful action by the last of the airpark people. A big hand-lettered sign said, ALL SHIPS ON STANDBY, MANUAL OVERRIDE. READ DIRECTIONS. Under it was a stack of dusty leaflets. They took one, put on their hats, and began to walk toward a pylon base with several ships floating at its tower. They had to duck under and around the web of dead moveways, and when they reached the station base there seemed to be no way in from the ground.

"We'll have to climb onto that moveway."

They found a narrow ladder and went up, helping the moondogs. The moveway portal was open, and they were soon in the normal passenger lounge. It was still lighted.

"Now if the lift only works."

Just as they were making for the lift shaft they were startled by a voice ringing out.

"Ho! Ho, Roland!"

"That's no voder," Peachthief whispered. "There's a live human here."

They turned back and saw that a strange person was lying half on and half off one of the lounges. As they came close their eyes opened wide: he looked frightful. His thin dirty white hair hung around a horribly creased caved-in face, and what they could see of his neck and arms was all mottled and decayed-looking. His jerkin and pants were frayed and stained and sagged in where flesh should be. Jakko thought of the cloth shreds around dead Ferrocil and shuddered.

The stranger was staring haggardly at them. In a faint voice he said, "When the chevalier Roland died he predicted that his body would be found a spear's throw ahead of all others and facing the enemy. . . . If you happen to be real, could you perhaps give me some water?"

"Of course." Jakko unhooked his canteen and tried to hand it over, but the man's hands shook and fumbled so that Jakko had to hold it to his mouth, noticing a foul odor. The stranger sucked thirstily, spilling some. Behind him the moondogs inched closer, sniffing gingerly.

"What's *wrong* with him?" Peachthief whispered as Jakko stood back.

Jakko had been remembering his lessons. "He's just very, very old, I think."

"That's right." The stranger's voice was stronger. He stared at them with curious avidity. "I waited too long. Fibrillation." He put one feeble hand to his chest. "Fibrillating . . . rather a beautiful word, don't you think? My medicine ran out or I lost it. . . . A small hot animal desynchronizing in my ribs."

"We'll help you get to the River right away!" Peachthief told him.

"Too late, my lords, too late. Besides, I can't walk and you can't possibly carry me."

"You can sit up, can't you?" Jakko asked. "There have to be some roll chairs around here, they had them for injured people." He went off to search the lounge office and found one almost at once.

When he brought it back the stranger was staring up at Peachthief, mumbling to himself in an archaic tongue of which Jakko only understood: ". . . *The breast of a grave girl makes a hill against sunrise.*" He tried to heave himself up to the chair but fell back, gasping. They had to lift and drag him in, Peachthief wrinkling her nose.

"Now if the lift only works."

It did. They were soon on the high departure deck, and the fourth portal-berth held a waiting ship. It was a small local ferry. They went through into the windowed main cabin, wheeling the old man, who had collapsed upon himself and was breathing very badly. The moondogs trooped from window to window, looking down. Jakko seated himself in the pilot chair.

"Read me out the instructions," he told Peachthief.

"One, place ship on internal guidance," she read. "Whatever that means. Oh, look, here's a diagram."

"Good."

It proved simple. They went together down the list, sealing the port, disengaging umbilicals, checking vane function, reading off the standby pressures in the gasbags above them, setting the reactor to warm up the drive motor and provide hot air for operational buoyancy.

While they were waiting, Peachthief asked the old man if he would like to be moved onto a window couch. He nodded urgently. When they got him to it he whispered, "See out!" They propped him up with chair pillows.

The ready-light was flashing. Jakko moved the controls, and the ship glided smoothly out and up. The computer was showing him wind speed, altitude, climb, and someone had marked all the verniers with the words COURSE SET—RIVER. Jakko lined everything up.

"Now it says, put it on automatic," Peachthief read. He did so.

The takeoff had excited the old man. He was straining to look down, muttering incomprehensibly. Jakko caught, *"The cool green hills of Earth . . .* Crap!" Suddenly he sang out loudly, *"There's a hell of a good universe next door—let's go!"* And fell back exhausted.

Peachthief stood over him worriedly. "I wish I could at least clean him up, but he's so weak."

The old man's eyes opened.

"Nothing shall be whole and sound that has not been rent; for love hath built his mansion in the place of excrement." He began to sing crackedly, "Take me to the River, the bee-yew-tiful River, and wash all my sins a-away! . . . You think I'm crazy, girl, don't you?" he went on conversationally. "Never heard of William Yeats. Very high bit-rate, Yeats."

"I think I understand a little," Jakko told him. "One of my aunts did English literature."

"Did literature, eh?" The stranger wheezed, snorted. "And you two—going on the River to spend eternity together as energy matrices or something equally impressive and sexless. . . . *Forever wilt thou love and she be fair."* He grunted. "Always mistrusted Keats. No balls. He'd be right at home."

"We're not going on the River," Peachthief said. "At least, I'm not. I'm going to stay and make children."

The old man's ruined mouth fell open; he gazed up at her wildly.

"No!" he breathed. "Is it true? Have I stumbled on the lover and mother of man, the last?"

Peachthief nodded solemnly.

"What is your name, O Queen?"

"Peachthief."

"My God. Somebody still knows of Blake." He smiled tremulously, and his eyelids suddenly slid downward; he was asleep.

"He's breathing better. Let's explore."

The small ship held little but cargo space at the rear. When they came to the food-synthesizer cubby Jakko saw Peachthief pocket something.

"What's that?"

"A little spoon. It'll be just right for a child." She didn't look at him.

Back in the main cabin the sunset was flooding the earth below with level roseate light. They were crossing huge, oddly pockmarked meadows, the airship whispering along in silence except when a jet whistled briefly now and then for a course correction.

"Look—cows! Those must be cows," Peachthief exclaimed. "See the shadows."

Jakko made out small tan specks that were animals, with grotesque horned shadows stretching away.

"I'll have to find them when I come back. What *is* this place?"

"A big deathyard, I think. Where they put dead bodies. I never saw one this size. In some cities they had buildings just for dead people. Won't all that poison the cows?"

"Oh no, it makes good grass, I believe. The dogs will help me find them. Won't you, Tycho?" she asked the biggest moondog, who was looking down beside them.

On the eastern side of the cabin the full moon was rising into view. The old man's eyes opened, looking at it.

"More water, if you please," he croaked.

Peachthief gave him some, and then got him to swallow broth from the synthesizer. He seemed stronger, smiling at her with his mouthful of rotted teeth.

"Tell me, girl. If you're going to stay and make children, why are you going to the River?"

"He's going because he promised to talk to his father and I'm going along to see he comes back. And make the baby. Only now he won't take any more pills, I have to try to find another man."

"Ah yes, the pills. We used to call them Wake-ups. . . . They were necessary, after the population chemicals got around. Maybe they still are, for women. But I think it's mostly in the head. Why won't you take any more, boy? What's wrong with the old Adam?"

Peachthief started to answer but Jakko cut her off. "I can speak for myself. They upset me. They made me do bad, uncontrolled things, and feel, agh—" He broke off with a grimace.

"You seem curiously feisty, for one who values his calm above the continuance of the race."

"It's the pills, I tell you. They're—they're dehumanizing."

"De-humanizing," the old man mocked. "And what do you know of humanity, young one? . . . That's what I went to find, that's why I stayed so long among the old, old things from before the River came. I wanted to bring the knowledge of what humanity really was . . . I wanted to bring it all. It's simple, boy. *They died.*" He drew a rasping breath. "Every one of them died. They lived knowing that nothing but loss and suffering and extinction lay ahead. And they cared, terribly. . . . Oh, they made myths, but not many really believed them. *Death* was behind everything, waiting everywhere. Aging and death. No escape . . . Some of them went crazy, they fought and killed and enslaved each other by the millions, as if they could gain more life. Some of them gave up their precious lives for each other. They loved—and had to watch the ones they loved age and die. And in their pain and despair they built, they struggled, some of them sang. But above all, boy, they copulated! Fornicated, fucked, made love!"

He fell back, coughing, glaring at Jakko. Then, seeing that they scarcely understood his antique words, he went on more clearly. "Did sex, do you understand? Made children. It was their only weapon, you see. To send something of themselves into the future beyond their own deaths. Death was the engine of their lives, death fueled their sexuality. Death drove them at each other's throats and into each other's arms. Dying, they triumphed. . . . *That* was human life. And now that mighty engine is long stilled, and you call this polite parade of immortal lemmings *humanity?* . . . Even the faintest warmth of that immemorial holocaust makes you flinch away?"

He collapsed, gasping horribly; spittle ran down his chin. One slit of eye still raked them.

Jakko stood silent, shaken by resonances from the old man's words, remembering dead Ferrocil, feeling some deep conduit of reality reaching for him out of the long-gone past. Peachthief's hand fell on his shoulder, sending a shudder through him. Slowly his own hand seemed to lift by itself and cover hers, holding her to him. They watched the old man so for a long moment. His face slowly composed, he spoke in a soft dry tone.

"I don't trust that River, you know. . . . You think you're going to remain yourselves, don't you? Communicate with each other and with the essences of beings from other stars? . . . The latest news from Betelgeuse." He chuckled raspingly.

"That's the last thing people say when they're going,"

Jakko replied. "Everyone learns that. You float out, able to talk with real other beings. Free to move."

"What could better match our dreams?" He chuckled again. "I wonder . . . could that be the lure, just the input end of some cosmic sausage machine? . . ."

"What's that?" asked Peachthief.

"An old machine that ground different meats together until they came out as one substance . . . Maybe you'll find yourselves gradually mixed and minced and blended into some—some energic plasma . . . and then maybe squirted out again to impose the terrible gift of consciousness on some innocent race of crocodiles, or poached eggs. . . . And so it begins all over again. Another random engine of the universe, giving and taking obliviously. . . ." He coughed, no longer looking at them, and began to murmur in the archaic tongue, "*Ah, when the ghost begins to quicken, confusion of the deathbed over, is it sent . . . out naked on the roads as the books say, and stricken with the injustice of the stars for punishment? The injustice of the stars . . .*" He fell silent, and then whispered faintly, "Yet I too long to go."

"You will," Peachthief told him strongly.

"How . . . much longer?"

"We'll be there by dawn," Jakko said. "We'll carry you. I swear."

"A great gift," he said weakly. "But I fear . . . I shall give you a better." He mumbled on, a word Jakko didn't know; it sounded like "afrodisiack."

He seemed to lapse into sleep then. Peachthief went and got a damp, fragrant cloth from the cleanup and wiped his face gently. He opened one eye and grinned up at her.

"Madame Tasselass," he rasped. "Madame Tasselass, are you really going to save us?"

She smiled down, nodding her head determinedly, yes. He closed his eyes, looking more peaceful.

The ship was now fleeing through full moonlight, the cabin was so lit with azure and silver that they didn't think to turn on lights. Now and again the luminous mists of a low cloud veiled the windows and vanished again. Just as Jakko was about to propose eating, the old man took several gulping breaths and opened his eyes. His intestines made a bubbling sound.

Peachthief looked at him sharply and picked up one of his wrists. Then she frowned and bent over him, opening his filthy jerkin. She laid her ear to his chest, staring up at Jakko.

"He's not breathing, there's no heartbeat!" She groped inside his jerkin as if she could locate life, two tears rolling down her cheeks.

"He's dead—ohhh!" She groped deeper, then suddenly straightened up and gingerly clutched the cloth at the old man's crotch.

"What?"

"He's a woman!" She gave a sob and wheeled around to clutch Jakko, putting her forehead in his neck. "We n-never even knew her name. . . ."

Jakko held her, looking at the dead man-woman, thinking, She never knew mine, either. At that moment the airship jolted, and gave a noise like a cable grinding or slipping before it flew smoothly on again.

Jakko had never in his life distrusted machinery, but now a sudden terror contracted his guts. This thing could fall! They could be made dead like Ferrocil, like this stranger, like the myriads in the deathyards below. Echoes of the old voice ranting about death boomed in his head, he had a sudden vision of Peachthief grown old and dying like that. After the Rivers went, dying alone. His eyes filled, and a deep turmoil erupted under his mind. He hugged Peachthief tighter. Suddenly he knew in a dreamlike way exactly what was about to happen. Only this time there was no frenzy; his body felt like warm living rock.

He stroked Peachthief to quiet her sobs, and led her over to the moonlit couch on the far side of the cabin. She was still sniffling, hugging him hard. He ran his hands firmly down her back, caressing her buttocks, feeling her body respond.

"Give me that pill," he said to her. "Now."

Looking at him huge-eyed in the blue moonlight, she pulled out the little box. He took out his and swallowed it deliberately, willing her to understand.

"Take off your clothes." He began stripping off his

jerkin, proud of the hot, steady power in his sex. When she stripped and he saw again the glistening black bush at the base of her slim belly, and the silver-edged curves of her body, urgency took him, but still in a magical calm.

"Lie down."

"Wait a minute—" She was out of his hands like a fish, running across the cabin to where the dead body lay in darkness. Jakko saw she was trying to close the dead eyes that still gleamed from the shadows. He could wait; he had never imagined his body could feel like this. She laid the cloth over the stranger's face and came back to him, half shyly holding out her arms, sinking down spread-legged on the shining couch before him. The moonlight was so brilliant he could see the pink color of her sexual parts.

He came onto her gently, controlledly, breathing in an exciting animal odor from her flesh. This time his penis entered easily, an intense feeling of all-rightness.

But a moment later the fires of terror, pity, and defiance deep within him burst up into a flame of passionate brilliance in his coupled groin. The small body under his seemed no longer vulnerable but appetitive. He clutched, mouthed, drove deep into her, exulting. Death didn't die alone, he thought obscurely as the ancient patterns lurking in his vitals awoke. Death flew with them and flowed by beneath, but he asserted life upon the body of the woman, caught up in a great crescendo of unknown sensation, until a culminant spasm of almost painful pleasure rolled through him into her, relieving him from head to feet.

When he could talk, he thought to ask her, "Did you—" he didn't know the word. "Did it sort of explode you, like me?"

"Well, no." Her lips were by his ear. "Female sexuality is a little different. Maybe I'll show you, later. . . . But I think it was good, for the baby."

He felt only a tiny irritation at her words, and let himself drift into sleep with his face in her warm-smelling hair. Dimly the understanding came to him that the great beast of his dreams, the race itself maybe, had roused and used them. So be it.

A cold thing pushing into his ear awakened him, and a hoarse voice said, "Ffoo-ood!" It was the moondogs.

"Oh my, I forgot to feed them!" Peachthief struggled nimbly out from under him.

Jakko found he was ravenous, too. The cabin was dark now, as the moon rose overhead. Peachthief located the switches, and made a soft light on their side of the cabin. They ate and drank heartily, looking down at the moon-lit world. The deathyards were gone from below them now, they were flying over dark wooded foothills. When they lay down to sleep again they could feel the cabin angle upward slightly as the ship rose higher.

He was roused in the night by her body moving against him. She seemed to be rubbing her crotch.

"Give me your hand," she whispered in a panting voice. She began to make his hands do things to her, sometimes touching him too, her body arching and writh-ing, sleek with sweat. He found himself abruptly tumes-cent again, excited and pleased in a confused way. "Now, now!" she commanded, and he entered her, finding her interior violently alive. She seemed to be half-fighting him, half-devouring him. Pleasure built all through him, this time without the terror. He pressed in against her shuddering convulsions. "Yes—oh, yes!" she gasped, and a series of paroxysms swept through her, carrying him with her to explosive peace.

He held himself on and in her until her body and breathing calmed to relaxation, and they slipped natu-rally apart. It came to him that this sex activity seemed to have more possibilities, as a thing to do, than he had realized. His family had imparted to him nothing of all this. Perhaps they didn't know it. Or perhaps it was too alien to their calm philosophy.

"How do you know about all this?" he asked Peach-thief sleepily.

"One of my aunts did literature, too." She chuckled in the darkness. "Different literature, I guess."

They slept almost as movelessly as the body flying with them on the other couch a world away.

A series of noisy bumpings wakened them. The win-dows were filled with pink mist flying by. The airship seemed to be sliding into a berth. Jakko looked down and saw shrubs and grass close below; it was a ground-berth on a hillside.

The computer panel lit up: RESET PROGRAM FOR BASE.

"No," said Jakko. "We'll need it going back." Peachthief looked at him in a new, companionable way; he sensed that she believed him now. He turned all the drive controls to standby while she worked the food synthesizer. Presently he heard the hiss of the deflating lift bags, and went to where she was standing by the dead stranger.

"We'll take her, her body, out before we go back," Peachthief said. "Maybe the River will touch her somehow."

Jakko doubted it, but ate and drank his breakfast protein in silence.

When they went to use the wash-and-waste cubby he found he didn't want to clean all the residues of their contact off himself. Peachthief seemed to feel the same way; she washed only her face and hands. He looked at her slender, silk-clad belly. Was a child, his child, starting there? Desire flicked him again, but he remembered he had work to do. His promise to his father; get on with it. Sooner done, sooner back here.

"I love you," he said experimentally, and found the strange words had a startling trueness.

She smiled brilliantly at him, not just off-on. "I love you too, I think."

The floor-portal light was on. They pulled it up and uncovered a stepway leading to the ground. The moondogs poured down. They followed, coming out into a blowing world of rosy mists. Clouds were streaming around them, the air was all in motion up the hillside toward the crest some distance ahead of the ship berth. The ground here was uneven and covered with short soft grass, as though animals had cropped it.

"All winds blow to the River," Jakko quoted.

They set off up the hill, followed by the moondogs, who stalked uneasily with pricked ears. Probably they didn't like not being able to smell what was ahead, Jakko thought. Peachthief was holding his hand very firmly as they went, as if determined to keep him out of any danger.

As they walked up onto the flat crest of the hilltop the

mists suddenly cleared, and they found themselves looking down into a great shallow glittering sunlit valley. They both halted involuntarily to stare at the fantastic sight.

Before them lay a huge midden heap, kilometers of things upon things upon things, almost filling the valley floor. Objects of every description lay heaped there; Jakko could make out clothing, books, toys, jewelry, myriad artifacts and implements abandoned. These must be, he realized, the last things people had taken with them when they went on the River. In an outer ring not too far below them were tents, ground- and aircars, even wagons. Everything shone clean and gleaming as if the influence of the River had kept off decay.

He noticed that the nearest ring of encampments intersected other, apparently older and larger rings. There seemed to be no center to the pile.

"The River has moved, or shrunk," he said.

"Both, I think." Peachthief pointed to the right. "Look, there's an old war-place."

A big grass-covered mound dominated the hillcrest beside them. Jakko saw it had metal-rimmed slits in its sides. He remembered history: how there were still rulers of people when the River's tendrils first touched earth. Some of the rulers had tried to keep their subjects from the going-out places, posting guards around them and even putting killing devices in the ground. But the guards had gone themselves out on the River, or the River had swelled and taken them. And the people had driven beasts across the mined ground and surged after them into the stream of immortal life. In the end the rulers had gone too, or died out. Looking more carefully, Jakko could see that the green hill slopes were torn and pocked, as though ancient explosions had made craters everywhere.

Suddenly he remembered that he had to find his father in all this vast confusion.

"Where's the River now? My father's mind should reach there still, if I'm not too late."

"See that glittery slick look in the air down there? I'm sure that's a danger-place."

Down to their right, fairly close to the rim, was a strangely bright place. As he stared it became clearer: a great column of slightly golden or shining air. He scanned about, but saw nothing else like it all across the valley.

"If that's the only focus left, it's going away fast."

She nodded and then swallowed, her small face suddenly grim. She meant to live on here and die without the River, Jakko could see that. But he would be with her; he resolved it with all his heart. He squeezed her hand hard.

"If you have to talk to your father, we better walk around up here on the rim where it's safe," Peachthief said.

"No-oo," spoke up a moondog from behind them. The two humans turned and saw the three sitting in a row on the crest, staring slit-eyed at the valley.

"All right," Peachthief said. "You wait here. We'll be back soon."

She gripped Jakko's hand even tighter, and they started walking past the old war-mound, past the remains of ancient vehicles, past an antique pylon that leaned crazily. There were faint little trails in the short grass. Another war-mound loomed ahead; when they passed around it they found themselves suddenly among a small herd of white animals with long necks and no horns. The animals went on grazing quietly as the humans walked by. Jakko thought they might be mutated deer.

"Oh, look!" Peachthief let go his hand. "That's milk—see, her baby is sucking!"

Jakko saw that one of the animals had a knobby bag between its hind legs. A small one half-knelt down beside it, with its head up nuzzling the bag. A mother and her young.

Peachthief was walking cautiously toward them, making gentle greeting sounds. The mother animal looked at her calmly, evidently tame. The baby went on sucking, rolling its eyes. Peachthief reached them, petted the mother, and then bent down under to feel the bag. The animal sidestepped a pace, but stayed still. When Peachthief straightened up she was licking her hand.

"That's good milk! And they're just the right size, we can take them on the airship! On the waycars, even." She was beaming, glowing. Jakko felt an odd warm constriction in his chest. The intensity with which she furnished her little world, her future nest! *Their* nest . . .

"Come with us, come on," Peachthief was urging. She had her belt around the creature's neck to lead it. It came equably, the young one following in awkward galloping lunges.

"That baby is a male. Oh, this is *perfect*," Peachthief exclaimed. "Here, hold her a minute while I look at that one."

She handed Jakko the end of the belt and ran off. The beast eyed him levelly. Suddenly it drew its upper lip back and shot spittle at his face. He ducked, yelling for Peachthief to come back.

"I have to find my father first!"

"All right," she said, returning. "Oh, look at that!"

Downslope from them was an apparition—one of the white animals, but partly transparent, ghostly thin. It drifted vaguely, putting its head down now and then, but did not eat.

"It must have got partly caught in the River, it's half gone. Oh, Jakko, you can see how dangerous it is! I'm afraid, I'm afraid it'll catch you."

"It won't. I'll be very careful."

"I'm afraid so." But she let him lead her on, towing the animal alongside. As they passed the ghost-creature Peachthief called to it, "You can't live like that. You better go on out. Shoo, shoo!"

It turned and moved slowly out across the piles of litter, toward the shining place in the air.

They were coming closer to it now, stepping over more and more abandoned things. Peachthief looked sharply at everything; once she stooped to pick up a beautiful fleecy white square and stuff it in her pack. The hillcrest was merging with a long grassy slope, comparatively free of debris, that ran out toward the airy glittering column. They turned down it.

The River-focus became more and more awesome as they approached. They could trace it towering up and up now, twisting gently as it passed beyond the sky. A tendril of the immaterial stream of sidereal sentience that had embraced earth, a pathway to immortal life. The air inside looked no longer golden, but pale silver-gilt, like a great shaft of moonlight coming down through the morning sun. Objects at its base appeared very clear but shimmering, as if seen through cool crystal water.

Off to one side were tents. Jakko suddenly recognized one, and quickened his steps. Peachthief pulled back on his arm.

"Jakko, be careful!"

They slowed to a stop a hundred yards from the tenuous fringes of the River's effect. It was very still. Jakko peered intently. In the verges of the shimmer a staff was standing upright. From it hung a scarf of green and yellow silk.

"Look—that's my father's sign!"

"Oh Jakko, you *can't* go in there."

At the familiar-colored sign all the memories of his life with his family had come flooding back on Jakko. The gentle rationality, the solemn sense of preparation for going out from earth forever. Two different realities strove briefly within him. They had loved him, he realized that now. Especially his father . . . But not as he loved Peachthief, his awakened spirit shouted silently. I am of earth! Let the stars take care of their own. His resolve took deeper hold and won.

Gently he released himself from her grip.

"You wait here. Don't worry, it takes a long while for the change, you know that. Hours, days. I'll only be a minute, I'll come right back."

"Ohhh, it's crazy."

But she let him go and stood holding to the milk-animal while he went down the ridge and picked his way out across the midden heap toward the staff. As he neared it he could feel the air change around him, becoming alive and yet more still.

"Father! Paul! It's Jakko, your son. Can you still hear me?"

Nothing answered him. He took a step or two past the staff, repeating his call.

A resonant susurrus came in his head, as if unearthly reaches had opened to him. From infinity he heard without hearing his father's quiet voice.

You came.

A sense of calm welcome.

"The cities are all empty, Father. All the people have gone, everywhere."

Come.

"No!" He swallowed, fending off memory, fending off the lure of strangeness. "I think it's sad. It's wrong. I've found a woman. We're going to stay and make children."

The River is leaving, Jakko my son.

It was as if a star had called his name, but he said stubbornly, "I don't care. I'm staying with her. Good-bye, Father. Good-bye."

Grave regret touched him, and from beyond a host of silent voices murmured down the sky: *Come! Come away.*

"No!" he shouted, or tried to shout, but he could not still the rapt voices. And suddenly, gazing up, he felt the reality of the River, the overwhelming opening of the door to life everlasting among the stars. All his mortal fears, all his most secret dread of the waiting maw of death, all slid out of him and fell away, leaving him almost unbearably light and calmly joyful. He knew that he was being touched, that he could float out upon that immortal stream forever. But even as the longing took him, his human mind remembered that this was the start of the first stage, for which the River was called Beata. He thought of the ghost animal that had lingered too long. He must leave now, and quickly. With enormous effort he took one step backward, but could not turn.

"Jakko! Jakko! Come back!"

Someone was calling, screaming his name. He did turn then, and saw her on the little ridge. Nearby, yet so far. The ordinary sun of earth was brilliant on her and the two white beasts.

"Jakko! Jakko!" Her arms were outstretched, she was running toward him.

It was as if the whole beautiful earth was crying to him, calling to him to come back and take up the burden of life and death. He did not want it. But she must not come here, he knew that without remembering why. He began uncertainly to stumble toward her, seeing her now as his beloved woman, again as an unknown creature uttering strange cries.

"Lady Death," he muttered, not realizing he had ceased to move. She ran faster, tripped, almost fell in the heaps of stuff. The wrongness of her coming here roused him again; he took a few more steps, feeling his head clear a little.

"Jakko!" She reached him, clutched him, dragging him bodily forward from the verge.

At her touch the reality of his human life came back to him, his heart pounded human blood, all stars fled away. He started to run clumsily, half-carrying her with him up to the safety of the ridge. Finally they sank down gasping beside the animals, holding and kissing each other, their eyes wet.

"I thought you were lost, I thought I'd lost you," Peach-thief sobbed.

"You saved me."

"H-here," she said. "We b-better have some food." She rummaged in her pack, nodding firmly as if the simple human act could defend against unearthly powers. Jakko discovered that he was quite hungry.

They ate and drank peacefully in the soft, flower-studded grass, while the white animals grazed around them. Peachthief studied the huge strewn valley floor, frowning as she munched.

"So many good useful things here. I'll come back some-day, when the River's gone, and look around."

"I thought you only wanted natural things," he teased her.

"Some of these things will last. Look." She picked up a small implement. "It's an awl, for punching and sewing leather. You could make children's sandals."

Many of the people who came here must have lived quite simply, Jakko thought. It was true that there could be useful tools. And metal. Books, too. Directions for making things. He lay back dreamily, seeing a vision of himself in the far future, an accomplished artisan, teaching his children skills. It seemed deeply good.

"Oh, my milk-beast!" Peachthief broke in on his rev-erie. "Oh, no! You mustn't!" She jumped up.

Jakko sat up and saw that the white mother animal had strayed quite far down the grassy ridge. Peachthief trotted down after her, calling, "Come here! Stop!"

Perversely, the animal moved away, snatching mouth-fuls of grass. Peachthief ran faster. The animal threw up its head and paced down off the ridge, among the litter piles.

"No! Oh, my milk! Come back here, come."

She went down after it, trying to move quietly and call more calmly.

Jakko had gotten up, alarmed.

"Come back! Don't go down there!"

"The babies' milk," she wailed at him, and made a dash at the beast. But she missed and it drifted away just out of reach before her.

To his horror Jakko saw that the glittering column of the River had changed shape slightly, eddying out a veil of shimmering light close ahead of the beast.

"Turn back! Let it go!" he shouted, and began to run with all his might. "Peachthief—come back!"

But she would not turn, and his pounding legs could not catch up. The white beast was in the shimmer now; he saw it bound up onto a great sun- and moonlit heap of stuff. Peachthief's dark form went flying after it, uncaring, and the creature leaped away again. He saw her follow, and bitter fear grabbed at his heart. The very strength of her human life is betraying her to death, he thought; I have to get her physically, I will pull her out. He forced his legs faster, faster yet, not noticing that the air had changed around him, too.

She disappeared momentarily in a veil of glittering air, and then reappeared, still following the beast. Thankfully he saw her pause and stoop to pick something up. She was only walking now, he could catch her. But his own body was moving sluggishly, it took all his will to keep his legs thrusting him ahead.

"Peachthief! Love, come back!"

His voice seemed muffled in the silvery air. Dismayed, he realized that he too had slowed to a walk, and she was veiled again from his sight.

When he struggled through the radiance he saw her, moving very slowly after the wandering white beast. Her face was turned up, unearthly light was on her beauty. He knew she was feeling the rapture, the call of immortal life was on her. On him, too; he found he was barely stumbling forward, a terrible serenity flooding his heart. They must be passing into the very focus of the River, where it ran strongest.

"Love—" Mortal grief fought the invading transcendence. Ahead of him the girl faded slowly into the glimmering veils, still following her last earthly desire. He saw that humanity, all that he had loved of the glorious earth, was disappearing forever from reality. Why had it awakened, only to be lost? Spectral voices were near him, but he did not want specters. An agonizing lament for human life welled up in him, a last pang that he would carry with him through eternity. But its urgency fell away. Life incorporeal, immortal, was on him now; it had him as it had her. His flesh, his body was beginning to attenuate, to dematerialize out into the great current of sentience that flowed on its mysterious purposes among the stars.

Still the essence of his earthly self moved slowly after hers into the closing mists of infinity, carrying upon the River a configuration that had been a man striving forever after a loved dark girl, who followed a ghostly white milch deer.

A Source of
Innocent Merriment

Ah! What avails the rational bent,
And what the official word,
Against the undoctored incident
That actually occurred?

(With apologies to R. Kipling)

HIS EYES DID not bear the look of eagles, his skin was not bronzed by the light of alien suns. Like most astroexplorers, he was a small, sallow, ordinary figure, compact and flexible, now sliding inconspicuously to paunch. His face, from the distance he had been pointed out to me, seemed ordinary too; boyish and a trifle petulant. He was sitting alone. As I came toward him through the haze and spotlights of Hal's place, he glanced up, and the very bright blue of his eyes was striking even in the murk.

"May I join you for a moment?"

He started to say no, and then looked me over. I'm not young and I never was Miss Galaxy, but I still have a companionable smile.

He shrugged. "If you want."

I sat down puzzled and wary. Clearly this was no situation to mention my being with GalNews. After what I hoped was a relaxed silence, I told him I was a historian —which was also true.

"I'm collecting data that will be lost forever unless somebody preserves it now. The scouts, the men and women who are the first humans to set eyes on an alien planet, sometimes have experiences so bizarre or improbable that it never gets into the official records. They have no witnesses. If they report honestly it's put down to cabin fever or nitrogen poisoning. Mostly they don't report. And then if some of it comes out later it becomes barroom gossip, and the facts are soon lost in hype and garble. You know? . . . Some of the stories may be nonsense, but some of them have to be true, and very important. I feel deeply that someone should get it all down straight, while there's still time. I'm trying."

He grunted; not hostile, but not forthcoming, either.

"Hal said you had quite a story."

Instead of answering, he shot a blue gleam of fury at Hal behind the bar.

"I use no names, by the way; I protect identities every way I can. My records are under number, which refer to other numbers, and the master set is in my safe on Pallas. Also I can disguise all the nonessential detail you want. . . . You did experience something extraordinary, didn't you?"

He really looked at me then, and I saw in the depths of the blue eyes a pain eating at him, a loss barely to be endured.

"Hal says you don't take the first runs anymore, after . . . whatever happened."

"No. I stick with the follow-up teams, where it's safe."

He had a good, patient voice, underlaid with obscure self-mockery. I saw he was drinking Hal's blue doubles, but they hadn't affected him yet. I knew he didn't mean physically safe; the teams going in to set up bases on Earth-type planets have an unpleasant casualty rate.

"Could you tell me why?"

He was gazing beyond me.

"Please, if you can. It's so important."

"Important . . ." He sighed; I sensed he really wanted to let it out, but the self-discipline of silence was strong. "Well . . . we were way outside the Arm, see, checking out a cluster of promising-looking second-generation stars —did you mean that, about the codes?"

I showed him my notebook: nothing but numbers. "Somewhere in here is a woman who saw a flight of winged hominids take off into empty space. And singing, where of course no sound could carry. Another is a man who fought a huge invisible hand in his cabin. They put the wreckage down to space-paranoia, he'd been out twenty trips. You see, I can't tell who they are myself until I get back and go through the locked-safes routine. Does it matter, so long as the facts are there?"

He sighed again, yielding. "Well, all right. . . . Anyway, we didn't find anything useful, just gas giants. I took the last run, out to a GS at extreme range. And I saw it had two inner planets in the life zone. One of them was nothing but a cinder, the atmosphere read solid CO_2, with the runaway heat effect. But the other was cool, it read out fine. I don't mean habitable yet, I mean it had its permanent atmosphere, nitrogen and water vapor, with the CO_2 going down fast, being taken up by calcium silicate rock. Not a trace of free oxy, of course—or rather, just a twitch from zero. Big ranges of volcanoes blowing like mad. It had to be changing fast. I hadn't heard of anyone catching an Earth-type planet right on the edge of atmospheric flip-over, so I decided to run on in for a look. I had plenty of fuel. The problem was air. Those scouts don't have a bionic regeneration like the big ships, maybe you know that."

"I thought you had some sort of catalytic recycler."

"Oh yes. Just enough to let you die slow after the tanks are empty. You have to figure close. But I had enough for two orbits easy. And the thing was, as soon as I got within tight scan range, I *knew* I had to get closer. There was . . . activity."

"The vulcanism?"

"No." He was staring past me, with his teeth bared. I was afraid Hal's specials were getting to him, but he went on very lucidly.

"It was a half-and-half planet, you see. All the land mass on one side, and the other all ocean. Not like our ordinary oceans, of course, not water. Hot and shallow and mephitic. What they used to call the primordial soup. Lot of electrical-storm action going on. My readout showed that ocean was loaded with protolife, bits and pieces of proteins and nuclear material—the precursors of our kind of oxygen-based life. Anaerobic, methanogenic —are those the words? I'm no biologist. The primitive stuff that doesn't use oxygen . . . People think of it as dumb, nothing, like a lot of clay that hasn't made bricks."

He drained his glass, signaled Hal for another.

"It was . . . beautiful. Not the land side, that was just

silicates where it wasn't igneous. The ocean. Like a sea of jewels, like a sunrise in the water. —Oh hell, anything I say sounds stupid. I can't really describe it. The atmosphere there had a kind of ruby cast, lit up blue-white from tremendous lightning bolts, and in between the storms you could see the surface swirling with colors— gold and sapphire and coral and lavender and lemon and dark purple, all changing. No true green, of course. Except in one place where there was a great round rosette of floating algae. It was photosynthesizing, making oxygen. I'd really caught it just as the change was starting, you see."

"Was that the—what did you call it, the activity?"

"No. I mean activity, movement. Not like wave action, not like boiling. When the clouds cleared off I saw that all over that huge ocean the surface was formed up into unnatural-looking shapes that moved and pulsed and transformed into others. At first I saw only the big ones, like towers and ridges and crevasses. And then I saw they were covered and intermixed with smaller and smaller shapings; hillocks, lines, dark fuzzy patches like forests, clusters of geometrical blobs. And everything moving, changing, some slow, some fast. The whole thing —well, it was like flashes of a populated landscape. If you took a still shot of it you'd swear it was inhabited land, with cities, roads, dams, traffic—although I was too high up to have any idea of the details. It was never still. A couple of times there were glimpses of what looked like great battles, with organized masses and weird objects surging, and fires and explosions—and then peace again. I realized that it was exactly as if you were running a film of the history of a whole planet at incredible speed. Centuries, millennia of history flashing by. I couldn't keep track of it, I couldn't imagine what it was. All I knew was that it was alive, and I had to get down closer. And then just as I was passing over the far shore onto the rocky side . . . it hit me."

His breathing had quickened almost to sobs. I kept quiet.

"The joy," he said at last, in a heavy, dead tone. "Oh God. That whole crazy sea of poison was exuding it. Radiating joy. At a thousand km up I was grinning like a fool, happier than I'd ever been in my life. It faded some while I was over land, and then came back stronger than ever as the coast showed over the horizon. I'd backfired down lower by then. . . ."

For a moment he seemed to be lost in pure wonder, and then noticed me again.

"You have to understand it wasn't anything we would call life that was doing it, see. It was some kind of pre-life, the transient forerunner. Doomed to die—in fact, it was starting to die. *And it knew it.* Somehow I was sure of that. And yet it was broadcasting this innocent gladness, this contagious, childlike glee. All alone by itself, it was *playing*. And when I came over the shore again I began to suspect what it had found to play with. . . . Say that somehow it could foresee the oxygen-based life to come, the life that would kill it. And it was amusing itself by running through a show of the whole damn future history of that planet."

"But—"

"I know. It's impossible. But I became absolutely certain, although I kept telling myself it was just a brew of mindless molecular fragments. By that time I was down to one-fifty km; my scope showed me the flickering forms of alien animals and people and their artifacts. If you could have *seen* it—the momentary panoramas of empires spreading out and falling, the huge engineering structures flashing into being and back to dust again, and everything growing more complex as it evolved and changed and vanished away—and always with this aura of delight, a great joyful play."

"You mentioned film—"

"No. I said 'if.' " His tone was abruptly savage. I understood that something had happened there. If his cameras had been running he must have destroyed the film. Why?

"You couldn't catch the essential thing," he said more quietly. "The incredible harmless happiness, the acceptance. It was enchanted just to be, to play its game of foreseeing, even if what it saw was based on its own death. It wasn't afraid or saddened at all, it was even using that damn lethal patch of oxygenating algae in its structures. . . . And sending out its joy. To me, to the universe

. . . I can't tell you what it felt like, all pain gone, all fear gone, all the crap—just deep total joy, that's the only word. Nothing like sex or drink or drugs, nothing like anything you've ever known, except maybe in dreams . . ."

He fell silent.

"Well, I do thank you." I started to close my notebook. "That is something I shall always remember."

He gave a short, harsh laugh. "There's more," he said painfully.

"Oh?"

"As I was on my second pass over—that should have been the last one—I saw a new change. And I realized it was becoming aware of me—of me personally, I mean. Suddenly an Earth-type spaceport formed below, and a familiar lake, and the flash of a house I knew. Like signals. And an increase of delight, as if it was discovering a fine new game. And then glimpses of more and more personal stuff—the lab, my aircar, the ship, roads and places from my childhood, all mixed up. It seemed to be reading me deeper and deeper, and it loved it. Believe it or not, I loved it too—I heard myself laughing. Ever notice how pretty a traffic tower is? . . . And people's faces—friends, even a guy I hated—big as a mountain. You must understand, the scale of sizes was chaotic, and things dissolved into each other. But all suffused with this gladness . . . And then my folks, my family, covering half the sea, and lit with this glow, this sort of sweet playfulness as if it was proud of itself and wanted me to share. . . . Funny, I've always felt better about what happened to Dad after that. . . . But I was coming over the shoreline, and then . . ."

"Then?"

He took a deep drink.

"Well, I had to cut out and go back, see. The oxy. But I couldn't. The last glimpse I had of that ocean, it seemed to be building up a big cliff of foamy white stuff—I couldn't figure what it was. It didn't change and vanish like everything else as long as I could see it. I *had* to find out what it was. . . . And, oh hell, the truth was I couldn't bear to leave that wonderful happiness. Couldn't. So, over the land side, I refigured everything and decided I could make one more orbit if I didn't mind getting back to the

ship half-dead. . . . Mind? What I really wanted was to
stay and go round that planet until I strangled. Or even
to dive down in and die in bliss. . . . How the goddam
training tells; I reset the program for automatic kickout
after one more turn. Oh God, I wish I hadn't."

He seemed to be out of words, looking at me as if I
were an ape or a robot who couldn't possibly understand.

"You wish you hadn't gone back to the ship?"

"No. Yes, that . . ." he said blurrily. His voice was getting very low. "It was . . . that last orbit, see."

"What did you find?"

"Find? Felt—got burned forever, I guess." He started
to take another drink, and then seemed to become aware
of what Hal's blues were doing to him. He put the glass
down and straightened effortfully in his chair. When he
spoke again his words were flat and clear.

"When I came around again, I saw that whole deadly
sea was edged with this beautiful creamy white lace. Joyful, like—like as if you could see laughter. And as I came
over it, it opened. It was a goddamned gift box."

He did take a drink then, looking far away.

"Most men don't have it, I guess. The lucky ones. But
some do—maybe women too, God help them. I'm one of
those that have it. The *dream,* you know. The ideal. Quite
explicit, vivid. Your perfect, ideal woman. The one you
long for, seek for, knowing it's hopeless. You take other
women because they seem to remind you of her body or
soul, for a time. Body and soul . . . There she was."

He was forcing his voice, the words coming out
harshly.

"She was lying on that lacy stuff, naked. Flawless. Perfect and flawless. And absolutely alive. I could see her
sweet belly breathe, her wonderful breasts blushed a little.
Her long thick lashes—her eyes were closed—were trembling on her cheeks. . . . She was as big as a planet of
course, and I was a midge in the sky, but it didn't seem
that way. She seemed normal-sized, or rather, we were both
the same. I slowed down as far as I dared, just drinking
her in. She stirred a little, I could see every intimate part
of her. Totally exposed, totally innocent. . . . . The sexual
impact was unbelievable. I wasn't laughing anymore. . . .
They—it—whatever had created her had even used that

deadly algae rosette to make a sort of flower bouquet in the crook of her arm, I could see it hurting her beautiful skin. . . ."

His face creased with pain.

"Yes. . . It—they—didn't mean to hurt me, you know. It just read what I wanted and gave it to me, in delight, as well as it could. And I think I could have stood the physical thing, the violent sexual lust . . . I think. But as I came over her she opened her eyes and looked directly up at me. And the deepest, wildest bliss a man can imagine enveloped me. All the joy that ocean could project was looking from those huge eyes into mine. Sex? God, it was ecstasy. She *knew,* you see—she knew all about me, and about herself, and we loved. How shall I say? A marvelous fond complicity, as if we had lived all our lives together. I tried—I tried to tell myself it was just a hundred billion shreds of proteins and viruses somehow reflecting me, but I couldn't. She was a living person, a living, loving person. And *mine* . . . Then she smiled, the most beautiful smile, with a sweet quirk of playfulness. Total sharing . . . Oh God, I was in heaven. If I hadn't been paralyzed with wonder I would have killed the orbit and gone down to her. But she wasn't calling or luring me down in any way, you understand, it wasn't any dumb siren stuff. She was just so happy I was there. . . . And then my orbit carried me to the coast. I saw her raise her head and push back her floating hair to look after me. And then just at the very last her expression changed. It only lasted an instant —it was like being mortally cut with a razor, you don't feel it at the time. One heartbreaking look of sadness— love and loss and good-bye. As I say, it was over in a flash, and all was joy again . . . and the lovely smile . . . but I—I—it nearly—"

He drank again, and then again more deeply.

"I had to leave then, of course. If I hadn't laid the course in on automatic I couldn't have. Couldn't. I almost punched it out. . . . If I had it to do over again, I would have. Just to keep tasting of heaven . . . As I left the system I could feel it dying away, the joy; the shit we call life coming back. I tried to hold onto it. I was still imagining I could feel it when I did run out of oxy. . . . When the scout docked and they peeled me out I remember the human air smelled like poison, and I tried to punch Grober, the crew chief. . . . Later on I told them there was nothing there."

He was silent a minute. Emotion seemed to have burned the drink out of him, but his eyes were sick.

"I keep wondering, do you suppose that happens everywhere? The forerunners, a strange unliving life, knowing it's transient and doomed, but foreseeing all, accepting all —and laughing? The most beautiful thing in the universe, existing only for cosmic seconds. Do you suppose it happened on earth, happens everywhere before the dull bloody grind of oxygen life begins? . . . The sweetness . . . and I left it."

He noticed me again.

"Do you see why I'm through scouting?"

"You mean, in case you run into another?"

He sighed; I saw I hadn't quite understood. Maybe no one could. "That. Yes. Dreading, wondering if there're more." Fatigue and liquor overcame him then, his head sagged into his fists. "I don't want to know," he mumbled. "Let somebody else get burned. God help them. . . . God help them. . . . I don't want to know. . . ."

Out of the Everywhere

ENGGI WAS A cold deep-space cub, out on his first lone venture. His co-grex didn't know where he was, nor even that he'd left them. Precocious as Enggi was, he was yet far too young—millennia too young and unprepared—to roam the galaxy alone.

Enggi and his kind resembled nothing of Earth, being nearly immaterial sentiences evolved in the energic vortices of near-vacuum and icy radiations, where life takes root in the complex molecular debris of stellar catastrophes. Yet, as with any earthly cub, the strayer from the pack meets mortal dangers.

At first all was exhilaration.

He was thrilled by riding real astral currents—excited by bombardments of radiations that had been only dull teachings—delighted by clearly perceiving cosmic wonders that had been no more than blurs from within the gas clouds of his grex's nest. The buffetings of an immense explosion shook him with real fright, but lit him with the exultation of unaided mastery. And above all there was no one to direct him! No one to say no!

On certain older star systems he even found fading sign of a foreign grex, and boldly obliterated it with his own. Yes! Perhaps in the future, Enggi might claim this territory for himself, when he had grown enough to contest any of the former owners who might be still about.

Vastly pleased with himself and all he was finding, Enggi wandered up the pressure gradient that was a great galactic arm, now propelling himself athwart the flow, again drifting with it. And after a short while, quite thoroughly lost.

Meanwhile his absence from his grex had been discovered. Alarm, search, confirmation. Two scouts from an experienced subgrex set out to trace Enggi's cold trail.

They were not alone.

Some star clusters back, Enggi had unknowingly picked up a third, much closer follower, who now slunk and circled just out of range, scarcely believing its luck.

Earthly predators do not include beings of such passive rapacity, such sophisticated yet oddly automatonlike evil. Call it the Eater. Eaters are rare, but very long-lived. In their normal form they lie in ambush in any gaseous tangle, waiting the chance to display their attractants to some innocent of space.

This Eater was presently certain that Enggi was not part of a trap, that he was just as he appeared: alone. Stationed itself in the path of the unwary cub.

The two scouts patiently tracking Enggi's spoor were quite aware of this danger. When presently they came on an Eater's deserted lair they knew Enggi *had* to be found, and fast. But this was not from benevolence toward Enggi.

What they expected to find was not a killed or partly eaten cub, but an apparently intact, normal Enggi, their own bright friendly grexling—who nevertheless must be killed, by the scouts themselves.

For an Eater does not attack its victim from outside. Instead, it attracts the prey to contact and is subtly ingested. Here it begins inexorably to eat out its host from within, always taking care, as long as possible, to replace vital structure with its own body matter. Thus an infestation may go undetected for a long time. Finally comes the bout of terminal agony, after which, where the victim was, are three or more strong young Eaters—ready and able to attack any nearby prey. A single unsuspected Eater can thus in time destroy most of a grex.

Enggi's race had learned no defense against the attractant, no signs of early infestation, and no cure or means of expelling or cutting out an ingested Eater. Hence their only solution was the destruction of a known parasite by destroying its host, no matter how beloved in the grex.

Thus when the scouts observed the Eater's empty lair they knew that Enggi was the obvious, indubitable victim-to-be. And Enggi had made himself dear to his grex, with his vitality and promising ways. Sadness came to the scouts. As they followed him to what must be his fate, a strange mourning music drifted from them amid the spectra of the stars.

But before Enggi was reached by any of his pursuers, a quite different disaster intervened.

He was idly investigating a busy little single-sun system, when he found himself gripped in an intense local field configuration too strong for his fledgling powers. Much too late, he recalled a teacher's warning about the anomalous magnetic fluxes which may invest certain types of stars. In the very moment of recall, he realized he was tumbling helplessly, faster and faster, toward the small yellow sun whose heat meant his death. Panic!

Why, oh why, had he not attended more closely? There was something he should do—but what? Was it to do with these planets, perhaps?

The Eater, observing the start of Enggi's trajectory, knew what should happen, and prepared to settle down and wait. It was not dissatisfied; the prey, when it re-emerged from defensive stasis, would be confused and highly vulnerable to the taking.

But what should happen did not, because Enggi had not recalled in time. The icy outer gas balls on which he should take refuge were already flashing past. Ahead lay only the small, fatally hot inner satellites. Puzzled, the Eater followed.

Desperately, as Enggi plunged on, he racked his memory. Something—there was something that might still be tried—*if* he could discern the axial topography in time, and *if* the planet bore something called life. Yes—he had it! A frantic emergency measure, his only hope. But the first of the small planets was already too near.

Wild with terror, he deployed his sensors to their utmost, and at the last moment he found it: the magnetic configuration that allowed him to deflect his sunward fall. And yes—yes! As the next planet's gravity seized him, he found the polar vortex they had told him of. Cold—life-saving cold might be here. The cold that might help him for a little while.

But his crash would be frightful. He would be terribly damaged, and need much time to heal, if he were not killed.

Again he pounded at his memory. What must he do? If he recalled right, he must physically encyst, and at the same time fling loose the vital components of his psyche, in the forlorn hope that they would find living lodgement, to be recalled when his body healed. But where? Which?

He was hurtling toward extinction, no time left. Desperately he cast from him all he could grasp—will, thought, love, technical knowledge—all but bare identity. In his panic he almost forgot the most vital of all—*directionality,* that he might someday reassemble, or be found. There! Already in atmosphere he hurled the vectors out, sheer will taking the place of expertise.

And then he could do no more but clamp himself into agonized encystment, bearing the horrible crash of his physical self among the icy molecules, feeling himself splash and reclamp. And then all space and time and stars closed away, and it was too late for anything but luck.

At that moment in the human world, three small events occurred.

In a corporation office in San Juan, California, a middle-aged woman felt an abrupt inner jolt: mild but enough to make her hands drop a sheaf of data printouts and go to the desk for support. Her gaze was blindly on the windows facing north.

Migraine, she thought first; and then, *heart?* It was all over in a second, her secretary hadn't even noticed. But as she moved to her chair, still absently gazing north, she decided to accelerate certain private arrangements she was making, for the good of Marrell Tech.

Simultaneously, in the maternity waiting room of a nearby hospital, a man clutching a huge sheaf of wilting yellow roses found himself staring north across the freeways, blinking away some kind of strange eidetic flash within his eyes . . . or had someone called his name? He shook himself thinking, Too much caffeine and stress on too little sleep.

And then a door opened and a nurse really was calling him.

"Mr. Paul Marrell?" Behind her a baby squalled.

The third small happening had just taken place in that delivery room.

As the doctor lifted the newborn by her ankles, the baby girl jerked and twisted with such extraordinary vigor that he had to use both hands to grab the slippery little legs. Still the tiny mite managed to contort herself round so that her large, light-blinded eyes were staring northward as she gave her first cry.

From the hour when his young wife died just after giving birth, Paul Marrell detested the infant and didn't care who knew it.

The blood clot had meandered its lethal way toward his wife's aorta slowly enough to let her gaze into her daughter's enormous violet eyes.

"We'll call her Paula. Hello, Paula!"

The baby twisted its head comically, still seemingly trying to sense something beyond the north wall. Her mother laughed adoringly.

And then all laughters stopped.

Two dreadful hours later Paul Marrell was roaring up the San Fernando Freeway alone forever, with a case of Jack Daniel's in the bucket seat beside him. He was thirty-nine, an A-1 aero engineer who had put his heart into building up his own company before meeting the real love of his life. Now he had lost her.

Some days later his long-time executive secretary got the baby Paula home and properly installed, with a real nanny. With the help of Paul's friends, she sobered him up and slowly got his attention, if not his heart, back on his company, Marrell Technologies, which was prospering inordinately.

Little Paula soon began to do the same, although that nanny left soon. The next one Miss Emstead found lasted three months before she had to be replaced. The home was chaotic; Paul would spasmodically fill it with miscellaneous party people—service-station attendants, fading movie stars, dentists—and then forget them all. Miss Emstead would discover them and tactfully cope. When he recovered enough he took to marrying random women, and forgot them too, and Miss Emstead coped again. Finally one night he proposed to Miss Emstead, on the intercom.

"Miss Emstead—Gloria—darling—you're the only good person in the world. Will you marry me?"

"I'm terribly sorry, Mr. Marrell. Thank you ever so much, but Tim and I have been married for over ten years. I'm truly honored though, and I'm so sorry. But you need someone young and jolly and sweet."

"Why have you turned against me, too? No, cancel that. Who's Tim?"

"Tim Drever, your chief draftsman. I thought you knew, you gave us a lovely present."

"Oh. Fire the bastard first thing Monday. No. Cancel that, too. Give him a raise. Give yourself both raises. And send me up a fifth of Jack Daniel's and get me that red-haired girl for tonight—you know, the one with the cats."

"Yes, Mr. Marrell. But about the raises, you gave us one last month and I think the company's cash flow is getting excessive. If you'd like to do something, we'd love another share of stock. I'll send you up the fifth right away, only it'll be just a little different, maybe with a snack and some black coffee and the Putnam Air Force contract draft. And Miss Fitz is in Honolulu now, I'll try Miss de Borch. You know, the black-haired girl with the boa constrictor. You seemed to enjoy her company last week."

She started to add that little Paula's new nurse was at the airport, but choked herself off. Paul had only looked at the baby twice.

"Okay. Okay. Great. Hey!"

"What, sir?"

"I really meant it, about marrying me. Tim's a fortunate man."

"Thank you with all my heart, Mr. Marrell."

She clicked off, smiling oddly. She had always been a hundred-percent sure that Paul had not the faintest memory of a rather confused evening long ago, when he and a very new young typist had worked till dawn in an office with a couch.

Certainly Gloria Emstead had never mentioned it to a soul, not even Tim, but she had found herself unable entirely to forget. The problem had been handled with her usual discreet efficiency, and the evening's result, a young lady known as Girta Grier, had been lovingly raised by a widowed relative in San Francisco whom she believed to be her mother. Girta was doing exceptionally well in business school. Miss Emstead smiled again, sighed, and turned to the airport problem.

It was strange about Paula's nurses. They wouldn't stay, although the little girl was sweet and well behaved. She was also very pretty, in a tiny, frail, dark-haired way, and the huge violet eyes of her early infancy stayed on. Party women would find her and coo over her. But something about the waif's questioning stare would silently turn the coos off. Apparently it did the same for the nannies and *au pair* girls and RNs Miss Emstead hired, even when Paul briefly married one of them.

That was when he had to see a little more of his daughter.

It was the night of San Juan's first snowfall in twenty years.

He and Frederika, the current Mrs. Marrell, came home late, and she excused herself to go up and check on Paula, leaving Paul to wander in the little-used quarters below. Presently he came to where a French window stood open in a foyer. As he closed it he noticed footprints in the paper-thin snow, leading away. He had been much in the woods as a boy, and automatically paused to look; one set of stub-heeled woman's tracks, one set of small fresh sandal tracks, and a fading set of very tiny child's bare footprints. He recalled that Frederika seemed to have been wearing sandals. She was one of the *au pair* girls who had taken care of Paula before she began taking care of Paul, a tall, shaggy-blond Belgian whom he thought of as tender and fun, with unknown competencies —in which last he was quite right.

It was a gorgeous night now, a half-moon glittering on the crazy whiteness, and the stars blazing through. Paul stepped out to follow the tracks.

They led him across empty gardens and straight up the side of the first big grass-covered berm that protected the house. From above came a burst of high-pitched voices and, in the distance, a growl that meant a guard dog being restrained. Suddenly a child's voice was crying, "I hate you, I hate it here." Then there came the sharp smack of a slap on flesh, and silence.

Paul reached the top to find his wife and the RN standing a little back from a tiny child, who must be Paula; she was crouched down, almost naked in a skimpy nightdress.

"What's going on here?"

"She attacked Miss Trond," his wife exclaimed excitedly.

"She sneaks out in the middle of the nights," Miss Trond smoothed her uniform, her accent regrettably Germanic.

"That's right—she did it with me and the girl before me," Frederika added. "She's had us all scared silly."

But their stories didn't go down too well, especially when Paula raised her head to gaze beseechingly at her father, revealing the dark print of a grown woman's hand, complete with ring scratch, on her small white face. There was also the mark of her supine body behind her, in the snow.

"Why did you have to hit her?" he asked slowly. This didn't seem to be the monster that had killed his beloved. In fact, it didn't seem to be a monster at all.

The women were jabbering something about the danger from the dogs, and not being able to sleep. The child's big eyes never left his.

Uncertainly, he moved toward her and reached down his hand. She gazed up a moment more, and then her own hand went up to his and she grabbed hold, her hand cool and tiny as a baby animal's. He lifted her the short distance to her feet.

"Check with Miss Emstead tomorrow, you two," Paul said. Leading his daughter, he went down and away to his old bachelor suite.

Paula was soaked and shivering, so he took off the filmy shortie, dried her, and wrapped her in his old camel-hair robe, looping the ends up over the cord. It never occurred to him that a six-year-old could dress herself. He hadn't seen a naked girl child before, and the little bare body confused him slightly.

She remained totally silent through his ministrations,

until he had picked her up and plunked her down on the dressing-room cot.

"You all right, kid?"

"Yes, sir. Thank you very much," she said politely. Then she suddenly sat up and burst out, "Oh, Daddy, could you help me please?"

"Help you? How?"

"Let me look at your library books! They won't let me read them and they only give me icky stuff. I wouldn't hurt your books, ever."

"What do you want to read?" he asked, purely amazed.

"Arithmetic," she completed his astoundment. "And about the stars. Astro-no-my."

"Why of course you can. You go in there and take any book you want. And stay as long as you want. I'll tell Miss Emstead. She can find you some beginner's things."

Seeing the look of joy turn wary, he had the intuition to add, "If you find you need them."

What had he spawned here? Now that he observed her more carefully he could find little resemblance to her mother, yet she reminded him of someone. Himself, as a boy, perhaps?

"What were you doing out there, anyway?"

"I like to look at the stars. I only know the name of one: Po-laris." She ducked her head down, ashamed. "They say it's un-natural."

Ah! He had it—his young brother Harry, who had been killed in a car crash at eight. She was a mini-edition of Harry. Harry'd liked star-gazing too, come to think. Had the gods sent him back his kid brother, and he all blind to it?

"Well, we can fix that too. Next time you want to go— any time of night—you just ring the guard station and they'll send a man in five minutes for as long as you like."

Again the dismayed look on the so-expressive little flower face.

"What's wrong now?"

"Oh, it's nothing . . . it's just that I like to look *alone*." So had Harry, he recalled.

"We can fix that. You just tell them when you go out

and when you've come back and you won't see a soul. Or he'll be fired in the morning."

"Ohhh . . . *thank* you, Daddy! I mean, sir. Thank you so much."

"Daddy's okay for now. Where did you get that 'sir' anyhow?"

"You said to, sir. I mean, Daddy. And to never let you see me."

He hadn't the dimmest recollection. "Well, I didn't mean it. I was—sort of crazy for a while. That's all over now."

Her face radiated joy. And then suddenly, babylike, the dark furry eyelashes dropped to her cheeks and she was asleep sitting up, slowly toppling into a pillow almost as big as she. He settled her down straight, and went to his bed to think. It had occurred to him that something had to be done about Paula's schooling, and the usual kindergartens were clearly not the answer. But he was too tired—he had only time to tape instructions to Miss Emstead to find a good tutor as well as a new nurse, and to get the divorce lawyers going again, before he was asleep, too.

All these matters were duly attended to, and in the next weeks and months Paul became accustomed to coming across his little daughter curled in a library corner with anything from an astronomy journal to a math text to his old science-fiction comics. Or he would look out and see her walking—more often, running hard—on the berms. She continued to be very undersized, but the doctor said she was in perfect health and very strong for her weight. "Regular gibbon," he said. "But a lot better-looking."

Strange considerations moved him. Paula and her new nurse got used to the erratic arrival of vans from Chez Niçoise bearing huge delicious platters of filet mignon, oysters, lobsters, which they—especially Miss Timms—enjoyed wholeheartedly.

And then there was the ludicrous affair of the Children's Party. It took place, not on her birthday, which was never referred to, but on Paul's; a stiffly rowdy afternoon assembly of strange youngsters of disparate ages, mostly the offspring of Marrell Tech executives, among whom Paula was supposed to find friends. Paul looked in and even he was able to interpret the sight of his little daughter standing frozen with terror amid the tumult, cake knife in her hand like a sword.

Miss Emstead reassured him. "Paula'll find her own friends, Mr. Marrell. Slowly, among children of similar interests and abilities. When she goes to a suitable school." And she handed him the brochure of a special school for gifted children.

"Too far away. Find one where she comes home nights."

And the right school was duly found, even though it entailed twice-daily use of Marrell Tech's helicopter.

After a year or so of this, Robby, the helicopter pilot, took occasion to tell Paul that his daughter was no ordinary little girl.

"That kid Paula, she's something else. You better watch out, sir. She knows every chopper model on the market, and she helps me do the tune-ups. Last week I tore the engine down, she came out and worked for me till eleven P.M. Her nurse like to went ape. And she's after George to take her up in the jet, I caught her crawling around the pods. I think she could fly the chopper if I'd let her. And if her feet would reach," he grinned.

"Hmm."

It was about this time that the school notified him that they wanted to run some special tests on Paula. It seemed she had independently found the general solution for a class of differential equations. For a time Paul was afraid that he had an infant Gauss on his hands.

But it turned out that Paula was not of that calibre; only very bright, very motivated, and very, very quick. Next term she was into computers and electronics. He found her trying to measure the piezo-electric output of an old crystal with a beat-up ammeter she had begged off the electrician, and fitted her up with her own little workshop, to which in due course were added a closed-circuit computer system and a photo lab.

Before that, however, had come the telescope, and the pathetic business of Christmas. In her first term at the school the science teacher had suggested to him that he get her for Christmas an equatorial-mount 'scope with maybe a camera attachment. When he asked Paula what she wanted, she looked perplexed. "Daddy—exactly what *is* Christmas?"

"Why, it's—it's—" he began, and suddenly realized that never, in her six or seven years of life, had he given her a Christmas present.

"Haven't people given you things for Christmas?"

She shook her head, still puzzled. "Miss Gibbs had me put some cards around, one year," she remembered slowly. "And Mrs. Finney gave me a hanky and said I should give everybody something. But I didn't have anything. So she showed me how to make some folding cutouts with, I guess, trees and deer on them. And a fat man. They weren't very nice."

He now recalled the strange sticky object that had been among his cards one year. It was, as she said, not very nice. But the whole thing moved him horribly, and he could only mutter, "I'm sorry, kid, I'm sorry." And then, "They said you wanted a telescope."

"Oh! Oh-h-h-h, Daddy! A *real telescope!?*" Her joy was so contagious that he forgot all about the pathos while they plunged into the wonders of Edmund's Scientific Catalogue, and all the delicious temptations and countertemptations of rich-field vs. long focal length. And space was found among the rooftops for a real mini-observatory, and the problem of Paula's night wanderings was solved for a time.

But he still worried about her apparent frailty, until Miss Emstead suggested that he take her on some camping and fishing trips in the nearby air force reservation. That worked out fantastically, with her delight and wonder at the wilderness, and his recognition of her surprising coordination and stamina. In outdoor gear she looked a lot more natural; he took to calling her Pauly and even Paul, and sometimes Harry by mistake. She was only fair at fishing, but he found her reassembling his old twelvegauge over-and-under, and it wasn't long before she had her own cut-down .475, and presently a real rifle with scope sights.

To no one's surprise she turned out to be an excellent shot, and he was only briefly disturbed when he had to give her a couple of lessons on hunting ethics. After all, at her age he had been fairly bloody-minded too.

It was curious how much they both enjoyed the cold, or rather, the experience of exploring ever farther north.

He took her to see the great Athabascar ice cap near Jasper, and they spent two happy shivering hours prowling the caves beneath the melting glacier's huge tongue. Deep green light struck through here; the glacier's vast icy udders dripped millennial snow water, and a cold foul breath, the melt of life killed a thousand years back, flowed from under the ice and made miniature storms and rainbows in the sunlight out beyond. A Mountie finally routed them out.

Afterward Paula pored over bundles of maps, and they gloated at the fun they would have when time allowed them to visit the real Alaskan ice fields far to the north.

"I bet Miss Emstead would love to go, too," Paula said.

Paul agreed instantly—without either of them noticing the utter insanity of the notion that an older, sedentary lady executive in uncertain health would "love" to leave her husband for the joys of exposing herself to the hazards and rigors of the world of ice.

These camping-trip years with Paula became the happiest of his life; certainly the most innocent.

Around her eighth year a new phase of life with Paula started. On a whim he let her stay through a small dinner party that ended early, and afterward he jokingly asked her what she thought of a man he was considering as division chief of his new aerospace facility.

"He waits to be told what to do. He pretends not to, but he does."

"And how do you know that, Miss Paulie?"

"I watched him with his knife and fork. And the wine. He didn't know if he liked it until he saw your face."

"Hmm. I thought he spoke right up."

"No. He watched you, first."

"Um hmm."

After that he took to letting the child play hostess at small gatherings, both at home and at restaurants, with a few coaching sessions from Miss Emstead. Paula proved a model of precocious tactfulness, silences, and charm. She was, it appeared, very interested in "serious" people; she watched everything, and was a memory machine. This actually proved useful to him; men tended to talk quite freely in her presence, taking her as even younger than she was.

But in his private chats with her, it was impossible to recall how short a time she had been alive. She was so interested in his work, first in the actual technology, and then in the business aspect, the contracts, the problems, the new aerospace venture. When she was ten she asked him for the history of Marrell Technologies, and sopped up all the literature he brought her. He found himself using her for a sounding board, and talking over people and projects with her as if she were an adult.

One weekend afternoon when Paul was in Chicago, his daughter received an unexpected caller. It was Miss Emstead, with a portfolio under her arm. Two pairs of eyes, one huge and violet, the other hazel and old and smiley, met in a wordless mutual examination and appraisal. There had always been an unspoken bond of congeniality and affection between the two. But this meeting was on a different plane.

Miss Emstead didn't bother with the "my dears" or "how you've growns" (Paula had not grown, much). She said directly:

"You have a great deal of influence with your father, on topics in which a quite young girl is not usually interested."

Paula, equally direct, simply nodded.

"We at the plant, we older ones, never thought that Mr. Marrell would have a child to carry on the enterprise after him. But I'm beginning to think your interest is sincere and enduring. Am I right?"

Paula nodded again, very affirmatively.

"Good. That's good. Of course, you might change your mind later, after boys and things come along. What do you think about that?"

"I can't be sure," the child said carefully in her soft voice. "People—grown-up women—seem so strange, some of them. But I don't think I'll change that much."

"There's no reason why you should," Miss Emstead said heartily. "Lots of grown-up women are deeply involved in business and have families, too."

"Like Mrs. Plum."

"Yes. Like a lot of us. Which brings me to the next point. Quite a few of us old-timers have invested our whole lives in Marrell Tech. It's all we have, it's all our security for our old age. Forgive me, but you still are very young, although your mind isn't. I would like you to take just a moment to—well, kind of appreciate that. Try to put yourself in our places. Recall that—forgive me again —Marrell T. isn't in any sense just a hobby for us, or a temporary enthusiasm. It's years and years and years of hard work, and putting everything we have into in bad times and good, so we'll be safe in our old ages. Try, just for a moment, would you?"

Gray eyes bored hard.

The violet eyes were serious in response. They only flickered once, briefly, to the briefcase under Miss Emstead's arm.

"I think I understand," Paula said carefully. "I—I don't feel it's a plaything, Miss Emstead."

"Yes. And it's all you have too, you know. Although you're young enough to start over, Marrell Technologies is your total security, the source of everything for you, now at any rate. To damage or lose it would mess your life up."

Paula's little lips set, she nodded hard.

Miss Emstead gave her one more long look and then smiled, relaxing.

"Good, Paula. And I think you might try calling me Gloria if you like. I've brought something along, in hopes you were serious. You remember that history of the company we sent you, the one on glossy paper?"

"Oh yes," the child said politely. "Thank you." But her little nose wrinkled slightly.

"Exactly," the older woman smiled. "I thought that if I found what I hoped, that it was time you had a *real* history. So I've put together a short account, just for you personally. I'm sure you won't mind if I stay here while you read it, and take it back to the safe. I'm told you have a phenomenal memory. But anytime you want to see it again, *any*-time at all, you just call me and I'll have it out to you by courier, who'll bring it back again. You do understand that, don't you?"

"Oh yes, Miss—Gloria. I really understand and I really

thank you. There isn't much, um, security around here. And people think they should walk right in on me."

"They could even read over your shoulder, or take it away from you. You see, some of this even your father doesn't know. Do you understand what I mean when I say we all decided to try to keep the business end off him? If your father isn't an engineering genius he's the closest thing to it I'm apt to see. We didn't want to make the mistake other companies have—spoiling a fine engineer to make a mediocre businessman."

"I think I understand that. It's like when they made Mr. Endicott school principal and he can't teach us anymore. Because he's an ad-ministrator."

"Perfect. All right, here you are. I think you'll want the next hour free, don't you?"

The little girl reached for the typewritten sheaf as an ordinary child reaches for candy.

"Let's go up to my darkroom!" And she bounced out of the big chair, for the first time showing her true age.

"Good."

And so began the strange alliance, by which the now-giant Marrell Technologies was run in the main by an aging woman and a ten-year-old child. And a carefree engineer filled the safes with his best work.

The congeniality or empathy between the three such disparate minds really was quite extraordinary; sometimes it seemed to go beyond speech. Tim Drever, Gloria's husband, with that combination of vagueness and essential acuity so often found in art workers, took a careful look at it. Perceiving that the strange bond did not threaten him, he continued his genial presence rear stage.

But not even he could have guessed that the sharing really was that of the fragments of one mind—still less that the body to which that mind belonged lay frozen in molecular stasis, two thousand miles away in northern ice, knowing nothing of humanity. All that Enggi, or what was left of him there, was aware of was that healing went on—and also that a faint discomfortable disturbance occasionally threatened him from beneath.

Halcyon days, when for a brief time the tempest and conflicts grow calm in the eye of winter, and the birds of halcyon nest together in harmony.

They did not end, at least on the surface, when at the age of eleven Paula sexually seduced her father.

It happened in the most normal way, as such things do, on one of their camping trips.

There had of course been outdoor intimacies before— like father and son, they swam nude. He had nursed her through dysentery, and she had rubbed his twisted ankle and later his strained back, the small hands very quick and strong. Once or twice he had found himself slightly aroused, and pushed the thought from him. She was still as sexless-looking as a minnow.

On this night the open tent was caught in a downpour and her sleeping bag got soaked. (Paula loved to sleep right in the door, where she could gaze at the stars.) As Paul had done long ago, he rubbed her dry, and then took the cold little body in his arms in his bag with him, and they slept so.

But in grey dawn he wakened to find her curiously touching his genitals—so softly, gently, it was like a dream whispering, "Oh Daddy, I love you so." Only after it had become far other than a dream, only after there were muffled yelps and writhings and a confused partial entry bringing his relief, did he begin to know what had happened.

But she was ready for him, strong small arms holding, trying to rock him soothingly. "It's *all right,* Daddy. We love each other so. Daddy, it's *all right.*" And telling him how she had read that such things happened a lot, and she was his girl, so how could it be wrong?

And then, very soberly, "Daddy—I have to learn about things, don't I? And I haven't anyone, no one at all. You're my teacher, you always have been."

He had barely time to take it all in before she was up and challenging him to race to the lake. The rain had quit; they had a fine breakfast and a great day's stalk of quail, and he took the subject as closed.

That night she went to her own dried bed. But before dawn she came into his sleeping bag as if by right, and this time she made him actually be merry, touching and asking questions like "How does this feel?" with giggles and squirmy demonstrations till the day broke on her—

so clearly innocent and happy in her newfound sensuality that he lost all but the last shreds of his guilt.

And there was, as she said, always this curious sense of *belongingness* in their joinings, of that which had been split apart again becoming one. He put it down to rationalization; how could he know how right he was?

And after all, it wasn't as if this had never happened before, he told himself. One or two of the new books about the house seemed to make quite a point of this, when he came to look.

And so began a last enchanted time of overt comradeship and covert delights. Paula was growing and rounding out a little now, but with her usual tact she hid it under boy's clothes and childish dress. At home all was as before; her hostessing of his parties became ever more winning and delightful. The parties themselves had long changed too; in place of the miscellany now came hardworking politicians, engineers, and scientists, always with a lovely girl or three for Paul; while Paula, who seemed totally unjealous, attended as zealously upon the wives as she did the men. She became adept at finding and charming people who could be of use, especially in the new aerospace aspect. She also suggested financial contributions to the PACs of certain aspiring politicians, some of whom proved definitely helpful to Marrell Tech.

Paul took to giving her joking rewards for her work, in lieu of allowance. Her simple delight in crisp new thousand-dollar bills amused him, and with money pouring in on all sides he could afford it. Marrell Tech was taking over a few struggling small firms; Paul depended on Paula to keep his memory straight, and indeed she once stopped him, at a party, from informally opening bids against himself.

So passed the last year of halcyon. Their sexual contacts, by tacit consent, were confined to camping trips. For a time that worked well. But Paula had underestimated matters; she had no real concept of the tumult she had unleashed. The poor besotted man developed an unnatural passion for the outdoors, and began dragging Paula out with him in all weathers and on any pretext.

Perhaps by coincidence, it was at that phase that Miss Emstead issued one of her rare warnings.

"Always remember, Paula, there're a lot of smart people out there, and few of them are friendly. There *are* other people as intelligent as you—I'm not one of them, but they exist. Some may even be smarter. No matter how well things seem to be going, it's always good strategy to run a trifle scared."

And she told Paula the story of the man who sold Stanley Steamers. The Stanley was an excellent early steam car, but it weighed tons and was a bitch to steer. In those days motor roads often consisted only of two deep ruts. So, as he crossed the West selling cars, the salesman told his clients, "When you meet another car, don't bother pulling her out of the ruts to pass. You keep right on going. That thing is a monster; when the other driver sees you aren't pulling out he'll yank his car aside and let you by."

It was good advice and worked well, until the day one Stanley Steamer driver met another.

Paula, in all her short life, never met another Steamer —or rather, when she did she didn't recognize it. For it was in part herself.

Whether it was truly, improbably, inadvertence; or pique at her first failure in a test of her power to charm; or simply a miscalculation due to ignorance—for she *was* still a child, unknowing of the strength of tribal mores, and everything had gone her way for a long time, so she may have actually failed to understand what being legally very much a minor could mean in terms, say, of gaining control of her inheritance; howbeit, whether from hubris or error, there came a party evening when Paula found herself alone with Nicky Benson.

Nicky Benson was a youngish man of great physical and mental charm. Paula may have temporarily forgotten that he was also a devout Mormon and his wife Joan a fanatic one. But it is barely credible that she could have forgotten that Nicky was also an executive with Nippon/Sterling, Marrel Tech's only serious competitor in several fields.

What was visible was that after an unclear twenty minutes alone with Paula, Nicky abruptly left the party, his face flushed angry red under his butter-yellow hair. He told the details only to his wife, which was little better than putting them on CBS News. For two days, while Paul was in Chicago, the phrase "Daddy shows me how" cascaded through that sector of the industrial-social world, gaining new color and specificity with every telling. On the evening of the second day, three of the household staff gave notice en bloc, and Robby the copter pilot quit. The phone was unnaturally quiet.

Paula spent an increasingly dismayed and horrified night; she was, as mentioned, very quick at extrapolation. She may have done some growing up.

At three in the morning she did one of the incontrovertibly decent acts of her brief life. She phoned Gloria Emstead. Appropriately, there was a wild electrical storm over San Juan.

"This is Paula. Sell all your Marrell stock."

"I know your voice, Paula." Miss Emstead did not sound sleepy. "Would you please repeat what you just said?"

"I said—" the young voice quivered and was under control again. "Sell all your holdings in Marrell Tech. And your husband's. And tell G-George Henry and the others too; you know. Right now, first thing in the morning." The last word trembled away as the storm spewed static.

"Paula. I'll never forget this, my dear. As a matter of fact, we already have sold out; we did it in little dribs and drabs, it never showed. But I'll always remember that you called tonight."

"Oh," Paula said exhaustedly. Then, childlike, she asked, "When did you sell, Gl—Miss Emstead?"

"We started over a year ago. Now you better try to get some rest. Draw out all the cash you can in the morning, and hide it. And remember this law-firm name— Armistead, Levy, and South. He's with them, he's—" a lightning bolt crackled the line. "Good-bye now. Keep that chin up, nothing lasts—"

The line went dead.

Paul bounced off the Marrell jet at nine next morning with nothing but plans for a trip to the Great Slave Lake wilderness in his head. He was met by a green-faced George Henry and two very polite senior policemen with a warrant.

For the whole next year everything went bad.

Paul was of course soon free under bail, but forbidden contact with his daughter. This was enforced by an ever-present police matron. Paula tried to charm her, but the catastrophe seemed to have spoiled her touch; it was as if the stress had caused her to revert to the childhood she had never known. Patrolwomen Haggerty, Kelly, or Wyskof munched Paula's liqueur chocolates, casually evading those which tasted a bit odd after a visit to Paula's workshop, and watched sleeplessly over her. Paula improvised a series of visits to museums in which she would stand for three excruciating hours at a stretch, apparently engrossed in the more insipid tableaux of Pueblo Indian life; the patrolwomen stolidly stood by. Paula spent whole days in the planetarium; the police-women did, too.

The only news she got was bad. Paul had started to drink heavily. And then Gloria Emstead developed a heart condition and came out of the hospital with all business communications forbidden.

The trial was disaster compounded. Pressure seemed to be coming from somewhere; despite all the Marrell side's protests the trial took place in open court.

Nor could Paula prevent old Mr. Northrup, the chief of Marrell Tech's legal staff, from defending Paul in person, armed with little but a metaphysical belief in his clients' innocence. It seemed to be his idea that he had only to let people see his principals and they would be smitten with a revelation of the wicked absurdity of the charge. He had never heard of *Lolita,* and let the term "nymphet" go past him unchallenged three times in the prosecution's opening remarks.

Worse, he caused Paula to appear in her little navy school dress with white collar and cuffs, in which she looked positively edible. Judge Dyson, who had read *Lolita* with care, took one look at her and began to pity Paul, who was looking abnormally haggard and dissolute in the dreadful executive-type clothes Northrup had clad him in.

At the first break, the prosecutor's female aide took a short stroll, eyes flickering to where Paula tried to sit composedly. When the trial resumed, Prosecutor Baylor unexpectedly changed the order of witnesses. He finished up with some repulsive expert testimony on the composition of stains in Paul's camp sleeping bag (which Paula had been unable to get to on that last night, although she had thought to destroy some of her own garments) and then recalled her governess to the stand. Miss Briggs was one of those who had quit on that final afternoon.

PROSECUTOR BAYLOR: "Miss Briggs, I want to ask you about the dress which your employer's daughter is wearing now. You can see her clearly, can't you?" *(General craning of necks.)* "Is that one of her normal school uniforms?"

MISS BRIGGS: "Yes, sir."

BAYLOR: "And do I see correctly that it has been shortened?"

MISS BRIGGS: "Oh yes, sir. Miss Paula is very small."

BAYLOR: "I see. The skirt was made shorter, and perhaps the hips and bodice were taken in a little, made to fit better?" *(Gestures suggestively.)*

JUDGE DYSON: "Counselor, I fail to see where this questioning is leading."

BAYLOR: "Your Honor, I wish to establish that it was evidently the practice to alter this child's clothing to make it unusually tight and seductive-looking, as Your Honor can see for himself."

JUDGE *(somewhat absently):* "Denied."

At this Paula herself spoke up. Her young voice was so quick and clear and indignant that Dyson stayed his gavel long enough to let her get out: "I'm *not* seductive—I'm embarrassed! I've grown while they made me wait for trial and there's nobody to sew my clothes!"

It might have made points.

But Paul chose that moment to break down, and in three minutes the courtroom was a chaos of strobe flashes, falling chairs, Northrup gibbering and shouting, and Baylor shouting back, the judge's gavel going futilely—and all in perfect time for the afternoon editions and TV, on an otherwise newsless day.

The headlines ran from the comparatively sedate MARRELL TECH HEAD ADMITS INCEST through the colorful MARRELL CONFESSES SEDUCING 10-YR-OLD DAUGHTER to

"GOD HELP ME I CAN'T KEEP MY HANDS OFF HER," CRIES POP; "I'M BETTER OFF DEAD!"

And when Paula tried to get to him to quiet him it was a photographer's picnic: PAULA RUNS TO COMFORT DAD WHO DEBAUCHED HER—PAULA MARRELL BATTLES POLICE TO REACH DAD AFTER HIS CONFESSION—PAULA VAULTS TO POP'S ARMS DESPITE POLICE—with a full view of her skimpy little-girl white underdrawers as she all-too-expertly one-handed the defendants' rail.

She had forgotten the damned dress, or the classic courtroom chase would have lasted longer than it did. One photo of Paula sailing flat-out between a fat policeman's legs became a collector's item.

The remainder of the trial was a quick farce.

Poor Northrup withdrew "for reasons of health," and the junior staff was able to inject a medical-psychiatric plea that had the effect of obtaining one of the new and controversial indefinite "psychotherapeutic" sentences for Paul.

As for Paula, her head seemed to clear. The explosive exercise of the courtroom scene may have been cathartic. Also instructive, when she came to notice it, was the fact that Nicky Benson's name had never appeared in the whole scenario. (Only one easily muffled female reporter associated "James N. Benson-Flitch, complainant," with the Nicky Benson who had just made VP at Nippon/Sterling.) Paula resolved that she would never again fight the world alone and in the open.

But when the dust settled, things couldn't have looked worse. Paul was out of contact, being done God knew what to in a minimum-security facility at Tehatchapi. Miss Emstead was recovering, but still allowed only one business conversation a week. Paula herself was a ward of the court under the governance of appointed strangers, attending P.S. 215 in San Juan, plus private tutors. Marrell Tech's common stock was on the ground, and the firm itself was living precariously on Paul's stored-ahead plans, under the wobbly guidance of old George Henry.

Paula dispassionately took stock, and bethought herself, belatedly, of a certain untaken piece of advice. But how to find the unknown?

Her "touch" was coming back. The weekday guardian

soon relaxed a bit, helped along by variants of the museum ploy. Paula worked on a driver well enough to establish written communication to and from George Henry, but he was no help in the central matter. So, gaining an hour free for "shopping for girls' things," she went to search head-on.

The secretaries at Armistead, Levy, and South were fairly used to appointments being made for a "Miss Smith." They were not used to having "Miss Smith" turn out to be a girl child whose feet didn't quite reach the waiting-room floor. Nor was Mr. Armistead used to opening notes consisting of a crisp thousand-dollar bill, to which was attached a modest card inscribed with a child's notorious name.

"I want you to get my daddy out. I'm sure he didn't get a fair trial and the business needs him."

Armistead hemmed and pontificated at Paula, who thoughtfully retrieved the $1,000 and retreated to try again. She perceived she had remembered sloppily; Miss Emstead had said he was "with" the firm—thus obviously not one of the senior partners.

She used one of Gloria's permitted visits to get the name, and after two more tries she caught her quarry alone in the elevator.

"You're Ellis Donohue?" Handing him the note.

The short but conventionally handsome, clean-cut young lawyer opened her note slowly, studying her in a way that told her he knew something of her previous calls. She was pleased to note the way he took hold of the bill; not quite the grip of a drowning man, but not far from it. His eyes met hers with an expression combining the gravity of the law with the activism of a man whose mistress has fifteen credit cards.

"I believe something could be done on a mistrial. For example, his lawyer never seems to have considered a change of venue. And there are several other aspects."

They made a coffee-shop date at the museum, and she hurried to swoop up random additions to the "girls' things" she was supposed to be shopping for.

When next they could talk, she had a list of requests, headed by "Free access to my lawyer" and, second, "Access to my bank."

"I'm pretty sure we can do that one fast," Ellis told her. "But . . . am I your lawyer?"

In answer she took out a frilly pink Kleenex case. Under the top Kleenex lay a wad of crisp new bills. She made a little napkin tent, and in its shelter started tearing the bills in neat halves. Ellis Donohue caught his handsome eyes starting to pop, and lost count at fifteen.

"I'm sure you'll forgive me, Mr. Donohue. You see, I'm very young, and people have played bad tricks on me. A story I read suggested this." She handed him one wad of halves, wrapped in another intact bill.

"Oh c-certainly."

"There's my guardian!" She waved childishly, and slipped from her chair, putting her halves back in the Kleenex case. "Mr. Meyers, I'd like you to meet Mr. Donohue. He was telling me about poor Mr. Northrup." She extracted a Kleenex from the case (giving Ellis fits) and blew her nose. "Maybe Mr. Donohue will find Daddy a new lawyer."

That night, as often, Paula stayed long in her observatory, scanning the familiar wonders somewhat absently. She had expected to feel more satisfied. Certainly everything humanly possible to her was underway, or being done. Only there was a pressure, a sense of unease she could not quiet. Almost as if some unheard voice was calling, calling her name. Again and again her gaze went to the northward smog, but nothing, of course, was there.

Paul sighed, putting away the scope.

Then she walked out onto the rooftop, casting off her little robe, and sat down and stared upward with an expression as unreadable as it was intense. Puzzlement—longing—a faint smile—a clenching of the small jaw. Finally her lids dropped, and she breathed deep and hard, shivering a little, before she took up her robe and went in. An acute observer might have noticed that the tile where she had sat was very slightly worn.

The tears that had been shed on that coping had left, of course, no trace.

Events of the next weeks moved right along, spurred on by the contents of the pink Kleenex case. The Armistead senior partners gave Donohue his green light, and he began to deliver: appeal, mistrial, change of venue to a backwoods portion of an adjoining state where the alleged offense was claimed to have occurred, and a quick and private hearing, with Paul and Paula clad in their normal outdoor clothes.

Nicky Benson proved to have no more appetite for blood, especially when some of it might be his own, and two more of the original complainants could somehow not be found. In four months the whole matter was dismissed from the courts and Paul was home, a free and technically innocent man.

Meanwhile Marrell Tech had scraped up a respectable PR budget, and its flacks succeeded in persuading a large section of the public that some slight incident, more the fantasies of overwork than real, had been used against Paul by unscrupulous rivals. Paula herself was duly seen about with a squad of healthy young American boys fresh from Central Casting.

When Paul came home Paula all but smothered him with determinedly sexless affection, and this, plus his now-personal hatred of Nippon/Sterling, put him well on the mend.

Even here fate took a helpful hand: before Paul's detestation of Nicky Benson could take on unhealthy virulence, the Mormon couple met with grisly disaster. While passing through a riot area, their car was caught and rolled. Its defenses weren't breached, but a tank full of a defense-security compound that Nicky was testing developed leaks as the car was righted. Nearby a liter of the stuff rained onto Nicky and Joan. The test worked all too well. It was hoped that the couple would recover some eyesight, but much of the other damage was beyond all plastic surgery's best skills.

Ellis Donohue found Paula reading about it.

"Your lucky day," she told him. "This was a job I was saving for you."

The young lawyer chuckled, and then suddenly peered more closely at his small client. She met his gaze unsmiling, watching him pale as the chuckle died in his throat. It had been the whim of a moment, but she found herself fascinated by the chance to guess at just how much power she might wield—were she to wish to, which she at present did not. Only—the Nicky Bensons of the world would never get their yellow hair through her defenses again.

"I better get this to Daddy right away. He'll probably want to send flowers. Perhaps some kind that can be smelled?"

Ellis tottered off, trying to look worldly.

But when Paula found Paul, they didn't discuss the Benson thing. She found him uncharacteristically moody; pacing, breaking off a sentence to stare out across the freeways, pouring out a Jack Daniel's and pushing it away untouched. This last convinced her he was suffering from more than the effects of Tehatchapi. Perhaps he was worried that irreparable hurt had been done to his beloved Marrell Tech? He had never seemed to care for their public image, but still, they had never had such a problem before. Certainly something more in the PR line could be useful.

But Paula had an odd feeling that this was all beside the point. He was acting the way she herself felt. But what *was* the point? She hadn't a clue.

At this point Paul's new young assistant, Girta Grier, came in to remind Paul that it was his and Paula's afternoon to visit Gloria Emstead.

"Good-oh. We need some air. Some good cold north air."

"Do you feel it too, Daddy?" Paula asked him in the car.

"Feel what?"

"Needing something—some north air, like you said."

Instead of replying verbally, he just looked at her, and they both knew the answers.

"Something's bugging us," Paul muttered at last. "I mean, more than all that crap. That's all over and past now. It's—it's like something we should *do*."

"Yes." And Paula added by one of those peculiar inspirations, that made no logical sense, "Let's ask Gloria. I don't think it would upset her. Maybe she'd know."

"Right-oh. I don't know why but that's a good idea, kid."

They found Gloria Emstead out of her chaise, making a shaky march around the room. She greeted them gasping, laughed apologetically as they helped her back to the couch.

"I'm just not fit for much yet."

"But there's nothing you have to do. Take it easy."

"*Isn't there?*"

"Gloria, do you mean what I think you do?"

It soon turned out that she too was suffering the same inexplicable malaise; as of something unknown, needing ever more urgently to be done.

But what? They couldn't define it, only discuss it by half-sentences and shared silences.

In one of the silences Paula remarked abruptly how she and Paul had once found great fascination in a glacier, and how much they'd wanted to experience the real ice-country to the north.

"We even thought you'd like to come with us. Of course that's crazy."

"No," said Gloria quietly. "Not crazy at all. Of course I can't get far right now. But—look." She reached behind her for a much-folded magazine, and handed it to Paula.

It was an account of a series of seismic tremors in the McKinley Range north of Fairbanks, which were causing several local glaciers to be shunted seaward. One photo of an ice-lined bay with a line of great bergs splitting and calving off drew Paula's eyes like a magnet. When she passed it to Paul she noticed her own heart thudding.

"What—what is it with us?" Gloria Emstead asked, only half-humorously, watching their reaction.

They didn't know. Who could?

But an idea suddenly was born in Paula's head, so intensely that she felt as if she were lighting up with a cartoon light bulb.

"Gloria—Daddy—listen! Let's go for broke. Los Angeles is already burning up with drought, the whole coast is, and the summer's barely started. The Colorado River is down to a trickle, people are starting to shoot each other over water. Fresh water! Everybody wants it, everybody has to have it. And Marrell Tech needs some really good publicity. People've talked about towing icebergs here for years—why don't we *do* it? It would supply I forget how much fresh water—years' worth. Suppose we tied into one of those really big bergs and towed it down here and grounded it right offshore where they could just run a pipe out to it? And suppose we did it free, the first one anyway, with 'Gift from Marrell Tech' all over it?"

"Hmm," said Paul. Gloria Emstead's eyes were shining as she looked from face to face. Paula suspected the idea wasn't new to her.

". . . currents. The California sets in somewhere along Portland, it'd help," Paul was muttering. He had produced one of his battered envelopes and was scribbling on it. "Shelf depths? Those things need channels . . . sea mounts? How to get a grip on it, storm-proof? Not to lose it. Lease dredges, tugs. Could a chopper turn it? Experts —do we need experts! Georgie Warner for a lead-in . . . And probably there's some damn book of regs saying, No Way. Lawyers. Bet that'll be the worst . . ."

There was no more formal discussion. From the moment the idea was voiced, it was settled: Marrell Tech would spend every penny it could muster, employ or invent every device needed, to bring that iceberg south.

Only once did Paul say lightly to Gloria Emstead, "Well, I guess we're going to see our glacier together, after all. If Mohamet can't get to the mountain . . . !"

Her smile was more than radiant.

And yet no one of the three ever really asked why? They only acted.

If questioned, they would have explained that they were helping out a drought-struck state for the good name of Marrell Tech, and seizing the initiative in what could become a new engineering field.

Experts galore were duly called in, and feasibility studies made—not in formal leather-bound presentations, but under forced draft through nights and dawns, recorded on Paul's crumpled envelopes. By this time Marrell Tech had a small work camp on Jackson Promontory, near several likely berg-calving points, and experiments with towage and grappling techniques were underway. Ice presents problems of variable strain tolerance, and of unpredictable slippage under pressure and friction. Paul soon found himself doing what he did and loved best, problem-solving, inventing, improvising in a new field. Paula and Gloria managed to pry enough data out of him to secure future patent claims, though somehow even that didn't seem important.

As he had predicted, the legal and governmental obstacles provided the worst hassles of all. By this time, various ecological groups had also gotten into a dozen facets of the project. But as the cruel drought worsened, and crops and toilets dried up, the loudest adversaries did likewise. And Ellis Donohue, now provided with ample staff, had sufficient needs and greeds to keep him tramping the halls of the Maritime Commission, the navy, the coast guard, and half a dozen others almost as fast as his principals demanded.

The final impasse came when they were denied permission to tow a berg into shipping lanes. This too was broken—in private by a few discreet transfers of funds to certain political action committees, and in public by commissioning the iceberg as a ship. When the proper berg was selected, and two special waterjet motors, at least in theory capable of deflecting it, were mounted, the documentation by which it would become the *U.S.S. Marrell Tech* under Panamanian registry, would be ready.

The actual selection of the berg came in two stages. Paul and Paula, on their first overflight of the upper shelving area, saw at the same instant a huge, snowy, crater-topped monster, newly separated and glittering in the morning sun amid a jostle of lesser ice. There was no need for either to point to it; it was almost as if a vector lit in their heads. Photos were taken, and rushed back to Gloria, who reacted exactly as they had.

But the engineers had already fixed on other, smaller bergs farther from the dangerous east-west Alaska flow. Paul overruled them curtly. As if to oblige him, the great berg soon wandered into better, less crowded water. It was also found to have a favorably broad and comparatively shallow underwater configuration. Then, too, its crater shape would facilitate and prolong meltwater collection. The engineers were pacified.

At last came the day when the first towlines tightened. Sirens blared, various fireworks and assorted explosions went up from the Jackson camp, now a small town, and the enormous white presence began imperceptibly to change course and ever so delicately to accelerate on its two-thousand-mile journey south. It was hoped to deliver it to Los Angeles in something under three months, about Labor Day. Dredges were already at work carving a berth for her at a safe distance from the oil drillers off Catalina.

As the voyage of the *U.S.S. Marrell Tech* became a reality, the events and excitements of the trip came more and more into the news, especially when the craft met and mastered her first storm without breakaway. But the most important event escaped all but perfunctory notice.

When the iceberg began its course, the suction wake created by the underwater passage of its huge, irregular volume caused a flotilla of small chunks and berglets to trail after it. These gradually melted or fell away, until only the largest was left—a respectable-sized small berg that seemed determined to accompany them. There was talk of exploding it, but since it too was fresh water, and not endangering anything at the moment, the decision was delayed. A surplus tugboat laid a couple of grapples on it and it gave no trouble.

When Paula was shown it from the air her small brows drew together. "I don't like that thing. It looks . . . dirty."

The pilot chuckled.

"I mean it. I wish we'd at least X-ray it or probe it; maybe there's something inside."

"Ah, it'll get lost pretty soon."

But it did not get lost. To the presence embedded in stasis deep inside, the stimulus-configuration of receding, escaping prey was acting as a tropism. Human eyes saw only that the harmless small berg seemed to be caught in the currents, maintaining a roughly constant distance from their tow.

While, in the tow itself, all oblivious of danger or of humanity or of the means which moved him or even that he was moving, the helpless cub Enggi continued to beam out his unearthly call for his own reassemblement. He felt only a tiny discomfort from the growing warmth nearby; overriding this was a contenting sense that slowly, slowly, regatherment was taking place. For some time he had felt faint twinges of anticipation as if parts of his missing selfhood were coming close. But the situation was incomplete; an important aspect or aspects was still missing. No less than all of him would serve.

In the human world, another event caused even less notice: one morning the smog-shrouded sunlight of the California coast was briefly dimmed by two tenuosities passing far, far overhead. The apparent passage of some gaseous wisps at orbital heights may have puzzled an astronomer or two. The phenomenon vanished eastward, and no one could have observed them taking up Earth-stationary positions in the 20,000-mile-out zone to await the moment when an alien cub would emerge and meet his fate.

Meanwhile the Marrell Tech fleet ploughed on, insignificant to astral senses, but becoming ever more stimulating to local humanity. It angled laboriously across the Alaska current, and accelerated as it picked up the southward California flow. Fishermen of Queen Charlotte Island sighted it, a moving mountain of shining snow, trailing fog like steam. Seattle and Portland sent marine excursions out to see it go by. By the time it reached California waters it was an Event, and San Francisco became the leader among cities suddenly demanding an iceberg of their own.

Inland the drought burned on, and jokes about bergjacking became loud enough to generate watchfulness in the coast guard escort. Obviously, a stolen berg could not be hidden, but the berg might be deflected and irretrievably grounded on a rocky shore, where its use could scarcely be denied. The escort was doubled. And then, as berg fever grew, and the general public began trying to join the flotilla in everything from kayaks to yachts, the escort doubled and redoubled again. A maniac almost crashed it with his helicopter, and an even crazier soul sky-dived onto it; a permanent air-safety patrol had to be set up. Marrell Tech was turning out its pockets to pay the security bills; it could not let go of its tiger, and it was becoming a financial disaster to proceed.

Yet the goal was now almost in sight, and just as total chaos threatened, the *Marrell Tech* solved her problems herself. Deceleration, the shedding of its enormous momentum, had to begin far to the north of target, not far from San José. And as the great ice mountain lost way, the fog which it generated, and which had been trailing it like smoke, caught up and closed over it, ever thicker as it slowed. Advantage was taken of this by slowing the berg even more than necessary. Soon, on all but gale-force days, nothing was visible of the whole enterprise but a vast shining slow-moving fog bank, etched here and there with rainbows, above which a glittering ice turret might appear at long intervals and vanish again.

The fog of course created its own problems, but these were manageable with ordinary care, and only a dozen or so idiots required to be rescued in their efforts to reach their invisible goal. The only serious injury came to a lunatic hang glider who broke both legs on the little maverick berg, which was still stuck in the suction wake of the *Marrell Tech,* causing no trouble.

"Two for the price of one," the tow captain grinned.

But Paula turned pale at the news that the small berg was still there.

She and Paul and even Miss Emstead had been causing the tow captain a great deal of trouble by their eagerness to fly out and land on the great berg. He had only just managed to use all his authority, plus Gloria's obvious frailty, and the heaven-sent fog, to keep them off it until it was officially "berthed" and out of his command. This was now a week away.

Meanwhile Gloria had improved enough to make visits to the office, which she spent supervising candidates to replace her. Girta Grier was one of these; the young business school graduate's "mother" had recently died, and slightly against her own better judgment Gloria had invited her down to try out at Marrell Tech. The girl was doing well. Gloria struggled to remain impartial, and to subdue a growing natural affinity between them. Girta didn't resemble her physically, but an artist might have traced out a similarity between Girta and Paula, minus Paula's intensity and diminutive size.

Miss Emstead was somewhat dismayed to note that there seemed also to be a strong natural affinity budding between Girta and Paul, which the senior office staff warmly approved. But she was a philosopher. If society had wrenched a man out of one daughter's bed only to push him into another's, who was she to defy Fate? She contented herself with seeing to it that Girta was as capable as possible in her grasp of Marrell Tech.

Thus it was that when the great day finally came, and the fantastic sight of an enormous iceberg being grounded in its channel near Catalina was before the people of L.A., Girta Grier, with Tim Drever, were part of the small unofficial advance party to copter out and land.

Coming in, they all fell silent with awe. There it sat at last! Resplendent in its pearly fog and rainbows, with just enough breeze to clear them a landing site on the seaward side, at the nearest approach to the crater.

Deep within that crater, a being so alien as to be incomprehensible to humans, stirred and relaxed its long icy clamped encystment. His stirring did not much disturb the earthly matter about him; the substance of Enggi's body was only loosely intermeshed in the molecular lattices of ice. He was conscious of little but great joy. A desperate hope had won out, his hour of returning life had come.

As the copter came down beside cliffs of ice, Girta and Tim Drever exclaimed in unison, "God, it's huge!" "I thought it'd be just a little hilltop," Girta added, "a big ice cube!"

"It's a landscape," Tim said. The Marrells and Gloria were silent as the pilot helped them all out. The copter had landed them on a big steel-mesh mat laid on a dry place in the shelving shore that ran around the berg. Beyond them farther out, men in wet suits were splashing in the shallows, securing mooring grapples. Out of sight around the blue-white cliffs were the mountings of the two motors, and the official "stern," flying the Marrell Tech flag.

Another copter droned by overhead on its way to deploy a big new Marrell Tech sign of netting, on the shoreward cliffs. There were no permanent structures on the berg, only a faint trail leading to the cratered summit above them. Since this was a potential drinking-water reservoir, all traffic had been kept to the wave-swept shelf around the edge. The melting process so far had done little but slightly widen and raise this water-level ledge; under it all hung the great volume of the ice.

To Tim and Girta's surprise, Paula, Paul, and Gloria had already started up the steep trail to the top. Paul was helping Gloria with an arm around her waist, and she was climbing up quite rapidly.

"Take it easy, honey," Tim called. A cold, damp downdraft blew in his face. He and Girta began to follow more slowly.

"Our iceberg nuts." Girta smiled uncertainly.

Tim grinned briefly. "I'll be glad when she's safe off this thing. Why does she have to climb up there?"

"I know what you mean," Girta said thoughtfully at the first pause. The climb was quite steep. For a moment the fog blew thinner around them, so they could see over the water. "Look, there's that other iceberg, the follower."

The maverick berg was moored a couple of hundred yards off, momentarily sunlit.

"It does look rather dirty, as Paula said."

"Probably just a layer of old volcanic ash," Tim told her. "What are they all shouting about, back there?"

The men on the shelf were hallooing to others who seemed to be out of sight around the cliffs. As Tim and Girta looked, the chopper pilot waded out to join them.

Meanwhile the three above them had reached a point where they could begin to see down into the great shallow irregular crater at the top.

"Look!" Paula cried. "There's a—a cloud coming up!"

Enggi's body did not reflect much visible light or heat, and he was not inordinately large compared, say, with the crater itself. As parts of him came free of its icy matrix, the humans saw only what might have been a whale-sized, peculiarly dense and defined white cumulus cloud beneath them. He did, however, emit and reflect a considerable UV and microwave spectrum; the commotion among the workers was caused by the fact that most of their electronic gear was going into overload or malfunctioning erratically as Enggi came into line.

The emerging cloudlet humped and swayed toward them, a beautiful prismatic white in the sun. As it did, the three humans unconsciously moved toward the brink to meet it.

They felt only a generalized glad rightness; warmth, welcome, perhaps. And for two of them there might have been a brief mild jolt of joining, as if something intangible had met or been passed. No words exist to express what is felt when a fragment of aspect of personality—a fragment of what had been the person—leaves. There is no "emptiness" because that which could have felt empty is simply gone. The only "feeling" left here was a kind of joy, as Enggi's own joy in his recovery of himself leaped the momentary link and overflowed into the abandoned matrices that had housed him. Neither Paul nor Gloria were harmed, or left mutilated; they had, after all, been fully functioning adults when they received Enggi's last desperate transmission.

But Paula—Paula who had been newborn . . .

Blinking away a brief sense of disorientation, the other two turned and saw that the girl had gone a little to one side and closer out, on the crater's lip, so that the strange snowy apparition seemed almost to touch her and light her up. She gave a strange wordless cry, and then seemed as if fighting to retain or maintain herself; her small arms hugged her own body. Then she flung back her head and screamed, or shouted, almost commandingly, "Take me, too! Take me with you!"

At that Paul found voice, though it was little more than a croak of "No! No, Paulie!"

But that moment something new happened. As if jerked by an invisible bond, the beautiful apparition towering above the girl visibly turned from her, and bent or curved its energies so directionally away that they all turned to look.

And they saw it.

Atop the nearby maverick berg, a smoky gray presence was exhaling, or writhing out. A gray tentacle extended toward them, and then *bloomed*, at its tip, into something half visible and wholly fascinating—a great smoke flower, set with stars of piercing, luminous, summer-sky blue.

It was that which Enggi had sensed, and toward which he was now drawn, his innocent cub's curiosity pulling him in every fiber. What—what was this wondrous new thing? All incomplete and unwary as he was, he must—he must draw closer!

But Paula, who had held—and still held—so much of his being, was neither unwary nor naive. With her whole human/unhuman soul she distrusted and dreaded this glowing lure. She had even seen such blue before, in Nicky Benson's eyes. With all her might she willed the white presence, which was somehow half herself, to reject it, to beware and turn away.

"No! No! No!" she cried to it, sending at Enggi all the force of her will.

And indeed she felt his fascination waver, his attention start back to her.

But the Eater brightened and enlarged its attractant, with mesmeric smoky involutions of the "petals," and ever brighter, bluer stars. To half-seeing human eyes it was a fantastically alluring sight, like looking into infinity itself. To Enggi's senses it was all but overpowering. He was yielding, turning fatally back toward it and away.

"No!" Paula shouted. She had no weapon but her naked will, yet that will was half his own, and she strove somehow to connect, to compel. "Come back here! Turn away!"

At this moment Tim and Girta, who had begun to run stumbling up the ice when they heard Paula's cries, burst panting onto the summit. They saw the girl poised straining on the utmost lip of the crater, half enveloped in a great alien whiteness that was pulsingly alive.

As they stared, Paula's head snapped back, and for an instant she stared sightlessly straight up, as if seeking or receiving some signal from the empty sky.

Then she screamed, with more power than seemed possible in her small body, "Get us away from it! Go!"

—And something like a bolt or umbilicus of diamond fire poured between her and the alien thing. The whiteness straightened itself skyward around her. And both Girta and Tim said afterward that for an instant they had seemed to see the outline of a naked girl, unbearably bright, curled within the glittering white cloud.

Then it was going, accelerating impossibly, bolting, streaking for the open sky above, dwindling to a pinpoint star—and vanished before they could draw breath.

And behind it, from the adjacent berg, a smoky thing with all jewels gone, shot up like a great squid in pursuit.

An Eater was no match for Enggi's speed in open chase, but this one's hunger and frustration were so fierce that it tried. It strove so hard that it did not sense until too late Enggi's two protectors awaiting it with their adult energies at ready.

The resultant flash at 21,000 miles set the astronomers of several nations searching to see whose stationary satellite had exploded.

But on the iceberg top off California, all human eyes were on what had been a living girl, lying like an empty glove at the empty crater's lip. Long before Paul and the others reached her they could sense that all life was gone. Paul could only hold her, stunned and disbelieving, and yelling for futile ambulance planes.

When the copter pilot finally screwed up his courage to respond to his employer's howls—there had been some fairly unnerving phenomena experienced below—he found Paul and Girta embraced in grief around Paula's limp form, while Tim Drever comforted his exhausted Gloria.

And thereafter matters on Earth took their purely human course.

The events of the Marrell visit, and the sad loss of Paula, were officially ascribed to accident and the premature malfunction of fireworks prepared for the evening. The electronic disturbances ceased and did not return. And the entire enterprise redounded to the eventual great profit of Marrell Technologies, the happy old age of Gloria and Tim, the satisfying if somewhat irregularly joyful conjugation of Girta and Paul, and a notable, if temporary, improvement in the coastal California water supply.

Elsewhere in space and time, Enggi and the two scouts were on their journey home, in travel mode.

For some time Enggi journeyed in silence, until he judged that he could be considered to have digested the angry and sobering lectures he had received. The next time they broke mode to navigate an eruptive complex, he offered respectfully, "I have learned another thing."

"Be silent, worthless young one," returned one scout. "You have caused enough trouble."

"Wait," objected the other. "This cub, reprehensible as it is, has yet faced an Eater at close range, all untaught, and survived. It is possible that something has been found. What is it, Enggi?"

"It is the—the life on these strange little satellites. My essence lived in their minds and thought their thoughts. I'm not sure even now that I'm wholly myself. There's a part of me that had never known of an Eater, yet knew at once it was evil and forced me to escape."

"So!" retorted the first scout. "Undoubtedly it felt no lure."

"It felt it," Enggi persisted. "It felt it strongly. I know. But that isn't it. It's that their lives are so different from ours. I believe," he signed formally, "that I have found my life's work. When I have completed my duties to the grex, of course," he added hastily.

"What do you mean, your life's work? What could you do?" asked the first scout.

"And all that matter is so short-lived," the other remarked thoughtfully. "A mere passing fritha-gust."

Enggi was silent for a long distance. In him lived one aspect of a human mind that had been tormented by a hopeless longing for the stars. Now he had the stars; their glories and infinite spectacles were around him as pebbles had been underfoot for the beings on that far-off Earth. And now, paradoxically, in this same part of him another longing was being born, a shadowy nostalgia for the soft-colored organic intricacies, the growing things and tactile breezes and blue skies and racing waters—all the micro-life he had loved as a human mind, or minds. Even for their strange mutual fevers and complexities, so intense, so meaningless to Enggi's kind, yet now not meaningless to him.

"I don't know," he admitted honestly. "But I believe there is something of value there. Perhaps on other satellites as well. If we could somehow manage to interchange, for short times, without all that terror and desperation, if we could know and experience different kinds, and learn which are most promising. It might be that some of their knowledge applies to us, as did the one who recognized the Eater without teaching. Yes, they are brief, but their minds are rich. Maybe their short lives force them to learn quickly, and then push beyond what they have been taught. This could be of use to us. And there is something strange about Time itself—it did not seem short while I was in their bodies. Could it possibly be that Time is not the same everywhere?"

"Youngling, your experience has unbalanced you."

"Perhaps so," Enggi persisted stubbornly. "But I am now not content to go on as before. I believe I will study these things."

"There was one who had some such idea," the first scout remembered.

"Where is he? I would seek him and learn!"

"You can't. A neutron sink got him. You haven't learned of *those* yet," the first scout made a sign of grim amusement.

But Enggi said, "What a loss. But see you, why do we learn so slow? The mind I shared could have absorbed that and the Eater and much else in a morn—in a very short cycle."

"It is our only, our right way."

"Nevertheless I am sure I shall do this thing. Perhaps some cycle I shall start by returning to the world I left, and trying to offer to exchange some parts of being for a time. If I could communicate with one of the star-longers, I'm sure something would be possible. I *felt* its need. And they might help me choose others."

The scouts were returning to travel mode; but the first scout, who had been most scornful, suddenly made an archaic sign, as if Enggi's thought had moved him.

"Fair faring . . . And now we must journey on."

With Delicate Mad Hands

CAROL PAGE, OR CP as she was usually known, was an expert at being unloved.

She was a sweetly formed, smallish girl of the red-hair-green-eyes-and-freckles kind, but her face was entirely spoiled and dominated by a huge, fleshy, obscenely pugged nose.

A nurse at the State Orphans' Crèche told her that a student OB had crushed it, in the birthing that killed her mother. What resulted was a truly hideous snout, the nostrils gaping level with her squinted eyes, showing hair and mucus. The other children called her Snotface.

As she grew older she became CP, and later yet, when her natural fastidiousness was known, the spacers called her Cold Pig, sometimes to her face.

Had CP been officially born to one of the world's ruling Managers, a few passes with a scalpel would have returned that snout to its dainty pixie form; her eyes would have been as nature intended, provocatively tilted green stars, and her lips would have retained their delicious curves. Then, too, her skin would have remained cream-and-rose petals, instead of its dry angry workhouse red, and her slim fingers would have stayed delightful. The lack of these amenities cost the world a girl of delicate, impish beauty—but this world was precariously recovering from many and much more terrible losses, and individual desolations counted for little.

CP was, in fact, lucky to be alive at all.

At fifteen her mother had been assigned to a visiting Manager who fancied virgins. She became pregnant through an unexpected delay in his schedules. He had become fond enough of the child so that when he saw how passionately she wanted her baby, and how she dreaded her destined future, he took the trouble to find a place for her in a State hospital. Here, of course, she died, but the baby, CP, retained her place-rights in the State Enclave.

This Enclave was one of a small number of city-form complexes on clean ground, where a shadowy form of old-style middle-class life was maintained. It served as a source of skilled labor and very occasional potential Managers. CP's basic health needs were attended to and she was placed in the Enclave's Orphans' School, where she became Snotface.

Here CP developed two traits, the first well known and the second totally secret.

What was known to all was that she was a hard, smart worker—tireless, unstoppable. Whatever came her way, she drove herself into the first percentile at it, and looked for more. It presently became clear what she was aiming at—in a school where mere survival was a feat, CP was dreaming of an all but impossible achievement: Space Crew Training.

She was doing it by simple hard work, undistracted, of course, by anyone who wanted personal relations with a Snotface. Whatever could conceivably be of help, she learned, fast and well. She plowed from arithmetic through calculus into vector math, she tackled metallurgy, electronics, computers of any and all kinds. Astronomy she devoured. Being a realist, she neglected no menial art—metal-cleaning, nutrition, space cookery, nursing, massage, the twenty-seven basic sexual stimulations, how to fix any common appliance, space laundry. She took a minor in space medicine. And always she went at engines, engines, more engines, and whatever she could find on orbital flight and thrust maneuvers. Her meager State allowance she saved from childhood until she could actually afford simple flying lessons at the Enclave strip.

And she made it—the incredible quantum leap into Basic Space Crew Training. A mathematician who had never touched a woman pushed her name, a State test administrator who wanted to up his school averages was of use. A general shortage of support personnel for the vital asteroid mining program helped. But basically it was her own unquenchable drive for the stars that carried her up.

Lots of people longed to go to space, of course; among other things, the spacers' life was thought to be a privileged one. And people admired the stars, when they could be seen. CP's longing wasn't unusual; it was only of another order of intensity. She didn't talk about it much —in fact, she didn't talk much at all—because she learned her fellows thought it was comical: Snotface in the stars. But, as one of them put it, "Better there than here."

In Basic Crew Training the story repeated itself; she simply worked twice as hard. And her next small savings went for a medical operation—not on her nose, as any normal girl would, but on the sterilization required of female students, for which they had to pay, if they wanted to get to actual flight. (For space-station workers it was desirable too, but not compulsory.)

And she made it there too, relatively easily. At nineteen she certified for work in space. She was ready to be assigned off-planet. Here, oddly, her dreadful looks helped. In her interview she had asked particularly for the far-out exploratory flights.

"Holy Haig," the young interviewer said to his superiors on the Assignment Board. "Imagine being cooped up for a year with that face! Stick her in the far end of station sewage reclamation, I say."

"And you'd be a damn fool, sonny. What caused the abort on the last Titan trip? Why were there three fatal so-called accidents on the last six Trojan runs? Why do so many computers 'accidentally' dump parts of the log on a lot of the long missions? We lost the whole mineralogical analysis of that good-looking bunch of rocks on the far side of the Belt. If you recall, we still don't know where we'll get our cesium. Why, junior?"

The young Personnel man sobered quickly.

"Ah . . . personality tensions, sir. Stress, clashes, unavoidable over long periods to men in confined quarters. The capsule-design people are working on privacy provisions, I understand they have some new concepts—"

"And to these tinderboxes you want to add an even reasonably attractive woman, sonny? We know the men do better with a female along, not only for physiological needs but for a low-status, non-competitive servant and rudimentary mother figure. What we do *not* need is a female who could incite competition or any hint of tension for her services. We have plenty of exciting-looking women back at the stations and the R & R depots, the men can dream of them and work to get back to them. But on board a long flight, what we need sexually is a human waste can. This—who is it?—Carol Page fits the bill like a glove, and she has all these skills as a bonus, if her marks mean anything. Talk about imagining a year with 'that face'—can you imagine any crew who wasn't blind or absolutely crazy experiencing the faintest additional tension over *her?*"

"I certainly see what you mean, sir—I was dead wrong. Thank you, sir."

"Okay, skip it. Hell, if she works out at all she may actually be a fair asset."

And so it was that CP went out to space, with a clause in her Articles certifying her for trial on long-run work.

On her very first run, a check on a large new incoming asteroid apparently dislodged from cis-Plutonian orbit, she proved the senior Personnel man right. She cleaned and dumped garbage and kept the capsule orderly and in repair at all times, she managed to make the food tastier than the men believed possible, she helped everybody do anything disagreeable, she nursed two men through space dysentery and massaged the pain out of another's sprained back; she kept her mouth strictly shut at all times, and performed her sexual duties as a "human waste can" with competence, although she could not quite successfully simulate real desire. (It was after this trip that she began to be known as Cold Pig.) She provoked no personal tensions; in fact, two of the crew forgot even to say good-bye to her, although they gave her superior marks in their report forms.

After several repetitions of this performance she began to be regarded by the Planners as something of an asset, as the Personnel chief had predicted. The crews didn't exactly love her, and made a great exhibition of groaning when Cold Pig showed up on their trip rosters; but secretly they were not displeased. Cold Pig missions were known to go well and be as comfortable as possible. And she could fill in for half a dozen specialties in emergencies. Things never went totally wrong with Cold Pig aboard. The Pig began to be privately regarded as lucky. She achieved a shadowy kind of status in the growing space network.

But not with Captain Bob Meich, on whose ship, *Calgary,* her story begins. Captain Bob Meich loathed her, and despised a certain fact about Cold Pig that was the most precious possession of her life.

Among the various Articles of Contract by which she was bound, there were two unusual clauses that were all she had worked for, and which she prized above life: Cold Pig, almost alone among thousands of women in space, was fully certified for solo flight.

She had insisted on a general flight clause at first signing, and she had the attested experience to back it up. Authority showed no particular resistance: space work includes thousands of hours of dull routine ferrying of stuff from here to there, which the men disliked, and quite a few station women were allowed to help out. Cold Pig's looks were helpful here too; clearly her goings and comings would never cause a ripple. But Cold Pig had her sights set higher than this.

Once in space, she set out to achieve a solo cert for every type of rocket going. She piled up flight time between all her assignments. She would fly anything anywhere, even if it meant three months done in foul air, herding a rock in an old torch with a broken-down air regenerator she could barely keep functional. Her eagerness to fly the lousiest trips slowly made her an asset here, too.

The payoff came when there was a bad rock-hit on a hot new short-run mission; Cold Pig not only saved a couple of lives, but flew the new model home alone and docked it like a pro. The wounded captain she had saved was grateful enough to help her get the second Article she coveted, the big one: it was formally stipulated that if a scout became disabled on a multiship mission, Carol Page would be assigned as replacement to take over his mission and ship, solo, until he recovered. This was extended to include flying the mother ship itself should all other crew be totally disabled.

Thus it was that one day Cold Pig came head to head with Captain Bob Meich of the *Calgary*, on the extreme-range mission on the far side of Uranus, with four of the ship's five scouts out on long exploratory flights. Don Lamb, the fifth and last, lay stranded helpless in his sleeper with a broken hip, and his scout ship idled in its berth.

"No cunt is going to fly off my ship while I'm breathing," Meich said levelly. "I don't give a flying fuck what your Articles say. If you want to make a point of it back at Station you can try. Or you can have a little accident and go out the waste hole, too. I am the captain and what I say goes."

"But, sir, that data Don's ship was assigned to is supposed to be crucial—"

He glared coldly at her; not sane, she saw. Nor was she, but she didn't know that.

"I'll show you once and for all what's crucial. Follow me, Pig." He spat out the name.

She followed him to the scout access tunnel; all the ports but one were empty. He opened the port of Don's scouter and crawled into the small capsule. *Calgary*'s pseudo-gravity of rotation was heavy out here; she could hear him grunting.

"Watch." He jerked the keys from the console and pocketed them. Then he yanked free the heavy pry-bar, and deliberately smashed it again and again into the on-board computer. Cold Pig was gasping.

He crawled out.

"Take your pants off."

He used her there on the cold grids beside the wreckage of her hopes, used her hard and with pain, holding her pants across her ugly face so she nearly smothered.

At one point a bulge in her shirt pocket attracted his notice: her notebook. He jerked it out, kneeling his weight hurtfully on her shoulders, and flipped through it.

"What the hell's this? *Poetry?*" He read in ferocious falsetto scorn: *"With delicate mad hands against his sordid bars*—aagh!" He flung the little book savagely toward the waster. It went skittering heavily across the grids, tearing pages.

Cold Pig, supine and in pain, twisted to see it, could not suppress a cry.

Meich was not normally a sexual man; several times she had felt him failing, and each time he slapped her head or invented some new indignity; but now he grinned jubilantly, not knowing that he had sealed his own fate. He jerked her head forward and, finally, ejaculated.

"All right. That's as close as you get to flying, Pig. Just remember that. Now get my dinner."

He was tired and withdrawn; he hit her covered face once more and left her. Cold Pig was grateful for the cover; she hadn't cried before in space—not, in fact, for years. Before dressing she rescued the little notebook, put it in a different pocket.

"Pig!" He may have had a moment's worry that he'd killed her. "Get that food."

"Yes, sir."

Quite insane now, she smiled—a doubly horrible effect on her bloodied face—and went to do as he ordered, smoothly, efficiently as always. Don was awake, too, by now, looking curiously at her. She offered no explanation, merely inquired what he'd like to eat.

The dinner she produced was particularly tasty; she used some of her carefully hoarded spices to disguise any possible taste from another carefully hoarded ingredient—though she knew from long-ago paramed school it was tasteless.

The fact that she was crazy was made clear by her choice. She had other capabilities; she could have served a meal from which neither Don nor the captain would ever have wakened. In fact, she did give one such to Don, who had always been minimally decent to her. But for the captain she had another, and as it turned out, more perilous plan. Cold Pig was human; she wanted him to *know*.

He ate heartily. Another type of person might have been made slightly suspicious by the niceness, comprising just the foods she knew he was fondest of. Or by her compliant, quietly agreeable manner. To Bob Meich it only confirmed what his father had taught him, that all women needed was a little knocking about, to be shown who was boss. He announced thickly something to this effect to Don, on his bunk in the next "room"; expecting no answer and getting none.

Don was young, the captain mused. Too soft. He still talked about his mother. When Don got better he would teach him a thing or two about handling women.

Presently he began to slump toward the special dessert CP served him. Feeling some irony, she put his "nightcap" bottle where he liked it, within easy reach. She was impatient now, there was much to do. Waiting, she had to admire his extraordinary physical vitality. A dose that ought to have brought quick oblivion took a few minutes to work fully on him. She began to worry that he might hear Don begin to hyperventilate, but he gave no sign of this. Finally Meich stared about, focused on her, shouted "Wha—?", and half rose before he went down for good.

She should have been warned.

But he *was* completely unconscious—she snapped her fingers by his ear, sprinkled salt on his exposed eye to make sure. She could get to work.

First she wanted to check on Don. She had saved enough of the substance she had fed him to serve her own necessities, and she wanted to see how painful it might be.

Don was half off his bunk, the last spasms subsiding into occasional leg jerks. His face was not excessively distorted, only sweat-covered, and the mouth was bloody. He'd bitten almost through his tongue, she found. But it did seem to have been quick. There was no heartbeat now except for one last faint thud that came during the minute she listened. Despite herself, she wiped his face a little, closed his eyes, and laid a hand for an instant on his soft brown hair. He *had* been considerate once.

Then she went to work, hard and fast. She blunted one scalpel and another—those suits and air tubes were tough —and had to go to pliers and other tools before she had things to her satisfaction. Next she got all essentials tied or taped in place. She also disconnected a few alarms to keep bedlam from breaking out prematurely. Early in the process, Meich startled her by sliding out of his chair, ending head down under the table.

One of the air cannisters she'd wrestled loose rolled under the table too, the cut end of its hose wagging. This she noticed only subliminally, it didn't seem to matter. She was busy undogging heavy seals.

The main air-pressure alarm in the pilot's chamber was very loud. It roused Bob Meich.

He rolled convulsively, and pushed himself half upright, overturning table and seats, opening, closing, opening his eyes wide with obvious effort.

What he saw would probably have stunned a lesser man to fatal hesitancy. The room was in a gale—papers, clothes, objects of all description were flying past him, snapping out of the half-open main port.

The port was opening farther. As he looked, the suited, helmeted figure of Cold Pig pulled the great circular port seal back to its widest extent and calmly latched it. Alarms were howling and warbling all over the ship as air left from everywhere at once and pressure dropped; total uproar. Then the sounds faded as the air to carry them went out. The last to remain audible was a far faint squeal from the interior of Don's scouter. Then near silence.

CP had wondered whether Meich would go first for his suit or directly to the door and herself.

His reflexes carried him, already gasping in airlessness, to the suit that hung on the wall behind, standing straight out as it tugged to fly. One heavy boot had already rolled and shot out the port—no matter, the helmet was there. Emergency suits were emplaced throughout *Calgary*, which was partly what had taken her so long.

He was halfway into it, staggered against the wall, when he saw the cuts. He grunted—or perhaps shouted, the air was now too thin to carry sound—and fell to his knees clasping the helmet. But he couldn't or didn't put it on—his dying eyes were still sharp enough to catch the neatly sliced air hoses. The helmet couldn't help him, it was now connected to nothing.

His mouth opening and closing, perhaps yelling curses, he toppled to the floor, taking great strangled gulps of near-vacuum. Finally he rolled again beneath the table.

His last gesture was to grab the bolted-down table leg with one strong pink hand, to fight the pull that would carry him out the port. He held there through the last spasm CP decided was death. She couldn't see him fully, she wanted neither to touch him nor to peer, but he was totally moveless. Man cannot live without air. Not even a Meich, she told herself.

In her savage heart she was a shade disappointed that he had not put on the useless helmet. Further, she would have been better pleased never to have to see that face.

The gale was subsiding, the pull from the port was almost gone. CP waited impatiently until the VACUUM light flashed on the console; it was time to get to work. Don should go first.

Outside the port was a rushing, flickering grayness— the starfields flashing by as *Calgary* rolled. Only ahead and astern was there relatively stable vision. Ahead lay steadier stars, she knew—she dared not, of course, lean out to look—while behind lay the great dim starlit disk of Uranus, flame-edged on one limb. They were orbiting in outward-facing attitude, to maximize the chance of observing any events on the planet. By chance—she hadn't had endurance enough to plan—*Calgary* was just coming into that arc of her orbit where the sun and the world of men were almost directly in line beyond the planet.

Good. She hooked a safety web across the open port, and walked, cautious of any remaining air pockets, into the chamber where Don lay.

She had prepared jato units to send the corpses as fast as possible down out of orbit and falling into Uranus. There would of course be no science-fiction nonsense about macabre objects orbiting *Calgary;* certainly not after she was on her way out and away forever—how she longed to start!—but more practically, she wanted no accidental discovery of the corpses. It would be, of course, a million-to-one freak. But freaks happen. CP knew that. In *Calgary*'s attitude, the temptation to set the jets directly at Uranus was strong, but she must arrange them to decelerate instead; most efficient.

She was figuring out the settings as she bent over Don. The hypo she had prepared in case Meich went for her was still clenched, almost hidden, in one glove. She must put it down somewhere safe.

As she reached toward a locker her body was touched from behind.

Terror. *What—*

An arm clamped hard around her neck.

As it passed her faceplate she had a glimpse of muscles and unmistakably pink, hairless skin.

A dead man had come after her. Meich had come back from death to kill her—was killing her now.

It would indeed have been Meich's impulse and delight to maul and kill her with his bare hands. But he was impeded. One hand was pressing the cut end of an air-tank hose to his mouth. And it is not easy in vacuum to batter a body in a pressure suit, nor to choke a neck enclosed in a hard helmet base. So he was contenting himself with yanking out her air hoses first, intending to get at her when she weakened, and keep her alive long enough to fully feel his wrath.

His first great jerk almost sent her reeling, but he had a leg hard about hers, holding her close.

Cold Pig, aghast to the bones, didn't keep her head. Adrenaline rush almost stopped her heart.

All was gone from her save only reflexes. The hand holding the hypo came round in one drive of horror-heightened power and precision—the needle he hadn't seen was there went straight in, against all likelihood not bending, not breaking, not striking plastic or bone, right through the suit he had pulled up, through liner, skin, and visceral sheath, while CP's clumsy gloved fingers found the triggers and her terrified muscles exerted impossible strength. The discharge shot directly into liver and stomach and ran out lodged in the lining of his renal vein. The strike was so clean Meich may never have felt it. He didn't know he was now truly a dead man. Or would be in seconds.

And seconds counted.

He had torn her air tubes loose, she was without air save only for the tiny amount lodged in her helmet and suit. And he was clamped to her, arm and leg. She began to choke, partly from sheer panic, as she twisted in his dying grasp, not understanding at first what was happening. The force of her turning blow had carried her partway round; she contorted frantically, and finally saw the air tank he was holding and the hose end he breathed from.

It took precious instants for her to understand that she must open her faceplate and get that air hose to her mouth.

Somehow, in spite of his mad battering and wrenching, she opened up. Dying girl fought with man for the hose end. She could not possibly pry loose his fingers, though she broke one. But the lethal drug was telling on him—she finally butted his head aside with her helmeted one, and managed to gulp air hissing from the hose he held.

In one last spasm of hate he tried to fling the air tank away from them both. But the tank struck her body. She held on.

And then it was over, really over at last. Meich lay slumped grotesquely at her feet, against Don's bunk.

It took infinite time for her to stop shaking. She vomited twice, fouling herself, but since the hose end was free she didn't aspirate it. She watched, watched, for any motion or breath from the twice-dead man. Only the fear that the wildly escaping air—so precious—would give out, finally got her moving rationally.

It was almost more than her fingers could do to reconnect her hoses, fit a spare for the damaged one, wipe out and close her faceplate. She would have to live and work for a time in her own vomit, which she found appropriate.

And there was much work to do, in vacuum, before she could reseal *Calgary*. It was now getting very cold.

She had a message to send, and she wanted to dump everything of the men's before repressurizing, to use the waste flush later as little as possible. The bodies she would send out first, right now.

This time there was no question of Don preceding; she laid shuddering hands on Meich's legs and dragged him to the port and the jato rig. She managed to stop herself from leaning out to make sure he had jetted clean away, not caught on some part of *Calgary* to clamber back at her. But she did permit herself to go to the stern port and watch his jet dwindle among the whirling stars.

Then Don. Then everything she could lay hands on or dump from lockers, even to letters, private caches, the pinups on walls, even the duty roster. All, all went out, and did orbit *Calgary,* but only for a time.

Finally she unlatched and wrestled shut the cold main port.

Then without waiting to repressurize, she was free to yield to heart's desire. She didn't even bother to sit down, she simply ran through the basic emergency ignition sequence—*Calgary* was already in perfect attitude—and slammed the main thrust over and on.

Softly, with slowly growing, inexorable power, *Calgary* departed orbit and headed at maximum acceleration away from Uranus, away from Sol behind it, away from humanity, outward toward empty space and the unreachable stars.

Now the message.

She activated the high-gain transmitter, and plugged her suit mike in. And then Cold Pig undertook the first and last literary-dramatic exercise of her life. She was, after all, as noted, human.

First she keyed in the call signals for *Calgary*'s four other scouts, plus a general alarm. Next, gasping realistically, "—All scouts, do not try to return to *Calgary;* repeat, do not . . . try return to *Calgary* . . . there's nothing . . . there . . . Head for . . . the . . . *Churchill.* —Wait, maybe *Calhoun* closer . . . repeat, *Calgary* . . . is not on station . . . do not try to return. . . . Wounded, will try to return log . . . so much blood . . . Cause: Captain Robert Meich dead, self-inflicted . . . gunshot . . . Lieutenant . . . Donald Lamb also dead by gunshot . . . inflicted by Captain Meich. . . . Both bodies lost in space . . . Captain Meich shot Don and . . . unsealed . . . main port. . . . He took Don's body, and . . . shot himself in the abdomen before . . . going out. . . . Cause: Captain Meich said we were docked at invisible spy station, when Don tried to stop him . . . open port he said." Here her words were coming in a soft fainting rush, but clearly, oh clear: "He said Don might be an alien and shot him, he was carrying gun three days . . . sleeping with it. . . . Cold, blood . . . he made me strip and tied me to galley post but Don threw me . . . helmet and air tank but I—have . . . shot wounds in body . . . since yesterday . . fear *Calgary* lost, Captain Meich fired escape course, broke computer . . .

cold . . . trans . . . mission . . . ends . . . will try . . ." And
then very weakly, "Don't repeat don't return . . ."

After a few more deathly sounds, she unplugged, leaving the transmitter on. It was voice-activated, it wouldn't
waste power, but she must be careful about any sounds
she made, especially when air came back.

Then she went carefully around the ship, sealing off
everything but necessary living space, to conserve air,
and turned the main air valves to pressurize.

Finally she snapped out the log cassette in a realistically fumbling manner, carefully tearing the tape head
off before where she knew her argument with Meich began. It would look as if she had simply torn it clumsily
loose. To add verisimilitude—they would test, oh yes—
she reopened one of the cuts Meich's blows had left on
her face and dabbed her fresh blood on cassette and can-
ister. The cannister went into a wall slot, which would,
when activated, encase it in its own small jato device with
homing signal to Base. She fired it off.

The data from *Calgary*'s exploratory mission would ar-
rive, some day or year, near Base, beeping for pickup.
That much, she thought, she owed the world of men.
That much and no more.

The air pressure was rising slowly. No leaks so far,
but it was not yet safe to unsuit. She checked the scanners once, to make sure Uranus and Sol were dwindling
straight astern, and set the burn to turn off in an hour. If
the fuel lasted that long.

Then she simply sat down in the co-pilot's chair,
leaned back in her filthy helmet in the comfortless suit,
and let herself lose consciousness. When she awoke she
would be far enough away to turn the transmitter off.

She was headed for the Empire. Whose name, she
knew quite rationally, was Death.

When she came to, the main torch was off. Had it run
out of fuel? No, turned off, she saw, checking the console; there was still some energy left. Her eyes, nose, and
lips were crusted, almost closed. Air pressure was back
to cabin-normal.

Gratefully she opened her face plate, unlatched and
lifted off the heavy helmet assembly that had saved her

life from Meich. Don't think of all that, she told herself. Never again. Never ever again to suffer anything of man. Think of the fact that you're dehydrated and ravenous and dirty.

Gulping juice and water alternately, she checked position. She must have been unconscious a long, long time, they had passed Neptune's orbit; still accelerating, slightly. She should have saved the main burn till she was freer of Sol's gravity; she was glad she hadn't.

She got herself unsuited and minimally washed. There was a big cleanup to do. But first she'd better make herself count up her supplies, which was to say, her life.

She had long ago made the rough calculation that it was somewhere in the range of a hundred to a hundred fifty Earth-days.

Food—no problem. The dehydrated supplies were ample to take six men and herself another year.

Water was more serious. But the reclamation unit was new and worked well, all tanks were full. She would be drinking H_2O that had passed through all their kidneys and bladders the rest of her life, she thought. But in the humans of her Earth such thoughts no longer could evoke revulsion. She had drunk unrecycled water only a few times in her whole life; it had been desalinated water from a far sea. The importation of water-ice asteroids to Earth had been one of Base's routine jobs. *Calgary* even had a small potential supply of fresh water, if she could reach it without too much loss of air. They had encountered a clean ice rock and lashed it to the substructure of the hull.

She was gazing about, checking around the main console, at which she had never been allowed to sit before, deferring calculation of oxygen, when an odd glint above caught her eye. She stood up in the seat to peer at the thing embedded in the ceiling. A camouflaged lens.

She had stumbled onto one of the secret spy-eyes and spy-ears placed in all ships. She put a screwdriver between its rim and her ear, and caught a faint whirring. Somewhere in the walls a tape deck reeled. It had of course recorded the true events on *Calgary*, and the fish-eye lens was set so that her present course-and-position readings would be recorded.

It was not, she was sure from former tales and trials at Base, transmitting now. People had confided that the eyes and ears sent off their main data in supercompressed blips, at rather long, random intervals. The detailed reading would wait until *Calgary* was back in human hands.

For that, they would have to catch her first. She smiled grimly through cracked lips.

But had it already sent off a data blip while she was unconscious? Or in the time before, for that matter? No way to tell. If so, her story would be only an addition to the catalog of her crimes. If not, good.

How to deactivate it, without tearing out the walls, or causing it to transmit in terminal alarm? Others must have tried it before her. She would have to think hard, and discard her first impulses.

Meanwhile she contented herself with taping over the lens. Then she thought for a moment, and continued searching. Sure enough, now that she knew what to look for, she found the backup—or perhaps the main one; it was much more skillfully hidden. She taped it, thinking too late that perhaps the blanking-out itself was a trigger to it to blip. Well, no help for that now. At least she was free of the feeling of being watched. This was actually a strange new sensation. People took the fact of being covertly observed almost for granted. Brash souls made jokes about what must be mountains of unread spy-eye data stored who knew where and how, perhaps an asteroid full.

She sank back down in the comfortable pilot's couch. If there was a third backup on her now, good luck to it.

The oxygen.

Even before she had dumped a shipful of air, the oxygen situation had not been very healthy. The regeneration system was old-style, dependent on at least some outside sunlight. The weak light at Uranus's orbit hadn't been enough for it; some of the bionic compounds had gone bad, and the regenerator was near the end of its life.

This had been well understood before the . . . incident. It had been planned to cut short the time in total shadow by establishing a semipolar semiorbit—Uranus rotated almost "lying down" relative to the solar plane—so as to maximize light. And the *Calhoun* was headed to an emergency rendezvous with them as far out as possible, to pass over oxygen and regenerator equipment. The water-ice rock might have had to be used inefficiently for air; they were on the lookout for others. Not a crisis, as such things went, but a potentially uncomfortable prospect.

Now she dreaded to think what a period of cold vacuum might have done to the system, and made herself go check. Damage, all right—some trays that had been photosynthesizing showed brown edges. Not a total wipeout, though, as she had feared. It would take care of some of her CO_2, more if she rigged emergency lights. She counted and recounted the suit tanks, and checked the high-compression ship supply of oxygen.

The answer came out surprisingly near her rough guess —oxygen for 140 days max, ten weeks. Actually the CO_2 buildup would probably sicken her seriously before that, unless she could contrive some help.

First was to supply all possible light of the correct wavelengths to the regenerator trays. She sorted out filters, power cords, and robbed all the lights she could spare from the rest of the ship, until she had all trays as fully lit as possible. She even found a packet of presumably long-dead culture starter—"seeds"—and planted them in the hope of restarting two dead trays.

That took hours, perhaps days; she kept no track, only stopping to eat and drink when the need was strong. The trays were huge and heavy, and she was sore. But she felt nothing but joy—joy in her perfect freedom. For the first time in years she was alone and unsupervised. But more: for the first time in her life she was truly free for good, accountable to no one but herself. Alone and *free* among her beloved stars.

The job completed, too tired to clean up herself and *Calgary*, she staggered back to the pilot's couch with a cold meal, and alternately ate and gazed out at those starfields straight ahead that could be seen through the gyro-stabilized scope.

It wasn't enough. She wanted it all. What did she have to fear from the physical deterioration of zero gee?

She sank into sleep in the big pilot's chair, planning.

Over the next two Earth-days she cleaned ship intermittently, between work on her main task: to stop the rotation that gave *Calgary* its "gravity." She was careful to use as little energy as possible, letting every tiny burst take fullest possible effect before thrusting more.

Outside, the stars changed from a rushing gray tapestry to a whirl of streaks, shorter and shorter, steadying and condensing to blazing stubs against perpetual night.

Her touch was very accurate. At the end she scarcely had to brake. The bright blurs and stubs shrank and brightened—until, with a perceptible jolt, there they were! Stars of all colors and brilliances, clouds dark and light, galaxies—tier beyond tier, a universe of glory.

CP toured the ship, unscreening every viewport. *Calgary* had many; she was an old belly-lander built originally to shuttle from the Mars sling, in the days when seeing outside with the living eyes was still important to men. *Calgary* even had a retracted delta wing, unused for who knew how long.

There were more cleanup chores to do as all gravity faded out and objects began to float. But always CP would pause as she passed a port, and revel silently in the wonders and beauties on every side. Her own wretched reflection in the vitrex bothered her; soon she turned off even the last lights, so that *Calgary*'s interior became a dark, starlit pocket of space-night.

Ahead of *Calgary* lay, relatively, nothing. She was flying to Galactic North, toward a region where the stars were relatively few and very far, without even a dust drift or any object closer than many human lifetimes. This didn't trouble her. She turned off most of the forward scanners and sensors, wanting to spend her last days studying and dwelling mentally in the richer, wondrous starfields on all sides.

The condition of weightlessness didn't bother her at all. She was one of those rare ones who found sustained pleasure in the odd life of free-fall. The exasperations of toolboxes squirmly unpacking themselves when opened merely amused her. And *Calgary* had many ingenious old zero-gee life and work aids. While CP's body healed, she was happy to be free of anything pressing her.

She was indeed grateful for all the comforts of the big

mother ship. She'd never intended to steal it. A scout, the scout Meich had denied her, would have sufficed. This trans-Uranus trip was the farthest out she could ever have expected to be allowed to go. When Don broke his hip it was simply luck: she had been debating how most humanely to incapacitate the last pilot, so that she could take his scout as her Articles promised. The small capsules weren't comfortable, little more than flying torches, but their ample power would have served to carry her out, and not been worth pursuit.

Out was all she craved. Out, outward forever, past Oort's cloud—would she be alive and lucky enough to detect a "sleeping comet"?—outward at greatest acceleration from Sol and all the world of men—out free, in freedom dying, all too soon dead—but her body still flying free. Never to be pursued, touched, known of by man or humanity.

Out to end among the stars. It was all she had dreamed of, worked and endured for, rationally.

No, not quite.

CP was not always rational, or rather, never "rational" at the core. There was always the thing she called for short the Empire.

It was noted before that CP had one total secret. The fact that she planned to steal a ship and fly out to her death she of course kept secret. But it was not her Secret, and it wasn't even unique. Others before her had now and then gone berserk under the strains of man's world, and taken off on death-flights to nowhere. Such loss of valuable equipment was spoken of rarely but very disparagingly, and accounted for much of the Managers' endless, stringent screening, testing, and rechecking practices in space. But this plan was not her Secret.

"The Empire" was. The Empire of the Pigs.

The Empire was everything and nothing. It was basically only a story, a voice unreeling endlessly in her head. It had started before she could remember, and gone on ever since. It accounted for the inhuman sanity of her behavior, for her unshakable endurance under intolerable stress. It was an insanity that kept her functioning with superior competence and rationality, and it was known or suspected by nobody at all.

Not even the prespace test psychologists with all their truth serums and hypnotic techniques and secret, ceaseless spy records over every private, drug-relaxed hour of her test month, not even their most artfully sympathetic human-to-human congratulatory wind-downs, which had in the end brought so many secrets to so many hard-guarded lips; none of it had unsealed CP's. Her Secret lived unsuspected, unhinted-at to any other human soul.

Somewhere in her early years she had seized a chance to study the disapproved findings of psychology. What she really wanted was to know if the voice in her head meant she was truly crazy, although she didn't admit that to herself. It probably did, she decided subliminally, and buried her Secret deeper. As usual, she also studied hard and efficiently in the brief time allowed, and this knowledge helped her later to fend off assaults on her mind and to gratify those who controlled her fate.

The story had started very early.

She'd always been told she looked like a pig. One day the honors children were given a great treat—a visit to the city zoo. Here she saw a real pig; in fact, a great boar and sow. She lingered to read every word on the cage-card. It told her how intelligent pigs were—and by nature cleanly, too. And somehow there started in her small head the story of the Empire of the Pigs.

The Empire was very far away, on Earth perhaps beyond the Chicago Pits. At first everyone in the Empire looked just like her, and life was simply very good. Every night, no matter how exhausted she was, Snotface would live there for a few instants. It took months of such instants to develop each satisfying aspect or event.

In the tale she always referred to herself as the Pig Person. At some early point things changed a little: she had volunteered to be surgically altered for temporary exile among Yumans.

And then one day she was taught about the stars. Right in the classroom her world gave a sort of silent snap, and the Empire moved off Earth, forever. Perhaps the Voice started too, she never troubled to make sure. She couldn't think then; she feared being inattentive.

But that night excitement fought off fatigue as she thought of the Empire in the stars. It was relatively quiet in the dormitory; she remembered that a star or something said very, very faintly but clearly, "Yes."

She fell asleep.

This starward move gave whole new dimensions to the physical Empire. She busied herself with adjustments and composing new, delicious stories of life there and the joys she would later return to.

Another quiet night the Voice said, stronger, "Come."

Such events she accepted tranquilly but happily. She would certainly come. Although even then a tiny part of her mind knew too that her return would also mean her end. This didn't disturb her; dying wasn't uncommon in Snotface's world.

The story soon grew very complicated, developed and abandoned sub-branches, and changed greatly over the years.

Quite early the Empire people changed from being literal pigs to a somewhat shadowy physical form—though always entirely real. In one phase they ceased to be of two sexes. About that time her unexplained exile also changed, first to an exciting spy mission. Real, Earthly pigs were sometimes failed spies, or persons being punished by some power. In one episode the Pig Person rescued them and helped them resume their real forms. "Pig" also took on an acronymic meaning, which she didn't use much: "Persons in Greatness." One of the main branches of the story, which tended to take over as she grew older, also had a title: "The Adventures (or Reports) of the Pig Person on Terra."

All this complex activity kept the deep inside of CP's head very busy, without in the least interfering with all her learning and work.

By the time she went to space, a typical entry might transcribe thus (in this branch she wasn't primarily a spy but a stranded, ship-wrecked traveler trying—successfully—to work out her way home):

Today the Pig Person judged best to open her legs twice to accommodate the hard, fleshy protuberances characterizing two male Yumans. One Yuman requested her to conceal her face during the procedure, so she improvised a mask from her underwear (see note on male-female Yuman attire). The Yuman appeared gratified. This is important because on return from this flight he will be promoted to Personnel Assignment, where he could help the Pig Person acquire more skills on some of these Yuman-type spacecraft. The Pig Person also made a mental note to improve this technique by making a real mask—better, masks of several types—as soon as materials can be procured. How her friends in the Empire will enjoy the notion that some poor Yumans cannot look at her fine Pig face without losing the ability to erect their absurd organs! But however amusing this is, the Pig Person must positively bend all efforts to returning to the Empire before all her information becomes obsolete.

So spoke the true, silent Voice of Cold Pig nightly—sometimes, in bad periods, hourly—in the dark shell under her shining red hair.

Or was it her voice?

Mostly, yes. By it she changed almost unbearable humiliation and pain into "funny" stories.

But there was another real Voice, too. The main one.

It didn't always speak in words. At first, and much of the time since, it "spoke" like a feeling, a sense of being listened to encouragingly, and responded to, quietly and often volubly, just beyond her hearing range.

But more and more, in those early years, the Voice rose to blend exactly with her own, as she composed-recited to herself the life and events of the Empire of the Pigs. Sometimes the Voice came alone into a mental silence, though what it told her wasn't usually quite clear. Very occasionally it rose to complete clarity; for example it had four times given her the answers during her myriad academic exams.

Since the answers the voice provided were actually known to CP, only lost from tiredness, she was subconsciously reassured. This proved that the Voice wasn't a craziness, but merely what the book had called a "projection" of her own memories, seeming to come from outside.

Such projections, she learned, weren't uncommon, especially under stress. And in dreams.

As for the Voice giving her new ideas, elaborating details about the Empire, she read that creators, artists and writers—usually the mediocre ones—often projected their inspirations onto some outside source like their "Muse."

CP was wholly Noncreative in any normal way, a personality deficit considered valuable, even essential, among non-Managers. Her secret Empire-story and the Voice must be some rudimentary Creativeness leaking out, luckily in a private way.

She took care to memorize every possible Noncreative test response and attitude, and sealed her Secret tighter.

And the Voice only rarely gave her totally new information. On a few occasions it had seemed to pull her from the Empire to tell her about—she was not quite sure what, only that there was often an accompanying large visual impression of blue or lavender, and once, very clear, a gray hand. It was doing something with a complex of fabric. . . . All meaningless, afterward.

What wasn't meaningless was an indescribable personal-reference "transmission." The voice *knew her*. And now and then it repeated, "Come."

Twice it said very clearly, "Waiting."

All this concerned space too, she was sure. Well, her one wish in life was to go to space. Projection again, nothing to worry about.

"I will. I will. I will. I will . . . The Pig Person shall go to the stars," she told the voice. "The Pig Person will end among the stars. Soon. Soon."

Now as she settled to her last days, on *Calgary*, she—or the voice—composed as usual a succinct account of all that had passed. But it was cast in quite new terms. Gone were the flat hard tones of unutterable sadness, the terse descriptions of the intolerable. She still spoke as the "Pig Person"—but this person had at last found freedom and joy, found her way to the stars. A way that would lead her back to the Empire, could her human life be long enough to reach it. It would not be. But she would at least end on her free way home.

Thinking this, it came to her that her chance-determined course might not be quite right. Perhaps this was even told her. Conscious with most of her mind that she was giving way to real insanity, she carefully scanned the forward field. Empty, of course, save for the faint far stars. And yes—the Voice was right—she was not quite on course. She must correct just a trifle. It was important.

On course for *where?*

For the first time she faced her madness abruptly, hard. *What* "right" course, en route to *what?* To nothing —nothing but icy vacuum and nothingness and dying. She proposed to waste fuel "correcting" to an insane delusion? A delusion she knew perfectly well was born of her human need for support amid ugliness, rejection, and pain?

But if nothing lay ahead, how could the spent fuel matter?

Slowly, almost but not quite amused at herself, she gave in.

Her fingers played delicately over the thrust-angle keys, her eyes went back to the scope. Where? Where shall I come, show me! She let her eyelids almost close, feeling for it. *Where, where?*

And dreamily, but clear, it came to her: there. *Here . . .*

Random nonsense, she told herself angrily, almost turning away.

But the shadowy vector persisted clearly in her mind. She peered through her strongest scope, scanned every band of EM radiation. Absolutely nothing lay *there.*

"Come," the Voice sighed in her head. "Come. I have waited so long."

"Death calling," she muttered harshly. But the fact was, she couldn't be truly comfortable until she turned *Calgary* to head precisely that way.

Carefully, deliberately, she set in the course correction for Nowhere. She punched to activate. The burn was very brief, she had been as usual, accurate. *Calgary* shuddered imperceptibly, the starfield crawled slowly slightly slantwise, then steadied to a rest with almost no braking necessary, pointing exactly *there.*

And as it did so, the Empire died.

For the first time she could remember, the story that had run ceaselessly in her brain, the Voice that was mostly a feeling, fell silent. What had hit her? What had silenced her? Startled, yet somehow accepting, she stared about. Nothing had changed; it was simply gone. There was no Empire, no one to "report" to, ever again. She was alone. Or . . . was she? It didn't matter. Everything was all right. Had not the Voice been commanding her too, in its way? Now she was truly free of the very last outside orders.

She went back to her quiet routine of gazing, observing, using the scope and other analyzers on interesting objects. Of them all, she preferred the eye. She found an old but serviceable computer-enhanceable high-power scope in a rear locker, left unused in recent years when no one had desire nor time to look at things too far to give promise of gain. To her joy, with a bit of work it proved functional. She pored over star charts, identifying and memorizing. In some peculiar way, this activity was all right too, beyond her own personal fascination.

By using all the ports, she had a 360-degree field of view in all directions—the universe—and she scanned at least briefly, but systematically, over it all. A feeling almost like the old voice-in-her-head encouraged her. Habit, she knew. I'm projecting my own pleasure back at myself.

As the early days stretched to weeks—she kept only the vaguest track of time—she experienced only comfort. Small events: one of the regenerator trays she had planted "took," the other stayed dead. She scraped together a last sprinkle of seeds and tried again. She also arranged a contraption, a double-inlet tube that would carry her breath from her habitual seat and bunk directly to the trays, which at this time were actually short of CO_2. The later buildup to saturation and ensuing degeneration would go fast; she installed a gas sampler and alarm to give ample warning of the rise.

Absurdly, she minded the prospect of dying from simple oxygen lack less than the notion of positive poisoning by her own wastes. This was nonsense, because what she knew of physiology told her that internal CO_2 would be an agent of her death anyhow.

Despite her comfort, she made every possible effort at conservation. The possibilities were pitifully few, consisting primarily of minimal use of the waste flusher, which lost air. Even when she had collected quite a pile of the men's overlooked leavings—including souvenirs of Meich—she denied herself the luxury of flushing them out.

Aside from the star work, and simply indulging in a rest she'd never known, she occupied herself with recalling and writing down such words as had once struck her as wise, witty, or beautiful: sayings, doggerel, poetry, a few short descriptions of old-Earth phenomena no one she knew had ever seen—a clear sunrise, a waterfall— the names of a few people, mainly women, she'd respected. Effortfully, she even composed a short account of a striking memory—an eclipse she and other children had been allowed to see in the open.

She mulled unhurriedly over practical matters, such as whether the expenditure of oxygen necessary to bring in that ice-rock lashed to the hull would repay her in oxygen theoretically extractible from it. Quiet . . . a blissful life.

But one day came disturbance. The lone bow scanner chirped. Doubtless a malfunction; she moved to turn it off, then paused. This might signal an oncoming rock; she didn't want to die so. She activated another. To her surprise it lit in confirmation. For one horrifying instant fear seized her—could the human world have somehow pursued her here?

She turned on more pickups, was reassured—and then so amazed that she peered out visually to orient the scopes. Not a rock, or a rocket, not small but vast: ahead and slightly "above" her floated something world-sized— no, nearly sun-sized—very dimly lavender, glowing and ringed.

For another sickening instant she feared she had, incredibly, flown a circle and was coming back among Sol's outposts. But no; the scanners told her that the body occulting the forward field was nothing in Sol's family. Huge, her sensors told her, but relatively small-massed. The surface gravity, if she was seeing the surface, would be a little less than Earth-normal. It was definitely, though faintly self-luminous—a beautiful blue-rosy shade she had no name for.

And very highly radioactive.

Was she looking at a dead or dying star? Possible; yet this body conformed to nothing she knew of in the processes of star-death. Perhaps a star not dead, but still below the threshold of interior ignition? A star coming slowly to be born? Or one destined to remain thus, never to ignite to birth at all?

Without even considering it, she had automatically activated thrust and set in a course correction that would fly her straight at the body. Equally automatically, she noted that *Calgary*'s pile was so used out that she hadn't possibly enough fuel to shed her now tremendous velocity and slow *Calgary* into any kind of close orbit. She ignited thrust.

What was she doing—unconsciously planning to die by crashing into this silent mystery? Or, if it had atmosphere, be roasted to death in the friction of her fall? It was not the quiet death she had intended, among the eternal stars.

Yet approach she must. Approach, see, and know it, orbit closely if only for a last fiery instant.

She lost track of all time, as the mystery grew in the ports, with her terrible speed, from dim point to far disk to closer, larger, port-filling nearness. She was retrofiring repeatedly, trying to get effect from every precious erg, willing *Calgary* to slow as if her naked desire could affect the laws of physics.

Finally the time came when she felt uncomfortably upside down to the great surface; she expended a precious minimum of energy slowly righting *Calgary*'s attitude. On crazy impulse, she suited up, leaving only the faceplate open, and strapped herself in the pilot's cocoon. It was all futile madness—despite everything she could do, her velocity was impossibly too great. Still she retrofired intermittently, trying to judge exactly optimum angles of thrust, fighting the temptation to torch everything once and for all, straining back in the cocoon, willing, commanding, imploring aloud to *Calgary* to slow—slow—slow—slow—

And luck, or something logically nonexistent, was with her. She was still moving lethally, hopelessly too fast, but *Calgary* seemed to have shed more velocity than the computer predicted possible. The thing must be faulty; she took over completely from it, and against all calculated chance, achieved a brief quasi-orbit in what seemed to be the equatorial plane.

She could see the "surface" now—a smooth, softly glowing, vast-dappled, racing shield, which the sensors told her was cloud. Two hundred kilometers beneath that lay solid "ground," some of which registered as liquid. Expecting nothing but nitrogen-methane at best, CP glanced at the spectroscope—and lunged against her straps to slap on the backup comparators.

Same readings!

That cloud cover was oxygen-hydrogen: water vapor. And the basic atmosphere was 25 percent oxygen on a nitrogen base. She was looking at an atmosphere of Earth-normal quality.

Hastily she ran through the tests for various poisons; they were not there. This was preindustrial, prewar air such as CP had never breathed on Earth!

Except, of course, for its appalling radioactivity, which apparently emanated from ground level. It would quickly destroy her or any Earth-born living thing. To walk on this world, to breathe its sweet air, would be to die. In days, perhaps only hours.

Her orbit was decaying fast. The visible cloud was no more than a few thousand kilometers below her now. Soon she would hit the upper atmosphere—hit it like a skipped rock, and perhaps break open before *Calgary* burst to flame. The ship's old ablatives had been designed only for Mars, and deteriorated since. Slower; slow down, she pleaded, using the last full thrust of the pile. In her mind was a vivid picture of her oncoming doom at her present inexorable speed. Only moments of life remained to her —yet she was content, to have found, in freedom, this great wondrous world.

Belatedly recalling that Don's scout capsule was still on umbilical, she managed to reverse-drain its small fuel supply into two of *Calgary*'s back boosters that weren't operated off the pile. Slow down—slow! she willed, firing.

The small backfire did seem to slow her a trifle. She had abandoned the instruments, which foretold only her death, and was watching the cloud tear by below. *Slow down, slow down!* She pushed herself back so hard she ached, sensing, dreaming that the death clouds were rushing imperceptibly slower. The atmosphere that would kill her extended, of course, far above them. She was all but in it, the molecule counter was going red.

Then, while she noticed they were over "land," *Calgary* seemed actually, undeniably to slow further. The clouds below changed from a featureless stream to show perceptible dark-light gradients flashing by. Still far too fast, of course; but it was as if she was passing through the backward tug of some unknown field. Perhaps the effect of the denser molecules around her? But *Calgary* wasn't heating up. Some utterly alien energy was at work. Whatever it was, she needed more. Slow, much more. Desperately she urged it.

And *Calgary* slowed.

What mystery was helping her kill velocity? It had to be physical, explicable. But CP, knowing with part of her mind that she had gone crazy, gave herself over to a deep conviction that this was no impersonal "field." She *knew* it was connected in some way with her need, and with her visualizing—"broadcasting" mentally—her plight. Mad, she was. But she was being helped to slow.

Perhaps I'm already dead, she thought. Or perhaps she would come to, drugged and manacled, in Base Detention. What matter? She had reached her Empire's power, it was saving her at last.

Over and over again she "showed" the unknown her needs, her vulnerability, the onrushing terrors of impact and heat, all the while draining every tiniest output from the dying pile, which seemed to have regenerated slightly while she'd rested it.

And *Calgary* slowed, slowed, slowed as if flying through invisible cold molasses—so that the first wisps of atmosphere came past her at little more than common supersonic speeds. A miracle. There were no smashing impacts, only a jostling of loose objects, and very little heat. And then she was down to where the first visible tendrils of cloud rushed by.

It was so beautiful she laughed out loud—the blue-lavender-pearl streamers against the star-blazed night. For an instant she looked for *Calgary*'s shadow, and then checked herself and laughed again; this world had no sun, it had never known a shadow from the sky—all its light came from below, within.

Then she was in it, blinded, dependent only on her instruments. *Calgary* was barreling down, its orbital direction curving to a fall. It occurred to her that the delta wings would help now. Would they extend, and if so, would they tear off? She had an instant's neutral memory of another life, in which a captain's potential madness had driven him to a compulsive predeparture checkout of *Calgary,* even to the old, never-used wing, even to insisting that it be serviced to function. Strange.

She activated the extensors, pulled with all her strength on the manual backup. Gratings, groans—and the delta lurched from its slots and extended in the alien air, slowing *Calgary* into a yawing roll. She thanked fate that she had strapped in where she could reach the old flight controls. Now her hard Earthside flight training served her well; she soon had *Calgary* on a rough downward glide. The wings vibrated violently, but stayed on, even at this wild speed.

Down, down through two hundred kilometers of brightening cloud. Until she burst abruptly out of the lowest, lightest layer, and saw—yes—a world-ocean far below. This ocean glowed. She looked up and saw the cloud ceiling lit grape-blue, krypton-green, by its reflection.

Next moment she was over land, too high to see anything but swaths of new luminous colors. Glowing orange, smoky turquoise, brilliant creams and crimsons, with rich dark-purple curves and flowings here and there; a sublime downscape, with tantalizing illusions of pattern. Above her the solid sky was lit up varicolored reflecting it, as if an immense stained-glass window were shining from below.

The ocean under her again, this time much lower. She could see the lucent pale-green V where it broke on a small island. The surface seemed very calm, save for long, smooth swells. More V's of green-blue light came under her—an archipelago? Or—wait—was there *movement* down there? Impossible. She strained to see—and suddenly there could be no doubt. Twenty or thirty somethings were each trailing its brilliant V of wake, moving contrary to others.

Life.

Life! Whalelike mythical beasts? Or was this perhaps a warm, shallow puddle-ocean, in which great creatures, like the Earth's Cretaceous saurians, sported? Or—she dared not think it—ships? Whatever, minutes from her death, she had found, or been found by, the first alien life known to humanity; on a dark solitary, unseeable almost-sun.

She prayed aloud to no god to let her slow enough to have one sight of this marvel. To the unknown power that had helped her she sent desperate, fear-lit images of her onrushing crash, explosion, death—unless *Calgary* could be slowed enough for her to belly-land it in one piece. She had the momentary sense that the power was reluctant, perhaps tired—but desire to know more of this wonder drove her shamelessly. She pled with all her soul to slow more.

And sluggishly, but in time, response came. Once the slowing was so abrupt that her glide fell below *Calgary's* high stall speed. She went tail down and began to drop like a stone, until she found one last unbelievable gulp of fuel to send the ship back into level flight. She tried to send in careful detail the image of her needs. They were almost unfillable—to glide *Calgary* to some sort of bare, level landing place, large enough to absorb what would be her ground momentum. If only she could, once, *see* these marvels! No matter how injured she was, she longed only to die with her eyes filled with them.

Nothing but death lay ahead, but CP was in ecstasy such as she'd never dreamed of.

Releasing the controls for an instant, she flung her arms wide. "I name thee Cold Pig's Planet!" she said to Auln. (Auln? Whence did that come to her?) But no, she was not falling to the satellite of any sun. "I name thee Cold Pig's Dark Star!"

Appropriate, she thought wryly, grabbing the controls, and strapping in tighter. All those weary hours of Earth-flight kept returning to her aid. Skillfully she nursed the awkward old ship over the pale fires of this shoreless sea; she was too low to see beyond the far, high horizon to where land might lie. She could only fly straight with the direction of revolution toward where she remembered the continent bulged seaward.

Unsteady breezes tossed her, sometimes bringing her so low that *Calgary* barely skimmed the crests—and once she all but nosedived in, as she caught a flash of strange life, dark-bodied, playing in the waves. Too fast, too low, *Calgary* could not survive splashdown here. Resolutely she ignored all wonders, made herself concentrate on staying airborne, above what seemed a world on fire. The horizon was so weirdly high! This world was huge.

And then a line of brighter fire showed on the horizon ahead, seeming almost above her. Shore! But forested, she saw. Those lighted shapes were a solid wall of trees— she was hurtling toward a fatal crash. Frantically she pictured, pled for what she needed—and then saw that the forest wall was not solid, there was a great opening, an estuary slanting out. She swung *Calgary* to aim into it; she could see now that it wasn't a wide river, but a relatively small stream edged with swamp, almost treeless. Perfect. But coming at her fast, too fast—if only there could be headwind! She was prepared for anything now, had no wonder left but only gratitude as the sudden shore wind struck and slowed her.

Into the opening they tore, over the margin that appeared barest. Then *Calgary*'s belly structures hit sticky marshland, crushed clangorously—the ship bounced and careened past flying trees—flat-spun twice, throwing CP about in her straps—and went wing up, the down wing breaking off as it plowed fountains. And finally, incredibly, all motion stopped.

CP slowly, dizzily, stared around her at the cabin. No broken walls or glass, air pressure reading constant. The cabin seemed to be intact. Intact. She was down safe! And, apart from a few bruises, herself uninjured.

Her hearing was deadened by pressure change. When her ears opened, she could hear only the clanks of cooling metal, and the crackle of a small flame by the jets, which died as she watched. No hiss of escaping air. But the silence outside had the unmistakable sense of density and resonance that told her the *Calgary* was no longer in vacuum but in air.

Weak almost to fainting, CP wiped her breath from the

vitrex to peer out. It was confusing—a world like a color negative, all light coming from below, with strange-hued shadows above. So beautiful. Only trees and shrubs were around her—a wilderness of trees; CP had never seen so many trees all in one place. And they stretched on and on, she knew, to the horizon. Beyond them she could just see the lighted sparkle of running river water, *free water,* presumably fresh.

A paradise—save only for the lethal radioactivity, which had her scanning dial stuck against its high edge. A paradise, but not for her.

Nevertheless her prayers were granted. She was seeing a New World. She could touch it if she wished. A deep, extraordinary happiness she could scarcely recognize filled her. Her lips trembled with a constant smile she'd never felt before. But she could no longer keep her eyes open. She knew she had spent some hours fighting the *Calgary* down; she didn't realize it had taken her three Earth-days.

As she lost consciousness, hanging sidewise in the straps, from somewhere outside a living creature gave a single, unearthly, echoing hoot, loud enough to penetrate the sealed cabin.

Her last thought was that she would probably awaken, if she did, in the bonds and cuffs of Base prison.

She woke up painfully stiff and thirsty, but with the same marvelous alien world outside the port. And the air-pressure reading had stayed constant! All essential seals were intact—a final miracle.

Calgary had come to rest nose down on its broken wing stub; the "floor" was at a 40-degree angle. As CP unstrapped and slid down, she saw how good this was: the big port at her chair gave her the view outside right down to ground level, and so did one end of the bow window. The opposite port gave her the treetops. She paused curiously to study their strange adaptations of form to utilize light coming primarily from below. There seemed to be two general types, a pad-leaved sort, and a big tree fern, but there was extraordinary intervariation.

How much sealed airspace was left her? Gone, of course, was the whole underbody, the scouter dock, and the trailing space equipment—including the ice rock. But she had the pilotage and observation chambers, and the door to the galley had sprung askew without causing leaks. So had the wash-and-wastes roomlet, and even the door of her own bad-memoried little cubicle—no leaks in there.

Gratefully she pulled off her heavy helmet and shook out her flaming hair. Her last days would be not only sublimely interesting but actually comfortable!

Her water supply was intact too, she had checked that when first slaking her huge thirst. She would have to conserve, but she would have quite enough for the twenty days or so of oxygen left to her. That lack would be her end, as had been foretold from the start.

Just as she settled by the window to open a food pouch, movement outside drew her eyes. *Calgary* had plowed a long open avenue through the swamp brush, and was turned so she could look right back down it to the far, high, green glimmer of the sea.

Now something she had taken for vegetation moved, moved again, and became a long, willowy, pale animal. It was clambering down from a low fork in a tree by the "avenue," where it had perhaps spent the night. Had it been watching *Calgary,* shocked by the crashing intrusion of the ship? Even at this distance she could see that its eyes were enormous. They were shining with reflected light, set very far apart on a thin whitish head. The head resembled that of a goat or sheep which CP had seen alive in the zoo. It was definitely watching her now. She held her breath.

As it swung down, she could see that its side-skin hung in folds, and a long-ago memory of her one picture book came back. Earth had once had "flying" squirrels and other gliding animals. Perhaps this creature was a giant form like that, and used its flaps for gliding between trees?

Down from the tree, it sat on its haunches for a moment, still watching her. *Please, don't be frightened,* she begged it mentally, not daring even to close her mouth, which was open for a first bite of breakfast bar. The creature didn't seem alarmed. It stretched, in a laughably human way, and dropped its short forelimbs to the ground. It had a short, stout, upcurled tail.

Now CP remembered a picture that was closest of all—the kangaroo. Like the kangaroo, this animal's rear end was higher than its shoulders on all fours, because of its long, strong hind limbs; and its neck was curved up to carry its long head level. Only its tail was much smaller and shorter than the picture she recalled.

To her delight, it began calmly to amble, or walk-hop, right toward *Calgary*. As it came closer she could see its draped pelt clearly.

It wasn't fur.

It wasn't bare hide or leather.

It was—yes, unmistakably—and CP's mind seemed to explode with silent excitement—it was *fabric*.

As it came closer still, she could make out that around the neck and along the back-ridge ran a pattern of what could only be embroidery. It was set with knots and small shiny stones or shells.

She simply stared at the approaching form, unable to take in all the implications at once.

A world not only bearing life, but bearing intelligent life.

Too much, that she had stumbled on *this*.

And yet—was she really so surprised? The feeling that something . . . or someone . . . was "hearing" and helping her down had been so strong. . . . Was she looking at the one who—?

Impossible. She could think no further, only stare.

The creature—no, the *person,* calmly returned her gaze, and then sat down again, upright. With delicate spatulate fingers, it unfastened the throat of its cloak—CP could clearly see its thumbs—and removed it, revealing its actual pelt, which was cream-white and short. It folded the cloak deftly into a long strip and tied it round its body, then dropped back on all fours and resumed its amble toward her.

But it did not head to her window, it detoured around *Calgary* on higher ground. As it passed, twitching one of its tall "ears" toward her, CP had a confused, faint mental impression of others—very diverse others—somewhere nearby, whom this one was going to meet. The notion vanished so quickly she decided she had made it up. Her visitor was passing out of sight from that port, into the undisturbed forest ahead of *Calgary*'s stopping place.

She clambered quickly to the side post, but the stranger was already beyond sight among the trees. Perhaps someone or something else would come from that direction? She made herself comfortable by the vitrex, and at last began to eat her bar, studying all she could see. She was over the broken wing stub now. *Calgary* had come to rest against a dry hillock, this side made a natural approach. Slowly, so as not to alarm anything, she extended the auditory pickup and tested it. It worked! A world of varied rustlings, soft tweets, a croak or grunt, filled the cabin.

After a moment's thought, she tested the sound transmitter and extruded that too, so that her voice could be heard outside.

Presently she became aware of a periodic crackling or crashing sound coming from the woods beyond the hillock. She watched, and saw a far treetop sway violently and go down. Soon another followed, a little closer, and then yet another smaller tree jumped high and disappeared. A big herbivore, perhaps, feeding?

But as the sounds came closer, they seemed clearly deliberate. Perhaps a path or road to *Calgary* was being cleared. If so, what would appear? An alien bulldozer? A siege ram? A weapon carrier brought to blast her and *Calgary* out of existence?

Yet she waited unafraid, only glad and fascinated. This world did not feel hostile. And had they not already helped her, saved her life? *Calgary* had rudimentary defenses, mainly of a ballistic sort, which in recent decades had been occasionally used only to break up rocks, but it never occurred to her to deploy them. Life here had saved her life, and she had intruded a great shipwreck upon them. Even if they wished to be rid of her now, whatever came she would accept.

And suddenly it was there—so different from her expectations that she didn't at first take it in. One—no, two tall-humped forms were pushing through the trees. Their sides and tops seemed hard, she could hear thuds as they brushed against stems. Why, they were great tortoises, or turtles! She had once seen a tiny live one, much flatter in outline. Or could these carapaces be, like the Watcher's cloak, artificial shells? No, she decided. Their limbs and necks were formed to them, she seemed to see attachment in the openings' depths. Could they be trained beasts, used here instead of inorganic machines?

As she watched mesmerized, one of them backed ponderously into a tangle of tree trunks, sending them down like paper trees. Then it turned, reared up, and began neatly to break up, sort, and pile the debris. Just behind it, the other was doing the same. Then it came past the first, selected an obstructive giant tree, and repeated the process. She realized how very big they were; the tops of their shells would be higher than her head, and their push-force must be in tons.

As she saw the results of their work, she realized these couldn't be animals, however trained. They weren't merely clearing a way, they were creating order. Behind them stretched a neat, attractive clearway, without the edging tangle of damage usual on Earth. It wound away quite far; she could see perhaps a kilometer.

As the creatures reared up, worked, dropped down to push, it was evident to CP that they had a generic resemblance to the first one, whom she thought of as the Watcher. The same heavier hind limbs, here ponderous and half-hidden by their carapaces; the same shorter forelimbs, here massively muscled. When they extended their necks, these too were long, though thickly muscular, coming from very large front openings in the shell. They walked with heads high and level. The heads, now retracted to their shells, were somewhat similar to the Watcher's. Not at all reptilian, with upstanding "ears," heavy frontals, and protectively lidded eyes.

As they came closer, working rapidly but always neatly, she could see that their carapaces carried decorations. Some self-luminous pebbles or seeds had been set among the designs; their undershells, seen brightly illumined, were beautifully scrolled, and seemed to have straps or tool pockets mounted on them. Logical, she thought; frees the front limbs to walk. And finally, as the closest one rose up to grapple a tree fern, came the most bizarre touch of all—she could clearly see that it was wearing cuffed, decorated work gloves.

This perception set off her overloaded nerves—she

nearly dropped the kaffy from her shaking hands as a gale of giggles swept her, turned into peals of laughter that rang through the speaker into the swamp. Abashed, she thought how inappropriate this was, that the first human voice heard on this world should be not a proper formal speech, but laughing. She couldn't help herself. She had laughed little in her life. No one had told her the sound was very sweet.

She had it under control in a moment. Wiping her eyes, she saw that the turtlelike workers had dropped their logs and come closer for a look-in. She hoped the sound she had made wasn't displeasing or ugly to them.

"Excuse me," she said absurdly through the speaker.

A vague feeling of all-rightness suffused her; one of the "turtles" made what was clearly an attempt at imitating her laugh, and they went back to their labor, now almost at the ship.

And when her vision cleared, she could see, in the distance, six or seven new shapes approaching up the path the "turtles" had made.

She finally bethought herself the binoculars, and peered with all her might. The glasses were of course set for celestial use, with a very small field, and she had trouble at first in counting how many were in the group.

Four—no, three of them closely resembled the Watcher, but she could pick him, or her, out by the paler fur, and the color of the tied-up cloak. This method of transporting stuff seemed to be common. The other two kangaroo-like ones diffused among themselves too—she had a glimpse of more strangely formed heads, possibly even an extra very small set of forelimbs—but she was too busy trying to see all the others to check.

Another of the turtle or tortoise types was with them, its carapace heavy with encrustments. She gained a quick impression that it was quite old. It was even larger, and differed from the tree movers in its eyes, which were enormous and very bright beneath the heavy lids. Indeed, her first sight of the group had featured eyes—huge eyes, so bright and reflective that some seemed almost self-luminous. She noticed that all of them, as they advanced, looked about continuously and carefully, but with their major attention on *Calgary*—almost like a group of advancing headlamps.

Touching, partly leaning upon the carapaced one, came a short figure so swathed in red fabric veils that CP could make nothing of it, except for the great eyes in a face much shorter and more pugged than the Watcher's. The fur on its skin was pale, too. CP had the impression that this creature—no, this *person*—was somewhat ill or weak, perhaps old, too. She or he paced upright, much of the time leaning on the big "tortoise," only now and then dropping to a quadropedal amble. Their slower movements seemed to be setting the pace for all.

Another veiled person of the same general type, but taller and blue-veiled, came behind, moving strongly, so that the limbs often thrust through its veils. CP could definitely make out two pairs of upper "arms"; the lower pair seemed to be used for walking. Its upper body was upright so that, walking, it resembled a creature CP had only once seen a child's picture of—a being half-horse and half-human. But its face was neither horse nor human —the features were so snarled that only the big eyes, and four tall feathery protrusions that might be ears, or other sensory organs, could be identified.

Two more figures with gray pelts brought up the rear. One of them attracted CP's attention by swerving off the path into a pool of water, and drinking deeply with webbed hands held to a kind of bill or beak. She guessed that it might be at least partly aquatic. Its companion waited for it. Behind this one's shoulders were two hard-looking humps that might be vestigial wings.

The party was close now; CP had discarded the binoculars. As they passed the tree-moving turtles the personages she thought of as the Senior Tortoise and its veiled companion paused, and the others halted with them.

There was a brief interchange, consisting of some short, voiced phrases mingled with odd, meaningful silences. CP could not tell which voices belonged to whom; only one was melodious, but they were not unpleasing. Nor did they sound tense, agitated, or hostile. She gleaned the notion that this visit was in some weird way routine, and also that the road had been constructed voluntarily, by nearby residents, perhaps.

Could it be that people were *used* to spaceships landing here? But no; the party gave no sign of familiarity with anything like *Calgary*.

Their first act was to tour deliberately around the ship —CP saw that the ground had been cleared around her while she slept—looking gravely at every detail. CP followed them around from inside. On impulse, when they could see both her and the remaining wing, she raised her hand and moved an aileron control.

There was a general, surprised backward start.

By this time, CP was sure that some at least were telepathic. She sent them the strongest feeling of friendship she could project, and then pictures of herself moving controls. The "kangaroo" types seemed to respond with eagerness, as did the "Senior Tortoise." They moved closer, eyeing her keenly. So CP spent a happy time moving and wiggling everything that functioned, at the same time naming it and its function through the speaker. The small red-veiled alien seemed particularly interested in her voice, often attempting to repeat words after her.

They all had no hesitation in touching anything and everything; the agile web-footed ones clambered over the remains of *Calgary*'s top, and all came up and peered into all the cabin ports by turn.

Several times CP stopped herself from trying to warn them not to approach the "hot" thrust vents, or the debris of the reactor chamber. It was hard to realize that any residual radioactivity from *Calgary* was as nothing compared to the normal blizzard of hard radiation just outside, in which these visitors had evolved and lived.

Presently the small red-veiled alien limped, or hobbled, to the extended speaker and laid a fragile, pale, apparently deformed hand on it. At the same time, a very clear image came to CP; she closed her eyes to concentrate on it, and "saw" herself with opening and moving mouth. The image flickered oddly. The alien had made the connection between her voice and the speaker. But how to transmit "yes" by mental imagery? She nodded her head vigorously—a meaningless gesture here, no doubt—and said verbally, "Yes! Yes. Uh . . . hello!," pointing to her mouth and the speaker.

The little alien made a peculiar sound; was that a laugh? Next moment its hand moved to the auditory pickup, and CP experienced something new—a strikingly sharp image of the microphone, followed by a literal blanking of the mind—indescribable. As if an invisible blindfold had descended. Next instant came the mike image again, and again the blank—and back to the image; faster and faster, these two impressions alternated in her mind, to a flicker sequence that made her dizzy.

But she grasped it—as clearly as a human voice, the alien was saying, "And this thing is—what?"

So that was how questions were asked!

How to answer? She tried everything she could think of, pointing to the alien, to her own ears (which were doubtless not ears to the alien), saying "Hello" repeatedly like a parrot, all the while trying to picture an alien's mouth speaking. She'd never seen the red-veiled mouth, so she imaged another's.

Something worked—with apparent eagerness, the small alien put its face to the mike, and nearly blasted CP from her chair with "ER-ROW! ER-ROW! ES!"

CP was childishly delighted. She and the alien exchanged several "Hellos" and "Errows" through speaker and mike.

But shortly a new question emerged. She began to receive a strengthening picture—as if from several minds joining in—of herself coming out of *Calgary* and moving among them. After a few moments of her nonresponse, this image began to alternate slowly with a scene of the aliens inside *Calgary* with her. Again, the two images alternated faster and faster, to confusing flashes. But the meaning was plain—"Will you come out, or shall we come in?"

It took her a long, laborious effort to try to transmit the impossibility. She concentrated hard on forming images of the port opening and air coming in, herself falling down, pictures of radiation (she hoped) coming from the ground. Suddenly, at those last pictures the old tortoise seemed to understand. He advanced and laid one heavy paw on *Calgary*, and then made a sweeping gesture that CP read as negation. Of course: *Calgar*y, alone of most of this world, was inert, nonradioactive.

At this point they seemed to have had enough, or were tired; in very human fashion they drew off to sit in a group at the edge of the clearing with the tree-fellers, and produced packets of edibles. CP stared eagerly, wishing she could see and taste. As far as she could make out, most of them ate with more or less Earthlike mouths, but the veiled persons inserted their food beneath their throat veils.

Then the small red-clad alien seemed to notice her staring and CP suddenly felt her mouth and nose filled with an extraordinary alien sensation—neither good nor bad, but quite unknown—which must be the taste of what they were eating. She laughed again, and daringly transmitted a faint replica of the cheese-and-peanut-butter packet she was eating.

Refreshments were soon over. Now the large blue-veiled alien and the kangaroo-types came forward to the window. Looking directly at CP, the veiled one stood up and made motions of turning. CP understood; it was her time to be inspected. Obediently she turned, extended an arm, opened her mouth to show her teeth, wiggled her fingers.

Then the veiled one raised her top arm, unfastened something, and deliberately let drop a veil. The implication was plain: undress. For a moment CP was overcome with an ugly memory of Meich, the countless other humiliations she had undergone. She hesitated. But the alien eyes were insistent and seemed friendly. When CP didn't move, the big alien pulled off another veil, exposing this time its own bare and furless belly and haunches. A strong feeling of reassurance came to her—of course, to these people her body was as neutral as a mollusk or a map. She unzipped her suit and stepped out of it and her underclothes. At the same time, as if to encourage her, the alien removed its own upper-body covering. CP noticed that the others in its group had turned tactfully away.

CP was amazed—in the crotch where human sex and excretory organs would be, the alien had nothing but smooth muscle. But its chest region was as complex as a group of sea creatures; valves, lips, unidentifiable moist flaps and protrusions—clearly its intimate parts. CP could form no idea of its gender, if any.

Not to be outdone in scientific detachment, CP demonstrated her own nude self, and made an attempt at transmitting images of the human reproductive process. She got nothing in reply—or rather, nothing she could interpret. She and the alien apparently diverged so widely here that thought could not carry across the gulf. Only excretion seemed sufficiently similar to be at least referrable to.

At length the alien gave it up, resuming its own veiling and indicating that CP should do likewise.

Then the whole group gathered round her windows and CP was astounded. Abruptly she was assailed by a thought-image that said, as plainly as a shout, "Go away!"

The image was of *Calgary* again taking to the air, and spiraling up and away. The feeling-tone wasn't hostile or threatening, merely practical. If she couldn't live here, she should go elsewhere.

"But I can't!"

Desperately she pointed to the wrecked wing, sent images of the empty fuel reserve.

A counter-image, of *Calgary* being literally lifted off and flung out of atmosphere, came back. Did they propose that the same presumably "mental" force that had slowed her should lift her back to orbit?

"No—no! It wouldn't work!" She sent images of *Calgary*, released in space, falling helplessly back upon them.

But the thought-send persisted. "You-go-away"—and the sequence repeated itself.

Then CP had an idea. But how to indicate time here in this never-changing world? Oh, for an hourglass! Finally she gathered up a handful of crumbs, broken glass, and other small debris of the wreck and let them trickle slowly and deliberately from one hand to the other. She held up her fingers, counting off a dozen or so—and acted out a scene of herself strangling in foul air, collapsing and dying. As an afterthought, she tried to express a feeling of contentment, even joy.

The Senior Tortoise got it first, and seemed to enlighten the others.

She would not be here long alive.

There ensued a brief colloquy among the aliens. Then one after the other came to her window, put up its "hands" to take a look around, and seemed to transmit something grave, and faint. She was not even sure she was receiving. The old tortoise-person came last, its great hands heavy on the glass as it shaded out reflections to look in. From it CP was sure something emanated to her. But she could not name it.

Then they all turned and walked, ambled, or hopped away as they had come, taking the "Watcher" with them. The tree-fellers brought up the rear. CP stared after them, surprised.

They had simply departed, leaving her alone to die.

Well, what more could she have expected?

But it was strange; no curiosity about the stars, for instance, nor whence she had come.

And what had they been trying to impart, there at the last? Of course: "Good-bye."

"Good-bye," CP said through the speaker softly, into the alien air.

Then began an unadmittedly lonely time, waiting to die there in the beauty of the swamp. CP began to wish it wasn't so viewless and closed in. She decided that soon, before the air was all gone, she would go out, and try to climb to some sort of view before she died.

On impulse, she set her Earth-day timer, which had ceased in the crash, to manual-battery operation. She who had fled the world of Earth forever yet had the whim to perish on Earth's time. Only so much of nostalgia persisted. That and her little copybook of poems.

She had long since smoothed out and repaired the captain's damage. Only one page was lost. She occupied herself in reconstructing it from memory:

With delicate mad hands against the sordid bars,
Surely he hath his posies, which they tear and
 twine—
Those—*something*—wisps of straw that miserably
 line
His strait caged universe, whereon the dull world
 stares.

Pedant and pitiful. Oh,—*something*—*something*—
Know they what dreams divine
Something—like enchanted wine—
And make his melancholy germane to the stars?
Oh lamentable brother, if these pity thee,
Am I not fain of all thy lost eyes promise me?
Half a fool's kingdom, far from—*something*—all
   their days vanity.
Oh, better than mortal flowers
Thy moon-kissed roses seem;
Better than love or sleep,
The star-crowned solitude of thine oblivious hours! *

Much was muddled, but she had the essential lines.
They had kept her company all those years behind her
sordid bars. Well, she had had the stars, and now she had
the moon-kissed roses, and the fool's kingdom. Presently
she would open the port and go out to possess it. . . .

It was late on Day Six of the perhaps fifteen left to
her, that someone else came. She had long ceased to
watch the path, but now she felt a tug at her attention.
At first there was nothing, and she almost turned away.
And then, in the far distance, she made out a single,
oddly shaped figure. Quick, the binoculars. It became an
alien something like the former Watcher, but ruddy and—
yes—carrying or being ridden by a much smaller alien on
its back. More—she saw the small alien was legless,
with very tiny arms. She had the strong impression of
fatigue, of a long-distant goal reached. They had, she
thought, come a long, long way.

Then she understood: this world was huge, and she
knew nothing of their means of transport, if any. Perhaps
those who wished to see *Calgary* must walk, so even from
the far side?

She watched, scarcely daring to blink, as these new
aliens continued their weary way toward her into naked-
eye view. The larger alien raised its head, and must have
seen her waiting. She was quite unprepared for the jolt

* *To One in Bedlam*, Ernest Dowson, *ca.* 1875, as all s-f
readers should know.

of feeling that shook her—like a shout of welcome and joy.

That she still lived! Had this alien been fearful it was too late, that she would have died before he or she could get here? That must be it.

As the alien came closer yet she noticed an oddity about the big one's head—where others had had upstanding "ears" or antlerlike antennae, this one had large, triangular velvety flaps that drooped toward its eyes. Where had she seen these before? Oh God—aching half with laughter, half pain, she recognized—the large, folded, triangular earflaps of a pig! And the alien's muzzle was pugged, like hers.

Dear stars, what cosmic joke was this?

The rest of the alien's body was not at all porcine, but seemed worn and gaunt from travel and bearing the weight of its companion. Built more ruggedly than the original Watcher, its pelt was dusty red and it was wearing a thin vest that covered the chest area and tied behind as a knot which its rider clung to. A cloak was also tied round it. Its eyes were not abnormally large, more like pale human eyes without visible whites. Walking quadrupedally, or walk-hopping as it was now, its shoulders were lower than its rump, and the stumpy tail stuck straight out behind, possibly from excitement.

As it approached *Calgary* its gaze shifted from her to the wrecked ship, and images of the starry night of space filled her head, alternating occasionally with a vision of the lavender cloud ceiling overhead, and the 200-kilometer thickness of cloud that had blanked her view coming down—and then back again to the stars—the stars as she had seen them in a hundred shifting views.

She began to receive a curious new impression.

When the creature, or person, came slowly right to *Calgary*, it sat up as far as it could without spilling its rider, and laid first one hand and then the other on *Calgary*'s broken wing. She became sure.

This was reverence. Here was a longing for the stars that filled its soul, the stars from which it was closed away forever by the implacable, never-ending cloud. As plainly as speech, its gesture said, "This—this came from the stars!"

When it raised its gaze to her, its face had changed to a strange openmouthed pursing, like a child trying to pronounce "th"; denoting she knew not what, until she received the image of what must be herself, weirdly exaggerated, among the stars; and understood, from her own experience.

"You—you, an intelligent alien—have come here *from the stars!* Life is out there, beyond our heavy sky!"

It was almost as if it were worshiping *Calgary* and herself—no, it was just that she and it were the most precious, exciting things in life to it. Perhaps, alone of its kind, it had insisted that there was life beyond the sky? And was now proved right? She had met a human astronomer who would have felt this way.

The alien had now clambered up onto the wing stub to peer in, pushing back its beautiful ears to see better. Close up, its muzzle was complex and pleasingly furred. As it alternately inspected the cabin and gazed at her, its small companion clambered off onto the wing, agilely pulling itself by its shrunken arms. She saw that it had a large, thick, apparently partly prehensile tail, which served to boost it along in place of the missing legs. Its bare skin was scurfy and wrinkled; CP understood that it was very old. It seemed to be interested in the length, the width, the sheer size of *Calgary*.

But the larger alien's head kept sagging; it was spent with exhaustion, she saw its eyelids droop, pull open again, and reclose despite itself. It sank down into the uncomfortable corner between the wing stub and the window, not even untying its cloak, looking toward her as long as it could stay conscious. For a moment CP feared it was ill or dying, but received a faint image of it waking up animatedly.

She wished she could at least undo its cloak to cushion its head. A moment later the little old alien dragged itself over and did just that, as if "hearing" her.

Then it turned its bright eyes on her, far less tired than its friend. It seemed to have something to convey: images of herself, her hands as she fought *Calgary* down, came to her. What could this mean?

As if exasperated, the little being pulled itself to the remains of the booster rocket by the wing base; showing an odd combination of the activity of a child with great age.

There it patted the booster, pointing first to her and then to itself. This was the first time she'd seen anyone here point manually.

Images of *Calgary* descending came again. She was baffled. Sensing this, the old creature seized a stout twig lying on the wing, raised it high, and dropped it.

The twig fell briskly—then slowed, slowed, halted before touching down—and as she stared, it reversed course and slowly rose upward, back to the alien's hand.

CP's eyes smarted with staring, she had consciously to blink. What had she seen if not movement-by-remote-will —telekinesis!

The act seemed to have tired the alien, but it looked at her intently, holding up one hand. In human gesture-language this would say, "Attend!"

CP "attended." The alien screwed up its small, wrinkled face, closed its eyes.

And *Calgary* rocked. A single startling lurch.

There was no question of some physical shift of weight doing it—the ship took a pull so strong she could hear mud sucking under the crushed hull.

She had to believe.

Incredible as it was, this tiny old being was, or exerted, the force that had slowed *Calgary* and brought her safely in. Somehow it had reached out all those thousands of kilometers, to the heavy, hurtling ship, and slowed it.

Saved her life.

She didn't know how to say thank you, even to show gratitude. She could only point to it and bow her head ignorantly, stammering "Thank you, oh thank you!" through the speaker. In the end she actually knelt on the tilted deck, but was not satisfied.

The little old being shied away from the speaker, but seemed to understand that she understood. It was panting with fatigue. But after a few moments' rest it did something new. Advancing to the speaker, it pointed to itself and said loudly, "Tadak."

Luckily it spoke loudly enough to reach the mike, too.

"Tadak," it said again with more self-pointing.

Its name, the first one she had known!

"Tadak. Hello, Tadak!" she said eagerly. But it seemed

exasperated again. Of course: she pointed to herself. "Cee Pee."

It imitated her roughly, too faint to hear well. She was distracted, but her longing to show her gratitude had produced an idea. It would lose her several liters of air; she reproached herself for even the automatic thought. Too much—in return for her life?

Motioning to Tadak, she laid hold of her most precious human possession, the golden flight emblem pinned to her collar. Tadak watched intently as she demonstrated how to pin and secure it.

Then she crawled under the console, disconnected an old lubricant-intake valve, and rapped loudly on the inside cover to guide its attention. When she heard taps outside, she placed the pin in the opening and recapped it. A considerable struggle to communicate ensued; this world —or Tadak—did not seem familiar with toggles and screw threads. In the end she heard a fearful grinding sound, and guessed that it had used its TK to rip the cap straight off.

Tadak crawled weakly back into view, panting and clutching the shiny trinket with apparent reverence in its old gnarled fingers, first to its chest, then over its upturned face as though marveling. Then its bright eyes went sidewise to CP, carrying an impression of both joy and—yes —mischief. The old face puckered hard.

—And *Calgary* jumped again, higher than before. It came down with a jolt that made CP a trifle nervous.

A protesting grunt came from the sleeping alien by her window.

But Tadak was really tired now. It seemed to take all its remaining strength to hump up to where its friend lay and to bed down, too. One tiny hand twitched up at her and slumped. CP was left to watch over the sleep of her new acquaintances.

She felt herself drifting toward sleep, too. This must be a world without the dangers normal to hers; its inhabitants seemed to have no fear of lying vulnerable in the open. With Tadak quiescent she could see how very old and frail it was.

Her drowsy attention and wonder settled on the head and softly folded "ears" of the larger alien. In all her dream life in the Empire of the Pigs she had never imagined a pig head of such beauty and dignity. There was a shining metallic chain about its neck too, with a medallion of some sort. And its poncho was beautifully embroidered. Evidently her wondrous new visitors weren't paupers, if such things existed here. Still studying them, she fell asleep and dreamed of stars, mixed with her old story of safe arrival home in the Empire.

They were all awakened by more visitors.

By the time she was conscious, the newcomers had filtered into the clearing and quietly surrounded *Calgary*. It was a spoken utterance by the open microphone that awakened her to confront two strange yellow-colored rotund shapes right by the window, squinting in at her. Beyond them she glimpsed pale or dark alien forms on every side.

She reacted with automatic panic, diving under the console. Police? Army? Enemy of some kind?

But a cautious peek out reassured her.

Her two new "friends" were greeting the arrivals calmly, even joyfully. While the flap-eared alien raised its arms to touch palms with one group of newcomers, Tadak clambered onto the carapace of a large turtle-type, and was being carried around *Calgary*, to hand-greet other arrivals. She noticed there were different nuances of position and length of contact in the double-palm greeting, like different human handshakes for old friends or new, formal meetings. She saw, too, that most of the newcomers looked travel-worn; only a few seemed fresh. It was difficult to count, but she decided that about thirty strangers had arrived. Here she noticed a novelty—subdued voices were to be heard all around. Evidently many of those new aliens talked in verbal speech. Had she been meeting only mental-projection specialists?

As they saw she was awake, voices rose excitedly and they began to gather round her window and settle down. Clearly these weren't idle tourists. A meeting of some sort impended. Perhaps some ultimatum or scheme to urge her off-planet?

CP splashed her hands and face hurriedly, conserving the water for a second use, and retired to the wastes cubby. When she closed the door on herself the wave of general disappointment was so strong it reached her. She grinned to herself; maybe, later, she would abandon all her Earth ways. Maybe.

Snatching up a breakfast bar and self-heating kaffy, she came back to the window. Her two new acquaintances had stationed themselves just outside, evidently as her official translators or keepers. All right. Now let's have it.

A truly strange-looking large alien advanced and held up its palms in formal greeting. It was dark ochre-orange and blue, wrinkled, and extravagantly horned, and it squinted. Its body was such a confusing combination of sluglike membranes and legs out behind that she never quite managed to separate it from its complex clothing and equipment. It was one of the road-worn—CP received a subliminal impression that others had waited for it as spokesman or leader.

Evidently it could mind-speak, perhaps assisted by one of the two on the wing. A misty image formed behind her eyes; she closed them to concentrate, and "saw" herself back in *Calgary*. She was—yes—going from port to port, scanning over the whole sky. This was the long, Voiceless last period, after the Empire had faded out, when she was contentedly—but systematically—studying the visible universe. The image turned to her star charts.

On impulse she opened her eyes and pulled the real charts from their locker.

The impression of excited joy that came to her was unmistakable. Unmistakable too, now, was an odd "tone" to the communications, especially those from the antlered one. Familiar!

While Tadak and its large friend helped her explain why she couldn't pass the charts out now, but they'd have them soon, she searched her memory for that "tone," and found it.

Why, it was these aliens to whom she had been "transmitting" all those days after she was on course. They were too weak-voiced to reach her, but she had felt not alone, "all right." Who could they be?

Oh! While she'd been puzzling, a new, very strong phenomenon had emerged: above and around every new head in the clearing came a small halo of stars. Some were weak, barely floating pinpoints of light, others were a full-blown circlet of blackness lit with glory, before all faded.

The astronomers of this world had come to her.

But how could this sealed sunless world, surely without space flight, have "astronomers"? How could they ever have found out the stars at all, unless perhaps the clouds cleared once in a while, like an old story she'd read? Here she was wrong, but she only discovered it later, during one of the most exhausting yet pleasant twenty hours of her life.

They wanted to know everything.

Each had formed its one most vital question, each in turn would walk, hobble, crawl, hop forward to "ask" it. But first the big antlered speaker "asked" a question so comprehensive that it obviated many other planned ones.

An image of a starfield bloomed in her mind, stars of all the types she had unwittingly "shown" them from *Calgary,* each clear and specific before merging into the whole.

This great image was followed by a startlingly strong blankout. Then the stars came back, then the blank, faster to the now familiar flicker-meaning:

"The stars are—what?"

Whew.

She had to explain the universe wordlessly to a race whose concepts and measures—if any—of distance, motion, forces, matter, heat she didn't know.

Afterward, she recalled mostly a mishmash, but she thought she must have given quite a performance. This was, after all, her own beloved study, at an amateur level.

She remembered first trying to convey some notion of energies and distances. She imaged this world's—Auln's —surface from above, then using old tape-teach effects, she "receded" down to a lavender point against the stars, then "pulled" one of the nearer small stars close for comparison, and showed the wild atomic fires of its surface compared with the colder weak processes of Auln. She "built" a star up out of a gas cloud, changed it through its life to red giant and nova, built another, richer one from the debris and condensed its planets. She "started life" on the planet, gave them a glimpse of her own Earth—typical astronomers, they cared little for this—then sent it receding again and built up the Milky Way, and galaxies beyond it, attempted the expanding universe.

It was there she had paused, exhausted.

While she rested and ate someone sent her the answer to her question: how did they know of the stars?

She received an image of a new sort—framed! Multiply framed, in fact, frame within frame. The image itself was oddly blurred in detail. Sharp, however, was a view of extraordinary metal wreckage, unidentifiable stuff strewn at a deep gash in the ground. Much was splashed with brilliant green, and there was a central ball or cylinder— no, wait, a *head,* not human. Had these aliens actually attempted space flight?

No. The framed image jumped to show a fireball streaking down through the clouds, then back to the green-smeared head. Wrecked as it was, it did seem generically unlike anyone she had seen on Auln. As if to settle her problem, "her" ruddy, flop-eared alien bent and pulled a wrap off its leg, showing a healing cut. Its blood was red, like hers.

So another, a *real* alien had crashed here! And long ago, too. The frames, the blur suggested many transmissions of the scene. But this space alien was obviously dead. How, then—

Into the image came a head like the beaked "aquatics" among her first visitors. Huge-eyed, somehow rather special-seeming. It laid its head against the dead astronaut's. And the image dissolved to faint views of the starry sky from space, an incoming glimpse of Auln, strangeness.

Generations back, then, they had learned of outside space, the stars—by probing a dead brain!

She was so bemused by this that she barely attended to another, clearly contemporary image sequence until a motion like wing beats caught her. She reclosed her eyes in time to "see" a birdlike creature flapping desperately, up— up—it seemed to be driven, or lifted, higher than its wings could sustain it, higher than it could breathe. The image changed. On the ground, a far-"sighted" alien was looking through the dying bird's eyes, seeing weirdly focused images of thinning, darkening cloud. Just before the bird eyes died, a rift opened above it; blackness lit by two bright stars was briefly there.

A living telescope! But the "tone" in which these sequences came through suggested some sadness or disapproval. CP thought that perhaps they used this ruthless technique only rarely and reluctantly. It certainly wasn't sustained enough to be useful, but it sufficed to reassure them that the stars *were* there.

The ensuing hours and hours of sending, trying to understand queries, to invent visual ways to convey the barely communicable, not to omit too much of importance, to share in effect all she knew of the universe, condensed in memory into a great blur, of which she recalled only two things.

The first was rooting out the magnificent star and galaxy color photos poor Don Lamb had collected, and pasting them up inside the ports. This was a sensation; the crowding nearly did tip *Calgary*.

The other was her own graphic warning of all that could happen on Auln if Earthmen or another aggressive species found them.

This changed the mood to a great sobriety, in which she sensed that the thought was not entirely new to all. She sent all she could on human nuclear space bombardment, robot weapons, and air-to-ground attack, which seemed to be attentively received. The idea worried her, but she had done all she could. This telekinetic, mind-probing, perhaps mind-deceiving race might be able to devise adequate defense. . . . How she hoped it!

And finally, after more than an Earth-day's wakefulness, they left as abruptly as they'd come, each giving her the two-handed gesture of farewell. Tadak left too, riding on the carapace of a strong young shelled one. But to her relief and pleasure, his larger, flop-eared friend seemed prepared to stay. Indeed, she didn't acknowledge to herself how carefully she had watched for signs of his intentions. It was peculiarly, deeply important to her.

As she watched them straggle up the road, hearing the last of their rather high-pitched, Asiatic converse, it seemed to her that one or two turned into a side path near the ship and disappeared behind a rise. Her attention was drawn to this by seeing the others pause and hand over cloaks, or packets of supplies. Perhaps these were headed another way, by a long route; she forgot it.

When they had all departed and the path was empty, the alien whom she was beginning timidly to think of as a friend, came up onto the wing stub at her window. It looked at her, the same look she'd seen at the very first. But now it was looking solely into her eyes, long, deep, searchingly. Peculiar images, apparently just random memories, came to her; the dormitory of her old school-days, the streets of the Enclave. Her first real desk. And always in them was a figure she reluctantly recognized: herself.

She began to tremble.

These were not . . . memories.

More images of the past. And weaving through them, a gleaming red-gold cap—could that be her hair?

No one but herself knew of all these past scenes.

None but one other.

Could this be—was she at last looking at the one who —was it this alien being who had "spoken" to her all her life? Was this her Voice?

She trembled harder, uncontrollably.

Then her "friend" reared up and placed both thin palms on the window by its head.

Cold struck her to her heart.

She tried to tell herself that this was just to see her better through the port. But that couldn't be, she realized dully; the light was not that bright, the vitrex wasn't that reflective.

This must be—oh, please, no, don't let it be like all the others, a final, formal good-bye. Not from the one who held her life, who had been with her lifelong, through all the dark nights, the pain. Who had said, Come.

The image of herself also holding her hands to the window came urgently to her. She was expected to respond.

Oh please, she pleaded to no one, not good-bye from *you*, too. Not you, my Voice . . . Don't leave me alone. To die. Grief pushed huge tears past all her guards. To distract herself she thought how rude all the others must have thought her, when she failed to respond to them.

This one really wanted her to respond properly. Evidently it had enough personal feeling for her to make this important. Well, she would, in a moment, when she had herself under better control.

A thud shook the wing. Humanlike, but with far more strength, the alien stamped. Perhaps it was impatient to rejoin the others? It stamped again, harder, and slapped both hands on the window, sending a peremptory image of her holding her hands up against the vitrex, matching its own.

All right then. Good-bye.

Blind with unshed tears, she stood up and spread her palms against the window opposite the red-and-cream blurs. The alien made an exasperated sound and moved its hands to cover hers as exactly as possible.

And something—began to flow. It was as if the vitrex grew hot, or not hot but charged. Almost alive. CP shook so hard her hands slid lower; feeling another stamp from outside, she tried to replace them. The "current" flowed again, carrying with it a bloom of feelings, images, wordless knowledge, she didn't know what, all bursting through her from their matched palms.

The alien's eyes caught and held hers, and slowly it brought its hands closer to its head. Hers followed jerkily.

Here the feelings strengthened, became overpowering. She sank to her knees, the alien followed, still holding her palm to palm, through five centimeters of hard vitrex. She couldn't remove her hands if she chose.

But she wouldn't have broken that contact for life itself. She was learning—she was understanding, oh incredulously—that all her life—

Suddenly a strong, rich sound from the audio startled her: the alien's voice.

It had to be repeated before she understood.

"Ca-rol."

Her name. It was known to no one here.

"Ca-rol . . . ehy-ou . . . Iye . . ."

Unmistakable, though strange and jerky here, she recognized her Voice.

There was no need now for the alien to explain that his gesture was not a good-bye, but communion.

But there was more to it than that. Ludicrously, neither of them had her word for it, because it was a word CP had never had occasion to use. It seemed important, for a while, to find it. They went at it the long way round, through her feeling for the stars, and for a rat she had once briefly been allowed to make a pet of. The recognition, the realization scared CP so badly that her teeth rattled. But the alien "held" her, insistently pressed the communication on her, out of its own need. In the end she had to know it fully.

Know that she—Carol-Page-Snotface-CP-Cold Pig— had walked all her days and nights embraced by love. Alien love, at first for a little-alien-among-the-stars, but soon, soon for her alone.

She had never been alone.

She, Carol-Page-Snotface-et-cetera was the Beloved . . . and always had been.

As this rosy, fur-clad, soft-eared, glowing-eyed one was of course hers, though she had never used the word. Her lifelong love.

When two long-parted, unacknowledged lovers meet at last and reveal their love, it is always the same. Even though a wall of vitrex came between them.

Long intervals of speechless communion, absorbing the miracle of You Too Love . . . that You Are Here, that Me + You = One. In other intervals her lover showed her all this world of Auln, about the Viewers, about the early training to become a Star Caller. The alien was still young too, she gathered. It had been on its first Star Search when contact with her occurred. She wanted to be shown everything, she couldn't get enough of images, even trivia of her lover's life. All hers was of course known in detail to her alien Voice.

As the current between them strengthened she took to thinking of the alién as "he," meaning no more by it than that "it" was insupportable and "she" or "sister" was not quite appropriate in a human sense. Like herself, she found the alien had never borne young. Besides, there were now no other "hes" in CP's universe.

Twice she touched on the violent acts that had brought her here, and each time the current jumped almost to real pain. Strongly, oh how strongly he supported them and her!

Rather wildly, they both sought ways of closer contact, ending whole-body-plastered to the vitrex. Neither could bear to cease contact long enough to eat much. Vaguely she thought that accounted for a slight unnoticed ill feeling.

Then came the day when her timer blatted so insistently that she saw it was past the red mark. The illness she'd ignored was real.

Calgary's air had ended.

It was time to come out—to him. She explained what he already knew, and received grave assent.

When the huge port swung open, the air that rushed upon her was impossibly sweet and fresh—spring air such as CP'd never breathed before. *Calgary*'s foulness made a fog at the port. The first thing she saw through it was his hand, stretched to her. He led her out, to a different end.

Again, when two lovers win to real bodily contact, it is always the same. But these two were still separated, not by a mere wall, but by being prisoned in wholly different bodies with wholly different needs.

Unnecessary to follow all their efforts in those first hours. Sufficient that they learned two things. First, mutual laughter, and second, what all Earthbound lovers find, that *nothing* suffices.

They blamed this on their differences, but they suspected the truth. Where love has been intense and silent and all-consuming, only the impossible, the total merger into one, could slake its fires.

On this world, such a consummation was only a little less impossible than on Earth. In the end, they found the physical palm-to-palm contact deepest and most poignant, and they stayed so.

Outward events were few and slight, but the most important in the universe. While she was still feeling wonderfully well, he led her up a nearby hill to a small glade with a superb view. She saw in reality the glorious self-lit colors of great Auln's cultivated lands, its wildernesses and rivers and, in the distance, a small city or town, the sky overhead reflecting all. Behind them lay the luminous sea, from which blew a gentle breeze, and where she glimpsed strange sea creatures tumbling. Presently her lover lured a few of Auln's "birds" and other strange or charming creatures to them.

At one point she flinched about her nose, and he "told" her in pictures how his own flopped ears were viewed as deplorable. Even on this world where individuals mutated so wildly as scarcely to seem of the same species, by chance all but a few heads bore upright ears or other sensors. His own rounded head was almost the sole feature seen by all as ugly. This revelation caused much time to be occupied by caressing reassurances.

She was weakening fast, but pain seemed absent or muffled for a while. Her exposed pale skin burned and blistered shockingly by the second day, despite the gauzy cover he had made for her by tearing out the lining of his cloak. The burns did not hurt much either. Later, when she saw him wince, she began to suspect why. They had a battle of wills, in which hers was no match for his trained one.

On the third day her beautiful hair was falling out in sheaves. He collected it, strand by strand, smoothed and kept it.

That day she had the whim to cut their names on a stone, and could scarcely bear it when he left her to bring one. Amazed and delighted by the novelty, they realized she had never known his name—Cavaná. She said it, sang it, whispered it a thousand times, built it into all her memories. Finally she did, with help, scratch *Cavaná* and *Carol* onto the stone, and tried to make other lines, but was too weak. He never left her again.

By this time they were lying with their heads on a cushioned log, their hands as if grown together.

One of the last things she noticed was the amusingly fluffed, mossy little vine that made the log so comfortable. He told her its future.

The Fountain had flowed since the Viewers had been here last. Two farmers from Pyenro were now putting in part of their town duty clearing vine from the alien sky-box. They passed on news of two new young ones, and a possible animal-sickness the Viewers should keep track of.

Their task inside the now open sky-box busied the Viewers for some time. Old Andoul, of course, could not enter. While the others were occupied she communed effortfully by sound with the three sky-obsessed ones who

had remained here. They had stayed discreetly out of
sight of Cavaná and the alien, but had caught nothing of
consequence in that time. However, the open sky-box
had given them much of overwhelming interest, including
a sheaf of extraordinary, flat, flexible, permanent images,
which they called "stars." They asked Andoul and
Askelon, a new young Viewer, to view them. This they
did. The images were of nothing recognizable, being
largely black-spangled, but oddly moving in addition to
their fascinating new technique.

The farmers had widened the summit path for Andoul.
When all was finished below, the Viewers started up. It
was steep. The deformed child Mir-Mir, who was so
young it hadn't yet chosen gender, had to clamber up on
Andoul's back, tucking up its red veils and complaining
aloud, "If you accept any more jewelry, *Saro* Andoul, I'll
never find a place to sit. I believe you do it on purpose."

"Speak properly, child," Andoul told it. "And if you
eat any more no one will be able to carry you. . . . Aah!
I View." All halted, and Mir-Mir slid off.

They had arrived at a pretty little glade near the summit. An elongated mound, green-covered by vine, lay with
one end on a green-clad log.

Looking more closely, all could see that the form was
in fact two, closely apposed and entwined at the log end,
where lateral mounding indicated arms.

Xerona and Ekstá advanced to it, squatted, and placed
their webbed hands gently on what might be two vine-
covered heads pressed tight together.

After a moment both touched one body and Xerona
sent them all an image.

"Cavaná," Mir-Mir said aloud. Andoul grunted in disapproval, both of Mir-Mir's vocalizing and what was in
its mind. Ferdil, one of the three very silent, hardworking Viewers who resembled Cavaná, was actually
Cavaná's cousin.

"See the bigger legs," Mir-Mir said defiantly. "Poor
Cavaná, so ugly. But she lived in the sky!"

The two beaked Viewers were indicating the other
form, transmitting a rather sketchy image of the orange-
maned alien. They were all silent a moment, refining and
supplementing the image. Finally Askelon sighed.

"I did ill," he mourned aloud. "It was my responsibility." He sent short images of himself inspecting the nude alien, and himself now, downcast with both hands drooped from the wrists. Shame.

Old Andoul gently corrected that image to raise the hands. "We all must begin," she said in words. "None of us considered it very important. Perhaps it isn't. Although—" She lapsed back to imagery, showed the alien in a framing of color that was short-speed for "Person of perhaps great soul," and then jumped to sketched-in multitudes of other red-headed aliens diving upon them with fantastic sky-boxes and explosions of flame.

The other Viewers sighed, too. Askelon revived slightly. Ferdil and her two friends went over by the feet of the dead ones, and gazed down at the hidden form of Cavaná, locked in death with her alien love. When Ferdil gave the sign of formal last farewell the others, after a polite interval, did likewise.

Meanwhile Xerona and Ekstá were hard at work, their own heads against first one dead head and then the other. At length they arose, their expressions very sober.

"Nothing . . . of interest or use to others," Ekstá said. "Cavaná . . . took much of the alien's pain."

Xerona was trying to hide weeping, but missed an indigo tear at his throat gills.

"Ah, look!" Askelon, scanning hard to redeem himself, had come upon an odd corner of rock. When he lifted and cleared it, they saw a flat stone with chasings or scratches on it.

"Alien writing!" exclaimed Mir-Mir, hobbling to it. "Ferdil!"

Ferdil and her companions were already Viewing the stone. With a confirmatory transmission to old Andoul, she produced a small container from her belly pack, inserted a straw, and skillfully blew a mist of moss-inhibiting bacteria over the stone. Then she set it on edge beyond the lovers' heads.

Unexpectedly, Ferdil spoke in words.

"I knew Cavaná well, we were deep friends in the early days, before . . . She had only just chosen gender when she made Contact. . . . Her love was very severe; changeless, unremitting. Almost a sickness. But she left us much.

And one thing more—we know now her communication was real. Many doubted. But the one she Called really heard, answered, and with much effort came."

The others were silent, admitting her right to important verbal speech.

Around them Auln lay in beauty, under the eternal, soft-colored cloud ceiling that was their sky. The plain in view here was vast, bioluminescent to the high horizon. Nothing had ever changed here, nothing would. No light of day, no dark of night, no summer, neither fall nor winter. Only their own works, like the *sumlac* fields, changed the tints reflected in the cloud. People came from great distances to watch the shifts at planting time and harvest, and for their enjoyment the farmers synchronized many crops. Now the sky carried pink bands that came from the simultaneous channeling of water into the *millin* lanes.

Characteristically it was the child Mir-Mir who broke the silence as they started to descend.

"I am going to change, and become a Star Caller!"

"Oh, child, you don't know what you're saying!" Askelon exclaimed involuntarily. "Look at the life Callers have, they must give up everything to Search and Search —and if they find and focus, they are—well—" He paused, gestured back at the mounds of the dead.

"Doomed!" finished Mir-Mir melodramatically.

Proper transmissions now came from all sides from so many fellow Viewers at once that they blurred. But it understood that this was all discouragement, dismal images of a Star Caller's totally dedicated narrow prison plus Mir-Mir's own flightiness.

"No. I think I really mean this," Mir-Mir said soberly. "I'm not going to become a very good Viewer. And I have this different feeling"—Mir-Mir put its head up to look raptly skyward, stumbled, and almost fell—"not just since this. Before. I didn't say it. I think I . . . I think I'm capable of that love." It had halted them all and was rubbing the hurt, twisted little legs with its frail hands.

Old Andoul spoke, surprising them all.

"I too have felt. Long ago . . . a hint of love. The love of all that is alien. Of the stars. But I believe that with me it was too generalized. Those who Call must focus, and so lose everything to perhaps gain one. . . .

More, in my youth we were not quite certain even that the stars were there, that it was not delusion. Think hard till you are sure, child. But more Callers are not unnecessary, now . . . and speaking of now we must move along."

"Yes," said Ekstá severely, pushing on at a determined waddle as he sent brisk images of the sessions now beginning at Amberamou, and the urgent matter of the flying herd. As he passed Mír-Mir he said, not unkindly, "Auln knows, Child, you're loud enough!"

Presently the path was empty; summit and *Calgary*'s hollow lay silent again. Above, more salmon-colored rivers streamed through the clouds, as the great farm channels filled. The pink light touched the stone, on which were scratched human letters, trailing off unfinished:

CAVANÁ + CAROL
OF LOVE & OXYGE

Mir-Mir's intentions held. Sometime later, somewhere a man or alien would turn his gaze up to the stars with ardent longing, would begin to imagine he could hear. . . .

The Saga of the Well World

Jack L. Chalker's series is a futuristic phenomenon!

Awarded the Edmond Hamilton-Leigh Brackett Memorial Award.